ARNE DAHL

Arne Dahl is a multi-award-winning author. He is the creator of the bestselling Intercrime series which was made into a critically acclaimed BBC TV series. His books have sold over four million copies, and have been translated into more than thirty languages. *Hunted* is the second instalment in the thrilling Sam Berger series and has proved a sensation, topping bestseller charts throughout Europe.

ARNE DAHL

Hunted

TRANSLATED FROM THE SWEDISH BY
Neil Smith

VINTAGE

1 3 5 7 9 10 8 6 4 2

Vintage
20 Vauxhall Bridge Road,
London SW1V 2SA

Vintage is part of the Penguin Random House group of companies
whose addresses can be found at global.penguinrandomhouse.com.

Copyright © Jan Arnald 2019
Published by agreement with Salomonsson Agency
English translation copyright © Neil Smith 2019

Jan Arnald has asserted his right to be identified as
the author of this Work in accordance with the Copyright,
Designs and Patents Act 1988

First published in the UK by Harvill Secker in 2019
First published with the title *Inland* in Sweden
by Albert Bonniers Förlag in 2017
First published by Vintage in 2020

penguin.co.uk/vintage

A CIP catalogue record for this book
is available from the British Library

ISBN 9781784705732

Printed and bound in Great Britain by Clays Ltd, Elcograf S.p.A.

Penguin Random House is committed to a sustainable future
for our business, our readers and our planet. This book is made
from Forest Stewardship Council® certified paper.

HUNTED

1

To Superintendent Desiré Rosenkvist

The first time I heard the sound was two months ago. It's hard to describe. It's as if someone's inside the wall. The sound doesn't seem to come from inside the house, and not from outside either, and there's no way it can be human. But now that I've had time to think about it, the police officers' suggestion the other week when two uniformed youngsters were here feels pretty insulting. At the time I didn't even know what house borers were.

I do now.

House-borer larvae live deep inside dry pinewood for up to ten years until they pupate and hatch. The wood ends up riddled with holes even though it looks intact from the outside. The only way to combat house-borer larvae is to burn affected wood and fumigate the building with toxic gas.

And apparently you can hear them gnawing their way through contaminated timber. They're not inside, they're not outside; they're hidden away in the darkness.

But that's not what I can hear. Unless I've got an evil house borer all of my own. Because it really does feel like someone's out to get me.

Where I live is very isolated. No one just turns up here spontaneously, no hikers who've lost their way, no estate agents trying their luck, no management teams pretending to relax by doing iron-man heroics. But there are plenty of animals, so obviously my first thought was that a reindeer, maybe even an elk, had got through the fence and was rooting through my carefully chosen perennials. But there was no evidence in the beds, and no sign of damage to the fence. And I know that reindeer and elk can't get over the fence: that was one of the main reasons I had it installed.

So if the noise was made by an animal, that animal had to be human. Because human beings can be inhuman too. It's not unreasonable to wonder if we, among all the millions of animal species on the planet, actually hold the world record for inhumanity. Even though we're supposed to embody humanity.

And scientists still think we've only managed to discover half of the species on the planet, at most.

Anyway, it can hardly be anything other than another person stalking me. And he – I'm assuming it's a man – can hardly have any other reason for being up here on the plateau. The snow has come now, and I keep examining the surface but haven't found any signs of life except the ones I myself have left. But in spite of that I know it's going on – it's going on the whole time.

Someone's spying on me.

I'm in Darkness.

Back in the nineteenth century women who fought for freedom and equality were locked up and dismissed as hysterical, and sadly we don't seem to have made much progress since then. I know the police think I'm hysterical, you have done for ages, even if these days you cover it up with labels like

4

'conspiracy theorist' and 'agitator', and no doubt have some handy neuropsychological diagnosis you can apply. Well, good luck with that is all I can say – I hope that sticks in your throats when you're staring down at my battered corpse.

Because this man definitely doesn't wish me well.

It genuinely saddens me that no one believes what I say. Or, even worse, thinks I'm mad. I could hear it in the two police officers' tone of voice when they were here. I heard them when they were getting back in their patrol car, laughing about house borers. As if I couldn't hear the difference between an angry grown man and the larvae of long-horned beetles. As if I'd somehow confuse the two sounds.

I've tried so many times before, but no one listens to me. I am totally in the dark.

You know as well as I do that Operation Gladio was real, and that American tobacco companies added addictive substances to their cigarettes. The CIA really do have a heart-attack pistol that leaves no evidence, and the Scientologists really did carry out Operation Snow White even though no one believed it.

I've pointed out plenty of times that Victor Gunnarsson was seen on Luntmakargatan just after Olof Palme was murdered – there's evidence to prove it – and I personally spoke to a police officer who admitted that two witnesses, independent of each other, saw a white sports car belonging to a local detective parked on the road by the café at Kinnekulle that July evening.

I have also done my best to get you to realise that no traces of Essam Qasim's DNA were ever found on the knife that was found in the drain in Strömstad, and that three years before the murder of Anders Larsson, Penny Grundfelt was active on Flashback under the hate-mongering profile of DeathStar. That the ink mark on Lisa Widstrand's buttock was even reported in the local press without the police bothering to wonder if that had implications for Karl Hedblom's guilt, and I've seen part of an email exchange between the Abubakir twins where the ammunition for the Ruger Mini 14 that blew Sanchez's head off is explicitly mentioned.

But you don't care about any of that.

You'll only care once I've been murdered. When I'm a dead body.

Yes, I'm using a typewriter to write this. I stopped using computers when I found out the truth about the NSA. That's how Edward Snowden has been able to stay under the radar in Russia: he never uses computers. And he of all people ought to have suffered serious withdrawal symptoms, but it's all perfectly manageable. I use a pad to access the Internet, concealed, obviously, but I never write a word electronically. It all exists for ever in the cloud, and can be endlessly copied and spread. If the Abubakir twins discovered where I am, for instance, I'd be in an extremely dangerous position.

I just heard the noise again, just now. Dear God.

The worst thing about writing this while it's going on is that he's bound to take these sheets of paper with him. With my blood on them. Then he'll get rid of them without giving it any real thought, as if it didn't matter at all.

Me, sitting here writing in my own blood.

The outside wall, down by the cellar. A sweeping sound, as if someone really is moving inside the wall, deep in the darkness. Obviously I understand he must be outside, moving through the snow out in the flower beds. I just don't understand what he wants.

Did I actually manage to leak a few undesirable truths on to the Internet before I gave up computers? Has someone guilty walked free and felt threatened by my actions? Or is it just some ordinary, unremarkable sadist who doesn't have any real motivation beyond the act itself? A burglar, a rapist, a hit man – I don't honestly care which one it is, but I would like to know why.

I want to know why I'm going to die.

I refuse to stand up, I refuse to stop writing. Dusk has fallen already, earlier again today, but I can still see that the sky is covered with cloud, that there's some kind of other darkness beyond this one.

The sound again. It's moved. A quick, sweeping, dragging sound along the wall, clearly moving towards the door.

If only it had been house-borer larvae.

I don't want to look up from what I'm writing. But I can't help feeling that I ought to be looking for a way out. My candle flickers gently in the darkness, almost goes out. Now there's no other sound but the clatter of the typewriter, a sound which in any other circumstances would be able to soothe my frayed nerves.

But not this time.

Because I can hear the noise again, the rapid shuffle, a swift dragging sound. It's never been this close.

Two months of this. Sometimes every day, sometimes an unbearable break of a few days. And now, as I hear the sound on the porch steps, it feels almost a relief: I couldn't have put up with the uncertainty for much longer.

The cellar that I stopped using a couple of years ago: I haven't even been down there since then. The moment I look over at the cellar door a sudden ice-cold wind sweeps through the bedroom. Just as the small flame of the candle blows out I hear . . .

2

His name is Berger. Sam Berger.

That was all he knew. Except for the fact that he had to get out.

Get away.

He put his hand against the kitchen window. It was so cold it felt like his sweat was going to stick his fingertips to the glass. When he quickly pulled his hand away the print was so clear he wondered if it was mostly made up of skin.

The first thing he saw in the window was his own reflection. He raised his right hand and extended his index and middle fingers, making his hand look like a double-barrelled revolver.

And shot himself.

Outside the window everything was white. Utterly white.

The thick covering of snow lay flat. It was covering a field or perhaps a meadow, and seemed to stretch to infinity. Until he detected movement a long way off in the distance, at a point where his vision could only just reach. If he strained his eyes he could just see that the rectangular block moving along the edge of the field was a bus.

That was where he had to get to.

There was a road there. A road out. Away.

The door to his room had been left unlocked for the first time, and he had managed to slip out just at the right time, in the post-lunch lull, and had managed to make his way to the kitchen where – as far as he was aware – he had never been before.

The kitchen staff had got everything ready for afternoon coffee; there were Thermos flasks on a trolley next to a plate of cinnamon buns covered with cling film. A number of white coats were hanging up beside the trolley.

He looked out through the window again, from close up: the cold hit his face. He looked down at his body. Below what could under other circumstances be taken for jogging bottoms his feet were bare. He wriggled his toes quickly. It was as if they themselves realised he'd never reach the road without shoes.

But he had to get out. He had to get away. He had been here too long.

He had been away too long.

He went and looked in the pantry. In the far corner there was actually a pair of wellington boots, and he put them on even if they were at least three sizes too small. His toes were scrunched up, but he could walk, maybe even run in them.

When he emerged into the kitchen again he heard cries through the door leading to the main corridor. The door was closed, but it was unlikely to remain that way for long.

He grabbed all three of the white coats hanging next to the trolley and hurried over to the other door. The pain in his pinched toes kept him alert.

He pulled on the first white coat, then the second, but by the time he was about to pull the third on top of the other two the noises from beyond the kitchen door were getting far too close. He carefully pushed down the handle of the door and slipped into the side corridor. He closed the door behind him as gently as he could, as he heard the main kitchen door being thrown open. As he ran down the dark corridor he pulled on the third coat. The boots made his ordinarily fluid running style look like the dragging steps of a madman.

Ordinarily? There was no 'ordinarily'. And certainly no running style. It was as if he had woken to a completely empty, completely white world.

A world without markers.

What appeared to be memories were no more than the phantom pains of his soul. Everything was gone, stripped away. It was as if his brain had consciously erased all traces of the past.

But he still remembered the door, he even remembered the little gap that let a billow of cold into the last dark metre of corridor.

He opened the door. The terrace was large, enormous even, like something better suited to a royal palace, but only a small square around the door had been cleared of snow. It was covered with cigarette butts.

He must have stood here smoking when he was still in the darkness. That must be it. How else would he have been able to find his way here?

But hadn't he stopped smoking?

Beyond the cleared square the snow lay a metre thick on the terrace. It had been swept aside in layers, forming a steep flight of densely packed steps leading up to a plateau of snow. The edge of the terrace was six metres away, and he didn't know how far it was down to the ground.

To the field that led to the road. To the road that led out of there.

Away.

He set off across the deep snow. The crust was so hard that even the disproportionately small boots didn't break through. Not until the end, anyway, when the struggle to reach the railings turned into a struggle to move at all. He reached the railings at precisely the same moment that he heard noises behind him from the terrace door.

The drop to what he had taken to be a wide field was at least five metres. The snow looked deeper there than up on the terrace, although if it was just as hard he could easily break his legs. But there was no alternative.

Without looking back, he swung first one leg then the other over the railing. The three layers of coat flapped around him like bizarre white wings. And they flapped for a disconcertingly long time.

He hit the snow and sank into it. Yes, he sank, and the metre-thick snow absorbed the impact. He fell forward and somersaulted into the white powder. His mouth filled with it and he couldn't breathe.

It went on slightly too long and he started to panic. An avalanche of panic. But he got to his feet, and this time his legs didn't give way. He spat out snow, blew snow from his nose, vomited snow, but he managed to start running across the field. Towards the road. His progress was painfully slow. Like moving through quicksand.

When he had got about ten metres he glanced back over his shoulder. Two thickset men were standing by the terrace railings, staring down at him. Then they vanished.

He kept going. The powder was simultaneously compact and porous, easy to move through horizontally, hard to move through vertically. It was a battle against the elements. And, in spite of the three layers of medical coat, it was insanely cold.

It started to snow. Large flakes drifted down from the darkening sky. The sun had already set by the time he noticed another sound beyond his own ragged breathing. He stopped and turned his face to the sky, let snowflakes settle on it like a fragmented face mask, held his breath, listened.

Listened hard.

In the thin weak light that followed sunset he could make out movement in the distance. After a while he was able to make out a shape. A rectangular block was moving through the whiteness.

It was heading in his direction. He set off again, taking an overenthusiastic step and stumbling at once, before overcompensating and falling backwards instead, with his legs buried deep in the snow. He couldn't get up, and dancing snowflakes settled on his eyes, making his eyes water.

He genuinely couldn't get up.

He had to dig deep inside to find a burning kernel of will, a hidden reserve of energy. A core of compressed, violent force. He stood up with a roar, spraying snow around him as the coats flapped like wings. He was a fallen snow angel, resurrected.

He rushed on. The bus was getting closer, its sides completely covered by driven snow, only fragments of the windows visible. The driver put the headlights on full beam, and cones of light shot out from the rectangular shape. And the rumble of the diesel engine was getting louder and louder.

The unlikely sound of freedom.

He could see the road now, winding, almost sunken in the midst of the expanse of white. He ran, suddenly he could actually run, the snow was no longer putting up any resistance. He saw the bus weaving its way closer. There were another ten metres to the edge of the road. He fell to his knees, got up again. The bus was close now. He raised his arms and waved frantically. There was no way the driver could fail to see this winged white creature enveloped in an aura of powdery snow.

He ran on, still waving, reached the edge of the road, summoned the last of his strength to leap across the ditch. The bus was coming, for a moment he thought he caught the driver's eye.

But it didn't slow down.

The bus didn't slow down.

He held his hand up to the snow-covered side of the bus, forming it into a claw, as if he might be able to stop the multi-ton vehicle by willpower alone. The bus roared past him without altering its speed at all. When it turned slightly he saw five clear but irregular lines in the snow on its side, made by his fingers and thumb.

He stared at his frozen right hand, his bleeding fingertips, but he felt nothing. Nothing at all. He slumped to his knees. He didn't even have the strength left to shout out.

As it disappeared into the distance, the bus left an impenetrable cloud behind it; he was in the middle of a sudden snowstorm. Slowly it dissipated.

From the other side of the fog of snow a shape gradually appeared. Movement, apparently focused on him. Two beings emerged, two thickset men. One of them was still waving the bus on, as if time was out of joint.

The other man crossed the road, raised his fist and punched him right in the face. He was convinced he was already unconscious when the blow struck him.

The last thing he heard was the snow falling breathlessly through space.

3

A white expanse. Nothing happened there, there was nothing to be seen.

But as his field of vision expanded a pair of parallel fluorescent lights slid into the whiteness. One of them was flickering faintly but quickly, spreading a nervous, pulsating glow over the white ceiling.

He recognised the glow. He had seen it before. Even so, it could hardly be called a memory.

A first conscious thought: how strange it was to be so empty, so devoid of everything. Just a body. There was a grotesque freedom in it. Freedom from the past.

But there was another feeling now, a completely different one. As if little by little, door after door was opening in his brain. As if for the first time he actually *wanted* to remember.

An authoritative male voice was saying, 'Severely chilled, but no actual frostbite.'

He lowered his gaze from the ceiling. The white-clad man, who also had a profusion of white hair, folded the bandage back over his right hand and fastened it with a couple of pieces of tape. Then he met his gaze.

The man looked him in the eye for a long time, screwed his eyes up thoughtfully and said, 'I'm Dr Stenbom. Do you recognise me, Sam?'

He shook his head. He didn't recognise the man in white. But something told him he should.

'Well, your hand looks OK, anyway,' Dr Stenbom said, and put it back down on his thigh, actually rather tenderly.

'The bandage is nothing to do with the cold – the tips of your fingers were badly hurt when you tried to claw the side off the local bus, we've strapped up each finger individually. Apparently the bus was going at approximately eighty kilometres an hour at the time, which would explain the nature of the injuries. But they'll heal within a week or so. Do you remember trying to stop the bus, Sam?'

To his surprise he nodded. He did in fact remember. He remembered the whole crazy excursion. He remembered the kitchen, the smoking area, the terrace, the field. He remembered the snow filling his mouth. He remembered the bus. He remembered the two large men.

'What I don't really understand,' Dr Stenbom went on, 'are the injuries to your face.'

But I do, he thought and smiled briefly. To himself. It made his face tighten in a peculiar way. He put his left hand to his face – his whole head seemed to be wrapped in bandages.

'Do you remember how you hurt your face?' the doctor asked.

He shook his head.

Dr Stenbom nodded slowly in response, slightly warily.

'I thought I detected a new awareness in your eyes just now, Sam, but your memory still seems to be failing you after all. Do you know what day of the week it is?'

He shook his head. He wasn't even sure he knew the names of all the days of the week. There were seven of them, weren't there?

'Monday,' he said.

'Not quite,' Dr Stenbom said and frowned.

'Tuesday,' he went on. 'Wednesday, Thursday, Friday, Sunday.'

'You forgot Saturday, Sam.'

He looked up at the ceiling again. He'd forgotten Saturday. He couldn't even count to seven.

'You've got concussion, Sam,' Dr Stenbom said. 'It might be because of that rather than ... your existing condition. Can you tell me your name?'

'Sam Berger,' he said.

'Good. And do you remember how you got here?'

Vague movement inside him, somewhere down by the back of his neck rather than up in his head. In his marrow? An image: heavy snow falling on a windscreen, a rapid reflection in the same windscreen, someone's head. Then gone again.

He shook his head. Dr Stenbom nodded.

'But you remember trying to escape?'

He nodded.

'Of course I tried to escape,' he said. 'I've got no idea where the hell I am. The North Pole?'

Dr Stenbom laughed but quickly adopted his serious demeanour again.

'Do you remember who brought you here?'

Vague memories again, incomplete images like torn photographs. He shook his head.

'Do you remember if it was a man or a woman?'

'A woman,' he said immediately, to his own surprise.

'Good, Sam. Do you remember what she looked like?'

'Blonde.'

'We've got security-camera footage from outside the main entrance,' Dr Stenbom said. 'And that fits well – there was a blonde woman. But she left you outside, in the snow. We had to go out and carry you inside, Sam. Who was she?'

He could feel himself blinking. Each blink made the bandage feel tighter. Was the whole of his head really wrapped in bandages?

'I don't know,' he said.

'Nor do we,' Dr Stenbom said, holding out his hands. 'And we haven't got the names of any next of kin we can contact now that you're starting to get better.'

'I'm starting to get better?' he asked.

'I think I'd have to say that, yes,' Dr Stenbom smiled and stood up. 'I think we're starting to get somewhere, Sam.'

'I've got no idea where that somewhere is.'

'Let's try to make slow, steady progress, Sam. If you don't know where that somewhere is yet, then there's probably no rush to get there.'

'What are you doing now?'

'I'm putting the infusion back in, the drip we've been using for the past two weeks now. The same dose. We can start to decrease it very gradually.'

'But what is it?'

'It's mostly a nutrient solution,' Dr Stenbom said. 'You haven't been in a fit state to absorb nourishment any other way, Sam. But also a sedative. You certainly needed it before, and you need it just as much now that reality is slowly coming back to you.'

He looked at the strips of plaster across the crook of his left arm. They were crowned by a yellow cannula. The doctor inserted the tube from the drip hanging above his head into it.

Then he stood with his hands by his sides, looking at his patient. He said with a frown, 'You tried to escape, Sam. If the staff hadn't found you, you'd have met your death out there in the cold. Normal procedure would be to strap you down now, keep you tied to your bed for your own good. I've decided not to do that, though, because I think you realise that it's not us you're trying to escape from. It's your memories, reality itself. And judging from what I and the rest of the staff have heard in the past few weeks, getting those memories back isn't going to be a painless process. I want you to think about that, Sam. Maybe even remember it. It *isn't* going to be painless.'

Dr Stenbom looked at him for a while, studying him. Then he was gone. There may have been a click as the door closed behind him.

Lying in bed, he did nothing but stare at the yellow object sticking out of his arm. Very slowly he started to pull at the strips of surgical tape holding it in place.

The skin around the point where the thick needle entered his arm wasn't just blue but also covered by plenty more needle marks at various stages of healing; there was no doubt that he'd been there for some time now. A couple of weeks, that was what Dr fucking Stenbom had said, but it could have been considerably longer than that. Time still didn't have any real meaning.

He pulled the needle out of his arm with a jerk. A relatively weak jet of blood squirted from the crook of his arm, as if there weren't really much pressure left. It quickly turned into a trickle, and he pulled the pillow from behind his head, tugged the pillowcase off and placed the pillow under his elbow. The blood slowly trickled down onto it and slowly expanded into a stain.

He bent the thick needle: it was harder than he expected. Eventually he managed to form a gentle curve. He held it up to the light and examined it. Then he inserted it into the still bleeding hole and poked about a bit, searching along the vein.

The pain kept him alert.

He looked at his skin. A few centimetres below the entry hole there was a slight bulge. He pressed a bit harder and the bulge grew. Eventually his skin burst from the inside. The crooked needle poked out from his skin. Blood seeped from both holes, the entry hole and this new exit hole.

He saw a hole made by a bullet. The image flickered past, tried to stay, insisted on staying.

But a clear liquid in the middle of the flow of blood pushed the image aside. The liquid was dripping from the point of the crooked needle. Drip, drip. The infusion liquid. It was no longer flowing into his veins and poisoning his body.

And his soul.

He replaced the tape over the wounds, forming a little tunnel in the surface of one piece of tape, and waited until he saw the first clear drop run from the tunnel onto the pillow. Then he adjusted the yellow cannula, and everything looked just as it had done before.

He put the bloodstained pillow on the other side of the bed, as if to let it dry, swung his legs sideways and sat up on the edge of the bed. Then he shifted his weight and stood up. He swayed gently, and flashes of pain shot through his head, but he remained standing. Then he took a first tentative step, then another. The steps may have been unsteady, and he may have had to lean heavily on the drip stand, but his legs didn't give way.

At the other end of the bare room was a basin with a mirror above it. He staggered towards it and saw the peculiar mummy's face, and found that logical. The man without a memory, the man without a face. It wasn't Sam Berger's reflection. He touched the bandages gently; it was as if he was looking at a completely different person in the mirror.

Someone completely different. A reflection of someone else. Suddenly the mirror was a windscreen, probably a car's, and suddenly it wasn't clear but opaque. Snowflakes, big, flat snowflakes hitting the windscreen, as if the car was driving through a confusion of rapidly flaring sparks of light. And in a momentary reflection he saw something different. It wasn't his reflection, it wasn't Sam Berger. Blonde hair. But there was no face, just hair. And then it was gone, all of it. He was left staring at the bizarre mummy's face. And not at a windscreen but a mirror in a comfortless, bare room in what presumably was some sort of clinic.

He moved away from the mirror, didn't want to see more. He stumbled over to the window. Looked out. The field that had been so white before was now completely black. There was nothing there, no moon, not a single star, just pitch blackness. It wasn't even possible to see if it was snowing.

It was probably snowing.

He couldn't escape his reflection. There was the mummy again. But now the mummy made a Sam Berger gesture, and raised its bandaged right hand and shot itself with a double-barrelled revolver.

Then he stopped dead. Like a figure at a table.

A lightning flash of confusion. Table? Figure?

The terrible feeling of remembering something he didn't remember at all. Just the gaping hole where it should be.

He remained standing by the pitch-black window. He could see his own reflection, his mummified image. In the background things slowly emerged, solidifying before his eyes. A room, a large, almost empty house. Rain beating hard against the window. A figure sitting on a chair in the middle of the room. An emptiness, a stillness that was unlike anything else. The room's furnishings gradually emerged – or rather its lack of furnishings. An almost entirely unfurnished interior. A scream of uncertain origin rising towards the relatively high ceiling. But no more than that. Nothing else. Except one thing, perhaps.

A head of hair. Blonde hair. His brain was spinning.

The seated figure. Everything unclear.

A four-leaf clover. And a sudden explosion of blood. Violence and blood. A house filled with pain. Bullet holes everywhere. In the floor.

Bullet holes in the floor.

A seated figure. A woman. Stillness.

Then there was a flight of steps, dark cellar steps. He couldn't bring himself to go down them. His brain went into reverse.

A whirring sound started up, he had no idea where it was coming from. Two people, even more distant, as if he were looking at them from a long way away through both space and time. They were walking at first, then they sat very still, very close.

The whirring sound was very loud.

Perhaps this was reality: the moon crept out from behind a cloud, the slowly tumbling snowflakes lit up. They were dancing rather than crashing against the windscreen. It was actually possible to follow every individual flake, untouched by time, by any sense of speed.

Because there was no speed. It was inside him, nowhere else. And there things were moving fast.

The unfathomable vagueness of memories: everything was slipping away. Just as he was on the point of capturing an image it slid out of reach.

The two people again, one large, one small. Close colleagues, partners. He forced himself to stay with them even though they were moving towards the table. The larger figure was him, it was Sam Berger, and beside him was a woman. It wasn't the blonde woman, but someone with dark hair, quite petite, with her hair cut in a bob. He tried in vain to remember her name. Desiré?

Yes, that made sense and it didn't make any sense at all. A different name, a nickname, maybe? Yes. Deer. That was right, wasn't it? And then he suddenly saw them from outside, Sam and Deer, partners.

Police officers.

Then they were sitting on the same side of the table in an interview room. Sam himself on the left, Deer on the right. Rosenkvist. Desiré Rosenkvist.

He saw his own expression, sombre. He saw Deer's, encouraging. Good cop, bad cop. He saw the mocking Sam Berger gesture.

There were three women. One of them was sitting perfectly still on a chair in an unfurnished room where the rain was pattering against the windows and there was blood on the floor, which was riddled with bullet holes.

Unless there were four?

Even more?

And then it all vanished.

Abruptly. As if his untrained shaken-up brain had had an overdose of impressions and just shut down.

He took an unsteady sideways step. The drip stand rattled. His arm hurt where the needle went in. He looked at the strips of tape on his arm. Nothing seemed to have happened. He waited. Eventually a drop of clear liquid seeped out from the little tunnel in the tape.

It was still working.

He turned and looked at the room. He had left a trail across the floor. No blood, just a few clear drops of liquid. A drip trail. An infusion trail. He hoped it would have time to dry before any of the staff returned to his room.

He stumbled towards the bed. The pillow lay there stripped of its pillowcase, with an obvious bloodstain on it. He felt it. The stain was still wet. He laid the pillowcase next to it and decided to wait until the blood had dried before putting it back on.

So he didn't leave any evidence. A trail of blood.

He went around the bed, back to where he had started, swung his legs up and lay back on the bed.

He stared up at the ceiling. Behind the nervously pulsating light it was completely white. Yet there were still plenty of markers there. Markers that were starting to resemble memories.

He would take a break. Empty his mind again, leave it on charge. Then he had to start remembering.

Seriously remembering.

4

There were no windows in the room. But plenty of people. And even more screens. It was like they were in some subterranean bunker. Below ground level, anyway.

In one corner of the large, frenetically active room sat two men, slightly separate from everyone else; they were sitting on either side of a desk, and they looked at each other's faces as often as they looked at their computer screens. One of the men was facing the wall, the other had a view of the rest of the room; they took it in turns because they both preferred looking out at the room.

The heavily built man who had drawn the short straw this week and was facing the wall glanced at the cheap diver's watch on his thick wrist. As if he'd just come up to the surface and was checking how long he had managed to hold his breath. He took a couple of deep breaths, then went back down again. Deep into the ocean of his computer.

Beside the screen was a brass sign announcing the man's name as Roy Grahn.

The man on the other side of the desk glanced at him. Neither of them would have been prepared to admit it, but there was an ongoing struggle between the two, a private battle to see which of them would be first to gain official status and be promoted to Internal Resources.

Because for the time being they were still both outside the system.

Beside the computer screen that was facing the wall was a largely identical brass plaque bearing the name Kent Döös. And Kent Döös dived into his own computer equipped with the same search parameters as Roy Grahn to ascertain whether anything new had cropped up.

As usual the search was less than straightforward. If, against all expectations, any of their subjects did crop up, it would be the result of a mistake. And it was those mistakes that Roy and Kent were looking for: bank card usage, Internet activity, any little slip-ups that would reveal their identities.

Kent Döös thought: Molly Blom.

Roy and Kent had worked with her, and she had been extremely impressive. She would never make a mistake of that sort. She was an internal resource, one of the most highly regarded, one of the near-legendary undercover operatives. She had been authorised to use a number of secret identities which not even the Security Service knew about – she was capable of staying below the radar for ever if she wanted. It was her partner, if you could call him that, the former detective Sam Berger, who was the weak link. Almost all their efforts were devoted to tracking down any mistakes Berger might have made. And for the past couple of weeks it was as if he'd vanished from the face of the planet.

Either Molly was keeping a very close eye on him, or he had gone underground of his own accord. The latter seemed unlikely. Sam Berger was *bound* to make a mistake, it was utterly inevitable. It was all a matter of patience. But on the other hand, patience wasn't exactly Kent and Roy's strong point.

The most common method was to look for out-of-the-way locations, the ones with least online presence. Hotels with manual check-ins, discreet health clinics, training camps in isolated settings, plane tickets where dubious identification documents triggered the alarm too late, border crossings with lax monitoring, anywhere in the area covered by the Schengen Agreement where no ID checks were made. And of course outside the Schengen zone. It was thought likely that Berger and Blom were somewhere in the EU, in the Schengen zone, and probably – in this most objectionable of months, November – somewhere with decent weather.

Even so, Kent wasn't entirely convinced by the idea that they'd fled abroad. He had spent a lot of time working with Molly Blom. He didn't think she'd left the country. He focused his searches on Sweden, on the most desolate corners of Sweden. Maybe somewhere in the interior?

Roy Grahn and Kent Döös hadn't been granted access to the most confidential information. So they didn't exactly know what Molly Blom and Sam Berger had done. Just that they warranted a position close to the top of the Security Service's most-wanted list.

Kent would soon bitterly regret pausing for a few seconds, but he couldn't prevent a number of contradictory memories from surfacing. He clearly recalled a crazy fight when Berger had broken into Blom's flat. Berger had fought like a hardened old lag and they had been forced to tranquilise him. He remembered Blom interrogating Berger hard, but then for some reason she had sabotaged the recording of the encounter. And finally he remembered the raid on a nightmarish flat in Sollentuna.

Berger and Blom were there together, having made a heroic rescue effort.

Kent couldn't get the memories to fit a coherent narrative.

Yet he couldn't help smiling as he remembered that Roy had thrown up. Kent hadn't.

All of this meant that he wasn't entirely concentrating when the search results arrived. He didn't know how long the window on the screen had been flashing, but he was quick to act as soon as he noticed it. He clicked through a number of databases, made his way past a couple of firewalls, bypassed a couple of password requests, then, just as he was on his way, he saw something he really didn't want to see. A hand.

A hand in front of the computer screen. A hand and a cheap diver's watch. Index and long fingers forming a V.

Roy leaped to his feet and exclaimed, 'Arjeplog!'

He was already halfway out of the room by the time Kent, with a look of distaste, managed to complete his own search. The screen said, 'Sam Berger, Lindstorp Clinic, Arjeplog.'

As usual it took a while before the door made the low humming sound that gave them access to the holy of holies. By then they had already been hanging about in the corridor for more than a minute. Kent couldn't help wondering what the head of the Security Service's Intelligence Unit got up to during this time. Was it really just a demonstration of power?

Roy opened the door and walked in. August Steen, the head of the department, was sitting behind his desk with his back perfectly straight. His cropped grey hair showed no sign of thinning, and his pale grey eyes looked like they'd been carved from frozen stone.

'We've got him,' Roy said.

August Steen very slowly removed his reading glasses, tapped them on the desk and said, 'Who has got what?'

'Berger,' Roy said. 'Sam Berger. We've got him. He's in a clinic outside Arjeplog.'

Steen's eyebrows frowned for a moment, but the rest of his face remained impassive. And not a word crossed his lips.

'May I suggest the fastest possible mode of transport, sir?' Roy went on. 'Every second increases the risk of him getting away.'

August Steen studied him carefully. Then he looked at Kent. It was never a pleasant experience.

Then he gave a curt nod.

Roy and Kent were out of the room in less than a second. Steen watched the door close behind them. He stared at it for a long time.

He stretched his neck, making it click audibly, before he reached for the bottom drawer of his desk. After a brief search he pulled out an old-fashioned mobile phone. He waited for it to switch on with a distant expression on his face. Then he picked it up and made a call.

Roy Grahn had expected 'the fastest possible mode of transport' to mean a helicopter all the way. There were, however, nine hundred and forty kilometres between police headquarters in Stockholm and Arjeplog, but he wasn't actually aware of that.

But they were in time for the morning flight, and if everything worked as planned there should be a helicopter waiting for them at Arvidsjaur Airport to take them the remaining hundred and fifty kilometres to Arjeplog.

When they stepped out of the almost empty plane they were confronted with a snowstorm that seemed much heavier than it had been when they had landed; evidently it was getting worse. And the wind was blowing alarmingly strongly.

They climbed into a very small helicopter and were tossed this way and that through a swirling white sky that occasionally cleared enough to give them a brief glimpse of endless mountains. Knowing that Berger possessed certain – albeit limited – skills when it came to close combat, they checked their weapons, a pair of sturdy Glocks, and as backup some easily accessible syringes with thick needles that could quickly be inserted into a carotid artery, for instance.

It was barely possible to make out the frozen little town that the helicopter was now passing before it was back over open country again. Kent saw a thin box-like shape moving along a serpentine line which upon closer inspection was probably a road. So the box-like shape was probably a bus.

Through the snowfall a building gradually emerged and grew larger. It looked like an old manor house, and in front of the building a field spread out, flat and featureless, with a circle cleared of snow so that the helicopter could land. The taciturn pilot hovered directly above the circle and slowly descended, and everything turned white. The engines and rotor blades fell silent long before the swirling snow finally settled again. Through the falling snow three people in thick coats hurried towards the helicopter. The door opened and Kent and Roy were struck both by the cold and the realisation that their clothes were far too thin; they both realised that they ought to have guessed that Arjeplog in the middle of November would be a particularly chilly part of Sweden.

The white-haired man at the front of the delegation walked towards them with his hand outstretched.

'Dr Stenbom,' he said. 'Welcome to Lindstorp.'

'Roy Grahn, Security Service,' Roy said, shaking his hand. 'And this is Kent Döös.'

'Also Security Service,' Kent added.

Dr Stenbom didn't bother to introduce the two men behind him, but there was no need. Kent and Roy knew the type: warders, guards. Instead the doctor turned and led the visitors along an untidily cleared path towards the manor-house building.

'So, Sam Berger?' the doctor said as they walked through the snow. 'I don't know if you're aware of the fact, but he tried to escape yesterday. We managed to find him just in time – he would have frozen to death.'

'Escape?' Roy said. 'Is he locked up?'

'Temporarily, yes,' Dr Stenbom said. 'He was in a very bad way when he arrived. He was left here in a severely confused and violent state by an unidentified person – we had to sedate him. He was very upset when he came round, made threats and seemed extremely anxious. He was so difficult to control that we opted to keep him sedated.'

'And when was that?'

'About two weeks ago.'

'You've kept him sedated for a fortnight?'

'This clinic may specialise in advanced psychiatric treatment, but we don't have the resources to act as a prison twenty-four hours a day. From time to time we've reduced the dosage and examined his condition. Yesterday morning was the first time he's been calm enough to be allowed to wake up, very gradually. But that calmness was evidently merely the prelude to an escape attempt. A fairly deranged escape attempt, I might add. He tried to stop a bus with his bare hands.'

'What condition is he in now?'

'Because he suffered a number of injuries we decided to revert to the maximum dose again. He's thoroughly sedated.'

'Injuries?' Kent said, shivering. 'Frostbite?'

'Not primarily, no,' Dr Stenbom said. 'Like I said, he tried to stop a bus with his bare hands. It appears that the bus in question also hit him and caused a number of facial injuries. He's heavily bandaged.'

'Bandaged?'

'Gauze bandages around his head, yes.'

They finally reached what appeared to be a back door. Dr Stenbom tapped in a code, ran his card through a reader and said, 'So I'm afraid you won't be able to question Berger yet, regardless of what the suspicions against him might be ...'

Roy and Kent chose to ignore his curiosity and brushed the snow from their thin jackets. The corridor they were walking along was completely bare, and the strip lights in the ceiling cast a cold, bleak light over the desolate passageway. They turned into a larger corridor. There was a nurse pushing a medicine trolley but that was all; there wasn't a single patient in sight.

Finally Dr Stenbom stopped in front of one of the identical doors and pulled out an old-fashioned ring of keys. He inserted one of them into what was presumably a high-security lock. Then both Kent and Roy saw him frown, briefly but unmistakably. As if on a signal they both unzipped their jackets and unfastened their shoulder holsters. Dr Stenbom pulled open the door, which he hadn't actually had to unlock.

On the solitary bed against the far wall of the room lay a figure covered by a blanket.

Roy drew his pistol and quickly secured the room. As Kent ran the few metres to the bed he too pulled out his Glock. He yanked the blanket and sheet back.

The person lying there was fast asleep.

Dressed in white.

A nurse.

An empty syringe was sticking out of her arm. Stenbom quickly checked her condition to make sure she was OK.

'What the fuck?' Roy yelled and turned towards the two carers who had just ambled into the room. They shrugged their shoulders in surprise.

A large wet stain had spread across the bottom sheet beside the sleeping nurse.

'What the hell is this?' Kent exclaimed. 'Did the bastard piss himself, or was it the nurse?'

Dr Stenbom leaned closer to the wet patch and sniffed gently. Then he shook his head and turned to the drip stand beside the bed. He took hold of the tube and followed it to where it ought to have been inserted into the cannula in Sam Berger's arm. And there was the yellow cannula itself, with fresh blood on it. Dr Stenbom looked at the needle and saw that it was bent.

'The infusion didn't transfer correctly,' he said.

'And in layman's terms?' Roy bellowed.

'He bent the needle,' Dr Stenbom said thoughtfully. 'The liquid in the drip has leaked out. He isn't sedated. When the nurse came in to give him a—'

'He was waiting for her,' Kent interrupted and pointed at the two warders. 'He escaped yesterday. Where did he go?'

The warders looked at each other a little too long.

'Just answer, for God's sake!' Roy yelled.

'The kitchen,' the larger of the two said. 'Then the terrace and out across the field to the road.'

'So get moving, then!' Roy bellowed.

They ran along the corridor. Dr Stenbom panted:

'There's fresh blood on the needle. Hasn't been there more than a few minutes.'

They rushed up a flight of steps into another corridor. One of the carers opened the door to a kitchen. There was the usual trolley laden with Thermos flasks and a plate of cinnamon buns covered with cling film, but otherwise the kitchen was empty.

'Start looking!' Roy shouted.

Slightly clumsily, the clinic's staff followed Kent's example and started to search the drab kitchen. The smaller of the two carers said, 'Here.'

They went over to the window where he was standing. Through the grimy glass they could see the helicopter. The pilot was standing outside in the snow with a cigarette. The smoke seemed to get caught by the snowflakes and be drawn towards the ground.

'Here,' the carer repeated, and they looked from the window down at the worktop. In one of four unwashed coffee cups a drop of blood had formed a star pattern.

And the blood was fresh.

There were two more doors in the kitchen. Roy ran over to one of them and threw it open, revealing a pantry. There was no one there.

'Get that secured!' he yelled and ran towards the second door.

He pulled it open. A gloomy corridor led off in both directions. He stepped out of the kitchen as a voice called behind him:

'Blood in here, too.'

Roy quickly worked out where the helicopter was and ran left along the corridor. After ten metres he stopped and looked at the sad, beige textured wallpaper. Kent caught up with him and saw his finger pointing at a faint red stain on the wall.

'He's dizzy,' Roy said. 'Knocked against the wall.'

They ran side by side towards a door at the end of the corridor. They threw it open and were met by the snowstorm. It took them a moment to catch their breath, and even longer before they could see. The snow was swirling in every imaginable direction.

They were on a sort of terrace, but no more than a few square metres had been cleared, forming a provisional standing space, presumably a smoking area. They could see fresh footsteps in the thicker snow, and there was probably some sort of railing or balustrade nearby, then a drop of some sort down to the field, where they could just make out the helicopter off to their left.

Roy raised his pistol as if his vision might improve if he had something to aim at, but that meant he lost ground on Kent, who was already moving across the thicker snow, balancing on the crust, which he looked likely to fall through at any moment. Kent reached the edge of the terrace and threw himself over the snow-covered balustrade. He sank deep into the snow and lashed out to free himself from it, then set off into the increasingly heavy snowstorm. He could see a sort of flapping motion through the raging storm. It was such an odd sight that under any other circumstances he would have stopped to look at it, but now he was chasing someone, and nothing got in the way of that. Nothing got away from him.

Not even this angel.

Because that was what he looked like. The wings spread out, white against the all-encompassing whiteness, and it looked as if the figure might take off at any moment and defy the laws of nature to shoot up through the snowstorm and whirl triumphantly through the tormented sky, then dive down towards him and give him that smug Sam Berger grin just out of reach before sailing off through the snow and disappearing.

But that didn't happen. The figure ahead of him was coming closer. No, it was Kent who was getting closer, it was Kent who was gaining ground, close enough now to see him properly. He could see a thin trail of blood on the snow he was forcing his way through, and he was so close now that he could almost touch the fluttering figure.

Kent did a quick calculation. He would get one chance, and only one. He tried to calculate the right moment to throw himself at the fleeing man, but just as he launched himself forward with both feet the figure seemed to find some extra energy and slip out of reach. It turned round and he saw the blurred white face stare at him as if he'd never seen him before, had never fought viciously with him in Molly Blom's flat on Stenbocksgatan back in a snowless Stockholm.

It was like he was a completely different person. A mummy. And the mummy raised his bandaged hand as if to shoot him with his fingers.

That made the mummy stumble, and suddenly the moment presented itself. Kent steadied himself as well as he could on the treacherous snow, leaped forward and reached out, caught hold of one arm and pulled the flapping figure onto the snow, which gave way immediately. He found himself eye to eye with the figure, deep down in the snow, took a firm grip of it using the forbidden shoulder-breaking hold, and forced the bastard down into the soft whiteness.

The eyes stared up at him over the figure's shoulder through the gauze bandages. Blue, stubborn, mildly panic-stricken. Kent rolled him over and placed his knees on the man's lower arms. He grabbed hold of the bandage somewhere at the back of the man's head. He started to unwind it. He caught sight of a cheek, a fleshy mess and a chin with several wounds in it.

Kent had Sam Berger's hateful face engraved on his retina; it was time to pay back the humiliation of the past few weeks. He wanted to see this bloody, frightened visage slowly transform into Berger's badly beaten face.

He took a degree of pleasure in the slow unravelling. More and more skin became visible behind the bandage. The large flakes of snow melted on the slowly revealed skin.

But the victor's cup started to leave an increasingly bitter aftertaste. As soon as the jaw was visible Kent started to feel something was wrong. He couldn't drag it out any longer, and pulled the bandage off as fast as he could.

And suddenly the cup was full of poison.

Kent looked at the wounded, bruised face for a good while.

Then he bellowed into the air, 'This isn't Sam fucking Berger!'

5

The snow was no longer falling. It just lay there now. Still, unmoving. The world was white. It was like treading on virgin ground.

Something was moving through the whiteness. A woman.

Her laborious footsteps formed the first signs of civilisation. Signs of struggle, of survival. Defying the atrocious conditions.

It had been a long night, and only in the morning had the snowstorm finally moved off to the south. The neatly cleared path was no longer particularly clear at all.

The woman reached the top of a ridge and saw the cabin huddled in its new guise, and glanced at her mobile phone. She had two minutes. Plenty of time.

That was when she saw him. He was stumbling through the snow, clutching the bright red padded jacket tightly around him.

She slowed down, took a quick look at the clear blue sky, then ran after him. The steps he left in his wake were deep and clear, but hers were slowed by the thick covering of snow. She was forcing her way forward rather than actually running, and he was whirling away ahead of her, as if the zigzag trail he left behind him also gave an indication of his mental state.

Even so she was gaining ground. She pulled out her phone again, but had no idea how long it had shown 10.29; it could move on at any moment, and then it would all be too late.

As she ran the last few metres, more like a snowplough than a gazelle, she unbuttoned her long white coat. The wind caught it and made it look like a spinnaker on a stormy lake. He turned. There was a look of confused, primal fear in the eyes, which were only just visible above the wild grey beard.

She landed on top of him, pressing the whole of his redness into the thick snow, letting her snowy white spinnaker sail over him as she glanced at her phone. It clicked to show 10.30.

They ended up eye to eye under the hastily improvised bivouac. He stared at her. She put her finger to her lips to hush him; he obeyed without a word.

It was strange to see him like this. He had changed so much. The fact that his beard was so mad was less remarkable than the fact that it had changed colour. His dark hair was also greyer than before; it was as if two weeks in Sweden's pole of inaccessibility had turned him into a different person.

She was still holding her finger to her lips, and he was still quiet, lying motionless, suddenly cooperative. She looked at her phone, let time pass. All she could hear was their own panting breaths, at two very different rates.

She was lying on top of him. His body felt limp. In the snow cave of her big white coat she realised she had managed to get through to him for almost the first time since the boathouse. The eyes above all that beard were clearer than they had been for a very long time.

A last glance at her mobile; it was OK now, it had passed. She slowly stood up, her coat no longer camouflage, falling surprisingly tightly around her upright frame. As if in response his red padded jacket lay splayed across the snow.

He got slowly to his feet and stood in front of her, eye to eye.

'Satellite,' she said. 'One of several.'

He blinked hard as if he were physically trying to fend off the remains of his confusion. He opened his mouth to speak, but verbal communication still seemed impossible. Instead she took him by the arm and led him carefully back towards the cabin.

A pole of inaccessibility is the furthest point you can get from any outpost of civilisation. For instance, one of the sea's poles of inaccessibility, in the southern Pacific Ocean, the furthest point from land anywhere on the planet, is known as Point Nemo.

But each country has its own pole of inaccessibility. Sweden's is located at the south-eastern inlet of Lake Kåbtåjaure in Padjelanta National Park in the district of Jokkmokk, not many metres from the improvised snow cave the pair had just left.

When she opened the door of the little cabin the gust of air from inside lifted her blonde hair.

The bed was empty, the sheets and covers all in a heap. The pills were still on the bedside table. The rectangular watch case was open for the first time since they arrived; one gilded chrome strap glinted faintly in the winter sunlight filtering through the windows.

The man pushed his way past her and sank onto the floor behind the rudimentary toilet, where he curled up with his back against the wall, his arms around his knees, his eyes staring off into the distance. He had a watch on his wrist for the first time in a very long while.

'It's been more than two weeks, Sam,' the woman said. 'But we're still not completely safe. I've got a timetable of when potential satellites are passing. It's important not to be outside then.'

He looked at her, stroked his thick beard, straightened his neck and said, looking away from her, 'This crap has to end.'

'It's not as if you're particularly easy to communicate with during this time, Sam. Have you stopped taking your medication?'

He shook his head and said, 'Molly, for fuck's sake.'

She crouched down beside him. They sat there for a while, she on her haunches, he against the wall. The only sound was the ticking of the radiator.

'I think it's running out,' Sam Berger said, gesturing towards the car battery.

'Apart from the satellite, you've picked a good time to wake up,' Molly Blom said. 'That makes the future look a bit brighter.'

'I've got no idea what you're talking about now.'

'You're right,' Blom said, getting to her feet. 'It's your fifth battery, and it's running out. It's nearly time for a bit of civilisation. As long as we bear in mind that we can't move freely. We're in hiding. We're being hunted. You remember that much, don't you?'

Berger looked at her. She looked back unflinchingly. His gaze was a cornucopia of questions.

'So many nightmares and hallucinations,' he said. 'A completely expressionless face keeps coming back the whole time. So, Syl's dead? Murdered by the Security Service? And with a fucking sock stuffed in her mouth?'

Blom observed Berger. He looked like he'd wasted away.

'I really hope I haven't been giving you too much medication, Sam. But you've been impossible to deal with. You don't remember any of it?'

'I remember us catching a murderer from the dim and distant past. I remember us freeing a load of hostages. I remember us getting fired from the police. I remember us being out in a rowing boat, making plans for the future. But my brain doesn't want to go any further than that.'

Blom leaned over next to Berger, picked up a dirty camping stove from the floor and put it on the table. Then she pulled out one of the wobbly chairs and sat down. She poured some water from a nearby plastic bottle into a badly dented saucepan and lit the gas stove. The sound drowned out the radiator.

'You need to eat,' she said.

'What the fuck am I wearing?' he muttered, getting laboriously to his feet and looking down at his body. 'A bright red padded coat with holes in, and filthy fleece trousers? What happened – did I mug a tramp or something?'

'We bought clothes along the way,' Blom said. 'From shops that definitely didn't have security cameras. And that restricted the choice. You don't have to wear that red coat any more, there's a white one.'

Blom pulled a small bag from one of the pockets of her coat, shook it gently and held it up.

'Beef soup?'

Berger shrugged and sat down on the other side of the table. Blom saw the confusion in his eyes, but at least now it was finally combined with a desire for knowledge. A desire to know rather than run away.

To confront the facts.

'I know I've been living in this barren shack for a hell of a long time,' he said. 'I've used that stinking composting toilet several times a day, I've drunk boiled water from the lake until I could use snow instead, I've eaten that hideous powdered soup. I haven't had a single shower. I know all that. But that's it. Where are we?'

'I've helped wash you,' Molly Blom said.

He looked at her and blinked several times. She went on:

'The lake is called Kåbtåjaure, and it's in Padjelanta National Park. It's as far from civilisation as I could get.'

'Padjelanta?' Berger exclaimed. 'Lapland? North of the Arctic Circle?'

'Yes,' Blom said. 'We had to get away, really get away. Because Sylvia Andersson's killers seem to be pretty good at finding people.'

'The Security Service.'

'Or an organisation linked to the Security Service somehow, yes. Do you remember the circumstances?'

'Not well enough,' Berger said. 'They killed Syl and left her five-year-old daughter Moira an orphan. And it was all my fault.'

'Sylvia was an adult,' Blom said, bringing the soup to the boil. 'And a police officer. She was capable of making her own decisions. A precondition for us being able to move on is that you stop beating yourself up. And get back on the pitch.'

'I pushed her too hard.'

'Do you remember what for?'

'Security Service files. She was going to hack her way through to some documents that had been erased from Security Service records.'

'And do you remember why?'

Berger screwed his eyes shut. Blom barely recognised him. He really was a different person.

'It was to do with our murderer,' he eventually blurted out. 'The Ellen Savinger case.'

'So are you ready to listen now? For the first time in over two weeks?'

He nodded. She took a deep breath.

'The murderer in the Ellen Savinger case was working indirectly for the Security Service, for their technical supplier, you remember that much?'

He nodded again. She went on, 'We thought it was a coincidence until we realised that he had also worked more actively for the Security Service, as a bodyguard for a family by the name of Pachachi, but that was the job that made him snap. Still with me?'

'Yes,' Berger said. 'I'm with you. The first girl he kidnapped. Aisha Pachachi.'

'Good,' Blom said appreciatively. 'We also managed to identify his father as a Norwegian mercenary called Nils Gundersen. This Gundersen was recruited back in the 70s by a young Security Service agent called August Steen, and went on to deliver vital information from the Middle East. Still with me?'

Berger nodded, frowning.

'August Steen. Current head of the Security Service?'

'Head of the Security Service's Intelligence Unit,' Blom confirmed. 'And he was the one who fired us.'

'But none of this is in Security Service files.'

'It's evidently been removed, fairly recently. Syl was in the process of tracking it down. Including the mysterious arrival of Ali Pachachi and his family from Iraq during the Gulf War. Why was that so secret? And why does August Steen appear to be prepared to kill to keep Gundersen's undercover work off all official records?'

Berger hadn't stopped nodding.

'What happened?' he asked. 'How did we end up here?'

'You remember the rowing boat,' she said. 'We thought we could relax, we were making plans for the future. You remember the boathouse?'

'Yes,' Berger said. 'I'm unlikely ever to forget that boathouse.'

'We even talked about buying it, going into business there, some sort of private detective agency. But instead Sylvia Andersson, your friend Syl, was sitting in the boathouse waiting for us. Dead. With a thick black sock stuffed in her mouth, just like one of the earlier victims, the senile old lady who gave us Nils Gundersen's name.'

'Fucking hell,' Berger said.

They didn't speak for a while, letting the long-suppressed past seep into the present until it started to get hard to breathe.

'Something happened to you there, Sam,' Blom said eventually. 'You became a different person.'

'After the rowing boat I only remember fragments.'

'We had made our way through a case that threw open all the shutters, that demolished all the firewalls you and I had both built up to keep the past at bay. Your feelings of guilt caught up with you. Guilt about me and a lot of other girls. But we got through it. Things were even starting to look a bit brighter. And then you got knocked completely off balance because you felt responsible for what happened to Syl and Moira. It's hardly surprising that you crumbled, Sam, and everything changed.'

'Crumbled?'

'I can't find a better way to describe it,' Blom said, pouring the soup out. 'I reacted pretty much on instinct; presumably my training as an undercover agent kicked in. All I knew was that we had to get away from there as invisibly as possible. They left Syl there for a reason. Either to frame us for her murder or as a warning, a sign that we'd been sentenced to death too; they could have got us then, while they were there – we were easy targets in that rowing boat out in Edsviken. Whatever this is, it really is that big. We blundered into it on the trail of a crazy killer, but he wasn't the main character in whatever this is. Something big was going on, and at the very most we were a couple of sacrificial pawns. So we had to get away from there, that was the only thought in my head.'

'You reacted instinctively, and I ... crumbled?'

'Have some soup, you're going to need it.'

Reluctantly Berger picked up the mug and took a sip of the hot liquid. It was immediately apparent, as usual, that there wasn't a great deal of beef involved in it. Blom drank some of hers, then went on, 'You literally fell apart. Like you'd been hit in the face with an anvil. I was left standing there with Syl's corpse and you unconscious on the floor, and I knew they were watching me, one way or another. I might have been able to get away, but then I'd have been forced to leave you. I had to bring you round quickly, Sam. And anyway the wound has healed now.'

'What, you cut me to bring me round?'

'I found an effective source of pain, yes. But you were impossible. You didn't seem to understand what was in your best interests, in our best interests. You were absolutely determined to go after August Steen, no matter what the cost. You wanted to go to the media, to shout it out from the rooftops. I had to calm you down.'

'Let me guess,' Berger said. 'Syringe to the neck?'

'I couldn't have you unconscious again, but I had to get you under control. I gave you half a dose. It worked, it made you more cooperative. Dizzy but cooperative. We escaped through the forest. The aspen trees, do you remember them?'

'The rustling of the aspen leaves,' Berger said. 'But they'd all dropped by then.'

'I held you up, and we stumbled through the forest, left our own car parked by the boathouses. We broke into a house and found a car key.'

'Seriously? *I* did that?'

'No, I left you on the porch steps and hoped no one would see you sitting there like a suspicious drunk. I've switched cars a couple of times since then. And now we've got this.'

Blom dangled a key in Berger's direction: the logo was unmistakable.

'A jeep.' He nodded. 'I'm guessing four-wheel drive?'

'It took me a while to figure out where to go. I couldn't contact anyone, not even once, that was the main thing. We had to stay below the radar the whole time. Off grid. These two cabins were what I ended up with, I remembered them from a hiking holiday a few years ago. No one ever comes up here, at least not in November. We've been lying low since then, no Internet, no phone calls, no transactions, no outside world at all. Plenty of existential angst, though. And a bit of skiing.'

Berger gestured towards the dangling car key and said, 'But now we're going to leave?'

'What do you mean?' Blom said.

'"Have some soup, you're going to need it." That's what you said.'

Blom drained her mug and looked at Berger. Their eyes met, as if they were each studying the other in detail.

Eventually Berger drank the last of his soup and said,

'So why do I need more energy than usual?'

Blom plonked her empty mug down on the table.

'Because I've got a surprise for you.'

6

The room is bare, claustrophobic, ice-cold, as if it's been blasted out of the rocks. Only the light from the screens stops the room being completely dark.

There are two screens, one above the other, and they show the same view but from different heights. The distance for screen visibility has been precisely optimised for the small desk, where a joystick controls the direction, zoom and focus. Right now the screens are showing still images, principally snow. The top screen shows two snow-covered cabins, one further away than the other, and the bottom screen only shows the closer of them.

Then the stillness is broken, over by the further cabin. Two people emerge, very small, very distant.

The hand wearing the thin leather glove zooms in on them with practised gestures; even from this distance the resolution is good. The woman is wearing thick white clothes, modern skiing gear, a tight-fitting woollen hat. The man is barefoot, and is wearing nothing but a towel wrapped about his waist. The woman leads him round the corner of the cottage, hands him a bucket, then walks back round the corner.

The camera remains focused on the woman for a while.

47

Then the left hand zooms in on the man. The right hand, also wearing a thin glove, makes notes on a small keyboard below a small screen:

'11.15: ♂ evidently awake; ♂ presumed ablutions; ♀ assisting from a distance.'

Then the man beside the cottage removes the towel and hangs it from a nail in the wall. His brown beard is streaked with grey. He steadies himself, pauses for a few moments, looking at the bucket.

Then he raises it above his head.

7

Waking up has many phases. Extreme wakefulness is usually only achieved by a sudden shock, primarily from cold.

When the bucket of meltwater washed over his naked body Berger certainly felt awake, to put it mildly. As if on a given signal a bottle of shampoo appeared from round the corner of the cottage. He swapped it for the empty bucket and the female hand disappeared again.

He soaped his whole body as the cold ate into him, millimetre by millimetre, apart from his feet, where it seemed to be taking greater strides. After a while the hand appeared round the corner again, this time with a full bucket. He tipped it quickly over his head and hung it back on the outstretched hand.

'Another one?' Blom asked.

'If it's not too much to ask,' Berger said through chattering teeth.

The bucket came back again. He emptied it over himself, grabbed the towel from the nail on the wall and had already started to dry himself as the water ran down his shins to freeze his feet to the snow.

But the water wasn't quick enough. He pulled free in a matter of seconds, rushed past Blom and into the cabin, half dry.

'Your normal clothes are in the bag,' Blom called from outside.

He quickly found them and pulled them on; everything felt disconcertingly normal apart from the thick snow boots that he'd never seen before but which fitted perfectly. When he stepped outside into the utterly silent winter landscape he wrapped a white coat over his padded white jacket. Molly Blom looked at him critically.

'What are we going to do about the beard?'

'That depends on what we're planning to do,' Berger replied.

She just nodded and set off. A relatively clear path led them up a hill, straight off across what looked like barren country. But instead another cabin came into view, slightly larger than his. There was a snow shovel outside it, but nothing else. Blom opened the door and went inside. Berger stood in the doorway while Blom gathered together a few things and tossed them into a rucksack.

He looked around the cabin. Just inside the door was a stack of car batteries, and on top of the stack was a large number of ordinary batteries, probably for lamps and torches. As in his own far shabbier cabin there was a wood-burning stove which evidently wasn't allowed to be used. He realised, in spite of his wretched condition, that this was because of the smoke. Smoke and satellites.

So this was where Molly Blom had been hiding for the past two weeks without any form of contact with the outside world, with a madman at an appropriate and manageable distance. He tried to see any sign of what she'd been doing. Cables led from a car battery beside the bed to a transformer from which more wires in turn led to a laptop on the bedside table and a basic printer just beneath it.

'No connection?' Berger said.

'Minimal,' Blom replied. 'And extremely secure. It was unavoidable.'

'You've googled the satellites?'

'Yes, I now know which ones the Security Service might have access to. They pass at fixed times, I've sent the schedule to your mobile.'

'So are you going to keep me on tenterhooks, then?'

Blom hoisted the rucksack onto her back, and as she pushed past she handed him a pair of sunglasses. The path through the snow led off across the landscape until it gradually petered out. Berger followed her, and soon they were pressing through the snow.

'Thank God it isn't too deep,' she said, leading the way. 'But it's still fifty kilometres to the nearest road.'

They moved on. The sun was still shining, and the ice-cold light reflected off the snow and somehow grew even colder. The sunglasses kept snow blindness at bay but couldn't stop the glare in their eyes.

Berger looked at his mobile, and despite the sunglasses he was able to see the satellites' schedule. They passed three times a day. But nothing for the next two hours.

The landscape was harsh, uneven, wild, mountainous. No vehicle could possibly drive across it, not even a four-by-four.

'How the hell did you get me all this way?' Berger asked breathlessly. 'I have absolutely no memory of walking.'

'The same way we made it through the forest at Edsviken,' Blom said. 'Regular, limited injections. You were able to walk but not much more than that. There was no snow then, the landscape looked completely different.'

Blom checked the compass on her phone and adjusted her course slightly to the south. They walked on for an indeterminate length of time without saying a word.

After a while the snow grew thinner and it became easier to walk; they had evidently reached an area where the prevailing wind was stronger. Trees started to appear; they may have been small and crooked, but they had evidently just crossed the treeline.

In the distance Berger saw something that looked like a wind shelter. Blom headed confidently towards it and began to clear the snow away. When she broke through and started to move some tree trunks Berger joined in. He wasn't in good shape, that much was abundantly clear. For the first time in his life he was reminded of the fragility of his body.

'Did you make this?' he asked, tossing a stunted birch branch aside.

'In case they decided to get really serious about satellite surveillance,' Blom said. 'Although I doubt that. Even the Security Service have to think about their budget. And, like I said, this isn't exactly the hiking season. But I didn't want to take any risks.'

The back of the jeep became visible. Military green – what else? Had she stolen it from an army camp?

Blom cleared a path to the driver's door, started the engine without any problem and reversed out. As Berger was getting into the passenger seat she was rooting through her rucksack. She pulled out a sheet of paper and passed it to him.

'It's a bit bumpy to start with,' Blom said. 'Hold tight.'

'What am I supposed to do with this?' Berger asked, waving the paper.

'Read it, maybe?' Blom said, and put her foot down.

'"To Superintendent Desiré Rosenkvist"?' Berger exclaimed and started to read.

When the intermittently non-existent path started to resemble a proper track for the first time in many kilometres Blom stopped and changed the jeep's number plates. Not long after that they reached the village.

In summer Kvikkjokk was the natural starting point for hiking trips in the Sarek and Padjelanta areas, but in early winter the village was considerably more desolate. By the time the jeep drove into what might be described as a built-up area they still hadn't seen a single person.

A bumpy fifty-kilometre drive through the wastes of Lapland in November ought to have left Berger feeling more astonished than it did. The reason was simple. He had just read a remarkable text written on a typewriter. It had even made him forget that he should have been feeling travel-sick.

He read out loud, '"The first time I heard the sound was two months ago. It's hard to describe. It's as if someone's inside the wall. The sound doesn't seem to come from inside the house, and not from outside either, and there's no way it can be human."'

She glanced at him, but otherwise didn't react.

'Who wrote this?' he asked as they drove past a sign announcing that they would soon reach Kvikkjokk Mountain Lodge.

'And what happened to her?' Blom replied, pulling into a car park between a number of long red wooden buildings. Water in the most stubborn section of some rapids was still forcing its way through an expanding covering of ice, but it was clear that the river was about to cease flowing for the next six months.

'You're seriously going to answer me with a question?' Berger said. 'You were the one who gave me this piece of paper. Which was addressed to my former colleague Deer? Using the wrong rank?'

'Has the detective in you suddenly gone into retirement?' Blom said. 'Yes, it was written on a typewriter, but is it an original document? Couldn't I have produced it using the little printer you saw in the cabin?'

Berger looked at his colleague as she got out of the jeep.

'Is this safe?' he asked, gesturing towards their surroundings.

'Supposedly,' she said. 'Keep your questions to yourself. And please be careful what you say for the next few minutes.'

'Supposedly?' Berger said, but he was talking to a closed car door.

He got out. The sharp icy air cut through his airways, and he had to jog to catch up with Blom. It felt oddly refreshing. They reached a flight of steps leading up to a sort of loft, the upper floor of one of the rust-red wooden buildings. There was still no one in sight; it was as if the entire universe had frozen solid. Blom led the way towards a door and knocked. While they waited for a response she turned to Berger and said, 'I hope your heart's feeling strong now.'

Berger just stared at her.

The door opened. He turned and found himself looking down at a woman with clear brown eyes and her dark hair cut in a bob. She pulled a little face and gestured slightly reluctantly to them to step inside.

Blom walked in, Berger didn't. Only now did his feet freeze to the ground, as if they had been waiting for just the right moment.

'Deer?' he said tentatively.

'Yeah, yeah,' the dark-haired woman said. 'Now come inside before someone sees that beard and calls the police.'

'What the actual fuck are you doing in Kvikkjokk?'

'Come in,' Desiré Rosenkvist repeated patiently as if she had done things like this many times before.

She gestured curtly towards a pair of chairs that had been placed next to what looked like a very small desk. On the desk were a pair of binoculars, three folders of varying thickness and a typewritten letter that looked a lot like the one Berger was still holding in his hand. Deer sat down opposite them and fixed her eyes on Berger's.

'Obviously I just happen to find myself in Kvikkjokk,' she said. 'We concluded that it was a reasonable place to meet.'

'We?' Berger said, looking out through the window at the desolate mountain scenery. 'Reasonable?'

'Quick in, quick out,' Deer said enigmatically. 'Day off after a weekend meeting under the auspices of the National Operations Department, direct flight to Kiruna, rented car, flight home. What the actual fuck are the two of you doing here?'

Berger met her gaze and felt how empty his own gaze was.

'Even if I understand every word you're saying, Deer, I can't make any sense of it at all. Except perhaps the word fuck, which seems pretty appropriate.'

Deer paused, looked at him intently, then said eventually:

'You got fired, just as I predicted. You disappeared in conjunction with Syl's tragic death. After a few days I sent a text to your private mobile. And Blom here replied. I've spent a fair while considering that reply.'

Berger studied the view through the window. Right now that was the most comprehensible thing in the vicinity.

'There are too many questions again,' he said. 'I'm shutting down.'

'As I understand it, you've been shut down for quite some time. And as I understand it, you were in the process of investing your redundancy money in the private sector. And as I understand it, it was extremely uncertain that you'd actually show up for this meeting.'

'I didn't even know about this meeting,' Berger said.

'But you've seen the typewritten letter?'

'I've just read it, yes. Who wrote it?'

'That's of secondary importance. The most important thing is if you reacted to anything.'

'Plenty of things, obviously. Is the woman who wrote it alive?'

'She's fine,' Deer said. 'The letter was written a couple of weeks ago, and she phoned from her cellar steps. The Jokkmokk police were there within an hour or so. There was nothing to indicate that anyone else had been there. And certainly not house borers.'

'But then she sent the unfinished letter directly to you?' Berger said. 'And called you Superintendent?'

'I am a superintendent,' Deer said. 'A temporary post with the National Operations Department.'

'The NOD? How did that happen?'

'Our unit fell apart. Allan retired, Syl had her stroke ...'

'Her stroke?' Berger exclaimed and felt Blom's hand squeeze his thigh hard. That was enough to make him shut up.

'Yes?' Deer said, looking at him intently.

'I didn't know the cause of death, that's all,' Berger said quietly.

'And you weren't at the funeral either ... What the hell are you doing up here? Hiding out? Making sweet love in an igloo?'

Blom pre-empted Berger.

'We got together in peace and quiet to discuss the future after the end of our respective careers in the police. Our relationship is strictly professional.'

Deer looked at her, shook her head and then turned demonstratively towards Berger, 'When a post at the NOD was announced with an immediate start date, I applied and got the job.'

'Congratulations,' Berger said.

'And the first thing that landed in my lap is Jessica Johnsson from Porjus. Just as she writes, she's a well-known troublemaker. Everyone in the NOD just shook their heads when I showed them the letter. They told me to burn it.'

'But you didn't.'

'And you know why, don't you, Sam?'

Berger wrinkled his nose but didn't say anything.

'If this letter is aimed at me,' Deer said, 'then it's also aimed at you, isn't it?'

'All I can see is a load of conspiracy theories,' Blom said.

Berger and Deer's eyes were locked. It took a good while before Deer looked away and said, 'Yes, Jessica Johnsson certainly trots through various conspiracies. But there's one name that stands out, isn't there, Sam?'

'Karl Hedblom,' Berger muttered.

'This is what it says: "... that the ink mark on Lisa Widstrand's buttock was even mentioned in the local press without the police bothering to wonder if that had implications for Karl Hedblom's guilt".'

'The first case we worked on together, Deer,' Berger said.

'And a bloody nasty case at that,' Deer said. 'It left its mark. A deep mark. Even though it was eight years ago, I can remember it like it was yesterday. A lot of sleepless nights later.'

'And you think she sent the letter to you personally all because of Karl Hedblom?'

'I can't see any other reason. Assuming that it was actually sent by her.'

'Ah,' Blom said.

Berger and Deer turned to look at her.

'I didn't make the connection with Hedblom's name,' Blom explained. 'It was a double murder, wasn't it? A mother and infant?'

'We were seconded to the National Crime Unit, as it was known at the time,' Deer said. 'The badly brutalised remains of thirty-five-year-old Helena Gradén and her fourteen-month-old son Rasmus were found in a ditch on the outskirts of Orsa. The child was still in his pushchair, at least partially. What sort of murder was it? Was it primarily the murder of a child or the murder of a woman? The detectives were tearing their hair out, looking into absolutely every option. It was heartbreaking. The father, Emmanuel Gradén, was the prime suspect for a long time, while he simultaneously tried to cope with overwhelming grief. It wasn't until the investigating team began to look at things from a different angle and think outside the box that they started to make any progress. It wasn't the child or the woman individually that was the principal target: they were looking for someone who wanted to kill a mother, a mother and son. It took a lot of psychological expertise – about as far from the Thomas Quick case as you could get – to shift the focus of the investigation. But in the end a man was found who was both severely disturbed and who had been on holiday not far from Orsa for a few weeks that summer with other residents from his sheltered accommodation. The man's name was Karl Hedblom, twenty-four years old, with a truly horrifying childhood behind him with the mother from hell. Helena and Rasmus Gradén weren't found until two days after they went missing. Karl Hedblom was pretty much able to come and go as he pleased, and in the end they found a freshly built shelter in the woods between the ditch where they were found and the place where the care-home residents were staying. And traces of blood and Hedblom's DNA were found in the shelter.'

Blom nodded, but she was frowning.

'This may be taboo seeing as Jessica Johnsson is a well-known troublemaker,' Deer said. 'But that's a secondary concern, really. The main reason it's untouchable is that the capture of Karl Hedblom was the crowning glory of many police officers' careers, Allan Gudmundsson's among them. It would take an awful lot to drag him back from his bridge tournament in Tahiti.'

'Bridge tournament?' Berger exclaimed.

'Didn't you know Allan and his wife are among the top bridge players in Sweden? Since they retired they've played all over the world.'

'Bloody hell,' Berger said.

Blom threw her hands out and said, 'So why would a brief passing reference in a letter from a conspiracy theorist have serious implications?'

'There was one question mark in the investigation that was never cleared up,' Berger said. 'Something that was never explained, which the police kept to themselves and eventually got overlooked altogether. A small ink drawing on Helena Gradén's left buttock.'

'I'd never heard of Lisa Widstrand,' Deer said. 'Jessica Johnsson mentions her in the letter. She turns out to have been a prostitute in Gothenburg who was brutally murdered by an unknown client. The case was never solved, but I've seen the photographs. And, sure enough, there's an ink mark on her left buttock.'

'What sort of drawing is it, then?' Blom asked. 'And how come the police didn't pick up on the connection?'

Deer held her hands up and said, 'Murdered prostitutes are more common than people think and often don't get any coverage in the media. It's not given top priority, sadly.'

'It was a very precise drawing of a four-leaf clover,' Berger said.

They fell silent and looked at each other. Intently.

'Jessica Johnsson addressed the letter to the NOD, and wrote *Superintendent* Desiré Rosenkvist. I became a superintendent just before she sent the letter. So she's been keeping an eye on me somehow. Which means she probably knows I was involved in the Gradén case. There's a strong probability that's all she wanted to say with this whole letter: that Karl Hedblom might be innocent. And she wanted to tell me specifically. Why?'

Berger nodded.

'And why are you sitting here in a secret meeting with a couple of cops who've lost their jobs and you think are *hiding out*?'

'A directive has been issued by the head of the National Operations Department saying that no one's to get involved with Jessica Johnsson at all. She's a classic pariah. In other words, I can't do anything myself. But I think she'd be just as happy to talk to you as she would to me, Sam. She knows something. I want the two of you to question her, unofficially, obviously. I want to know if it's worth the effort and anxiety that reopening the case would cause.'

'And the two of you have already agreed on this?' Berger said. 'I don't know if I'm well enough to play at being a private detective.'

Deer pushed the three folders across the little table towards them; the one on the left was considerably thicker than the others.

'The Gradén case,' Deer said, tapping it with her finger. 'The Widstrand case. And this is the file on Jessica Johnsson herself. You go and see her as representatives of the NOD, mention me as your reference, no one else. I'll send fake ID and business cards. And everything has to happen entirely unofficially; I shall deny all knowledge if you mess up. I've called Jessica Johnsson and told her you'll be paying her a visit. It needs to look like you're investigating this mystery man who's supposed to be watching her. But you'll really be there to find out what she knows about the murders of Helena Gradén, Rasmus Gradén and Lisa Widstrand.'

Berger turned to Blom. She nodded slowly.

'Where the hell's Porjus?' Berger asked.

'It's the next village,' Deer said and stood up.

Then she handed them a sturdy satellite phone.

8

In Lapland 'the next village' doesn't mean nearby. On the contrary, the phrase is used with conscious irony.

But compared with the winding path from the pole of inaccessibility, the road from Kvikkjokk to Vaikijaur was extremely well maintained. As the sun sank behind the mountains in an enchanted cauldron of colours just after two o'clock in the afternoon, they had almost reached their destination on the longest road in Europe.

Roads designated as European highways cross this way and that all over the continent, but none of them runs so far and so straight between north and south as the E45. It covers five thousand kilometres from Gela on the south coast of Sicily to Karesuando, the northernmost built-up area in Sweden; from the southern tip of the EU to its northernmost point. In the north of Sweden it's known as the Inland Highway, and from Vaikijaur in Lapland it rushes north towards Porjus.

The jeep had been silent all the way from Kvikkjokk. Information was being processed on either side of the gear stick.

'So you didn't know?' Berger eventually said.

'I knew Rosenkvist wanted you for some reason,' Blom said. 'But not what.'

'Deer sent a text to my private reserve phone? From hers, I assume? Two anonymous pay-as-you-go phones in the infinity of cyberspace. What exactly did she say?'

'"How are you? I can't get hold of you any other way. Important."'

'"Important"?'

'That's what made me answer,' Blom said. 'Briefly. As if you didn't want to be disturbed.'

'There was mobile coverage up at Copter-yowler, then?'

'It's *Kåbtåjaure*. No, not really. But under certain atmospheric conditions there's a bit of a signal if you're standing in the right place. Rosenkvist asked to email an address that didn't look official. I got a connection by going to the right place, admitted that it was me writing but from a long way away, said you were out of action for a while – I said you had an upset stomach – and got that typewritten letter in reply. When she asked if we were up north I clammed up. Because maybe the Security Service had got to her too. But she explained the situation, and I did my best to figure out how much truth there was in what she was saying and replied that we were flexible. Then I suggested meeting in Kvikkjokk, as something approaching neutral territory between us and Porjus.'

'I assume you were given the name Jessica Johnsson in the email?' Berger said. 'Have you checked her out? Who is she?'

'Untouchable, like Rosenkvist said. She's been sending letters to the police for years. The sort who always takes everything too far. One of the impossible ones.'

'I've reread the letter. Our Jessica really is in the dark.'

'Yes, Darkness with a capital letter and everything,' Blom said. 'Tell me about Helena Gradén.'

Berger stared out into what was now complete darkness.

'I've tried not to think about it,' he said after a while.

'Bad?'

'There was a video ...'

Silence settled inside the jeep. Half a minute passed before Berger went on, 'Fourteen-month-old Rasmus taking his first steps. Helena Gradén was so happy, laughing so much that Rasmus started to laugh as well. That laughter has tormented me. A mother and child's laughter, woven together into some sort of undeniable ... tapestry of life. I can't really explain it. It *got* to me. One week later they were both dead. Slaughtered.'

Blom said nothing for a while. Eventually she cast a quick glance and said, 'We can turn round if you like.'

'No,' Berger said firmly. 'I was Allan's sidekick during the decisive interview with Karl Hedblom. Allan was so on the ball in those days, he managed to bring out the worst in Karl, who turned out to be both mad and violent. He really did hate women who happened to be mothers. His placement in a poorly supervised care home was obviously a mistake, and it was even more of a mistake to take him on a trip with the other residents. Something had gone very wrong with the diagnosis of his mental state – a senior consultant lost his job over it – but at the same time there was something about the deed itself that Karl seemed completely oblivious to. Allan pushed hard, everything made sense until it was time to talk about the two days in that shelter.'

'What happened?' Blom asked.

'Karl Hedblom confessed. Without reservation. But his account of the circumstances left quite a lot to be desired. Because the physical evidence was overwhelming the court determined that he appeared to have been in a psychotic state and was simply unable to remember the details.'

'And you were convinced too?'

'I was at the time, yes,' Berger said. 'By the bigger picture.'

'Did Hedblom say anything about the ink drawing?'

'He admitted he had drawn it, but it wasn't discussed beyond that. Compared with the rest of it, a small drawing on her buttock seemed completely insignificant.'

'I assume you're going to tell me about *the rest of it* ...'

'If not, I dare say it's all in here,' Berger said, holding up the folders in the darkness inside the jeep. A couple of business cards fell out of the bundle. Berger picked them up from his lap and managed to focus on the lettering. He grimaced in disgust.

'We're there,' Blom said.

The jeep's headlights lit up the wall of a house some fifty metres away. When Blom pulled the key from the ignition only a very faint glow remained. It was coming from the porch, at the top of a flight of steps leading to a nondescript old house on a plateau out in the wilderness. There were no other lights in sight, not even any stars, and definitely not the moon.

Blom got out and Berger followed her. Beside the parking space they could make out a garage wall, and on the other side of the jeep a path led towards the house; Blom shone her torch at it. The snow lay thick and completely undisturbed. There was no doubt that any stalker would have left obvious tracks.

They climbed the steps gingerly and rang the bell. Berger turned away from the faintly lit porch towards the bitterly cold Lapland night. It wasn't much past three o'clock in the afternoon, but it was already completely dark. He tried to remain in the present, but the darkness was dragging him inexorably towards a ditch outside Orsa.

The pushchair. The mother's hand still holding it in spite of the position of her body. The blood.

Berger hadn't seen the scene of the crime. Not at the time. But he had seen photographs, intrusive, close-up photographs. And he had seen the crime scene later, when they were no longer there. That made it even worse; his imagination filled in the gaps.

The opening door quickly pulled him out of the dark depths of memory. The woman who appeared in the doorway didn't make much of an impression, she turned away before Berger was able to take a good look at her. All he could see were a thick knitted sweater and a pair of matching slipper-socks.

They went in and sat at a dimly lit dining table in an even more dimly lit living room. Berger placed his phone on the table and idly fingered his teacup as he glanced surreptitiously into a bedroom. He could see a desk with an old typewriter on it.

'Are you going to talk about house borers?' the woman asked, lighting a candle.

That was the moment when Berger saw Jessica Johnsson properly for the first time. The candlelight lit up her pale face. She was somewhere between thirty and forty, and there was something nervy about her whole being. She wasn't wearing make-up, her hair was fairly short, and her blue eyes were sharp even if they kept darting about.

'No house borers,' Blom said.

'I'm grateful for that.'

'What happened when you stopped writing?' Berger asked. 'You stopped in the middle of a sentence.'

'I don't understand.'

'Here. The last sentence in your letter reads: "Just as the small flame of the candle blows out I hear …" Then it just stops. And then you sent it to the police – without finishing it. Why?'

Jessica Johnsson chose to stare at the business card in front of her instead of the man opposite.

'Detective Inspector Lindbergh?' she said. 'With an h? What does the C stand for? "C. Lindbergh"?'

'Just answer the question,' Berger said. 'What did you hear when the cold breeze blew through the bedroom? Just as the candle blew out?'

'The front door opening,' Jessica Johnsson said and looked at him for the first time; her gaze seemed simultaneously open and guarded.

'And what did you do then?'

'I ran to the cellar door and threw myself in. Then I called the police from the cellar steps. I didn't want to go down there; I haven't been in the cellar for a couple of years.'

'If you think a crazed killer has just come through the front door, maybe your first instinct would be to hide?'

'I wasn't thinking rationally. Sorry. And the mobile signal was better from the stairs.'

'So you were thinking rationally when it came to that?'

'Instinctively. I didn't know I was thinking rationally.'

Berger nodded and looked at the woman. In his life as a police officer he had been a good judge of people. That ability could hardly have vanished in the space of two weeks. But Jessica Johnsson was hard to read. There was no sign of the manic energy that shone from the eyes of truly paranoid people. On the other hand there was none of the glow of crystal-clear intelligence like there came from Molly Blom beside him. It was almost as if the look in her eyes had gone into hibernation, it was apathetic and nervy at the same time, and a strange little smile was playing at the corners of her mouth. Berger saw Blom looking analytically at Johnsson. He wondered if she was having as much trouble evaluating her as he was.

'How long did you sit on the cellar steps?' he asked.

'Until the police arrived.'

'And during that time you didn't hear anything.'

'I heard the boiler.'

'The boiler?'

'The oil-fired boiler,' Jessica Johnsson said. 'It makes a rumbling sound. I don't like the noise. That's why I stopped using the cellar.'

'But nothing from upstairs?'

'Like I said to the police constables: nothing. I'd locked the cellar door and had found an old fire axe beside the steps. I was clutching it so hard they had to prise my fingers off one by one.'

'So you didn't go back up the stairs at all until the police arrived?'

'No. Not until they shouted: "It's the police, Jessica, where are you?"'

'Did they sound worried?'

'No. I know what they think of me. One of the first things I heard was "house borers".'

'And the letter was still in the typewriter then?'

'Yes, they didn't even look at it. When they left I got the idea of sending it. So you'd realise what it's like for me here. To get someone here who wasn't from the useless Jokkmokk police.'

'And now here we are,' Berger said. 'So talk to us. Why did you address the letter specifically to Superintendent Desiré Rosenkvist?'

'I saw her on television a few weeks ago,' Johnsson said. 'There was a kidnapping in Stockholm, Ellen something or other. She was interviewed. She came across well, and when I looked her up a bit later I found out that she was a superintendent at the NOD. I thought she might take me more seriously than the local police.'

Berger nodded and said, 'Obviously the man stalking you isn't a stranger. You know who he is, don't you? Why don't you want to tell us?'

Jessica Johnsson looked at him. Yes, there was sharpness there when she actually managed to focus, but there was something else too. Fear? Did it look like she knew that someone was out to get her?'

'I really don't know,' she said.

Berger leaned back in his chair and kept quiet. He hoped Blom would pick up the signal and take over.

She did.

'You've chosen to live in an extremely isolated place, Jessica,' Blom said. 'As far as I understand it, you haven't got a job, a husband or any children. Are you running away from something?'

'I just want to be left in peace,' Johnsson mumbled.

'In peace from what? Did you move here to get away from someone?'

'People in general. Like I said, I just want to be left alone.'

Blom fixed her eyes on her. Berger noticed and looked on intently, casting just a quick glance at his phone: the recording seemed to be working OK.

'You're from Stockholm, Jessica,' Blom said. 'You grew up in Rågsved, but a lot of your file is blank.'

'Why would you even have a file on me? I haven't been accused of anything.'

'We try to keep an eye on people who contact the police disproportionately often,' Blom said. 'But when there's a suspicion of a crime we have to look more closely at the individual.'

'Suspicion of a crime?'

'Withholding evidence,' Blom said and turned towards Berger.

Berger nodded sternly and said, 'I think we're going to have to dig a bit deeper into Jessica Johnsson's background, yes. That's probably where we're going to find the house borers.'

Jessica Johnsson's eyes swivelled towards Berger. He met her gaze. No one enjoys talking as much as conspiracy theorists; it's almost a law of nature for them to have to give voice to all the truths that people in power are trying to keep quiet. But Johnsson was restrained, she hadn't said anything she didn't have to so far. But she had still shouted very loudly to attract police officers who weren't local.

To get Deer here.

And now she wasn't talking.

Why?

'Who do you think is watching you?' Berger asked.

Jessica Johnsson just shook her head unhappily. Berger tried to pick up all the nuances of her movements, the constant shifts in her gaze, her unspoken words. There were discrepancies between what she had written and the way she was behaving now, between her paranoid temperament and the look in her eyes.

He needed to look more closely at that difference.

He remembered a previous interview, a life-changing interview with a woman called Nathalie Fredén they didn't have enough on to arrest. He glanced at Molly Blom again. This time she looked back and nodded almost imperceptibly.

Berger nodded more noticeably, switched the recording off on his phone and slipped it into the inside pocket of his old jacket. Then he got to his feet and said, 'I think we'll need to conduct a more formal interview, with video cameras and better lighting. We can do that at the police station in Jokkmokk if you like. It's practically next door, after all.'

Jessica Johnsson just looked at him.

'Or we could do it here,' Berger went on. 'Then you'll get shot of us sooner. Up to you, Jessica.'

'Here,' Johnsson said.

'OK,' Berger said. 'We'll get some lights set up and so on. But first we have to check the house.'

'Check the house?'

'You show us around the house and immediate surroundings. I don't suppose the Jokkmokk police took the trouble to do that?'

Jessica Johnsson stood up and gave him an inscrutable look. For the second time in a very short while he regretted that they weren't recording everything on video.

She led them upstairs. There wasn't much to see. Blom kept her mobile raised the whole time, taking pictures. Berger looked inside an attic in the eaves. The torch that had formed part of Blom's escape kit didn't pick up anything but motes of dust carried by air currents beyond human perception. They swirled round for a while before settling back down on top of four ancient trunks a bit like those migrants to America used to make dehydrated horses drag across the prairies.

'Those were here when I moved in,' Jessica Johnsson said.

'And you've never looked to see what's in them?'

She shook her head. They moved on. Two bedrooms, each with an attic under the eaves in the lowest part of the roof. In the first bedroom the solitary bed was bare, its wooden slats standing out like exposed ribs. In the second the attic was dusty but empty, while the bed and an armchair were covered with white sheets of the type well-to-do nineteenth-century families used to cover their furniture when it was time to leave their summer homes for the winter.

'Did you do this?' Berger asked.

Jessica Johnsson just shook her head. But Berger didn't back down. He kept watching her in the harsh light from the torch.

'It was like this when I moved in,' she said eventually. 'I've washed the sheets a few times, that's all.'

They left the bedroom. Berger lingered for a moment and ran his finger over the white cover of the sofa. Then they walked back out onto the landing. There were armchairs and a sofa there that didn't look like they'd been sat on since the turn of the century. They went back downstairs and into the kitchen. It was clean, a bit worn, but there were no signs of neglect. Berger saw Blom run one finger surreptitiously over an out-of-the-way surface.

Most of the rest of the ground floor was occupied by the large living room, which curved around the stairs and was divided into three distinct areas: a porch where the hall merged into a space containing a group of three chairs; an open space where a small television was mounted on the wall in front of a sofa; and then the dining area where the short interview had taken place. Finally they walked into the downstairs bedroom; Berger looked at the old typewriter and glanced over at the bed, which was just as neatly made as he had suspected.

'The basement,' he said.

'Do we have to?' Jessica Johnsson said.

'Yes,' Molly Blom said, switching her phone on. 'We're with you, there's no reason to be alarmed.'

Johnsson led them to a white-painted door with an old key in it. She turned it and cast a wary, almost slightly amused look at them. She smiled her strange, thin smile and opened the door.

'I'm not usually this faint-hearted,' she said.

The darkness that rose up from below almost seemed to push its way out through the doorway. Berger saw Blom take a step to the side as if to let the darkness past, and as they took the first steps down the staircase they were met by a smell of disuse.

Blom switched her torch on, shone it down the stairs and let the others go past her. Behind their backs she wedged her phone beside the handrail.

Then they took another step.

9

To start with, everything is very shaky. A white door with an old key in it. A hand turning it.

Then darkness, thick darkness. A strong torch, steps appearing, one after the other. The cellar stretches out of sight on either side of the staircase. Everything is still very shaky.

Then the image stops moving, becomes steadier. The far right is suddenly obscured by a dark surface, probably a beam somewhere beside the staircase. The image is now completely steady.

A woman comes into view, moving down the stairs. Then another figure, a man, and finally another woman, blonde with longer hair; she's the one holding the torch. Halfway down she turns and looks up the flight of steps as if to check that everything is still in position.

She seems to have the best overview of what's going on.

They stop at the bottom of the stairs, some distance away now. But there's very little distance between them. They're being drawn together, almost magnetically. Quiet words are exchanged; the only noise is a rumbling that sounds like an old-fashioned oil-fired boiler. Another torch is switched on. Beams of light spread across the basement.

The man with the recently turned-on torch is following the first woman, the one with darker hair. The other beam of light is moving separately, off towards the right. The blonde woman is rarely visible, but when she does appear she's rooting through clutter: ancient garden furniture, rusty bicycles, a surprising number of car tyres, moth-eaten canvas covering indistinct objects.

The man and woman to the left move out of shot. Every now and then the beam of the torch comes into view, but not much else. Then they move off towards the door that seems to be the source of the noise. They stop in front of it. The darker-haired woman waves the blonde woman over. The man follows. Fragments of voices occasionally drown out the sound of the boiler.

The man raises his hand towards the door handle. But he doesn't reach it.

He doesn't quite reach it.

Instead the door is thrown open hard from inside, and the rumble of the boiler suddenly becomes an awful lot louder. The door hits the man's head and he stumbles back. The blonde woman raises her torch as if to strike out with it, and its light sweeps across the ceiling, but she's too slow, what looks like a lump of wood hits her in the temple. The man gets unsteadily to his feet and gets hit in the head by the same piece of wood. He falls.

Only then does a figure emerge from the compact darkness of the boiler room. A large, shadowy figure, almost a silhouette. The boiler is roaring too loudly for any voices to be audible, it's like a pantomime, a silent film, and all movements seem oddly angular.

The figure strikes the prone man again with the block of wood, then turns towards the blonde woman, who is crouched on her knees. He hits her on the back of her head, and she slumps to the cellar floor and stays there.

He quickly looks at the two fallen bodies, then pulls something from his pocket. The dark-haired woman is covering her face with her hands, and the figure pulls her sideways and quickly ties her hands to the handrail with a cable tie. She sinks to her knees with her arms pulled awkwardly upwards, obscuring her face.

The figure drags the fallen man to the right-hand wall and fastens his wrists to a radiator, then repeats the procedure with the blonde woman. They sit there tied to their respective radiators, five metres apart, and the man turns his attention to the dark-haired woman by the stairs. He pulls a large hunting knife from his pocket and walks towards her. For the first time a voice clearly drowns out the clatter of the boiler as a shrill woman's screaming cuts through the basement.

The silhouette comes closer and raises the knife towards the woman. Then he cuts the cable tie, grabs hold of her and carries her flailing body up the staircase. Just as he passes the camera, in the weak light from the half-open cellar door above, his face becomes visible. And it isn't a face.

It's a black balaclava, and it's only visible for a fraction of a second before he moves past. There's the sound of a door slamming shut, and suddenly there's chaotic movement. Then everything becomes still again; the only thing in sight seems to be the very faintly illuminated corner of a plastic bag.

A metallic female voice rose above the noise of the boiler, 'Is that the end?'

'The camera fell over,' a more normal-sounding female voice explained.

'And Jessica Johnsson? What the hell happened to her?'

'Traces of blood in the house and out in the snow, and an open garage door. Too much blood for her to be alive, it was a real bloodbath. All the evidence suggests that the attacker murdered her and drove off with the body.'

Only then, when the tinny female voice let out a deep groan, did Berger properly recognise Deer's voice over the satellite phone. It was standing on the dining table where they had sat and tried to question Jessica Johnsson just a few hours before. He lowered the napkin from his head and looked at the blood. It was several different shades of red, at different stages of coagulation; it was like a déjà vu experience.

Blom was sitting on the other side of the table with a similar napkin pressed to her head, holding the phone to her ear.

'Christ, you were only supposed to go and ask her a few questions,' Deer roared down the phone. 'Instead you're dumping one hell of a mess in my lap.'

'He attacked us, Desiré,' Blom said. 'We were taken completely by surprise.'

A silence followed. Even from a distance Berger thought he could hear Deer swallowing a great mass of words. Eventually she spoke.

'So you went down into a pitch-black basement in an isolated house with a person who has reported that she's being stalked, *completely unprepared*?'

By now the silence was a third person in the room, and a very intrusive one at that.

'And there's nothing else on the recording?' Desiré asked after a while.

'It goes on for another ten minutes,' Blom replied. 'Until the phone battery ran out. Pointed at a plastic bag caught on the staircase. I came round before Sam, and by then I'd been out almost three hours. Then I spent twenty minutes chewing through the cable tie. Eventually I was able to slide over to Sam and shake him until he regained consciousness.'

Berger looked around the gloom. The house was now a completely different place. As was the world.

'And you're certain there isn't anyone left in the house?' Deer said.

'We were very groggy when we woke up,' Blom said. 'And like I said, three hours had passed. We weren't sure of our physical condition, we may be suffering from concussion. In the end we dragged ourselves up and did our best to secure the house. I put the phone on charge and went to get the satellite phone from the car, and that's when I saw the trail of blood on the snow. It wasn't like an ordinary trail, more like someone was being carried and put down on the snow every now and then, in something like a coffin.'

'But you haven't gone upstairs?'

'We did try ...'

'For God's sake, tell me you've got something else,' Deer roared.

Blom closed her eyes briefly and wrinkled her nose even more quickly.

'Like I said, we haven't looked upstairs. But we've covered the ground floor.'

'With the camera?'

'Yes.'

Deer let out an audible sigh. Berger grimaced and tasted blood in the corner of his mouth. He wiped his face again, but the napkin was as good as useless now. He needed a fresh one.

Blom tapped at her phone and attached it to the satellite phone's base station.

'Now,' she said.

The living room is brightly lit, as if someone wanted to drive out a long period of nightmares. The picture swings towards the dining table. No satellite phone yet but an awful lot of bloodstained napkins. Then the image moves through the open-plan living room, turns left towards the room with the television and sofa. The floor beside the sofa suddenly glistens, and the reading lamp beside the sofa is reflected in a large pool on the floor. When the camera gets closer it becomes obvious that it's a pool of blood. At its centre it is completely smooth, with a slightly coagulated surface. Various tracks lead away from the pool, including three footprints from a shoe at least size 45. But also two relatively clear lines, as if someone had been dragged away. These parallel lines lead towards the hall, before suddenly veering off towards the staircase to the upper floor. The camera follows them to the first step. Then the already shaky image becomes even more shaky and everything starts to spin, and suddenly the screen shows just the ceiling. Berger's face flickers past, his eyes full of concern. A drip sails through the air from his passing face and gets larger and larger. There's a splat, and the screen goes red.

'You fainted?' Deer asks over the phone.

'Let's just say that we didn't get upstairs,' Blom said.

'We've been taking it in turns to pass out,' Berger said out loud.

Deer evidently heard him, because she said, 'You've left so much of your DNA around that it's probably going to be very difficult to get rid of it all. But I can't have you showing up in this investigation, not in any form. And certainly not as suspects.'

'We can spend a few hours getting rid of evidence,' Blom said.

'Have you turned the lights out?' Deer asked. 'The recording was so brightly lit that the house must have stood out like a beacon. No curious neighbours have shown up?'

'Lights all switched off now,' Blom said. 'And no curious neighbours. I'd say that no one can see the house unless they're already on their way here.'

'So what's your best guess at the sequence of events?'

'The perpetrator broke into the house at some unknown point in time, probably when Jessica Johnsson wasn't home. He settled down in the boiler room and waited. While he was there he found a block of wood that he got ready to use on her whenever she deigned to appear.'

'Have you found the wood?'

'No,' Blom said.

'It doesn't sound particularly premeditated,' Deer said. 'A block of wood?'

'We'll have to come back to that.'

'You're not going to come back to anything. You're going to get out and stay away, that's all. We'll take over now.'

'The National Operations Department?' Berger said, taking the receiver from Blom.

'We can hardly keep the Jokkmokk police out of it,' Deer said, 'but we'll be working with them. For God's sake, make sure you get upstairs so we know what we've got to work with. I'll have to spend the rest of the night trying to figure out a solution, a way of reporting this crap and heading back up to Lapland. I should never have got you involved. Bloody amateurs. Just bear in mind that there's a small chance that the perpetrator is still hanging around up there. He could be a complete lunatic. Who knows, maybe he's waiting for you upstairs wearing Jessica Johnsson's skin?'

'What about the blood on the snow? The tyre tracks from the garage?'

'Have you ever heard of red herrings, Sam? At least take a kitchen knife with you. Call me later.'

'We'll send a recording,' Berger said to the already dead phone.

At that precise moment there was a clatter on the dining table in front of him. A kitchen knife spun to a stop on the top. Blom was also carrying one.

'Two,' she said. 'We'll take two.'

Then they set off. Berger went first; Blom filmed their movements over his shoulder. In the dark living room the now completely congealed pool of blood seemed to be spreading darkness from under the ground. Berger switched his torch on and started to climb the stairs. There were signs of someone having being dragged on pretty much every step, marks that could have been left by the heels of slipper-socks.

They reached the landing. Everything looked very different in the pale light of the torch, as if they weren't the same rooms, not the same house, not the same universe. The trail led to the left-hand bedroom. The door was open.

Berger raised the kitchen knife but kept it away from the beam of the torch. He could feel Blom's breath against his shoulder; she was very close to him. They stepped towards the door.

The first thing that came into view was the bedspread, which glowed unnaturally white through the night. Berger pointed the torch at the armchair. There was no sound, nothing to indicate the presence of anyone but them. Then he turned the torch towards the covered bed. And saw the outline.

The outline of a body. It looked like there was someone lying in the middle of the bed with their arms and legs stretched out, as if they were trying to make a snow angel in the whiteness.

Even so, it wasn't a body. There was no depth to the outline. Berger felt the torch quiver, and took a step closer. He felt the sheet, the outline. It looked like it had been painted on the fabric of the sheet. Whatever had been used to paint it had dried.

And a few hours ago it had been considerably redder than it was now. The blood had coagulated now. And it had coagulated in the shape of a lying human figure.

The outline stood out darkly in the bedroom. Berger heard Blom groan behind his back. Whoever had been lying there could hardly have been alive then, and certainly wouldn't be now, several hours later.

Berger shone the torch around the room, then pulled open the door to the attic under the eaves, still holding the knife ready. He aimed the torch into the small space, which was as good as empty and looked just as it had done a few hours earlier. The layer of dust was intact.

They moved on to the other bedroom, where the bed looked even more naked now, its slats even more like stripped ribs. But the low, narrow door to the attic in the eaves looked different.

It was open slightly.

They took up position in front of it, knives at the ready.

Berger took a deep breath, pulled the door open and shone the torch inside. The layer of dust looked undisturbed there too, but something was different. Berger looked around. Blom went on filming for a while, then walked off.

Berger remained where he was and counted the ancient trunks. There were three of them now, not four.

'One of the trunks is gone,' he said.

He crept back from the attic again. Blom had put her knife down and switched her torch on. She was moving it around the bleak bedroom. Then she seemed to catch sight of something in one corner. She moved closer, crouched down and half disappeared behind the skeleton of the bed.

Then she let out a deep groan.

'Dear God,' she said.

Berger walked round the bed and moved closer. He crouched down beside Blom. It was difficult to understand what they were looking at. At first glance it looked like a stranded jellyfish.

The object was lying on a rug, and a circular red stain had spread out around it. They moved a little closer. Blom shone her torch on it from close range.

'What the hell?' Berger said. 'Is that human skin?'

Blom zoomed in with her mobile, focusing on a small patch of skin that was a different colour. It looked like a drawing.

And then Berger saw what it was. It was a small ink drawing.

A four-leaf clover.

He stood up quickly, making his badly aching head spin. He closed his eyes and thought he was going to fall over. His vision seemed to form a crazy spinning mosaic.

But he didn't fall. He opened his eyes again. As if through a red mist he saw a man standing a few metres away. He looked utterly mad. Berger raised his knife. The man did the same.

The seconds that passed before he recognised his own reflection in the dark window would haunt his nightmares for a very long time.

10

Stillness reigns. Neither of the two screens in the ice-cold room shows any movement whatsoever. Not even the wind is whistling. The front cabin is just as quiet as the one further away.

Waiting is the key. There are moments when other things appear, other images. Internal images. Images conjured up by waiting.

The smell of pine follows the rays of the morning sun as they dance across the large terrace, gentle veils of dawn light. The tall rock in the distance stands out through the sea mist; a soft silhouette that seems to be floating on the still water.

It's the house. It's that house. Still being able to sit for a while in the morning warmth on the terrace and see. See properly. Be able to see. All movement, all effort is expended to that end. There is a time limit. A deadline.

There is an end to this. A good end.

No longer loneliness; they exchange glances, they see each other see, and for the briefest of moments the boundary between two people ceases to be absolute.

And that's never been experienced properly. Only in the dream. In the images conjured up by waiting. In minutes that pass, impossible to count.

There is a goal. There is a moment when everything is ready. When the tension of recent months suddenly eases. And then loneliness no longer reigns, that was decided long ago.

That's when the man appears in the top screen, already ten steps outside the far cabin. The images of waiting fade away, grim reality returns, the thin gloves tighten across the hands. Zoom.

The man is wearing a white coat, he pulls it tighter around his body, moves through the snow. No fresh snow, no wind, just the man's strange white silhouette. Like a snow angel.

Now the man appears on the lower screen, his head turns aside, he stands still, sees or hears something. Then she comes into view.

On the top screen the woman comes closer. Zoom in. Her skiing has been getting close to perfect in the past few weeks. Her muscles flex under her tight ski clothes. Zoom in for a moment.

It's her. The woman who is going to dissolve the boundary between two people.

Then the thin leather glove clicks the joystick, changes screen. The two figures are now both on the lower screen. A sigh passes through the ice-cold room. Keyboard, profanities.

The other hand writes: '10.24: ♂ and ♀ arrive together at ♀'s cabin. No urgent activity detected. Presumed collaboration initiated.'

The hand stops writing. Instead it puts a Sig Sauer P226 pistol on the table.

11

Berger woke up. Fragments of dreams drifted through him like a swirling shower of snow. But he couldn't make out a single individual snowflake, couldn't see a unified pattern. The only thing he was sure about was his raging, throbbing headache.

He sat up in bed and for the first time became aware of just how small the cabin was; the sleeping bag around his body didn't feel that much smaller. The walls were pressing in on him. For a brief moment his hand seemed to reach out towards an unfamiliar door that seemed to blur into the door to the toilet, but before his hand reached the handle the door flew open and hit him hard in the forehead. And then confusion. A roar that came simultaneously from outside, from the suddenly revealed boiler, and from inside, from a brain that seemed to be tossed about, torn from its moorings. And from the cold floor he saw the block of wood hit Blom's temple. He started to get up, but his brain wasn't with him, his body wasn't with him. The only result was that he got hit again and felt consciousness fading away. He focused what remained of it upwards, tried – in case he managed to survive, against the odds – to fix his rapidly narrowing field of vision on the figure's face, but it wasn't there, it was too dark. All he could see was the piece of wood in the hand of the elusive black figure, and then it came closer again. And then there was nothing but darkness.

Unprepared, Deer had said. He remembered it word for word: 'So you went down into a pitch-black basement in an isolated house with a person who has reported that she's being stalked, *completely unprepared?*'

But they weren't there because she had reported that she thought she was being stalked, there was a single purpose to their visit, and that had managed to block out any threat, not least because their attention had been ultimately completely focused on Jessica Johnsson's character, which had been so difficult to pin down. Their starting point had been that she was a conspiracy theorist, a troublemaker, and that the stalker only existed in her own paranoid consciousness, but it later became very apparent that she was stretching the truth in very different ways as well.

It had been him, Sam Berger, who had broken off the interview instead of simply rigging up a video camera and carrying on without interruption. It had been his stupid idea to search the house before the issue of the ink drawing had even been raised.

And now there was another one.

And it looked like it had been drawn on a slice of Jessica Johnsson's buttock.

Pain washed over him; it was nothing to do with his pulsating headache. He curled up, thinking about how useless he was and what a fucking hopeless team he and Molly were. Knocked out by a complete lunatic, perhaps two, and incapable of even rudimentary self-defence. And on the run from a justice system that had stopped being just.

The cabin came back as itself again. Empty. Completely empty. Even though he was inside it.

He tried to think of something that could calm him down. Not medication or drink, nothing like that. Something that could soothe his turbulent inner landscape. He grabbed his watch case, looked at the six wristwatches, which went on ticking, unconcerned, and waited until the remorseless passage of time softened to a gentle, almost synchronised ticking. Exhausted after the crazy hike through the winter night, dizzy from the blows to his head, wiped out by the explosion of violence that had hit the pair of them, he had still reset the watches one by one so that they all showed the right date, all showed the right time. And that had taken a while. And it had calmed him down. The tiny cogs' skittish resurrection, as if they had been waiting to catch up, waiting for the chance to tick him with terrible gentleness a few steps closer to death.

He pressed his ear to the case, separating each ticking from the others: two IWCs, two Rolexes, one Jaeger-LeCoultre, one Patek Philippe. As if they were counting a friendlier time than ours.

But they weren't enough to calm him down. Not really. That would take something stronger.

He reached for his mobile phone. Pulled up the pictures. Swiped backwards. Found the right picture. The twins in the coltsfoot ditch. They were eight years old, wearing clothes that were a little too bulky for the weather. Oscar was smiling, Marcus laughing. The last picture, the fixed point. Before they acquired the surname Babineaux. Before they lived in Paris and slowly but surely let their real father slip into the merciless realm of forgetfulness. But for Sam Berger they remained the Pole Star, the still point of the turning world.

They were there as the heaven he would never reach.

The pole of inaccessibility, he thought. That was where he was. As far from other people as you could get. The low-water mark. The bottom. Absolute zero.

Absolute pain.

That was where he was.

He looked out through the window, saw the vast whiteness. Emptiness. It seemed to mirror Sam's performance as a father. Marcus and Oscar had a different father figure now, a Frenchman. Sam Berger was probably unusually easy to replace.

The role of father, so different to the role of policeman, the only role he had never had to play. But Sam Berger the policeman was still a more plausible father than Sam Berger the human being.

He needed to become a policeman again, that was his only way back to becoming a human being. He missed his sons so much that it hurt an awful lot more than the concussion or any sense of professional failure. He missed their physicality, their smiles, their squabbling, their lives being lived. He was no longer part of anyone else's life. He was a loner, a failed loner.

Who had been saved by Molly Blom. She had managed to keep them away from the Security Service, from the whole mess that had led them to this point. And he had trusted her, implicitly and completely. Even though everything after his first glimpse of Syl's dead body was extremely unclear. He had been pretty much unconscious for over two weeks. Was that even possible?

But he *had* to trust her. She was the last straw he was clinging to.

He stood up, pulled his clothes on, put on his Patek Philippe, slipped his feet into the strange boots and caught sight of himself in the grimy mirror. Leaving aside his crazy beard, hadn't his hairstyle changed? It struck him as so asymmetrical that he had to look away. He must been sweating heavily while he was asleep.

Then he threw open the door to the winter landscape.

The interior of the country. How desolate it was.

A world without markers.

Wrapping the strange white coat tightly around him, he set off along the path through the snow. At least it hadn't snowed in the hours since he had stumbled half-dead into the cabin. Soon Blom's cabin came into view beneath its white covering. It looked completely abandoned.

Until he caught sight of a white figure moving quickly across the snow a little way in the distance. For a moment he found the jagged movements unsettling until he realised that the figure was skiing.

They approached the cabin from different directions and arrived at more or less the same time. Her breath hung around her in clouds as she unclipped her skis.

'Look at you,' Berger said.

'Well I had to do something while I was waiting for you,' Blom panted. 'Satellites can't pick up ski tracks.'

'But I noticed them yesterday.'

'You don't notice everything I do.'

'I'm very aware of that,' Berger said, trying not to imbue his words with too much subtext.

She opened a narrow door beside the real door. It concealed a small space that looked like it was meant for skis and nothing else.

'You've got one too,' Blom said, then shut the small door and opened the larger one.

'With or without skis?' Berger asked.

'With,' Blom said with a short smile, then stepped inside the cabin.

The computer was switched on, and the screen saver's odd pattern was dancing across it. Berger noted that it was connected to Deer's satellite phone.

'You've been skiing,' Berger stated. 'No trouble with your head, then?'

Blom stroked her white ski helmet and said, 'I've been a bit worried my skull might be fractured. Hairline cracks in my cranium.'

'So in response to that worry you set out into the wilderness on skis? What if you'd fainted? You'd have frozen to death. If nothing else, the half past ten satellite would have spotted your fallen body.'

'I needed to move about,' Blom said through blue lips.

Berger shook his head, pointed at the computer and said, to draw her out, 'Deer told us to stay away from the case.'

Blom didn't answer, just pulled off her thick ski glove and nudged the mouse pad with a sweaty finger. The swirling pattern of the screen saver was replaced by a face.

It was Jessica Johnsson.

It was like coming face to face with the dead.

Yet it was still less than twenty-four hours since he had done precisely that: he had sat opposite her, and at the time she had been very much alive. With that exact expression on her face. Unexpectedly sharp but twitchy, with a hint of a smile at the corners of her mouth. And simultaneously very obstinate, determined not to let anyone in.

'There are huge holes in Jessica Johnsson's biography,' Blom said, pulling her white coat off and sitting down.

Berger pulled the only other chair over and sat down beside Blom. Information was streaming across the screen.

'Born 1980,' she said, pointing. 'Looks like a fairly unremarkable childhood in Rågsved. Nothing in any police records. Did health care at high school, trained to become a nurse. Spent the summers working in hospitals while she was training, night shifts in psychiatric and geriatric wards.'

'No gaps until she hits twenty-five, then?'

'Apparently she spent a year in the USA when she was eighteen, nineteen. Unclear where and to what purpose. But it looks like a standard gap year; she came back and started training to be a nurse. Worked at St Göran's Hospital for a few years, in some sort of nursing pool. Then we have an incident that I managed to dig out while you were getting your beauty sleep.'

'I doubt even my own mother would be able to call that beauty sleep,' Berger muttered. 'An incident?'

'It wasn't in the material Rosenkvist gave us. I got hold of it a different way. At the age of twenty-five Jessica Johnsson met what's usually called "the wrong sort of guy". His name was Eddy Karlsson, and he seems to have been both a full-blown junkie and a full-blown psychopath. This is ten years ago now. She reported him for assault. He was banned from contacting her. Further incidents followed. She reported that he'd raped her, so the South Stockholm police set out to arrest Karlsson. And then it all died down.'

'Died down?'

'Eddy Karlsson has a police record going back to when he lived in Mora, but he didn't get picked up ten years ago. He just disappeared. The last thing the police file has to say about him is that he probably fled abroad under a false identity.'

'And I presume that's when the holes in Jessica Johnsson's biography start to appear?'

'Yes,' Blom said. 'A classic case of protected identity.'

'But she went back to using her real name? That must mean Eddy Karlsson is dead, if she dared to go back to her old life. So Eddy Karlsson can't be the man with the lump of wood. He can't be what she's been so afraid of that she moved to Porjus and hid herself away in an isolated cottage in Lapland.'

Blom looked at him for a while, frowning.

'Good to have you back,' she said.

'Neither of us is back,' Berger snapped. 'Not after what happened in that fucking cellar. How did we fail to see that coming? How the hell could we be so unprepared?'

'Has it occurred to you that it was your Desiré Rosenkvist who prepared us to be unprepared? That she actually *unprepared* us?'

Now it was Berger's turn to pause. He stared at her.

'What do you mean?' he asked eventually.

'The Security Service are after us,' Blom said. 'We can probably count on some unorthodox tactics from their side. If we'd been given the job without comment, without being told that Jessica was just a nutter, wouldn't we have been more on our guard in the cellar?'

'But if Deer is working for the Security Service we'd never have been given the job in the first place. They'd just have picked us up in Kvikkjokk. Deer would never have turned up there, just fucking Kent and fucking Roy.'

'Back to Eddy Karlsson, then,' Blom said, nudging the mouse pad. 'You guessed right: Eddy Karlsson is dead. Died of an overdose four years ago, no one was even aware that he'd come back to Sweden – from Thailand, evidently.'

'And soon after that Jessica Johnsson reappeared?'

'The missing ID number reappears, yes. But without any apparent source of income. She didn't have a job when we saw her, and I can't really figure out how she was supporting herself. I can't see any state benefits, no social security, no unemployment support. But it looks like the first documented use of the resurrected ID number is to buy a house. With cash.'

'Porjus?' Berger exclaimed.

'Yes.'

'So the moment the threat disappears, she isolates herself? Doesn't that seem like a paradox?'

'Maybe she was telling the truth,' Blom said. 'Maybe she did just want to get away from "people in general".'

'But that wasn't the impression we got from talking to her, was it?'

'No. She'd met someone new. It probably happened while her identity was protected, which makes it harder to dig out.'

'But not impossible?'

'Not if we dare to trust this thing,' Blom said, indicating the satellite phone.

'You mean if Deer *unprepared* us?' Berger said darkly. 'No matter how I look at it, I can't see any reason for that. It all gets unnecessarily complicated. The Security Service are hunting us, they manage to turn Deer, maybe buy her off with promotion and transfer to the NOD, and then they get her to give us this weird job and make sure that she *unprepares* us so that we can get murdered by some violent nutter up in fucking Porjus. No, that's pushing it too far.'

Blom shrugged her shoulders.

'I just get the feeling that nothing's the way it seems.'

Berger bit his tongue and shook his head. Blom went on, 'If we can trust the satellite phone, I can still get into the archive. That goes back to my time undercover, it's completely secure. We can rig up your computer on the other side of the table and link you up as well. Then we get to the bottom of this. Agreed?'

Berger tried to compose himself as best he could.

Then he nodded.

12

The picture shakes, and a fairly messy living room flashes past. Then a child comes into view, a little boy, a few metres away. He's wearing a tiny pair of jeans and a yellow top with a banana on it, and when he gets to his feet, using a pile of books to help him, his movements are very tentative. But he remains standing, albeit unsteadily. One of the picture books is dangling from his hand. He looks up curiously and smiles as if he's got a secret. A woman's voice says in a soft Dalarna accent, 'Do you want to read about animals, Rasmus?' And the boy takes a step, then another one, with the book still hanging from his hand. He stumbles but remains upright. Once he's taken five steps he throws himself forward towards the sofa that has just come into view. A pair of female hands catches him, and the voice says triumphantly, 'Those were your very first steps, Rasmus! You're such a clever boy!' As the boy settles down in his mother's lap, he opens the book and says, 'Read animals!' Then the woman's face comes into shot; she's smiling and wiping the corners of her eyes. She has fairly short brown hair and rosy cheeks, and she opens the book. The boy looks at her expectantly, repeats, 'Read animals!' but the woman is staring into his eyes. She leans forward and hugs him tenderly, and his little hand lets go of the book and reaches for her hair. She laughs warmly, from the depths of her heart, and that makes him laugh too; their laughter weaves together. Then she kisses him on the cheek, and everything stops.

'Ready for the next one?' Berger asked.

'Not really,' Blom replied.

The image of the mother's lips pressed against the child's chubby cheek is replaced with a completely different picture. A green ditch, dark and damp, a woman's body and an overturned pushchair whose handle the woman is still holding. The banana top is still partly visible, but is no longer particularly yellow.

'Oh, dear God,' Blom groaned, looking across at Berger. As he zoomed the picture in a tear rolled slowly down his left cheek; he didn't bother to wipe it off.

'This was the first case Deer and I worked on together,' he said in a subdued voice. 'And we were only involved on the periphery. Allan Gudmundsson was one of the three detectives responsible, under State Prosecutor Ragnar Ling. This abrupt contrast is one of the things I remember most clearly, the switch from fourteen-month-old Rasmus Gradén taking his first steps – his mum Helena's uncontained delight, the obvious love between them – to the pair of them lying slaughtered in the ditch. I don't think I've ever really got over it.'

'Was the murder weapon ever identified?' Blom asked, taking over the task of enlarging the picture.

'No, it was never found,' Berger said and pointed at the screen. 'But in among the sludge down there splinters of wood were found. Birch.'

'Birch? As in a ... a block of wood?'

'Potentially, yes. More splinters were found in the shelter.'

'Tell me about the shelter,' Blom said.

'Freshly built, not exactly professional but well camouflaged, in the deepest part of the Orsa forests. Halfway between where they were found and the hostel where the residents from Karl Hedblom's care home were staying. Traces of blood from both Helena and Rasmus Gradén were found inside the shelter. Hedblom's DNA was also found in fragments of skin. Back then there was never any doubt. We'd found our perpetrator.'

'I'm going to read through the whole case,' Blom said. 'But give me a quick summary. Why was the father a suspect?'

'Emmanuel Gradén.' Berger nodded. 'There was some doubt about exactly what happened when the mother and son set off on their walk to the supermarket. He didn't care if he was a suspect or not; his life was over.'

'Really?'

'Pretty much. He committed suicide six months later, after Karl Hedblom had been convicted. Drilled a hole in the ice on Lake Orsa and dropped himself in with fifty kilos of lead strapped to his body.'

'Lead?'

'A couple of weeks earlier he'd been to see his brother in Skellefteå. He bought a load of lead that he could wrap around his body from Rönnskärsverken in Skelleftehamn. It was all very carefully planned.'

'So his body was found, then? And it was definitely him?'

'I understand why you're asking. But yes, it was definitely him. DNA.'

'Otherwise you might wonder if he started with his own family, got a taste for it, carried on – and ended up murdering Jessica Johnsson eight years later. The man in the boiler room. But OK. Doubts about the walk?'

'They'd had a row,' Berger said. 'That autumn day when Helena Gradén went out with Rasmus in his pushchair she'd had a bad argument with her husband. She called a friend to say Emmanuel had been yelling that Rasmus wasn't his son.'

'Really?' Blom said. 'So he must have been the prime suspect right from day one.'

'The friend didn't come forward until a few days later, there was some problem with her mobile phone. But after that, yes. For a week or so.'

'Do you know if it was true? Was Emmanuel Gradén Rasmus's father?'

'As soon as the suspicion was raised a paternity test was conducted,' Berger said. 'He was definitely the father. And the fact that the last thing he yelled at his wife was a baseless accusation was probably the final nail in his coffin.'

Blom said nothing for a while. Then she went on.

'What do we know about the chain of events?'

Berger sighed.

'So, eight years ago. Helena Gradén set out at quarter past one on 18 October, and was found just after nine o'clock in the morning of the 20th by members of a search party who'd just finished their shift. The search had passed the place they were found six hours earlier, in the middle of the night: there hadn't been anyone in the ditch then. And they didn't die there. But the post-mortems indicated that they had been alive for around forty hours, probably in the shelter. Both victims showed signs of repeated abuse.'

'A search party?' Blom said. 'When did that set out? How could they have missed the shelter?'

'This was before the Missing People initiative was set up, before properly organised search parties,' Berger said. 'It seems to have been pretty haphazard, and it's easy to underestimate the size of the forests around Orsa.'

'The interior of the country again.' Blom nodded. 'So how did Karl Hedblom get caught then?'

'With the help of psychologists,' Berger said. 'No one actually knew there was a group of care-home residents from Falun in the area; they'd left before there was any idea of looking for other suspects apart from Emmanuel Gradén and were only called in for interview later. We were looking for specific types of disorder – hatred and previous violence against mothers with small children – and one of the clearest matches in the whole of Sweden was twenty-four-year-old Karl Hedblom. When it became clear that he'd been in the area at the time of the murders a DNA sample was taken. Unidentified DNA from the shelter turned out to be a match for Hedblom's. After that it was just a matter of questioning him.'

Blom nodded.

'Were there any other suspects apart from the father?'

'Not really,' Berger said. 'But a hell of a lot of people were interviewed.'

'And you conducted some of those with Rosenkvist? Nothing that stood out?'

'It wouldn't surprise me if the police questioned half the population of Orsa. Deer and I did at least twenty, maybe thirty. People living nearby, neighbours and work colleagues of the Gradéns, other residents from the care home, people who'd driven past that morning, truck drivers, you name it.'

'But by the time you were brought in the suspicions of Emmanuel Gradén had already been dropped?' Blom asked.

'As I recall, yes. We asked very few questions about him. Deer tended to focus on the drawing on the buttock, the four-leaf clover, while I looked for leads to the shelter. Things like who had built it, had this crime been prepared long in advance, who might have constructed it?'

'And there are transcripts of all the interviews in the file?'

'There should be, yes. But gradually it was scaled back. Like I said, I was present when Allan conducted the conclusive interview, when Karl Hedblom confessed. I was Allan's co-interviewer, but I don't think I said a single word.'

Neither of them spoke for a while. Then Berger took a deep breath and said, 'Did you find anything else on Lisa Widstrand?'

'Worked as a prostitute in Gothenburg. Brutally assaulted five years ago, found dead in the Gothia Towers Hotel just before the book fair, in a room paid for in cash booked in her name. She didn't have any relatives, and the murder came at a time when no one was interested in negative publicity, which probably explains why it escaped the attention of the media. But the four-leaf clover on her buttock is definitely on record. The only thing I haven't been able to find is the article in the local press that Jessica Johnsson mentions in her letter. But there are probably quite a few local papers that have gone out of business now whose archives I can't find. They may not even exist any more.'

'There's still a chance that it could be a copycat,' Berger said. 'Someone who read about the drawing of the four-leaf clover when Karl Hedblom was convicted.'

'Clearly a possibility,' Blom said.

'Any other similarities?'

'Yes, a certain similarity in appearance. Otherwise nothing. In purely social terms it's quite a long way from a primary-school teacher and young mother in Orsa to a heroin-addicted prostitute in Gothenburg.'

'What about the cause of death, and the amount of violence?' Berger said.

'Fairly similar. Hit with a blunt object, body badly beaten, blows concentrated on the face. Lots of cuts. But no child this time, thank God.'

'Did Lisa Widstrand have any children?'

'Not as far as I've been able to see,' Blom said. 'And Jessica Johnsson has no children. Or had, rather.'

'Had,' Berger echoed. 'Everything really does suggest that we allowed her to be murdered while we were still in the house.'

'We need to look forward,' Blom said. 'Remorse only leads to stagnation. Rosenkvist said she wanted us to stay away from the case, but it wouldn't surprise me if she'd be happy with a parallel investigation. She trusts you.'

'The only person in the universe who does,' Berger muttered.

Blom cast a sideways glance at him.

'It's two o'clock. Forensics ought to be finished in Porjus now. Dare we risk calling her?'

Berger looked at Blom. It was impossible to see anything other than professional ambition in her; she really did want to solve the case, find the man who had hit her in the head with a lump of wood and murdered the woman who should have been in their care. He couldn't detect any ulterior motive, any concealed intent.

But, on the other hand, that was exactly the sort of thing Molly Blom was an expert at hiding.

He nodded. Of course he was also keen to contact Deer, he wanted to know what was going on. And he wanted, most emphatically, to get hold of the man who had hit him with a lump of wood. But most of all he wanted to be a police officer again, wanted to become absorbed in a case that could fill the emptiness inside him.

'It would be better coming from you,' Blom said, handing him the receiver of the satellite phone.

It felt like a tiny breakthrough in their relationship.

13

The phone had rung ten times and Berger was about to hang up when it suddenly roared, 'What did I say to you about this case?'

'That we shouldn't go anywhere near it,' Berger said. 'So have we? Have they found any trace of us?'

Deer let out a deep sigh and said, 'Not yet. You cleaned up after yourselves well. But it had already been very well cleaned.'

Blom leaned closer to the receiver. Berger held it at a slight angle, and Deer's voice echoed out into the cabin. Blom nodded, Berger understood.

'She made us tea,' he said. 'We washed the cups afterwards. But it was already very tidy. We checked the corners of the kitchen too. What about the bathroom? That's where you're most likely to find DNA.'

'I'll be sure to pass on your forensic tips to Robin,' Deer said sharply. 'The preliminary results show just one type of DNA in the bathroom, on the toothbrush and hairbrush among other places, and from the look of it, it's a match for the blood. Jessica Johnsson's DNA obviously isn't on record, but the match looks pretty conclusive.'

'What about the boiler room, then? Where the perpetrator was hiding out?'

'Robin's just got started with the examination,' Deer said. 'But his first reaction was that boiler rooms tend to be an awful lot dirtier than this one.'

'Jessica Johnsson said she hadn't been down in the basement for a couple of years,' Berger said.

Deer replied, 'Either she was lying and trying to hide the fact that she had OCD – which could fit with the paranoid aspects of her personality – or the most likely explanation is that the perpetrator cleaned up after himself.'

'So before it all happened, then? He was in the middle of a brutal murder and had two ex-cops tied up in the basement. I can't believe he'd scrupulously clean a whole boiler room after that.'

Deer let out an even deeper sigh, and exclaimed, 'For God's sake, look at the mess you've got me into! Now I'm sitting here with a fucking parallel investigation and I already know more than all the other officers involved, and I can't even let on that I know that the murderer was lying in wait in the boiler room. It's just like with you and the Ellen Savinger case, Sam. And a fat lot of good that did you.'

'Mind you, Deer, you helped make this rod for your own back. You were the one who involved us, not the other way round. So make the most of it, stay ahead of the investigation. Then we can catch this bastard and you'll get all the credit.'

'Yeah, because the two of you have done a hell of a lot of good so far ...'

'If he cleaned up the boiler room, then it was probably him who cleaned the rest of the house,' Berger said. 'He must have done it without Jessica Johnsson noticing anything when she got home. It was all extremely well planned. And then he uses a lump of bloody wood as the murder weapon. The exact opposite of well planned.'

'But that could have been planned too. His weapon of choice.'

'You're thinking of …?'

'Yes, just like you are, Sam. I'm thinking of Orsa and Helena Gradén, and I'm thinking about Allan Gudmundsson's session with Karl Hedblom.'

'Can we visit him?'

'Allan? Well, it turns out his bridge tournament wasn't in Tahiti after all, but out on Frösön. So that ought to be possible.'

'Not Allan,' Berger sighed. 'Can we go and see Karl Hedblom and say we're from the NOD?'

'He's in one of the biggest secure psychiatric facilities in Sweden, Säter. I don't know exactly where you are, but I know that's a very long way away.'

'About a thousand kilometres straight down through the middle of the country,' Berger said. 'We can see him first thing tomorrow morning.'

He cast a quick glance at Blom. To his surprise, she showed no sign of protesting.

'Anyway, we don't actually know that the lump of wood was the murder weapon,' Deer muttered. 'What we do know is that some sort of extremely sharp knife was also used. To slice off that piece of her buttock. Which, according to the preliminary report, happened after death. The quantity of blood on the sheet, however, does indicate that he was using the knife while Jessica Johnsson was still alive.'

'So it was from her buttock? Bloody hell …'

'The knife hasn't been found. Nor the wood. Which you should probably thank your lucky stars for. That, if anything, ought to be dripping with DNA from two notorious ex-cops.'

'Do you know when he got there?'

'Seeing as the investigation is still in its infancy, there isn't even a *he* yet. But we know that Jessica Johnsson visited three different shops and stopped for coffee in Porjus between approximately ten o'clock and one o'clock yesterday.'

'And we got to her house just before three ...'

'But *we* don't know that. Only *you* know that.'

'It's going to be hard to remember what you can say from now on, Deer – trust me, I know.'

'The house is roughly ten kilometres outside Porjus,' Deer said, 'so she probably left home at twenty to ten, and got back at twenty past one. Meaning that the house was empty for just over three and a half hours. For most of the very limited daylight up here. So she walked around her DNA-scrubbed house for an hour and a half without noticing a thing while a killer hid in her boiler room.'

'Did she drive?' Berger asked. 'Has she even got a car?'

'Yes, double garage. Her Ford Fiesta is still there. But the other parking space is interesting. If you'd been acting remotely like cops you'd have noticed that there was another vehicle there. Then you might have taken the illegal weapons I know you've got into the house with you. Then all of this might have been avoided. Then Jessica Johnsson might still be alive.'

'Obviously we should have looked in the garage,' Berger conceded. 'We're clearly out of practice.'

'For God's sake, you're not cops!' Deer exclaimed. 'You're just using this as some kind of nostalgia kick ... as pillow talk. I have no more use for you, Sam. Go to ground again.'

'The other vehicle?'

'A trail of blood heading in that direction across the snow, like you said. Also signs of a trunk being put down a couple of times on the way to the garage, as if it was too heavy to carry all the way in one go. Each time in line with the trail of blood. The size matches the three remaining trunks in the attic, which were empty, by the way. The last of the blood is on the cement floor in the garage, and stops abruptly as if the trunk was lifted into a vehicle. There are tyre tracks to suggest that it was a small van, a Volkswagen Caddy, and potentially a small paint mark, as if the vehicle touched the garage wall when it was reversing out. Unfortunately the forensic situation is being confused by a set of tyre tracks that made Robin exclaim: "If those aren't from a jeep I'll eat botulinum toxin for the next six months." I have no idea what botulinum toxin is, but I'm wondering whether you lovely people might perhaps be using a jeep?'

'It's the strongest poison we're aware of,' Berger said, glancing at Blom. 'Half a teaspoon would be enough to kill everyone in Sweden. In its diluted form it's sometimes known as botox.'

'Have you got a jeep?'

'You know we have,' Berger said. 'You saw us in Kvikkjokk; I spotted the binoculars.'

'What I don't know is how to downgrade the jeep in the investigation. Something else to add to the list of things I have you to thank for. Couldn't you have driven a bit more carefully?'

'I don't think you quite appreciate the state we were in at the time,' Berger said. 'We managed to get rid of all the evidence inside the house. You're still a police officer, no one knows you sent a couple of freelancers. Your gratitude is justified, and warmly received.'

'At half past four this morning I got hold of one of my old informants, Sam, one of my decoys. He phoned the emergency call centre anonymously, reading from a script I'd given him. The Jokkmokk police were here an hour later, and then the

NOD were informed. We caught the first flight this morning, four detectives, with Superintendent Conny Landin in charge, and a whole battery of forensics experts under Robin. That's a big deal for the interior of Norrland, and my main concern so far has been to keep the two of you out of it. So I wouldn't mind a bit of gratitude as well.'

'Freely given, Deer. Yes or no?'

The line started to crackle, and in the background they clearly heard a male voice asking:

'Who the hell are you talking to, Deer? Get off there now, we need you in here.'

Deer called out:

'Sorry, Conny, trouble with the childminder. I'm coming.'

She half-whispered into the receiver:

'I have to go now.'

'Yes or no, Deer? Can we go to Säter or not?'

Deer frowned as she looked up at the overcast sky. The snow was starting to leak into her mid-length boots, she could feel it melting against her calves. The sun was already low in the sky, and the tops of the trees in the forest surrounding the field around Jessica Johnsson's house looked almost luminous. It didn't feel like a coincidence that the interior of Norrland was the last part of Europe to emerge from glaciation.

'Yes,' she said as she reached the bottom step leading up to the house.

Then she clicked to end the call and walked through the door of the isolated house ten kilometres from Porjus. A box of blue shoe covers had been left where none of the police officers could miss it. She took her boots off and placed them where she hoped they might soon dry, pulled shoe covers over her wet socks and walked into the living room from the hall.

To her left, on the floor next to the sofa, the forensics team had erected a couple of powerful spotlights. A couple of them were on their knees, in protective white suits, picking with tweezers at the now completely congealed pool of blood. Deer looked at the three trails of blood and stopped at the staircase. Light and sound poured down from above; Robin's technicians were hard at work up there too. She looked at the dragging marks that led up, step by step; it really did look as if the person being pulled had been wearing slipper-socks. Jessica Johnsson couldn't have been conscious at the time; the question was whether she had been alive.

She skirted the brightly lit area and headed towards the dining table. Superintendent Conny Landin, a robust man with a more robust moustache, was standing there staring at it.

'I'd like to know what this table was scrubbed with,' he said.

Deer waited, let herself fall into the role of less knowledgeable subordinate, waited for Uncle Conny to start mansplaining and thought about something else.

She was actually thinking about Berger and Blom. Against her better judgement she had stuck her head in the beehive and – for old times' sake – had decided to trust them. Berger, it was Berger she trusted. Blom seemed reliable, but Deer's encounters with her so far hadn't been particularly confidence-inspiring.

Why were they hiding north of the Arctic Circle? They had received decent redundancy payments, and if they pooled their resources they could start some kind of private detective agency; that seemed all the rage these days – and it was hard to think of anyone more suited to it – but why here? Why in the interior of Norrland? In a part of the country that was actually losing population? Surely there had to be more opportunities in Stockholm, Gothenburg or Malmö.

Unless there was something else going on? Were they really – as she had guessed – on the run? Had they gone into hiding, were they hibernating? Blom had intimated that Berger wasn't in particularly great shape, although a stomach upset would have had to be full-blown dysentery to stop the Berger that Deer knew. But when she saw him with that wild grey beard, she had realised that something had changed. Properly changed.

No more than three weeks had passed since she had last seen him. Deer tried to remember exactly what had happened at the confused conclusion of the Ellen Savinger case. The Security Service had slammed a lid on it, but Berger and Blom had evidently played a decisive role; the question was, in what way?

And then there was Syl's death; that had hit her hard, knocked her flat. How natural was it, really?

Deep down she really didn't want to have to go back to the Gradén case. It had affected her far too badly last time. Was she up to going back to her younger more neurotic self and remembering exactly what it was about the case that had affected her so strongly? She tried to think back to her and Sam's first case together, even if they were only involved on the edge of it. They had been a good match, and it hadn't taken him long to come up with the nickname Deer (which, although she never liked to admit it, she was actually quite fond of), and they had worked well together.

It was the mother. The mother who had clearly been so devoted to her child.

And the four-leaf clover. Because she had climbed the stairs to the upper floor in Robin's solid company, the shock hadn't been as great as it should have been. A slice from a woman's buttock. And exactly the same four-leaf clover, the same ink drawing. She had been particularly struck by that eight years ago. It had felt so specific, so deliberate. As if it really did mean something. But then

Karl Hedblom had confessed to everything, and she – along with everyone else – had seen the light. Everything fell into place, and obviously Karl was guilty.

But he could never really explain the four-leaf clover.

There had never been any doubt. Superintendent Desiré Rosenkvist wanted her old boss Sam Berger to visit Karl Hedblom in Säter psychiatric hospital. The goal was to get him to talk to Hedblom, talk in a way that hadn't been possible before. And she herself could remain beyond criticism, free from any blame from her superiors.

There was no point denying it. She was in the middle of a secret parallel investigation, just like Sam had been only a few weeks before.

A voice forced its way through the walls of her thoughts. And it wasn't the first time it had said, 'For God's sake, Desiré, who the hell called this one in?'

'Sorry?' Deer said. 'The whole thing just got to me for a moment.'

'Well stop letting it get to you,' Conny Landin snapped. 'A man without a Norrland accent calls to say that he saw a murder being committed in this house. But no one could see a murder being committed here unless they were standing right outside. And we know no one was standing right outside because of the snow.'

'You think the murderer himself made the call?' Deer asked, looking at him with her best deer's eyes.

Conny Landin blinked in surprise, stopped for a moment, quickly requisitioned the thought and made it his own.

'I'm starting to wonder if that might be the case. And this whole damn place has been so carefully cleaned. He wanted attention, admiration. Was he creating a stage where this was all supposed to play out? Are we his audience? The police?'

'That sounds like a previous case,' Deer said calmly.

Conny Landin slowly stroked his moustache, gestured towards a nearby white door.

'Anyway, he wants you to go downstairs.'

Deer nodded and walked off. She opened the door with the old-fashioned key sticking out of the lock. She found herself on the stairs leading down to the basement; the scene was familiar from the video film she had seen the previous evening at the desk in her garage in the Stockholm suburb of Skogås. She hadn't had access before, but now a very large man in protective white clothing was waiting for her at the bottom of the steps. The light was different – spotlights everywhere – but everything else was very familiar.

Berger had been right.

It was her turn to run a secret investigation.

And it was probably going to be a tough one to manage.

She went down the steps to the accompaniment of a loud rumbling sound. The operational boss of the National Forensics Centre was standing below in imposing, white-clad majesty.

'Christ, I can't talk to Ronny Lundén,' Robin spluttered.

'Conny Landin,' Deer duly corrected.

'You and I have always got on well, Deer. I think I might make you my liaison officer in the Porjus case.'

'I'm honoured,' Deer said. 'What message would you like to pass on?'

Robin pointed at the half-open door to the roaring boiler room.

'It's all been scrubbed clean, so there's really fuck all for me to do here. We're dealing with someone who knows how to get rid of DNA evidence. Someone with size 45 shoes, as we saw upstairs, and *someone who's done this before.*'

'But you still said "really"?' Deer said.

'I haven't actually got anything definite to go on,' Robin said. 'Not yet. But this boiler room feels ...'

'Feels?'

'I know, I know. But intuition is nothing but ...'

'... accumulated experience, I know.'

'How do you know that?'

'You'll have to assume that I've had some experience too, Robin.'

'Sorry, of course,' Robin said. 'It's just that ...'

'Spit it out.'

Robin filled his impressive lungs with air, gestured towards the boiler room and said, 'Some bastard's been living in there.'

14

The main road running through the interior of the country gradually emerged from the darkness. At some point during the night they had crossed the snow boundary, and now the E45 highway stretched out grey-brown and grimly autumnal. Berger had forgotten that the long, stretched-out country could contain so many seasons.

They had been driving in shifts. The main problem wasn't the driving itself but finding petrol stations without security cameras. They made sure they were using different number plates each time, kept their hoods pulled up and relied on the fact that petrol stations didn't tend to store security-camera footage for long.

When they passed Orsa, Berger noticed that Blom was asleep in the passenger seat for the first time all night. He saw the turning that led to the crime scene of eight years ago flash past. He decided not to wake her – they would be making the same long drive back soon enough, and he preferred a driver who'd had at least a few hours' sleep. Besides, it wasn't the right time to visit the scene; that could happen on the return journey.

He wondered if the shelter was still there.

She didn't sleep for long anyway. When they finally left the E45 at Mora and followed the road skirting the north of Lake Siljan, Blom woke up and looked about her blearily.

'One hundred and twenty kilometres to go. Another hour or so. Get some more sleep.'

She picked up the thick folder from her lap and went on reading as if nothing had happened. Then something suddenly occurred to her.

'What if he recognises you?' she asked, looking at him intently.

'How do you mean?'

'You're visiting him as "C. Lindbergh" from the National Operations Department – nice little in-joke there from your Desiré – but what if Karl Hedblom remembers you as Sam Berger?'

Berger nodded and muttered, 'We'll have to regard that as a calculated risk. It was years ago, and Karl was already pretty unstable. He might recognise me in spite of the beard, but the chances of him remembering my name are pretty negligible.'

'We need to do something about that beard,' was all Blom said.

Just over an hour later they pulled up in front of the entrance to the vast yellow building that housed the Säter Secure Psychiatric Clinic. It contained ten wards, seven of them high-security wards. What lurked behind those butter-yellow outer walls hopefully wasn't a reflection of the country's mental health.

'I'll warm him up,' Berger said. 'Then when it comes to the crunch, you take over.'

'A woman,' Blom nodded. 'Right age, too.'

Deer had evidently prepared for their visit well. A guard led them through one security check after the other until they found themselves in a reassuringly familiar sterile interview room, sitting on the same side of a desk with a little too much graffiti on it. And there they sat.

Ten minutes later the door opened and two well-built guards came in with a man who looked grey and careworn even though he was no older than thirty-two, but the boyish set of his features was intact. He paused and looked at Berger, and when he turned towards Blom with no visible change of expression they both assumed he was drugged.

The smuggling of knives, guns, drugs, even petrol and drones, was a well-established catch-22 in secure psychiatric clinics. It all took place through the postal system, and because the chief medical officer had to decide personally which parcels should be checked, there was a veritable torrent of dangerous goods pouring into psychiatric clinics, to the most dangerous, unpredictable criminals in Sweden. And without a change in the law there was nothing anyone could do about it.

It wasn't just time that had left its mark on Karl Hedblom's face, nor ordinary medication. In all likelihood it was methamphetamine as well.

'Do you recognise me, Karl?' Berger asked.

Hedblom's right eyebrow twitched, he began to scratch the left corner of his mouth and didn't stop, and his enlarged pupils darted about within irises that had once been bright blue. This definitely wasn't a man on the road to recovery and rehabilitation.

'No,' he eventually whispered.

Berger nodded.

'We're police officers,' he said. 'We'd like to ask you some questions.'

'Everyone asks questions,' Hedblom said with a crooked smile; he had several teeth missing.

'Do you remember what you were found guilty of, Karl?'

'I get judged every day, I swear.'

'Who judges you?'

'Everyone who knows.'

'A daily reminder of what you did? A reminder that hurts every day?'

'Not any more,' Karl Hedblom said and smiled.

'You find comfort in the post? How do you afford it?'

'It doesn't cost anything.'

'Do you pay in kind?'

'What?'

'What do you have to do to get the letters?'

'Nothing. They just come.'

'Have you kept any of the letters, Karl?'

'I'm not allowed to. If I do, I won't get any more.'

'How do you know that?'

'It said so in the first one.'

Berger and Blom exchanged a quick glance. Blom nodded, and Berger went on, 'Do you remember exactly what it said?'

'I don't remember anything any more. It's great.'

'But you still remember the first letter.'

'Not exactly. But ... the last sentence.'

'Can you describe what the letters look like?'

'I'm not allowed to.'

'You're not allowed to show anyone the letters, no, but you're allowed to describe them.'

'I don't know ...'

'I don't think it's crystals. Is it powder? Is there enough room in an ordinary sheet of folded paper? Does it say anything on the paper?'

'I want to leave now.'

'Does it say who sends the letters, Karl?'

'Ordinary white envelopes. No writing. I want to go now.'

'See, you *can* remember, Karl, well done. Do you remember what you were found guilty of?'

'They scream it at me every day.'

'Who does?'

'The idiots. The morons in the day room. The dribblers.'

'Dribblers?'

'Stefan who killed his brothers when he was a child. Åke who hit twelve people with a metal pipe on the underground. Kjell who ate his mother.'

'But all the dribblers think what you did was worse?'

'It was the child ...'

'Do you remember that too? Do you remember what happened?'

'I don't know ...'

'You confessed, Karl. I saw you, heard you. Tell me about the shelter.'

'The shelter? I talked about my mum most, didn't I?'

'So say it again.'

'You get born. You don't know anything. Someone has to take care of you. But the person who takes care of you hurts you all the time. If she wasn't already dead, I'd have killed her.'

'How old were you when she died, Karl?'

'Eight. But by the time she jumped in front of the train it was already too late. Nothing could get better.'

'But it did get better, didn't it? A stable, friendly foster-home in Falun, a normal school. But the scars were still there?'

'Andreas keeps going on about this stuff.'

'Andreas?'

'You know who Andreas is. The new doctor.'

'Of course we do, Karl. When did you start to hate mothers and pushchairs?'

'That was the worst time. Andreas says my first memory is of sitting in a pushchair, just as I'm being hit. With a lump of wood.'

'Always a lump of wood?'

'A lot of the time ...'

'Then there were a couple of incidents, weren't there, that meant you ended up living in a care home?'

'I don't know ...'

'Of course you know, Karl. A couple of incidents with mothers and children.'

'I didn't hurt anyone.'

'Only because you were stopped, though. You were sixteen years old, and your terror had started to turn to rage. Then you were moved to a care home, even though you should probably have gone to a different sort of institution. Like this one. Because at the care home you could come and go as you pleased. When you'd been there for a few years you all went on a trip to Orsa and stayed in a big hostel, and you built a shelter in the forest, it was lots of fun, but one day you saw a young mum who was out walking with her little son in a pushchair ...'

Berger leaned back. Blom took over.

'What happened then, Karl? When you saw them? What did you feel?'

'I don't know, I don't remember,' Karl Hedblom said, staring strangely at her.

'You'd just started building your shelter, you were happy. And then you saw the mother with the pushchair. What happened inside you then?'

'Have you got children?'

Berger saw Blom lose her thread slightly, but she quickly recovered and answered, 'What do you think, Karl?'

'No,' Karl Hedblom said, shaking his head. 'You're more like a man.'

Under other circumstances Berger would have laughed out loud, but this was hardly the time. Blom gave him a quick glance and said, 'You're in the forest, Karl. You've finished building your shelter. You see the woman with the pushchair. What happens next?'

'I've answered that before.'

'But did you tell the truth then?'

'I think so. Things happen to me when I see that. It's best that I'm here. Andreas thinks it's best.'

'Do you often see it, Karl?'

'I'm in here, I don't see anything. Sometimes I see it on television.'

'Do you get angry when you see a mother with a pushchair on television?'

'I don't know ...'

'We need to go back to the forest now. It's autumn, a bit chilly in among the trees. Can you smell the forest? The ground is covered with yellow leaves. There's a faint smell of decay. Were there mushrooms, Karl, was it mushroom season?'

'The mushrooms were rotten. It was them making the smell.'

'What were you doing out in the forest, Karl?'

'I got to be on my own. It was nice.'

'It can't be easy to built a shelter. Who taught you how to do that?'

'I didn't build any shelter.'

'Did you just find it in the forest? When you were out there on your own?'

'I don't know ...'

'Eight years ago you said you'd made it, Karl. What happened when it was finished? What happened inside it?'

'I want to leave.'

'It was almost two whole days, Karl. There must have been a lot of noise.'

Hedblom was no longer answering. He looked down at the table and shook his head with a slight smile. Blom made one more attempt, 'Had you planned to use the block of wood the whole time? Like your mother?'

Then the door was pulled open. The two huge guards walked in. Then they moved apart slightly, and a man in his forties looked up from his iPad and pushed his glasses up onto his head.

'This just stopped being OK,' he said. 'Come with me.'

It wasn't as if they were being given a choice. The guards helped usher them out into the corridor. Berger cast a last glance into the interview room before the door closed. The guards were approaching Karl Hedblom, who was still sitting there shaking his head.

The man was dressed informally – jeans and an untucked shirt – and he didn't say a word as they walked down a considerable number of Säter's corridors. After passing through a couple of security checks they reached a door marked ANDREAS HAMLIN, without any title or job description. He tapped in a code and used a passcard to open it, then gestured towards a couple of chairs. He walked around the desk and sat down. He pointed at his iPad.

'You crossed a few boundaries there.'

'I'm wondering if you might have just done the same thing,' Blom said. 'By letting us do it.'

Andreas Hamlin shrugged his shoulders.

'It's been a long time since Karl has talked to any strangers. I thought that perhaps you'd be able to find some perspective we've missed. Sadly that isn't what happened.'

'You were watching us the whole time?' Berger said.

'I think you had a good idea that I would have been,' Hamlin said with a brief, mirthless smile.

'What boundaries were you referring to?' Blom asked.

'Boundaries behind which he hides. You sensed them. The shelter, the mother, those two days. The block of wood. But the description of the forest in autumn was good, it might have been possible to progress from that.'

'The description of the forest in autumn?' Berger exclaimed, and felt Blom's hand on his thigh.

'Were you aware of the letters?' she asked.

Andreas Hamlin shrugged again.

'Obviously we know he's on something more than just lofepramine and nortriptyline, but it hasn't been easy to figure out how he's been getting hold of it.'

'Why do I get the feeling that you don't see Karl very often?' Berger said.

'Probably because it's true,' Hamlin said in the same gently amused tone of voice. 'Fundamentally all these patients need high-intensity psychoanalysis, and we're so understaffed that we can't do much beyond keeping them medicated. But when I started work here three years ago I made a fresh start with Karl. Went back to the beginning again. He certainly didn't build a shelter of any sort, he's completely impractical.'

'Anything else?'

'Difficult to say,' Hamlin said. 'He shuts down at certain points. I honestly believe that he doesn't remember. But I've seen inside his rage, and it's not the sort of thing you can just laugh off. It would be hard to find a stronger expression of human emotion, frankly.'

'Towards his own mother, or mothers in general?'

Andreas Hamlin nodded for a while; it was the first time he looked like a doctor.

'Primarily towards his own mother,' he said. 'But of course he has a history of attacks against mothers.'

'Two incidents when he was sixteen years old,' Berger said.

'And one single opportunity since then,' Hamlin said. 'And he grabbed it.'

'Is that your professional conclusion?'

'That was the professional conclusion of the police and judicial system. I just have to deal with it.'

'Stop that,' Berger said.

Andreas Hamlin cast a professional eye over him.

'You'd be an interesting case to take on,' he said.

Berger's reply drowned out Blom's unexpected snigger:

'But I wouldn't be satisfied with anything but "high-intensity psychoanalysis". Is he guilty or not?'

'I don't know,' Hamlin said. 'I honestly don't know. He's got the anger in him – he's clearly violent, so it's good for everyone that he's in here – but it comes in waves, like fireworks exploding. Keeping someone captive for two days is a different matter. A completely different psychology.'

'You think he's innocent?'

'You'll never get me to say that.'

'I suspected as much.'

'There is something else I've been wondering about,' Hamlin said quietly. 'No matter how hard I look through the investigation into the double murder of Helena and Rasmus Gradén, there's one thing I can't find.'

'What's that?' Berger said, as his pulse rate increased slightly.

'There's no mention of a police officer by the name of C. Lindbergh.'

'What?'

'No matter how I try, I can't find an officer of that name in the police file. And you said very clearly in there that you were present, that you both heard and saw Karl Hedblom confess to the double murder. But you weren't there, were you?'

'I was only peripherally involved,' Berger said with a slight frown.

'I thought I might raise the matter with your boss, what was her name, Superintendent Rosenkvist? Maybe take it a bit higher than that. What does the C stand for?'

'Charles,' Berger said in a strained voice.

'Charles Lindbergh? With an h? Seriously?'

At that moment Blom squeezed Berger's thigh so hard that he started, and she asked, 'Tell me something. Why was Karl assaulted in his pushchair? Doesn't violence between family members usually take place in the seclusion of the home? This feels like the exact opposite.'

'That was when his mother Ulla was left in peace,' Andreas Hamlin muttered.

'In peace to assault her son in his pushchair? While they were out walking in Falun? With a—'

'With a block of wood, apparently, yes. It was kept beneath the pushchair the whole time, well rinsed. But of course there's no way of checking that. Unless he's found.'

'He?'

'Like I said, I've only been in charge of this case for three years,' Hamlin said. 'And that was when it first came to light.

It would appear that no one was bothered enough to look before that.'

'What exactly are we talking about here?' Blom asked.

Dr Andreas Hamlin leaned back in his chair and looked at them carefully. Then he said, 'There was a father. And a brother.'

15

Eight years doesn't sound like much, but for a house it can mean the difference between standing and falling. And in this case it was definitely a matter of falling.

They were standing beside a large neglected storehouse look-ing out at what had once been a smallholding. Now the forest had swallowed it, greedily and ruthlessly, and Berger had no idea which direction they should take.

'So the care home was located in Falun?' Blom said.

'Autumn trip,' Berger said as he set off. 'There were nine of them, fifteen counting the staff, and they were here for just over two weeks that autumn.'

As they made their way into the dense forest it started to snow. The flakes sailed gently through the few gaps between the trees, and as Berger and Blom pushed their way onward the branches around them began to turn white. There was no doubt that the country's snowline was mov-ing south.

'So, a father and a brother?' Blom said.

'They weren't in the police investigation,' Berger said. 'They must have disappeared pretty early on.'

'But the forensic psychiatric report wouldn't have missed that, surely?'

'We only got to see the summary. Which means it can't have been considered important.'

They walked on. The snow fell breathlessly through space. The forest grew even denser, and silence settled around them.

'Karl's mother hit him in his pushchair,' Blom said eventually. 'Was that because she couldn't do it at home? Because there was a family?'

'A father and an older brother.' Berger nodded. 'But after his mother's death Karl Hedblom was placed with a foster-family straight away. So the father couldn't have been an option for custody. Why not?'

'We need to find out more about this,' Blom said. 'One thing's clear now, though.'

'What?'

'Karl Hedblom is hardly the sort of person a copycat would want to imitate.'

'No,' Berger agreed. 'He looks a lot worse now, with a serious drug problem and all that, but he was just as pathetic back then, a psychological wreck. A murderer needs some sort of charisma to warrant the honour of a copycat.'

'Which makes it more likely that it's someone within the family,' Blom said. 'A blood relation. A brother who went through the same crap. A father who was even worse than the mother.'

'And who wouldn't hesitate to pin the blame for the murder on his own brother or son? I don't know ...'

The words sank in. They themselves were sinking deeper into the forest. Berger consulted the compass on his mobile and adjusted their course.

'That would at least explain the lump of wood,' Blom said after a while.

'I don't know ...' Berger repeated.

'If Karl is innocent, who'd know about the lump of wood outside the family?'

Berger let out a deep sigh and gestured towards an almost entirely overgrown clearing. 'Or else Karl Hedblom walked this precise route every day for a week, first to build the shelter, then to come back day after day to torture his captives, Helena and Rasmus Gradén. Until he finally killed them and dragged them out to the road.'

With a bit of imagination it was possible to see that what was sticking out from beneath the heavy and now almost completely snow-covered fir branches had once been a shelter. A collection of logs from a mixture of conifers and deciduous trees lay in a heap, like a game of pick-up sticks for giants.

Berger walked over and touched the sawn end of one of the trunks, and ran his hand along a rotten length of rope.

'He sawed down trees, removed the branches, tied the trunks together, built a relatively stable construction in which he kept a child and a mother captive for two days without anyone suspecting a thing. Would you have been able to do that? Would I?'

'Maybe the shelter was already here? Maybe he just found it?'

'First it had only just been built, and second no one else came forward to say they'd built it. But sure, it's possible. And it was never really proved that they spent those two days here. But their blood and Karl's DNA were found here and nowhere else.'

Blom nodded and walked about a bit in the swirling snow. Berger pushed a large fir branch back until there was a dull cracking sound. The half-broken branch stayed back, revealing a space that looked more like a room than it had done before.

'If walls could talk ...' Berger said.

'They're talking to me,' Blom said firmly. 'They're saying: no one was held captive here for two days. They're saying: different perpetrator, different crime scene. They're saying: the evidence was planted. It was October. No matter how carefully wrapped up the fourteen-month-old boy was, there's no way he'd have survived in this shelter. He'd have died of the cold long before he was beaten to death. And probably the mother as well. If she hadn't already died of grief.'

'There was actually some evidence of hypothermia ...'

Blom went on undeterred:

'It's only now, now we know that the killing has continued, one way or another, that we can see Karl Hedblom clearly. Someone is sending drugs to him in the clinic. Someone wants to keep him as out of touch as possible. Could that be anyone except the true perpetrator? Karl didn't have the skills to build this shelter, and he wouldn't have been capable of tying up two unpredictable individuals inside it and keeping them quiet. He's an entirely different type, his violent outbursts have always been spontaneous. The police investigation stinks. So does the verdict of the court.'

Berger stopped and looked at her. Her blonde hair was covered in a layer of snowflakes that were so light they seemed to float above her head, like a nebula in microcosm. He hated the fact that he didn't feel able to trust her completely.

'You seem to feel very strongly about this,' he said tentatively.

Blom stared at him. She shook her head.

'Neither of us really warmed to Jessica Johnsson, we only met her for a few minutes, she was awkward, difficult. But all the evidence suggests that she was slaughtered in her house while we were there. We were there, Sam, we allowed it to happen. The person who killed Helena and Rasmus here has carried on for eight years, eight long years, and I'd put money on the fact that the victim in Gothenburg, Lisa Widstrand, is only the tip of the iceberg.'

Berger met her gaze; he couldn't see any trace of dissembling, of lying, in it. What happened after the boathouse was one thing, this was something else. That was how he had to think about it, divide his brain into two halves where one trusted Molly and the other one doubted her. He nodded.

'I've been doing my utmost not to think serial killer ...'

Blom pulled her mobile from her pocket and held it out towards Berger. An image appeared on the screen, a dark face in front of two sources of light lying at the bottom of a flight of steps. It was a balaclava, and from it shone a pair of eyes that seemed to have their own internal light. Blom zoomed in closer, they were bright blue.

'All the things these eyes have seen,' she said.

'You're thinking of Karl Hedblom's eyes?' Berger asked.

'Clouded now,' Blom nodded. 'But they looked like they used to be bright blue.'

'His father must be around sixty years old now. Could this man have been sixty?'

'Maybe. But he feels younger. The blows felt younger.'

'The brother?' Berger said. 'But we're fumbling in the dark now.'

'We need to find out more about the family history.'

'And what a history it seems to be.'

Blom clicked to close the image of the man in the balaclava.

'I don't want to stay here any longer.'

*

It was on the outskirts of Brunflo that Berger saw the sign, just before the E45 merged with the E14 for a while. At first the sign didn't prompt any sort of reaction, but somehow it must have taken root inside him, because when the name appeared on another sign a few kilometres later he said out loud, 'Frösön.'

Blom looked up from the file she was reading but said nothing. Berger went on, 'Why is the name Frösön setting off alarm bells inside me?'

Blom closed the file and frowned.

'Now you come to mention it ...' she said.

Then she fell silent again.

The longest road in Europe – the highway that ran the length of the interior of the country – would shortly curve right and leave its temporary companion behind. To their left lay the city of Östersund. And the island of Frösön.

'Not Tahiti,' Blom said.

'Ah,' Berger said.

The hall, which was usually used as an auditorium or dance hall, was now filled with tables. Each of the ten square tables was covered with playing cards. There were four chairs around each table, and on those chairs sat people who, almost without exception, had grey or white hair.

Berger almost didn't recognise him. He had let his beard grow and was wearing a loose-fitting Hawaiian shirt. He raised his hand in triumph, stood up from the table, put his arm around a woman and walked towards them.

Then the now-retired Detective Superintendent Allan Gudmundsson's jaw dropped.

'Sam,' he said tersely when his face no longer resembled a black hole.

'And you remember Molly Blom?' Berger said.

Allan whispered a few words to the woman, presumably his wife. She walked off slowly towards a table set for coffee, and Allan drew them aside.

'One year's salary as a retirement payment. An excellent opportunity to learn bridge. A magnificent sport.'

'Is there somewhere we can talk undisturbed?' Berger asked.

'Preferably not,' Allan said. 'Neither of us is in the police any more. We have nothing professional to discuss.'

Berger just stared at him, and in the end Allan gave up and shrugged his shoulders.

'Follow me.'

They ended up in a smaller conference room, and sat down at a square table that looked very like the bridge tables.

'I thought you were going to Paris,' Allan said.

'Do you remember Karl Hedblom?' Berger asked.

Allan Gudmundsson grimaced.

'I have no reason to remember either him or you, Sam. You let me down. You lied to me.'

'You know why, Allan. You know it was necessary.'

'So you say, yes. And why would you, an ex-cop who got fired, be interested in one of Sweden's worst ever murderers?'

'Some new facts have come to light ...'

'If that was the case I'd be talking to the police now, not you.'

'We're trying to establish ourselves as private investigators. We've been asked to check out this new information.'

'Asked by whom?'

Berger cast a quick glance at Blom.

'By Karl Hedblom's father.'

'Rune?' Allan exclaimed. 'What the hell?'

'Rune Hedblom, yes,' Berger said attentively.

'Is he still alive?'

'He thought it was odd that he didn't feature in the police investigation.'

'He got dropped, it wasn't worth investigating him any further. Is *that* your new lead?'

'Of course not. Why wasn't it worth investigating Rune Hedblom any further?'

'Serious alcoholic. Homeless in Borlänge. Has he sorted himself out now, then?'

'Yes. But he must have said something to you even then that made you drop him from the investigation?'

'He moved out when Karl was seven. Wanted to get away. Ended up on the streets.'

'And the other son?'

'Anders.' Allan nodded. 'Three years older. Disappeared even earlier, went to live with an aunt down in Skåne. I seem to recall that someone spoke to him on the phone and ruled him out of the investigation. So he got dropped too. Probably somewhere in the archives in Stockholm now.'

'Did he say anything memorable?'

'I don't remember. I doubt it.'

'Try.'

'He'd never been anywhere near Dalarna since he was sent away. Lived in Malmö, worked as a salesman somewhere. I seem to remember him saying something else, but there was no connection to the case and we dropped him. OK, it's time for you to tell me what you're doing.'

'You say he said something else. What?'

'Something that felt a bit peculiar, but I don't remember what.'

'Of course you remember, Allan. You were leading the investigation, you were watching everything like a hawk.'

'Not on my own. That lunatic Ling was hovering above the whole thing like a ramshackle helicopter, way above this old hawk. And do you remember Robertsson? He was fucking crazy.'

A smile crept up on Berger out of nowhere.

'The catalogue,' he said.

'A compendium of the country's escort services,' Allan said. 'And all in his bloody lunch breaks.'

'I wonder what a man like that would be doing today, eight years later?'

'He used to secretly film other people's interviews as well.' Allan laughed. 'With an old VHS camera, through a window in that crazy hotel in Orsa.'

This was what Berger had been looking for. A short moment of connection that might be enough to break the ice. He needed an Allan who wasn't as tense as a spring.

'So what's this new information that's come to light?' Allan asked when they emerged from the pleasant bathwater of memory.

'Someone's sending drugs to Karl Hedblom at Säter.'

'What sort of drugs?'

'Not sure. Methamphetamine is certainly a major component, anyway. Someone thinks it's a good idea to keep his mind and memories clouded.'

Allan fixed his eyes on him.

'You were there when Karl confessed. You were sitting next to me, Sam, you were there. Did you ever doubt, even for a second, that we'd found the right man?'

'No,' Berger conceded. 'Not at the time.'

'But now something has changed? Sweden's most obviously guilty criminal is suddenly as innocent as a lamb? Are you sure you're seeing things clearly now?'

'More and more sure.'

Allan shook his head slowly for a long time.

'Do you know what the difference between the police and private investigators has always been?'

Berger waited.

'The employer. The police serve the people, a private detective is a paid employee. And now that you're in the pay of Rune Hedblom, his son is suddenly innocent. Pull yourself together. And get rid of that fucking beard while you're about it.'

Berger stroked the beard in question, still surprised by its existence, and said,

'The four-leaf clover.'

For an indeterminate length of time Allan stared off into space. Then a penny seemed to drop.

'But that was just a drawing done with a ballpoint pen. The two of you kept going on about it, but it turned out to be completely irrelevant. Did you actually see the other injuries? And the two of you were banging on about a drawing on her buttock?'

'The same drawing cropped up a few years later on a victim in Gothenburg ...'

'Not that again!' Allan exclaimed.

'Again?'

'There was some nutter who spent years going on about that book fair tart as if a little drawing on a buttock meant there was a serial killer at work. And as you know all too well, we don't have serial killers in this country. We had to block her in the end.'

'And your nutter was going on about that in particular? No other conspiracy theories?'

'There was some other stuff as well – we were forced to block her.'

'Do you remember her name? The nutter?'

'Johanna, Josefin, and a similar-sounding surname.'

'Could it have been Jessica Johnsson?'

Allan nodded.

'Yes, that was it. That only started a year or so later, though.'

'If I told you that yesterday another ballpoint drawing of a four-leaf clover was found on another buttock, what would you say?'

Allan fell silent and frowned.

'I haven't stopped being a police officer altogether,' he said. 'The creases don't fall out that easily. There was an article in today's paper that reeked of a cover-up. Norrbotten?'

'The victim was Jessica Johnsson,' Berger said. 'The body's missing, but her buttock was left behind.'

Allan was now openly staring at him.

'Oh fuck,' he eventually said.

'Does that affect your opinion of Karl Hedblom's guilt?'

Former Detective Superintendent Allan Gudmundsson leaned back in his chair and tugged at his Hawaiian shirt.

'I've just remembered.'

'What?'

'What Anders Hedblom said on the phone.'

'What did he say?'

'That Karl inherited the pushchair from him.'

The sun was going down. Berger was still behind the wheel.

'Bridge doesn't exactly seem to improve your thinking,' Blom said.

Berger laughed as he drove up the Inland Highway.

'We did learn a few things, though,' he said.

'Like the fact that this Robertsson character was secretly filming the interviews,' Blom said. 'Shouldn't they all have been filmed?'

'There were too many of them,' Berger said, shaking his head. 'Routine questioning, mostly. To be honest, I reckon Robertsson was more interested in filming cleavages. But I'll try to find him. What else?'

'The father's name is Rune Hedblom, homeless in Borlänge.'

'And the brother is Anders Hedblom, a salesman in Malmö.'

'Who, more or less spontaneously, appears to have said that Karl "inherited the pushchair from him". By which presumably he meant that he had also inherited being beaten with a block of wood.'

'It's a very long way to Skåne,' Berger said.

'He was living there eight years ago,' Blom said. 'Salesmen tend to move about. We need to look him up. What else?'

'When we saw Jessica's typewritten letter we thought that the line about Karl's guilt was of secondary significance. But she'd clearly written about it a lot, and specifically about the four-leaf clover.'

'But she only started after the murder of Lisa Widstrand. So what happened then?'

'Jessica's tormentor Eddy Karlsson died,' Berger said. 'It wasn't until she resumed her former identity that she started to badger the police with her theories about the cases being linked with the four-leaf clover.'

'What she was trying to say, without being able to do so explicitly, is that the murderer is still walking free out there. And she couldn't do so explicitly because she had some form of connection to him. Back to square one, in other words.'

'I don't think so,' Berger muttered.

'Allan did say something else interesting, though,' Blom said.

'What's that?'

'That you and Desiré *kept banging on* about the four-leaf clover.'

16

It was lying on the table when he woke up. He hadn't put it there.

Woke up wasn't quite the right way to put it. There was no longer any boundary between dreaming and being awake. Everything blurred together.

They got back in the middle of the night. When Kåbtåjaure finally broke the undulating landscape with its clean, flat darkness, they were both so tired that they parted without a word.

Berger collapsed onto his bed like a dead man, without even taking his jacket off. The only thing he did was to toss his mobile on the table before he instantly slid into clean, flat darkness, a darkness that was probably a lot like death.

But gradually things happen in the darkness. A pair of bright blue eyes appear from it. A half-illuminated block of wood sweeps quickly, raggedly past, leaving a patch of white behind it, but the centre remains dark. The darkness takes on shapes, and they're the shape of a person, a bloody outline on a sheet. Then the moon reflects off a knife blade, a dagger, and the dagger sinks through skin, breaks the skin, and an image gradually emerges in glowing lines, a four-leaf clover whose leaves turn into the four wheels of a pushchair against the backdrop of light glinting between loosely bound tree trunks. When a pair of bound hands fades into ever increasing light a woman is sitting at a table, facing the other way. And in her mouth is a thick sock, as black as the darkness itself.

In a no-man's land between dream and wakefulness his reptile brain sent his hand towards the bedside table. But what it found was completely different to a cold mobile phone. Different enough for him to sit up abruptly in the bed, switch the bedside light on and stare in a deranged state at the thick black sock that was lying across the bedside table.

It lay there like a lump of death.

His tongue felt dry; he had been sleeping with his mouth open. Anyone could just have stuffed the sock in his throat. He wouldn't even have come round enough to put up any resistance.

He tried to think rationally. Had he left it there himself? When was the last time he had even touched a black sock like that?

But he had rummaged through the piles of clothes before their long drive down the Inland Highway, and Molly had brought an odd assortment of clothing when they first came up here.

The sock was there now, anyway. Laid out like a pennant across a fallen warrior's coffin.

No, it was just his imagination. No one had been in his cabin, not at the Swedish pole of inaccessibility. No one could have been.

No one but Molly Blom.

He sat on the edge of the bed. What sort of world was he actually in now? Nothing was certain. Nothing was as it seemed, least of all himself. Images started to rise, forgotten, suppressed.

The boys, the twins. Freja, his former partner, her long, sweeping hair. And what looked increasingly like their escape to France. A frightening figure chasing them at Arlanda Airport, a figure he only realised much later was himself. The failed father.

It was as if he were two people.

As if he lived two different lives.

He stood up unsteadily and felt his own unsteadiness as if from a peculiar distance.

Had he put the black sock there himself during the night?

In a different state, as a different person?

Longer than two weeks unconscious, as a result of a purely mental shock? There was no question that he felt guilty about Syl's death, but was it actually even possible for shock to affect someone that severely? Had he really been unconscious all that time?

Had he been living a different life during that time?

He stumbled towards the toilet and switched on the weak battery-powered light. The cubicle was tiny and cramped, the composting toilet smelled rank, there was a half-full bottle of water perched on the edge of the grimy washbasin beside a lump of soap that had failed to repel the dirt; it lay like an island in a puddle of filthy, frozen water. And crowning all this misery was a mirror that was so dirty that he could only just make out his bizarre, grey-bearded reflection.

What was going on? So far Molly had persuaded him to believe everything – the weeks of unconsciousness, their crazy flight up the length of this stretched-out country, her whole hero-status thing – but now everything was starting to teeter.

He looked at himself in the mirror for a long while, managing to see through the grime for the first time. That beard really was bizarre, could it really have grown so much in two weeks? And his hair still looked extremely odd; he tugged at it above both ears, and it was clearly much shorter on the left-hand side. He was thinner than ever, which made the fateful bite mark on his upper arm stand out more clearly than usual. And it looked like his cheeks had sunk somewhere behind that beard.

No, he thought and flicked the mirror with his hand before walking out. No, it was time to restore a bit of order. And he instinctively knew that the only way for him to restore order was to work. Investigate, do detective work, dig as deeply as he could into an absorbing case.

And now he had a chance.

He looked out through the window. The sun hadn't yet risen, but its rays were etching the mountaintops against the sky, making the ice-covered surface of Kåbtåjaure glisten; the rosy glow encouraged him to switch the bedside lamp off.

He quickly consulted the satellite timetable fixed to the wall and checked that none of them was due at the time shown on the wristwatch he had just pulled on, then he took a last glance at the grotesque sock and went outside.

Dawn came quickly. He left his cabin in semi-darkness and reached the other one in full daylight. He knocked. There was no answer, no obvious reaction. He opened the door, not the main one, but the narrow one. The skis were gone. He opened the main door to Molly's cabin and walked in.

The sleeping bag was laid out on top of the bed, the pillow perfectly plumped against the wall, it looked freshly laundered. Opposite was her makeshift whiteboard: a pine wall covered with pinned-up pieces of paper. The notes covered everything they knew, and he had a feeling that they had multiplied since yesterday.

How long had she been awake?

He stepped closer. There was a timeline of Jessica Johnsson's life, a plan of a familiar house in Porjus, a list of people questioned in the Helena Gradén case, selected photographs from the case file, a very graphic photograph of the dead Lisa Widstrand and a man in a balaclava rushing up some basement steps. Beside the familiar photograph of Karl Hedblom was a new one, showing him eight years older and considerably more drug-addled. And that wasn't the only new photograph; there was also one of a ramshackle storehouse, three pictures of the half-snow-covered shelter and even a fresh photograph of Allan in his Hawaiian shirt.

Blom had got even better at taking pictures without anyone noticing.

Berger pulled back from the wall slightly, looked out of the window and saw the sun glide above the mountains. He had no idea how long Blom had been gone. She could come back at any moment. Even so, he felt overwhelmed once more by the same feeling he had experienced in his own cabin, the feeling that order needed to be restored.

He stood there in the middle of the cabin, which was identical to his own, and saw the laid-out black sock before him as clearly as Blom's sleeping bag. Then he got going. He went into her bathroom, which was obviously a lot cleaner than his. He tapped on the walls, ceiling, floor, got down on his knees and explored all potential gaps in and around the composting toilet. Only when he was certain that there was nothing hidden in there did he go back out into the main room of the cabin. He burrowed deep into the wardrobe without finding anything, and repeated the procedure from the bathroom. Nothing in the walls, no obvious differences in the sound when he tapped the ceiling, nothing under the mattress, which left just the floor. He got down on his knees and put his ear to the wooden boards, then tapped frenetically and increasingly disconsolately as he made his way across the relatively small area.

Until suddenly there was a different sound.

It was right beneath the head of the bed, tucked away in the corner. He stopped, listened, slipped out from under the bed, peered out through the window, opened the door and looked around. The world was cold, white, silent, there was nothing out there. He went back inside, pulled the bed away from the wall, crept in behind it, tapped carefully until he identified a small area in the corner, looked for gaps, found nothing but the natural cracks between the floorboards, pulled open his penknife, slipped it into one of the cracks, wiggled it. Repeated the process. The knife blade looked like it might break at any moment and fly up into his eye. But then something moved slightly, slipped sideways. He prised the board a little more, closed his eyes as if his eyelids might provide protection from the spinning blade of a knife, until he finally managed to slide the tip of one finger into the crack in the floor. He grabbed hold of the other side and pulled out an irregular section of pine floorboard no more than thirty centimetres square.

Darkness opened up beneath it, but also a shape. He stuck his hands through and took hold of it, and lifted out a lumpy object.

On the table, in between their laptops, stood the satellite phone they had been given by Deer. There was a small space beside it, and that was where he placed a second, largely identical but rather more modern satellite phone.

She had already had one.

Molly Blom had brought a satellite phone with her when they arrived here. During the two weeks when Sam Berger had been doing his Sleeping Beauty act she had had full access to both phone and Internet. It was her first flagrant lie.

He heard a muffled rattling outside on the cabin steps. He stiffened when the door opened.

But not this door. A smaller one, the door to the ski closet. A brief respite. Berger grabbed the satellite phone and slipped it as quietly as he could into the hidden compartment under the floor. He heard the door close again as he slid the floorboard back in place, pressed it down, then slid the bed back into position as silently as he could manage as the door handle was pressed down. He pulled up the screen of his laptop and adopted a thoughtful posture by the wall, staring at the collection of notes and photographs. When Blom walked in he threw his hand out towards the paper-covered wall.

'You've extended it,' he said, hoping he didn't sound falsely jovial.

'And you've been asleep for a long time,' she said as she started to remove her ski boots.

'I'm trying to figure out what's new,' he said, stepping closer to the wall and trying to keep his heartbeat under control; he wasn't exactly born to be an undercover cop.

'You won't find the most important stuff there,' Blom said, standing there in her socks.

'Oh ...?' Berger said.

'The most important thing is what I *didn't* find.'

'Namely?'

'Anders Hedblom,' Blom said, opening her computer.

'Karl Hedblom's brother?' Berger said.

'I found the father, he died two years ago in a hostel in Borlänge. Sure enough, he did drink himself to death. But Anders Hedblom, a salesman in Malmö, doesn't appear to exist. There are around twenty other Anders Hedbloms in Sweden, and any one of them could be him of course. Sadly I haven't managed to find out his date of birth.'

'A bit of classic police desk work, then?'

'Unless you were planning another car trip,' Blom said, picking up a small bundle of paper from the table and coming over to stand beside him in front of the note-covered wall. He looked down at her; her cheeks were glowing as if they had been exposed to a long dose of sunshine.

'The sun rose something like twenty minutes ago,' he said. 'So it can't be that that's given you such a fetching rosy glow. You must have been out skiing for a long time. Did you set out while it was still dark?'

'The satellites don't appear before dawn,' she said. 'And don't worry, I keep a head torch in the ski store. It hasn't snowed recently, so the existing tracks were still there. Any more questions?'

'When are you going to shower?'

'When I've stopped sweating,' Blom said indifferently, and started to pin small notes with numbers on them up on the wall. 'One: look into the missing years in Jessica Johnsson's life. Two: get hold of more forensic results from the house in Porjus from the NOD. Three: go back to the Helena Gradén case and look through all the interview transcripts from eight years ago. Four: contact Dr Andreas Hamlin at Säter to make sure he keeps an eye out for letters sent to Karl Hedblom. Five: keep working on Gothenburg and Lisa Widstrand. Six: scour every police database in the country for any four-leaf clovers drawn anywhere on any bodies. Seven: find Anders Hedblom. What do you think?'

Berger sighed. 'What's the best option for the Gradén case? For you to look at it with fresh eyes, or me with my new-old ones?'

'You with your new-old eyes, I think. You've always had trouble dealing with the past; if you're forced to go back to it, maybe something you've suppressed might come to the surface.'

'That's one of the main tasks,' Berger said. 'The other one is investigating the missing years of Jessica Johnsson's life. That feels more like Security Service work. I take it you still have contacts there?'

He hoped he didn't sound too heavy-handed.

'I might well have,' Blom replied simply. 'So you take two, three, four and six. If I carry on with Widstrand, you can look for four-leaf clovers. OK?'

'OK,' Berger said.

Gentle steam rose from the gently undulating surface. He lifted the bucket carefully towards the end of the cabin, and a hand shot out from round the corner and grabbed it. A voice said, 'Hot water? Seriously?'

'I warmed it up a bit,' Berger said.

Instead of gratitude there was a splashing sound, then a gasp. The bucket came back, empty. He took it and started to mix some of the water from the saucepan with snow and said, 'One, then?'

The unmistakable sound of hasty washing was accompanied by an indistinct voice.

'No progress so far. Those secret years of Jessica Johnsson's life are still secret. I haven't managed to get anywhere with the Security Service, it's got top-level confidentiality. Two?'

'No more DNA in Porjus,' Berger said, passing the bucket round the corner again. 'But Robin, the lead forensics officer, has found evidence to suggest that someone was actually *living* in the boiler room. He's vacuumed the whole of that deafening room with a hyper-modern bit of kit borrowed from the FBI. Deer says they'll be getting results back about the tyre tracks some time today.'

'What about three?' said the voice as the empty bucket was passed back.

'I've read through the Helena Gradén case carefully,' Berger said, mixing more water. 'You were right about it stirring up a whole load of old memories. Deer and I were never at the centre of the investigation, we just dealt with peripheral figures on the edge of the case. One thing that has struck me is just how *good* Allan was back in the day. He asks all the right questions, in the right way. His colleague, Robertsson, on the other hand, made a number of basic mistakes.'

'Have you contacted him?' Blom asked from round the corner.

'I've managed to track him down, at least. Not entirely unexpectedly, Richard Robertsson has sunk through the ranks, he's now a lowly desk jockey in the police store. I'll give him a call. In the meantime I've been reading through his interviews, there are a couple that look promising.'

'What sort of people did you actually talk to?'

'I don't imagine you want names, but I've had time to memorise a lot of them by now.'

'I want names. And why they were questioned.'

'Four main categories. I'll take the names I can remember. Possibly responsible for building the shelter: Lennart Olsson, Magnus Bladh, Peter Öberg. Care-home residents: Linnéa and Elin Sjögren, Reine Danielsson, Johan Nordberg and obviously Karl Hedblom. Care-home staff: the manager Sven-Olof Lindholm, Juana Galvez, Lena Nilsson, Sofia Trikoupis. Neighbours, friends, et cetera: Per Eriksson, Göras Egil Eriksson, Elisabeth Hellström, Grop Åke Ek, Olars Fredrik Alexandersson ...'

'I didn't really mean in that much detail...'

'Seriously, though, what is it with those Dalarna names? Göras, Grop, Olars ...'

'I'm getting a bit cold here ...'

'Ah,' Berger said and handed her the bucket again; most of a naked female arm came into view.

'Point four then,' he volunteered. 'Dr Andreas Hamlin at Säter is going to keep an eye out for post for Karl Hedblom. And he's going to get Karl's blood checked. Five?'

'They're farms,' Blom said.

'What?' Berger said.

'It used to be fairly common in Dalarna for people to add the name of their farm to their given name. A lot of people have started to revive the old tradition.'

'Right,' Berger said, nonplussed.

'Point five then,' Blom said from round the corner. 'Lisa Widstrand. I've been in touch with a Superintendent Sjölund in Gothenburg, who as good as admitted it was a sloppy investigation. No one cared about the four-leaf clover on the victim's buttock because no one really cared about the victim. It was during the run-up to the book fair, and the instruction to sweep the murdered prostitute under the carpet was unspoken but very clear. I've got a Skype session booked with Sjölund in a few minutes' time.'

'Might be as well to finish showering then,' Berger said.

'Pass me my towel and give me point six.'

'Number six,' Berger said, passing the towel round the corner of the cabin. 'The four-leaf clover. To start with I tried to expand the search parameters. Not just "four-leaf clover" but "clover", "ballpoint drawing", "drawing on body", "ink sketch", "buttock", "arse cheek", "backside" and so on. I've got a couple of promising leads. Can I come round there yet?'

The muttering from beyond the corner of the cabin could possibly be interpreted as positive, and he walked round. Her blonde hair was sticking up, she had the towel wrapped around her body and a pair of bright-blue Crocs on her feet. He stared at them.

'All serious cold comes from below,' she said.

'Old Siberian saying,' he said.

'Go on.'

'The search is still running,' he said. 'I got a couple of hits on "four-leaf clover", but I don't know where they're going to take me. I turned into a shower assistant just as I was about to look them up.'

They went back inside the cabin. The radiator was working away doggedly, spreading heat that had never felt so welcome. The thermometer on the outside of the window read minus eighteen degrees: the winter chill had arrived in the interior of the country with a vengeance.

Berger crouched down beside the radiator and held his hands up so they were almost touching the hot surface.

'Who is he? What does he want?' she said.

'We won't know who he is,' Berger replied, 'until we find out more about Jessica Johnsson's past; that's where he is. As for what he wants ...? I think this has the feel of someone who kills for pleasure. I doubt the motive will match Karl's – hatred of mothers, revenge for past wrongs. No, this is too structured, too planned. This is about pleasure. He abuses and murders because he gets a kick from it. There's a lot that suggests we're dealing with a genuine sexual sadist. Are we absolutely certain that there's no trace of semen at any of the crime scenes?'

'Not as far as I've seen, not even in Gothenburg, where the victim was a prostitute.'

'Strange,' Berger said. 'Because everything seems to be pointing to one single thing. Sex.'

Blom nodded. 'Point seven. I think I've found Karl Hedblom's older brother Anders. He's the only one in the right age range. According to the files he lives nearby. But I haven't managed to get hold of him.'

'Nearby? Does every fucker live in the interior of the country these days?'

'Sorsele. So it's possible to imagine a potential sequence of events. Eight years ago Anders Hedblom was living in Malmö and went up to Orsa to visit his brother, sees a woman with a pushchair walking down the road through the forest, and it rouses his killer instinct. He does some planning, builds a shelter in the woods – he trained to be a carpenter but ended up selling work tools – then kidnaps the mother and child. After the double murder he cleans the shack of his own DNA but leaves his brother's and the victims'. Somehow he comes into contact with Jessica Johnsson, who's living under an assumed identity in Porjus and has a tendency to pick the wrong men; they start a relationship, he moves nearby, to Sorsele, but then he lets slip what he did, maybe tells her about the four-leaf clover and threatens her. Jessica dumps him but doesn't actually want to report him, so instead she gives the police little clues in the form of conspiracy theories. Until reality catches up with her. Just when we happen to be there.'

Berger nodded.

'Not entirely impossible. But that doesn't explain why Jessica sent her letter specifically to Deer. I don't really buy her explanation about seeing Deer on television and thinking she seemed trustworthy.'

'I've been thinking about that too,' Blom said. 'We should try to find that film clip. Do you remember when it might have been?'

Berger shook his head slowly and said, 'There was a lot of media attention at the start of the case, then it tailed off. I can try to find out. But I still think your hypothesis about Anders Hedblom justifies a trip to Sorsele.'

Blom nodded.

'I've got a Skype session first, though.'

'Are you going to sit face to face with Superintendent Sjölund in Gothenburg dressed like that?' Berger asked, gesturing towards the towel she was still wrapped in.

'I wasn't planning to, no,' Blom said and let the towel drop.

17

The man and woman have been in there for a long time now. What little focus remains is directed at the lower screen, the closer of the cabins, but to be honest there's precious little focus left. As usual in times of waiting the focus ends up somewhere else. On images conjured up by waiting. And they even manage to drive out the breathtaking cold of the little room.

Dusk sweeps in across the large terrace, the smell of pine merges with the thyme and rosemary from the steep slopes leading down to the sea and up to the mountains. From time to time a hint of lavender drifts past on air that will remain warm all night through. They can choose to sleep outdoors if they feel like it. Everything is possible here, everything allowed, everything so astonishingly alive. They will experience the same thing, with the same somehow elevated, doubled sensory apparatus.

While they can still see each other.

The contract is lying briefly on the desk of the lawyer on the balcony of Europe. The signature glows as if written in silver. The lawyer returns, he's had the payment date confirmed by the bank, signs the contract on the dotted line. His name glows as if written in gold.

When the door of the snow-covered cabin opens the cold comes so abruptly. The door closes again, but the Mediterranean warmth doesn't return. The observer is back in his bare room.

The thin leather glove on his left hand stretches as the screen zooms in on the cabin door. Which opens again. The man comes out first, he's wrapped up warm and is carrying the camping stove. He crouches down by the corner of the cabin. Then the woman comes out, draped in a towel and carrying a bucket which she puts down before she goes round the corner. The man lights the stove, fills a saucepan with snow, and steam starts to rise. The woman round the corner waits for a short while; the observer zooms in on her face, clearly sees how the cold starts to eat into her.

I can warm you, the observer suddenly thinks. There's a place where we can warm each other.

Then she removes the towel and hangs it on a nail in the wall. The man empties the steaming saucepan into the bucket and adds some snow, feels the temperature and hands the bucket to her. The woman takes it, lifts it above her head, and just as she tips the contents over her body the observer sees the vaguely star-shaped birthmark just below her right breast.

That's when he reaches into the desk drawer and pulls out something black. It's made of elasticated fabric, and he lays it out across the table. Only then does it become apparent that it's a sock.

A thick black sock.

The pistol, a Sig Sauer P226, is lying on the desk in front of the observer. The leather glove spins it round: a one-handed version of truth or dare. The barrel of the pistol slows down, eventually stops, pointing right at the observer's chest. The observer always chooses dare; the truth is far too complicated, not least the truth about the illness.

Profanation.

The right hand writes: '14.24: After spending hours together in ♀'s cabin it is time for ablutions. ♂ assists ♀. No evident results from time spent together.' The observer contents himself with that. That's his task.

One of his tasks.

18

The large white-clad man was moving in slow motion through his evidently limited space; the bluish-lilac light made him look like a solitary fighting fish in an aquarium. Ordinarily that pattern of movement would have caught her interest, but now she wasn't thinking about anything but the football match that kicked off at three o'clock. The girls' match.

It was actually Saturday.

First she had to get home from police headquarters, rush into the terraced house in Skogås, grab a hopefully ready-changed Lykke and race off towards Nytorps Mosse Sports Ground, where the nine-year-old girls in Skogås-Trångsund FC were playing their local rivals, Boo FC.

But right now she was standing here in a cramped laboratory watching this strange piece of choreography.

'It was on the wall,' Robin said, leaning over something on a table that appeared to be completely bare.

'It?' Deer said, adjusting the always uncomfortable white overalls. 'And why isn't *it* in Linköping?'

The National Forensics Centre, the NFC, was still based in Linköping, but these days it had a subsidiary branch on Polhemsgatan, in police headquarters in Stockholm.

Robin looked up at her with an affronted expression.

'It's actually Saturday today.'

Without bothering to try to interpret the remark, Deer replied.

'So, what is *it*, then?'

Robin straightened his back.

'We might as well call it a thread.'

'And why was the thread so important that I had to rush over here straight away?'

'It wasn't,' Robin said, returning to the invisible thread. 'Not yet, anyway. But I haven't exhausted all the options yet.'

'You want me to ask questions,' Deer said. 'So the thread was on the wall? Am I to assume that you mean the wall of the boiler room in the house in Porjus?'

'It was the only thing in there. So I can't actually prove that someone was living in the boiler room. Which means that I can't go and talk to Benny Lundin, the most inflexible superintendent in the long and heroic history of Swedish policing.'

'Conny Landin,' Deer corrected patiently. 'Why is there any uncertainty about us calling the thread a thread?'

'Because it's so small,' Robin said. 'It's more of a fragment of a thread, a fibre. It was caught on the rough cement wall, at head height if a reasonably tall man was sitting on the floor.'

Deer saw a film sequence playing out in front of her, a film sequence of a man in a black balaclava, a film sequence that she shouldn't have seen at all. For a fraction of a second she was on the verge of forgetting her new duplicitous status and exclaiming 'Black?' but she managed to bite her tongue.

'What colour?' she asked instead.

'White,' Robin said.

She looked at him a little too long before saying:

'What sort of thread is it, then?'

'That's why I need to look at it a lot more closely,' Robin said. 'This isn't necessarily what it is, but the same material is used in gauze bandages.'

'A gauze bandage? Blood?'

Robin nodded.

'That's why I'm talking to you rather than Sonny Landén. The answer is no. Initial analysis shows no trace of blood, but that doesn't mean that there isn't any. We need to get down to the molecular level, and that's why I had to be here.'

'And call me in? To tell me that you *haven't* found any blood?'

'Like I said, that's not why I called you in. It's because of this.'

Robin held up a small plastic bag that looked as empty as the table in front of him. Deer stepped closer and examined it. The bluish-lilac light glinted off tiny fragments inside the bag.

'We've had a bit of luck here,' Robin said, shaking the bag.

'Is that from the car?'

Robin nodded.

'Scraped paint from the getaway vehicle, yes. Are you familiar with the concept of foil wrapping?'

'I can't say that I am,' Deer said.

'You basically wrap the vehicle in thin foil which comes in all sorts of colours. Among the fragments in this bag is a bright blue foil from a range called Oracal 970 Premium, and the colour has been identified as Fjord Blue. On top of that we've got traces of the original paint, a sort of yellowish white that we haven't yet identified. That needs to be done chemically and is going to take a while.'

'A yellowish white vehicle that's been covered in bright blue foil?'

'And if it was done legally and was registered, it ought to be possible to track down for an ambitious police officer who's working on a Saturday,' Robin said before turning back towards the invisible thread. With his bent back facing her, he added:

'Well, don't just stand there wasting my time.'

Deer stared at the overweight senior forensics officer until she eventually said, 'Thanks, Robin.'

Without looking up he replied, 'The documentation is in a folder by the door.'

The rest of Saturday was very odd. Deer removed her protective overalls, ran down to the garage beneath police headquarters and drove out into the unrelenting, European November fog, a static form of rain that was dramatically different to what she experienced on her far too many visits to the interior of Norrland. As she accelerated unreasonably hard along Nynäsvägen she found herself missing the clear, unforgiving air – perhaps not least because things kept appearing out of said fog. A pair of bright blue eyes wasn't the only clue provided by the knitted black balaclava – there was also a microscopic white thread with blood on it. A blue van, a Volkswagen Caddy, reversed out of a garage and ended up with a yellowish white scrape on its side. And she was at least two seconds late cheering when Lykke for the first time in her nine-year-old life *headed* in the decisive goal against Boo FC, seconds that were reflected in her daughter's eyes. She saw the disappointment, and found herself staring directly into her own bottomless sadness when her dad had failed to show up for her dance demonstration.

No way was she going to let herself turn into Sture Rosenkvist, the man who refused to back down when his entire working-class family protested against him giving his newborn daughter a stuck-up name like Desiré.

Even during her sadly unvalidated ballet years she allowed herself to be turned into Dessie, but when she got a new professional partner soon after she qualified as a detective her name fell into place. She had never felt so happy with a name as she did with Deer, and now it was already starting to fade. The spell was broken. At the National Operations Department she was back to Desiré again; it was like a change of identity.

Sam, what the hell are you playing at up in Norrland?

Deep down Deer understood a bit more than she let on. Because she now had what she had wanted for a long time, a job with the NOD, she had let it go, but she would have liked to look into the link between Syl's sudden death and Sam and Molly's disappearance. There could hardly be any doubt that they were actually hiding up there, staying away from anything connected to the Security Service. Deer's duplicitous behaviour was, in the harsh glare of hindsight, less coincidental than she had pretended. It allowed her to hit two birds with one stone: resurrect the question of Karl Hedblom's guilt *and* find out what had really happened with Syl, Sam and Molly.

But instead the whole mess had blown up in her face.

And then, to her own surprise, she found herself sitting behind the wheel looking at her own considerably younger reflection. The same brown eyes – Sam's stupid 'deer's eyes' – and the same smooth flat brown hair, and the same almost-bob of a hairstyle. Often when she looked at Lykke she felt she was looking into a mirror through time. She would imagine a mirror that could show all the ages of a person, and right now Desiré was nine years old and on the point of turning into Dessie. But this nine-year-old didn't do ballet dancing, she played football, and she was impressively muddy as she sat in the passenger seat looking sullenly back at her.

'You played really well,' Deer managed to say, stroking her daughter's mud-spattered cheek.

'Do you even know what the score was?' Lykke asked, and the look on her face opened up yet another Sture-chasm inside Deer. Now wasn't the time to fall into it, though. Not now.

'Eight–four, wasn't it?' she said.

Lykke's features relaxed and she smiled broadly.

'I scored three goals,' she said proudly.

'I'm really proud of you, Lykke,' Deer said, rather more formally than she had intended.

Her daughter's smile meant she'd been forgiven. But she was unlikely to get a second chance that Saturday.

A cosy night in. She'd always had trouble coming to terms with that ultimate expression of middle-class smugness. But as Lykke grew up Deer had realised that time was finite; perhaps her daughter would rather spend Saturday evenings with her friends in just another year or so. Deer had promised herself that she'd make the most of the limited number of proper, exclusive cosy nights in they had left together.

While they waited for the right-hand door of the double garage to open, she looked at the terraced house in the murky dusk. An unremarkable terrace in a suburb wasn't exactly what she'd had in mind when she imagined her life; but on the other hand she hadn't exactly had any definite plans. Nothing beyond being a really good mum, wife and cop, and having a good life.

Deer was actually better than most of her colleagues at leaving work behind when she left the office. But not this time. She recognised the symptoms. Something was nagging at her. It wasn't just the fact that she had something definite to be getting on with – a task that really ought to be slotted into an existing investigation – but that she had painted herself into a corner. And she needed to find a way out of that corner at all costs. Never before had she broken the rules and been forced to keep things secret from her colleagues.

She was suddenly living a double life.

She had sent Lykke into the shower, and just as she was thinking the words *double life* and taking the last few ingredients from the fridge, the door opened and Johnny walked in with his arms outstretched, still wearing his ambulance driver's uniform. They hugged. Johnny ruffled her hair in his usual, annoying, wonderful way.

'So, how did it go? Did they win?'

'Eight–four,' Deer said, switching the stove on. 'She scored three goals. One with a header.'

'A header? Bloody hell. Didn't I say that a bit of personal coaching would do the trick?'

'So you reckon a few throws with a plastic ball in the garden count as personal coaching?'

'It's the amount of training that counts,' Johnny said as he started to take off his work clothes. 'That's the key.'

Deer watched her husband as he ambled towards the living room. She couldn't even say anything to him.

Double life ...

Dinner passed with long discussions of the match. As they ate she looked at her little family. They would have liked more children, but it wasn't to be. Anyway, Lykke was more than enough. Deer couldn't remember having had that much energy when she was nine. But on the other hand Johnny wasn't Sture, he was far, far better. Lykke's remarkable reserves of energy probably came from him, because in terms of Lykke's appearance she had only managed to find one thing, the curve of her ear lobe, which reminded her of Johnny; in every other way her daughter looked like a replica of her.

An improved model.

One that wasn't living a double life.

Dinner came to an end, Deer poured two more glasses of wine, slurped down the last strand of spaghetti and waited with a degree of anticipation that she wasn't altogether proud of. Eventually Lykke asked excitedly:

'Can we watch Liverpool? Please, Dad?'

This in fact was what Deer had been hoping for. Liverpool's classic demolition of Manchester United in March 2009. Four-one. One of the gems in Johnny's ridiculously comprehensive collection of Liverpool games. And she knew she wasn't expected to participate. She'd been given a ninety-minute break. Then the cosy night in would get her undivided attention.

Lykke knew it too, bounced over to her mother, gave her an apologetic hug and said, 'See you later.'

Deer stroked her daughter's cheek fleetingly and watched her bounce off towards the living room. Johnny gave her a kiss and turned on his heel.

'I'll clear up here,' Deer said. 'Then I might pop out to the garage for a bit.'

Johnny paused for a moment.

'On a Saturday evening?'

'Only for a little while,' she lied.

She almost managed to convince herself that it was a white lie.

As white as the microscopic thread from the boiler room in Porjus.

As soon as her little family had settled down in front of the television she sneaked out. She slipped through the ordinary garage to the far side of the double garage. That was her holy of holies. Or, in more prosaic terms: her workroom.

It was very sparsely furnished: a desk, a chair, a computer and a seriously large whiteboard with all manner of material on it. There was one unifying connection between the notes on the wall: they all related to the last few days. Jessica Johnsson, Helena Gradén, Lisa Widstrand, Karl Hedblom. And also Sam Berger and Molly Blom.

Maybe she was addicted to her work after all.

Beside the computer lay Robin's file. She opened it and looked at the time. Eighty minutes left.

A series of quick Google searches told her that foil wrapping was carried out by quite a number of paint workshops around Sweden, and that most of them offered the Oracal 970 Premium range and the colour Fjord Blue, so that didn't look like a fruitful line of inquiry, particularly not on a Saturday evening. Which left the advanced search option on the vehicle registration database: vehicles that had once been registered as yellowish white, if that was even a colour – she typed plenty of synonyms in the search box – and which at some point had been repainted bright blue. Possibly but not necessarily a small van, a Volkswagen Caddy.

As the search started up and the computer – which was considerably more modern than her official computer in police headquarters – appeared to wheeze with exertion, she looked through Robin's file.

There was some impenetrable but rudimentary chemical analysis, followed by a plan of the house in Porjus with all the finds marked and numbered. Deer noted that the white thread wasn't currently listed; she suspected that Robin didn't want to mention it until he had extracted the very last molecule from it. But the rest of the sketch indicated a sequence of events that was as yet incomplete. She supplemented it with information from her new, dark, secret world.

Jessica Johnsson goes down the steps to the basement accompanied by Berger and Blom. It's pitch-black, they've got torches, but if a light had been on inside the boiler room it would have seeped out through gaps at the sides of the door: that had been tested and proven. Inside the deafening darkness of the boiler room a blue-eyed man in a black balaclava is waiting. She estimated that he was about 1.85 metres tall, wore size 45 shoes, and *had been living in there* (here she trusted Robin's well developed intuition). The man is standing ready with a lump of wood, and goes on the attack before Berger even has time to push the door handle down. He acts with disconcerting efficiency: Berger and Blom don't stand a chance. Jessica evidently screams loudly, he ties her to the staircase with cable ties, then drags Berger and Blom over to the wall and ties their unconscious bodies to two separate radiators. Then he cuts Jessica free and drags her up the basement steps. He takes her into the living room, to the sofa facing the television, where he knocks her out with the block of wood. The quantity of blood suggests a brutal assault; maybe he's already started to use the knife, which is probably either an extremely sharp scalpel or a hunting knife. She doesn't die there in the living room, however, and the attack continues upstairs. He steps in the blood a number of times, and considering how carefully he had already cleaned the house it's odd that he leaves footsteps on the parquet floor. There are also trails left by the slipper-socks that Jessica Johnsson was wearing at the time. These lead to the upper floor, where the knife attack continues, and Jessica's body is so drenched in blood that it leaves a red silhouette on the white sheet. That's where Jessica dies, and the perpetrator draws a four-leaf clover on her buttock before slicing that section of skin off and leaving it behind. Why does he leave it behind? He's extremely careful not to leave any DNA evidence but has no qualms about leaving both footprints and something as obvious as the four-leaf clover. Why? Deer thought she could detect a number of carefully chosen clues, consciously left, as a message to someone.

Someone who had *banged on* about a four-leaf clover drawn on a buttock.

Why the hell had the now-murdered Jessica Johnsson sent that cryptic letter specifically to her?

She shook the thought off and went on with her run-through. After killing her, he pulls a trunk from the attic and stuffs the body inside it. He drags it downstairs, and eventually it starts to leak, in the snow outside when he has to put it down. Then he finally reaches the garage. Fortunately for him Berger and Blom's jeep isn't parked in the way, and as soon as he's got the trunk inside the small van he reverses out and drives off. And nudges the garage wall while he's reversing, leaving traces of paint behind.

An uncomfortable thought strikes Deer. What if Berger and Blom were so careful about removing their own DNA that they also managed to get rid of the murderer's? If that was the case, Deer had not only obstructed the investigation but actually sabotaged it. If her parallel investigation was uncovered she wouldn't just get the sack but would probably face criminal charges as well. Life as she knew it would be over.

Fortunately her train of thought was interrupted by a pinging sound which brought her back to reality. It came from the computer.

The search was finished. The screen was covered by a list.

Potential vehicles all around Sweden. Small vans and van-like vehicles with something approaching yellowish white original paint which had been covered by something approaching bright-blue foil.

There were nine of them.

Örebro, Helsingborg, Lund, Fittja, Umeå, Sorsele, Borås, Karlstad and Halmstad.

She studied the list and thought. To start with her thoughts were wordless. Then a word appeared: interior.

The interior of Norrland.

Sorsele.

She picked up her phone and noted that it was now 19.16; she had eight minutes left courtesy of Liverpool.

Then she made a call.

To the world of her double life.

19

Sorsele may have been located on the Inland Highway, the ever-present E45, but even for a seasoned Norrlander the almost three hundred kilometres that separated the little village from Porjus stretched the definition of *nearby* a little too far. From the pole of inaccessibility it was even further, but now the jeep was finally getting closer through the long-descended darkness. A faint glow hovering on the horizon suggested civilisation. An unusual number of elk had joined them on their trek, running along behind the wildlife fencing which could have come to an end at any moment, as if they had been seized by a collective urge to commit suicide. Fortunately the fencing had remained intact, and so far the pair in the jeep had remained unharmed by the wild, incomprehensible wildlife of the interior.

Unharmed but not unaffected.

Blom was driving. Berger was watching her surreptitiously; maybe she noticed, maybe she didn't. The look of concentration on her face was bathed in a dull bluish glow from the dashboard. There was nothing to read there; the secrets were all hidden elsewhere. If there were any.

'The bikini was a surprise,' he eventually said. 'I wasn't expecting that.'

Blom gave a thin, crooked smile.

'It's not a bikini. A sports top and sports pants, that's all.'

'What I still can't understand is how I could have been unconscious for so long,' Berger said bluntly.

'You weren't unconscious the whole time, but you were pretty heavily drugged. There was no other way of doing it, I'm sorry. You were talking about killing yourself.'

Berger stared at her.

'Was I?' he blurted.

'As soon as I eased up on the medication you tried. I had to wrestle you to the ground twice. You have to understand it was a genuine psychosis. And you have to try to understand how hard I had to work with you. It was a real emotional roller coaster. Yes, I sedated you, I drugged you. Because there was no other option. I was so relieved when I finally ... recognised you again ...'

Berger fell silent. He looked out at the pitch-like blackness. A sign swept past, informing them that they were entering the province of Västerbotten. As if that made any difference; it was all still Lapland. And no animals now, just forest. Forest and mountains.

Impenetrable, impassable.

'I don't understand how I could have got so out of control,' he said simply.

Blom shook her head.

'It's impossible to understand psychosis, there's no point. Reality and the ego dissolve. It's an entirely different state of consciousness. Everything approaching the super-ego disappears.'

'Sounds like you've dealt with it before,' Berger said. 'Evidently I got through it without serious injury, and you found just the right medication and treatment. Did you rob a pharmacy?'

'I have dealt with it before, yes. I have a younger brother . . .'

'Oh shit.'

'You can call it post-traumatic psychosis or acute reactive psychosis. So yes, I've seen it before. And treated it before. It was part of growing up for me.'

'But it is really possible to get it, just like that?'

Blom smiled unhappily.

'It only affects people who already have a dissociative way of dealing with the problems in their lives.'

'I have no idea what you're saying now.'

'People who have trouble integrating different aspects of their personality. You're just going to have to trust me on this.'

Berger fell silent again. He did trust her on this. He disappeared into himself, into his *unintegrated, dissociative* self. He'd felt it before, that he had different personalities living parallel lives. But his super-ego had come to life, he kept watch on himself, and a voice inside him.

Right now I'm having a moment of awareness of my illness.

He wasn't sure if the voice convinced him.

'I didn't know you had a younger brother,' he said.

She just grimaced.

'Did you buy anything else when you bought your sports top and sports underwear?' he asked.

'What do you mean?'

'Did you buy any other sports equipment?'

'A bit, yes. Skis, ski suits, the head torch. Intersport on the outskirts of Sundsvall, if you really want to know. Without any functioning security cameras.'

'Did you buy any socks?'

Blom took her eyes off the road, which was inadvisable considering the way the road was currently twisting and turning. She stared at Berger.

'Yes, I bought socks. Black socks. Basic, and good for most types of physical activity. But not all.'

'Hmm,' was all Berger said.

'OK, listen up, Sam. I know that Sylvia Andersson, your old friend going back all the way to those carefree days at police academy, your Syl, died with a black sock stuffed in her throat. I was there too, as you may recall. That doesn't mean that every black sock has suddenly turned into a murder weapon. What is it with you?'

'Did you lay a black sock on my bedside table last night?'

'What the fuck?!'

'I thought you didn't swear.'

'I've been hanging out with the wrong crowd,' Blom spluttered. 'What the hell's got into you?'

Berger shook his head.

'The last thing I did before I went out like a light last night, with all my clothes on, was toss my mobile onto the bedside table. I woke up in exactly the same position, and there was a black sock neatly laid out across my phone.'

Blom stared at him again. Then she shook her head and said, very clearly, 'I didn't put it there, I haven't been inside your cabin for ages. You were probably sleepwalking. You're still in the aftershocks of the psychosis, and you got smacked in the head with a lump of wood. It's hardly surprising that your brain is doing things you're not completely in control of. And that includes having all sorts of suspicions about the people around you.'

Berger pulled a face. The car rolled on towards the approaching lights, which no longer formed a dome on the horizon but were spreading out across the sky. They had started to pass the first houses.

'Did you find out any more about Anders Hedblom?' Berger asked.

'A bit,' Blom said. 'Three years older than Karl and, confirming what we already knew, a carpenter who moved into selling tools. He paid cash for his house on the outskirts of Sorsele when the tool company in Malmö went bankrupt four years ago. He's been living on unemployment benefit since then. No known involvement with the local community beyond gym membership. I got hold of the manager of the gym, who let slip that Anders is the fittest guy in the whole of Sorsele but that he hadn't been to the gym for a while. He also estimated his height to be around 1.85 metres.'

'Did he say anything else about him?'

'Only that he keeps to himself. That no one really knows him.'

'And was Deer right?'

'About what?'

'About us being in possession of "illegal weapons"? I don't want to make the same fucking mistake as Porjus again. If the extremely fit Anders Hedblom tries to rush me again with a block of wood, I'd like to be able to shoot him.'

Blom reached across Berger and opened the glove compartment. It was empty.

'It's like your watch case,' Blom said.

Berger felt that the way he was looking at her was at least as vacant as the glove compartment. Until the penny dropped. He took hold of the sides and pulled upwards. Beneath the empty space lay two sturdy firearms. He picked up one of the pistols and weighed it in his hand.

'OK,' he said simply.

'We're nearly there,' Blom said.

The car slowed down and turned off onto a side road, then drove on through the darkness until some faint lights appeared through the wall of fir trees. Blom stopped at once and switched the lights off.

'He's probably already heard us,' Berger said.

'Not necessarily,' Blom said, opening the door and squinting towards the lights in the forest.

She picked up her pistol, checked the magazine, released the safety catch and crept along the narrow road. Berger followed her, fumbling with his own gun until he got the hang of it in the darkness. The lights vanished then reappeared, now strong enough for them to see that they were coming from what looked like a fairly run-down little house. The light was shining from two windows, not very brightly but enough to illuminate the porch steps and front door. A small track led through a wild garden, where it split in two, one path leading towards the house, the other to a garage. There was no car in sight.

They followed the track towards the house. As they got closer it started to snow, fine gentle flakes powdering the drab scene.

On either side of the porch steps now, pistols ready. Listening. Not a sound. There was no wind. The only movement was the snowflakes drifting breathlessly to the ground.

Berger took the first step, as quietly as he could. He could feel Blom right behind him, understood that she was covering him, had his back. They reached the door. Blom crouched down and looked at the lock. Then she reached out her hand towards the handle, looked at Berger. Berger raised his pistol and nodded.

Blom pushed the handle and raised her own gun, opened the door, and a gust of air from the deepest pits of hell washed over them. It was as if the whole house had been pressurised and was only now allowed to let out its truly appalling bad breath. It was like opening a can of fermented herring, but in a completely different league.

There was no doubt whatsoever.

There was a dead body inside the house.

Blom hunched her shoulder, and Berger's vision momentarily went dark, but that couldn't happen, not now. The fact that someone inside was dead didn't mean that the house wasn't dangerous. It could even make it worse. Someone could be in there, messing about with the corpse. Or there could be an entire cemetery's worth of corpses, complete with a raving madman.

A highly intelligent madman armed with a lump of wood.

They readied themselves, honed their senses as they fought to suppress their sense of smell and made their way into the building. The house was filthy, a classic tasteless bachelor pad. Hall, then kitchen – no one there. Still no noise. A living room with very little furniture. Nothing.

Just the constant, painful difficulty breathing.

A flight of steps leading upstairs, and more steps leading down behind a half-closed door. They had no intention of splitting up, and followed their well-honed instincts towards the cellar door.

Berger opened it wide, aimed his pistol down the dark staircase. Blom located an ancient light switch and flicked it up and down several times. Nothing. She pulled out her torch, and Berger followed suit. Two beams of light swept across the low ceiling and claustrophobic walls.

Another flight of cellar steps.

Step by step. It was impossible to tell if the stench was getting stronger or weaker, their olfactory senses were already numb. The flares of green on the ceiling and walls indicated that they should be smelling something different, a smell of damp and mould. It was a mouldy house, but the mould didn't stand a chance.

First they shone their torches around the walls to check for hiding places and corners, then aimed them at the middle of the cement floor.

That was where he was lying. They shone their torches at him, standing completely motionless, listening. The sound they could hear wasn't the dull rumble of the boiler room but the higher-pitched buzz of flies.

His face wasn't visible at all; it lay pressed against the floor, and tangled hair lay over his ears, spreading out across the floor. A sturdy metal chair was half-lying on top of him, and when they looked more closely they saw that his shins were tied to the thick chair legs with cable ties. His arms were hidden beneath his sturdy upper body as if he had fallen with his hands clasped in prayer.

It had once been a very muscular body.

The blood surrounding it had not only congealed but had long since been sucked up by the cement floor, leaving just a faint trace of colour behind.

Berger looked at the toppled chair. On the left armrest hung the remains of a cable tie. A snapped cable tie.

Blom cleared her throat and regained at least some semblance of a voice, 'He was tied to the chair and tortured. But Anders Hedblom was strong. He didn't die. With the last of his strength he snapped the cable ties around his wrists. He tried to get up, fell, couldn't get up again, and died where he lay, face down on the cement floor.'

'The perpetrator must have thought he was dead,' Berger said hoarsely. 'But once he'd gone Anders Hedblom had enough strength left for one final act. Something he needed to do at all costs before he died. Are you ready for the hard bit?'

Blom held up a hand to stop him.

'We need to think,' she said. 'Shouldn't we secure the house first? Upstairs?'

Berger pointed at the body.

'There's dust on him,' he said. 'No one's been here for weeks. Just keep your gun handy.'

She stopped him again.

'The police will come here, sooner or later. Where have we left evidence?'

'The front door.' Berger nodded. 'Have you touched anything else?'

'It's the same as Porjus,' Blom said. 'We may have dropped strands of hair, particles of skin. If we do what you're thinking of doing we'll leave even more evidence.'

'Have you got a better suggestion?'

'No,' Blom said but did at least pull some plastic gloves from her jacket pocket. She handed a pair to Berger. With their hands shaking they pulled the awkward gloves on.

They took hold of the side of the corpse and braced themselves. Then they turned what had once been a very solid body over. It was surprisingly easy; the insects buzzing round in the stagnant air had emptied the body of any flesh that hadn't already dried out. The maggots already seemed to have left the sinking ship. It was like looking at an Egyptian mummy after it had been embalmed. Experience told Berger that Anders Hedblom had been dead at least three weeks, perhaps a month.

And no one had missed him in all that time.

There wasn't much left of the arms but the bones, and they were clasped tightly against the chest, the position he had died in. But his hands weren't clasped in prayer – they were clutching something.

There was a pen in his right hand, and a piece of paper in his left. It was a bill, an electricity bill. Berger carefully angled the blank back of the bill towards the beam of the torch. It wasn't blank. With the large, ragged writing of a dying man, one word had been written. And that word was, 'Berger.'

Berger stared at the sheet of paper. As did Blom.

'What the actual fuck?' he managed to say.

Blom looked pale. 'The perpetrator left him for dead. But he still had the strength to do one last, vital thing. He tore off the cable ties through sheer brute strength, which is quite an achievement, then got a pen and piece of paper from his pocket, simply because his urge to write a message was so strong. The urge to write the name Berger.'

'Christ. I've never been here before,' Berger said limply. 'When he wrote that we were trying to find Ellen Savinger's kidnapper.'

'We have to roll him back into the position we found him in,' Blom said.

'Not with that in his hand,' Berger said.

'We can't remove evidence from a crime scene,' Blom said. 'Besides, Robin is bound to figure it out, and that combined with the fact that your DNA is here really wouldn't be good. You're OK, you've got an alibi. There are lots of Bergers in Sweden. And he may have meant something else entirely. We roll him over and try to make it look like he hasn't been moved.'

Berger looked at her intently. This was hardly the time for nuance, but wasn't there something odd about her reaction? Wasn't she rushing things a bit too much? Did her reasoning actually make sense?

He made up his mind to trust her anyway. Besides, he wanted to get away from this hellish house at least as much as she did. Together they took hold of what was left of Anders Hedblom and turned him over. Blom adjusted his position, rearranged some of the details, and in the end everything looked just as it had when they arrived.

And then they left, pistols raised, giving cover to each other, not bothering to check upstairs, and emerged into the fresh air. Never before had it felt so very fresh, so crystal clear. Berger found himself taking deep, deep breaths in the increasingly heavy snowfall. With each snowflake he breathed in, his head cleared a little more.

He turned round on the porch. Blom was crouched in front of the door, wiping the handle. Then she walked off, and Berger followed her. Neither of them said a word.

They reached the car, put the guns back in the glove compartment, turned on the narrow and increasingly snow-covered road, and accelerated away from there. It was a long time before either of them could speak.

'So what the hell was that?' Berger said when they were back on the European highway.

Blom shook her head.

'I'm completely incapable of processing that right now, I'm still trying to get my breathing back to normal. But the one thing that's abundantly clear is that Anders Hedblom isn't our murderer.'

'Unless he's a zombie,' Berger said. 'He looked like one.'

Blom shook her head as if to make sure it was firmly screwed on.

'Why did he write my name?' Berger went on. 'That took the last of his strength. It must have been vital for him, one last clue for the police. Did his murderer say his name was

Berger? Was it actually a name? Could it have been something else? The beginning of a word? The end of one?'

Berger felt Blom's lack of engagement like a physical presence, an extra person squeezed in between them. A very cold person.

The ringtone, wherever it came from, felt like a liberation. He looked around, noting in passing that the clock in the jeep said it was 19.16, finally saw that the satellite phone in the compartment between the seats was lit up. He looked at the number on the display and answered on speakerphone.

'Yes, Deer?'

'Sorsele,' Deer said.

Berger and Blom exchanged a glance.

'I'm listening,' he said.

'The vehicle that drove off with Jessica Johnsson's body looks like it's in Sorsele. Isn't that somewhere in the area of where you two are?'

'It's nearby,' Berger said and got an electrified stare from Blom. 'Tell me more.'

'That's all I've got,' Deer said. 'A very specific vehicle, and the other eight are in other parts of Sweden. I'm reading while I'm talking now. So, it was definitely a Volkswagen Caddy, yellowish-white, but covered with bright blue foil. Registration LAM 387.'

'Have you got the owner's name as well?'

'I'm just looking it up ... hang on ... Yes, here it is. Hold on a moment ...'

'I'm waiting,' Berger said.

'The vehicle's owner is called Anders Hedblom. Hedblom?'

Berger was thrown forward and felt a sudden hard jolt across his chest. It took him a moment to realise what had happened. The jeep had stopped halfway across the Inland Highway. Berger looked instinctively for an elk running off. But there wasn't one. There was nothing but darkness, snowflakes falling through the beams of the headlights, and Blom's rigid, distant profile lit up from below by the pale blue light of the instrument panel.

'What the hell's going on?' Deer's slightly tinny voice echoed through the car. 'You just yelled, Sam, what's happening?'

Berger looked at Blom, who was still sitting there stiffly. Eventually she reversed and turned the car round. To start with they drove back along their own tyre tracks before changing lane.

'An elk,' Berger said with his eyes glued on Blom. 'Nothing to worry about.'

'OK ...' Deer said hesitantly. 'Hedblom?'

'Yes, that's Karl's brother,' Berger said. 'We tracked him down and got into his house in Sorsele.'

'For God's sake, what did I say about that?'

'You called us, Deer, you didn't call your colleagues in the NOD. So can we stop pretending? You're running a double investigation, you can't back out of it now. You want us to carry on.'

'You went into his house ...?'

'I'm afraid it's going to be a long Saturday evening for you.'

An audible sigh rang out through the jeep.

'I've got four minutes,' Deer finally said. 'Then Liverpool will have finished.'

'Anders Hedblom is dead,' Berger said. 'He was tortured to death around a month ago. He's lying on the floor in his basement.'

At that moment Blom put her hand on his thigh, just like that. He turned and looked at her. She wasn't looking at him, the expression on her face was just as distant as before, but she shook her head. Berger understood. He said nothing more.

Desiré sighed deeply, then asked in a clear voice, 'How much harm would it do if I waited to activate my anonymous decoy until tomorrow morning? Can the call wait? I'm having a cosy night in with the family.'

'Funnily enough, we're not having a cosy night in with the family,' Berger said, then added: 'No harm at all, Deer.'

'Thanks,' Deer said. 'Anything else?'

'Nothing else,' Berger said.

And then they were back. Blom stopped in the same place as before, and they made their way back through Anders Hedblom's half-overgrown garden and headed towards the garage. Blom shone her torch through the garage window.

There was no van parked inside.

She nodded and looked at Berger.

'OK, let's go back inside and get the note.'

20

At a small place called Slagnäs Molly Blom suddenly turned off the Inland Highway and carried on driving due north. When a road sign flashed out from the snow-flecked darkness and announced that they were fifty kilometres from Arjeplog, Berger couldn't hold back any longer.

'OK, you really do need to explain what you're doing now.'

It took a little while for her to answer.

'You remember I said that I still have one or two trustworthy contacts in the Security Service?'

Berger was looking at her carefully, trying to take in every little nuance of what she had said and her facial expression. He replied:

'Yes, although they haven't been able to give you any help with Jessica Johnsson's secret identity.'

'They probably can, the right moment just hasn't arrived yet. They're having to do covert work for someone who's being hunted unofficially as a traitor to the organisation. I dare say you can appreciate the difficulties.'

'Unofficially, but openly within the organisation?' Berger said. 'Everyone working there knows that we're being hunted? But not the rest of the police, the NOD?'

'Looks that way. And the operation seems to have pretty much the scope we feared. At least two full-time posts are now dedicated to the search for us. And they're my former colleagues, my external resources Kent and Roy, if you remember them?'

'I did run into them at one point, yes,' Berger said coolly.

'A few days ago, before you surfaced again, Kent and Roy apparently got some sort of hit from one of their online searches. For your name.'

He looked down at his lap, at the back of a dimly illuminated electricity bill, at a dying man's last message in the form of Sam Berger's surname.

'A hit?' he said simply.

'A man who had been admitted to a psychiatric clinic in Lapland, the Lindstorp Clinic outside Arjeplog. His name was Sam Berger.'

Berger said nothing. He disappeared deep inside himself, unless perhaps it was outside himself. He was thinking about the strength of post-traumatic psychosis, about the extreme boundary erosion that accompanied acute reactive psychosis. The ego and reality dissolved entirely, leaving none of the usual boundaries intact.

How strong was the psyche?

He had never believed in anything supernatural. He had always believed that every mystery could be explained rationally. But all of a sudden it felt perfectly plausible that his psychosis had been so severe that it had burst the bounds of reality and taken place in the outside world. That there had been two of him. That he had a doppelgänger. Was it possible that all the evil and guilt and egotism and griminess inside him had taken physical form? In which case it may have been a legitimate question to wonder which was which.

Perhaps he was the doppelgänger.

'What happened?' he finally asked.

'Kent and Roy went up there. It wasn't you. After a quick investigation it was dismissed as a coincidence and dropped without further action. There was no connection to you.'

'Dropped without further action?'

'After a short interview Kent and Roy were ordered to return to Stockholm as soon as possible to avoid attracting any more attention.'

'A short interview?'

'They soon realised they were looking at a complete lunatic. No one knew who he really was. They took his fingerprints, but that didn't help. When I heard about it I dismissed it as a coincidence. All the evidence suggests that the man was a full-blown schizophrenic and kept switching between imaginary personalities. The fact that he had picked the name Sam Berger looked like a complete coincidence.'

'Until ...'

'Not even when we found the note in the mummy's hand,' Blom said tersely. 'It wasn't until Desiré called and told us about the van that I reacted. That links Sorsele, Arjeplog and Porjus. I just don't know how.'

'Me neither. Are you suggesting that the murderer could be mentally ill? And using my name for some unknown reason?'

'I could imagine that it might revolve around an extreme form of bipolarity. Periods of clarity, focus and bloodlust inter-spersed with psychosis, angst and utter confusion. But that would need a lot more investigation. And that's why we're currently heading towards the Lindstorp Clinic in Arjeplog.'

'Just so I'm up to speed,' Berger said, rubbing his forehead. 'What would the sequence of events look like?'

Blom frowned and took a deep breath.

'With the proviso that this involves a fair amount of speculation, something like this: while she was living under an
assumed identity Jessica Johnsson meets the murderer, they
have an affair, but as time passes she realises how dangerous
he is and ends the relationship. He stalks her. She meets Anders
Hedblom; maybe she contacts him because she thinks his
brother is innocent of the murder of Helena and Rasmus Gradén, because she knows the real killer. Who somehow finds
out that Jessica is in touch with Anders and goes to Sorsele,
where he tortures and kills him. At this point the murderer is
heading for a psychotic phase, claims to be the fictitious Berger,
steals Anders' van, drives as quickly as he can towards something resembling an emergency psychiatric unit, his psychosis
hits him, he gets admitted and spends a couple of weeks there.
Then he improves, gets discharged or runs away – it doesn't
really make any difference – jumps back in Anders Hedblom's
van and drives to Jessica Johnsson's house in Porjus. He keeps
watch on her, then sneaks into the house while she's out.
He's in some sort of manic phase, cleans the house obsessively,
hides in the boiler room, then goes on the attack. And we
happened to be there.'

'Bloody hell,' Berger said.

They didn't see the bus coming. Suddenly it appeared round a
bend and swept past with a thunderous roar. They couldn't see
a thing, the car was completely swallowed up by an impenetrable cloud of snow. Blom slowed down and drove round the
bend with great care as the swirling mass settled again.

Out of the snow a building appeared. It looked like an old
manor house, a beacon of civilisation. In front of the implausible
building a snow-covered expanse spread out, a field, perhaps.

They drove on past the field and manor house until they reached what seemed to be the grand main entrance. They were met by a very odd sight. An elderly white-haired man in a smoking jacket was standing on the terrace waiting for them; behind him stood two care assistants with their arms folded across their broad chests. The terrace and entrance were imposing, with a colonnade of Doric columns, a balustrade with vase-shaped balusters crowned with urns, pots and even a statue of an ancient Greek, probably that father of medicine, Hippocrates, but not even he could quite conceal the security camera poking out from beneath the eaves.

Berger stopped as he was getting out of the jeep. A completely irrational thought seized him. What if they recognised him? What if Sam Berger really was here? What if he really did have a double who was using his name?

The white-haired man looked on with a stern expression on his face as they approached the flights of steps. But there was no trace of recognition there.

Blom held her hand out towards the man, and there was a slight pause before he took it and said, 'I'm hosting a dinner this evening, so I'd like to get away in reasonable time.'

'It's very good of you to see us, Dr Stenbom,' Blom said. 'I'm Detective Inspector Eva Lundström, and this is my colleague, Lindbergh. I hope we can get this done as quickly as possible.'

'Whatever "this" might be,' Dr Stenbom muttered as he walked through the main entrance flanked by the two carers.

The corridor they found themselves in was in marked contrast to the glamorous exterior of the clinic. Suddenly they were in an unremarkable care home with standard-issue textured wallpaper and linoleum floors. Dr Stenbom led them to a nearby

office whose door bore a sign announcing that SENIOR CON-
SULTANT JACOB STENBOM could be found within.

The furnishings of the office were strikingly functional. It was full of books, with loose files – mostly scientific reports, seemingly – cluttering every available surface. This was an office worthy of a man who lived for his work. There were two visitor's chairs. Berger and Blom moved the papers from them as carefully as they could and sat down.

'So, the National Operations Department?' Dr Stenbom said, looking at their fake business cards.

'Formerly known as National Crime,' Berger said helpfully.

'Thanks,' Stenbom said tartly and pushed the cards back across the desk.

'We're here to talk about a patient named Sam Berger,' Blom said. 'Do you remember him?'

'Let me see what I can do,' Dr Stenbom said in a tone of voice that didn't bode well. He looked through a pile of papers and pulled one out, read from it, nodded to himself and said, 'Yes, that's right. I can't do anything for you at all.'

He thrust the document towards them, and they both instantly recognised the unmistakable letterhead of the Security Service. They read it quickly: a classic gagging order.

'Yet here you are,' Berger said. 'Even though you have a dinner to get to. Dressed up in your smoking jacket and everything.'

Stenbom looked at him intently. For a moment it really did feel as if the senior consultant had seen him before.

'And how do you choose to interpret that?' Stenbom eventually asked.

'Curiosity,' Blom said. 'Professional curiosity. You weren't happy with the Security Service's explanation.'

'Explanation?' Stenbom exclaimed with a dry laugh.

'I know,' Blom said. 'Our colleagues can be a little brusque. My guess is that they swept in, ignored you completely, then vanished without a word of explanation. Might I hazard a guess that their names were Roy Grahn and Kent Döös?'

Jacob Stenbom leaned across the considerable expanse of desk and tapped the document.

'Even if what you say is true, Miss Lundström, there's still this.'

'Undeniably,' Blom said. 'But our visit this evening has two aims. Firstly to fill in the gaps of a lamentably succinct report from our colleagues, and secondly to offer the Lindstorp Clinic a somewhat belated explanation. We have our own oath of confidentiality. This document is primarily concerned with the media, not internally within the police service. And we don't want you to talk to the press either. Our goals are the same as theirs. But you deserve an explanation.'

'I hope so,' Dr Stenbom said, focusing all of his attention on the more amenable of the two visitors.

'Please, tell us all you know about Sam Berger,' she said with a smile that Berger wasn't entirely happy about.

But Senior Consultant Jacob Stenbom evidently was because he didn't hold back any longer.

'Sam Berger was in a terrible state when my staff found him outside the main entrance. He was simultaneously exhausted and very aggressive, and nothing he said was comprehensible except his name. It was immediately apparent that he was suffering from psychosis, and his violent tendencies led us to decide to sedate him. He was also given psychoactive medication. Over the course of a couple of weeks we reduced the sedative dose roughly every third day to see if he had calmed down. It took two weeks before he reached that point, on 12 November. The prognosis looked good when he woke up: there was a new awareness in his eyes, and he was calm, albeit still with plenty of sedatives in his system. Unfortunately the nurse on duty was called away to an emergency in another room just as she was unlocking his door. Berger noticed that the door was open and sneaked out. He made his way to the kitchen, put on several white coats and a pair of boots that were too small for him, rushed out to the smoking area on the terrace, climbed over the balustrade and jumped down onto the field. Then he ran towards the road, where he had evidently seen the bus driving past. And the bus did actually appear as he was laboriously making his way across the snow-covered field. He managed to get there and tried to grab hold of it, but obviously it didn't stop for someone who was almost the perfect embodiment of an escaped mental patient. In the process he suffered fairly serious injuries to his right hand and face. So I decided to sedate him again, but he bent the needle so that the drip soaked into the bed instead, and the following day he managed to overpower a nurse and escape again. Unfortunately that happened just after your colleagues arrived, so they ended up pursuing him themselves. One of them caught up with him out on the field and wrestled him to the ground. What happened after that was all conducted in private, we were shut out completely. Grahn and Döös questioned Berger behind closed doors and then left, after making everyone involved sign a gagging order. Since then I've had a long conversation with Berger myself, and there is no doubt that he had improved significantly and was very keen to leave Lindstorp. We kept him in for observation for another twenty-four hours, then discharged him on Sunday 15 November.'

'Discharged him?' Berger exclaimed.

'In spite of everything, to us he's a John Doe, an unidentified patient. We only had his word that his name was Sam Berger, and he never gave us an ID number or date of birth. No ID card or anything else that could help identify him. We may be an independent clinic specialising in privately funded psychiatric treatment, mostly the rehabilitation of people with various dependencies, but when space permits we take patients from the public health service too. But in cases like that we need the patient's ID number.'

'To be able to claim back the cost of the treatment?'

'That's something of a simplification,' Dr Stenbom said. 'But for just over two weeks he certainly cost us money.'

'In other words, you had no objection to discharging a patient whose treatment was clearly not complete?'

'We couldn't do any more for him.'

Berger felt Blom's hand on his thigh. He knew what it meant, and once again her touch managed to calm him down. He fell silent. All the poisonous remarks he had on the tip of his tongue vanished. Instead Blom spoke.

'Is it true that our colleagues from the Security Service took Berger's fingerprints?'

'Without any success, yes. Which was hardly surprising; he'd just run his fingertips along the side of a bus that was going at eighty kilometres an hour.'

'His right hand, yes,' Blom said. 'What about his left hand?'

'The fingertips were badly damaged, so they weren't any use either.'

'Damaged?'

'There were so many scars on them that they couldn't be used.'

'Scars? As if he'd tried to remove his fingerprints on purpose?'

'I can't answer that.'

'What about DNA, then? Did Grahn and Döös take samples?'

'Not as far as I know,' Stenbom said. 'We didn't either.'

'But you do still have organic material from Sam Berger? Urine samples, blood tests, samples of skin tissue?'

Stenbom shook his head.

'I'm afraid not. There's nothing of his left here.'

'Can we take a look around?' Berger said, getting to his feet.

Senior Consultant Jacob Stenbom just stared at him.

'We'd like to walk in Sam Berger's footsteps,' Sam Berger said.

Stenbom pulled a face and looked at his watch.

'I'm giving a speech to Goodyear's management team in less than an hour,' he said.

'Goodyear?' Berger said.

'They're important business partners,' Stenbom said. 'They test their winter tyres up here. And keep their addictions and breakdowns hidden from the world.'

They passed a staircase that must once have been very imposing – it was now covered with linoleum – and entered a beige corridor lined with a number of identical doors equipped with sturdy lock mechanisms. Stenbom walked over to one of them.

'Right now the son of a member of Audi's senior management team is being treated for cocaine addiction in Berger's room. But this one is exactly the same.'

He unlocked the door and they walked in. The head of the bed was pushed against the far wall beside a drip stand and a small table on wheels. On the opposite wall, next to the door, was a mirror and handbasin, as well as the door to the toilet. The window looked out across the snow-covered field; it was barely visible through the snow which was now falling heavily.

Berger stopped by the window and looked out. It was as if he'd seen it before.

'He spent a lot of time looking out there,' Stenbom said.

'At the field?' Berger said. 'And the road where the bus goes past?'

'I believe so. His flight instinct was very strong.'

'Anything else?'

'He made a particular gesture, we noticed it several times.'

'A gesture?'

'Possibly towards his own reflection. He formed his right hand into a pistol and shot himself with it.'

Berger put his hand against the cold windowpane and said, 'Where did he go from here?'

They followed Stenbom back out into the corridor, up the stairs, into another corridor, towards a door with no lock but a far larger handle. The consultant opened it and said,

'The kitchen. He was here for a while. He was barefoot, looking for shoes, and found a pair of boots that were too small for him in this cupboard. And here, beside the coffee table, is where he stole the white coats. That was an element of rationality in the midst of his irrational behaviour, he knew he'd freeze out in the snow, on his way to freedom.'

Berger felt the white coats and said, 'It wasn't these ones, though?'

'They went straight in the wash. But it could have been these, of course. Washed several times since then.'

Blom nodded and walked into the pantry and looked around. Berger went over to the window above the sink. There was a better view of the expanse of white from up here despite the falling snow.

The field, the field of freedom.

He looked carefully, so intently that his perspective changed and he began to see other things, rather like seeing the naked woman in Freud's face.

'So Berger liked to stand at the window?' he said.

'In his room, yes,' Stenbom said and shrugged.

Berger raised his hand towards the glass but held it slightly away from it with his fingers splayed.

'Did he used to touch the glass as well?' he asked.

'Occasionally. But, as I said, in his own room.'

'I wonder if he might have done the same thing here. How often does the kitchen get cleaned?'

'Daily ... But if you mean the windows, the cold makes that harder.'

Berger nodded and pulled on a pair of plastic gloves. He took out his penknife and a very small ziplock bag from his pocket. He picked gently at the windowpane and said, 'He stood here, saw the field, pressed his hand against the ice-cold glass. His fingers must have been moist.'

'Psychoactive medication tends to make people's hands sweat.' Stenbom nodded.

'Come over here,' Berger said. 'You can see it against the light, from a certain angle. The impression of the five digits of a right hand. No fingerprints, sure enough, nor from the hand itself before it got injured. But he must have pulled his hand away quickly, so I think that these impressions mostly consist of skin.'

Then he scraped the frozen fragments of skin into the little plastic bag and sealed it. Stenbom frowned momentarily.

'If you like I could fast-track the DNA analysis.'

'Curiouser and curiouser,' Berger said, putting the bag in his pocket.

'I'm not a psychiatrist for nothing,' Stenbom said. 'I detect a power struggle between the NOD and the Security Service. And in this instance I have a definite preference for the NOD. We conduct our analysis privately, samples never go through any official channels.'

Berger and Blom looked at each other and came to a decision. Blom nodded and pulled an identical ziplock bag from her jacket pocket. Blom held the empty bag open while Berger very delicately transferred half of the potential skin cells from the first bag. Blom handed one of the bags to Stenbom and said, 'We're *half*-relying on you.'

Stenbom gave a wry smile.

'I can start the process this evening. Fast-tracked.'

'As long as you don't miss your big speech,' Berger said.

'I was lying,' Stenbom said calmly. 'I'm not giving a speech. Just having some drinks with a number of businessmen. That can wait.'

Blom took a deep breath.

'OK, Sam Berger stood here for a while, held his sweaty fingers against the glass, put some extra clothes on. Then, what, he ran out through the other door?'

'Correct. Out to the main terrace. The only part that's kept clear of snow is the little smoking area. He'd been out there before to smoke, once when I mistakenly thought it was time to bring him outside. He had an episode out there and we had to sedate him on the spot. But he must have had some sort of memory of the terrace. Do you want to see it?'

'I don't think that will be necessary,' Blom said. 'Actually, something else just struck me. I saw a security camera out by the main entrance, didn't I? Is there any chance that the moment when Berger arrived in the car park was caught on film? When he first arrived?'

'The Security Service took the recording,' Stenbom said. 'And made sure there were no copies.'

Blom saw Berger grimace, and said, 'Do you remember the recording? What vehicle was Sam Berger driving?'

'He was hardly in a fit state to drive.'

'How do you mean?'

'He didn't drive here. He got dropped off.'

Berger and Blom exchanged a quick glance.

'So someone drove him here? Did you see the vehicle?'

'It was a small van, brightly coloured paint, possibly blue or green.'

'Did you happen to see the person who dropped him off?' Blom asked breathlessly.

'Very briefly,' Stenbom said. 'It was a woman.'

'A woman?' Blom exclaimed.

'Definitely a woman.'

'What did she look like?'

'Blonde,' Stenbom said. 'In fact she looked rather like you, Detective Inspector Eva Lundström.'

Berger felt the world quiver on its axis. He managed to turn his head to look at Blom. He imagined he could read her thoughts behind her wide blue eyes. He imagined she was thinking: Is there a parallel universe?

III

21

They've been active since long before dawn. The night-vision camera caught the man as he stumbled towards the woman's cabin, more unsteadily than usual. The man went inside, and indeterminate activity has since taken place, the observer has noted his lack of knowledge, but he has not noted his pain. Now there is nothing left to do but wait.

This maddening wait.

The screens have finally switched to the daylight cameras; darkness's share of the day is growing unexpectedly fast now. The daylight cameras are better considering the illness, the illness that threatens the whole of the observer's future.

RP, wretched retinitis pigmentosa, which means that the observer has to be absolutely precise about the distances to ensure screen visibility. Its progression has been so rapid recently that it feels important to make the most of every sensory impression. And he has to find a way to sit on the terrace in the warm sunrise, looking at the rock of Gibraltar through the haze before it's too late.

A shared view. Then the observer will have to take over her gaze, see beauty and calm through her eyes.

The observer lets time pass, lets the minutes tick away. He sees the date on the contract as if written in gold. Sees everything that remains, everything that has to be exactly right.

All the elements.

The previous day looked so promising. The observer thought he was going to be able to see it again. But when she let the towel fall she was wearing a bikini; all he saw was the star-shaped birthmark beneath her concealed right breast. The observer hoped that his disappointment didn't show in his report.

But now the door opens at last, and she emerges. The hand in the thin leather glove zooms in on her face, it's so lovely. Then the observer goes back to being an observer again, zooms out slightly, swears, writes: '09.50: ♀ outside on veranda, takes out phone, makes call. On this occasion no sign of ♂.'

The observer doesn't write that this is the preferred state.

No sign of ♂.

22

Berger recognised the voice at once. The years, and probably quite a lot else, might have drawn a partial veil over it, but it was undoubtedly the same voice that eight years ago had ranted about the country's escort industry.

'I don't remember any fucking Berger,' the voice was saying uncooperatively.

'I think you would if you thought about it, Robertsson,' Berger said. 'I helped interview witnesses in Orsa. You filmed us through the window with your VHS camera.'

'I still don't understand why everything wasn't filmed.'

'But you sorted that out. And now you're working in the police store. Have you got access to the films?'

'There's a hell of a lot of stuff from the Karl Hedblom case. There's no fucking way I'm going to look through all that. Anyway, you're calling on a Sunday morning.'

'If you can get there this afternoon and dig out the films, there's some money in it.'

'Why the hell would the NOD slip me money under the counter to get me to do something you can ask me to do in office hours?'

'It's urgent,' Berger said, pulling a face. 'Besides, it's all a bit off the record.'

There was silence on the line. Then Robertsson said, 'Five thousand cash. Five o'clock.'

And then he was gone.

Berger nodded and went back to his computer screen. A list of hits began to appear. Then it vanished.

Blom was standing with the connection cable in one hand and the satellite phone in the other.

'I need to call Stenbom,' she said and went out onto the porch.

It was bitingly cold. The sun had risen a fair way up the clear blue sky and was sending sharp, slanting rays across the chalk-white landscape. Blom sought protection from the strong sunlight beneath the cabin's projecting roof and held the satellite phone up in the shade so she could see. Then she dialled the number.

Berger was watching her through a crack in the door. When she got through he silently closed it. Then he turned towards the wall. There were even more documents there now, scraps of paper, photographs. There were a number of secretly taken photographs from the Lindstorp Clinic in Arjeplog; at the top was a less-than-flattering picture of a man with an unruly mop of white hair, Senior Consultant Jacob Stenbom, to whom Blom was currently talking.

Berger looked across the slightly chaotic pattern on the wall. He had always believed in this, absolutely, perhaps more than anything else in life: the art of police work, bringing order to chaos, finding the right threads to pull on to form a rational, comprehensible pattern, to understand the perpetrator, motives, driving force – to find a solution.

Find the truth.

And put the past right.

But even the most firmly held beliefs can be shaken, he'd learned that the hard way, and for the first time in his life he was no longer certain. Could there really be a rational explanation if there was a *parallel universe*?

The night had been tormented with nightmares – a normal occurrence these days – but this time a new and troubling element had appeared. He had seen limbs, sexual acts, extremely vivid scenes, abstract bodies in definite motion, as if his brain was trying to remind him of the sick connection between murder and sex.

He interpreted this to mean that he shouldn't forget that they were dealing with someone who killed for pleasure.

And he mustn't forget to act like a police officer.

Berger shook his head, did his best to drive out any irrelevant thoughts and forced himself to look at the wall again.

Blom brought a cloud of steam back in with her and flapped her arms to warm herself up, still holding the satellite phone.

'I need the Internet,' Berger said.

'Yeah, yeah,' Blom said and plugged the phone back in.

'So?' he said as she sat down and touched the mouse pad.

'The samples went off last night,' she said. 'To England. The fastest DNA lab in the world, if Dr Jacob's telling the truth.'

'Good,' Berger said. 'Anything else?'

'Not really,' Blom said. 'Just lots of ideas. What did we actually find out yesterday? That "Sam Berger" got a lift to the clinic from a woman. If we try to get rid of any unpalatable connotations, any parallels to *us*: who was she? I can see two possible scenarios. One of them sticks to our basic theory: that the murderer was alone at Anders Hedblom's house, heading for some sort of psychotic episode, but managed to steal the van and drive off, perhaps to a girlfriend, something like that, and she drove the increasingly debilitated man to Lindstorp. The other scenario is more uncomfortable: that this woman was *with* him when he committed the murder. She was there in Sorsele. What does that do to our theory?'

Berger shook his head.

'I don't know,' he said. 'But it feels very tenuous. She sits there and waits while he tortures a man to death down in the basement? I doubt that. What's the situation on the Jessica Johnsson front?'

'I spoke to my Security Service contact early this morning,' Blom said. 'He hasn't been able to get into the register of protected identities but did discover a contact, a social worker who dealt with Jessica Johnsson's relationship with Eddy Karlsson in the early stages. Her name's Laura Enoksson – she took early retirement, sounds like she was just burned out. I've got a mobile number. I'll try calling later today.'

'Interesting,' Berger said.

'Sure,' Blom said. 'But I've been thinking about something Superintendent Sjölund in Gothenburg said yesterday. Lisa Widstrand, the prostitute, was evidently pregnant.'

'Bloody hell,' Berger said.

'Maybe we're back to the motherhood angle again,' Blom said. 'Is he going after mothers after all?'

'We both sat opposite Jessica Johnsson in Porjus,' Berger said. 'There's no way she was pregnant.'

'We don't actually know that, she was wearing a thick sweater and she could easily have been hiding – what? – four months of pregnancy behind that.'

'It's possible to find that out from a blood test, isn't it?' Berger said, looking quizzically at Blom.

'It's Sunday today,' she said, shrugging her shoulders.

Berger picked up the satellite phone and dialled a very familiar number. No answer. He called again. After five rings Deer's tinny-sounding voice said, 'No unnecessary calls.'

'This isn't,' Berger said. 'What are you doing?'

'What I'm definitely not doing is making small talk with you. What do you want?'

'Did Jessica Johnsson's blood show that she was pregnant?'

The line fell silent. It sounded like Deer was leafing through some papers. Which she apparently had right in front of her. Which meant that she was working, probably at home in that spare garage where Berger had visited her so often in another life. Eventually she answered. 'Yes.'

'Yes?'

'I'd missed that,' Deer admitted. 'It's in Robin's final report. What does that mean for the investigation?'

'Don't know. But Lisa Widstrand was also pregnant. Fifth month.'

'So is he killing mothers after all? Are we back to that line of inquiry?'

'Don't know,' Berger said. 'Thanks, Deer.'

They hung up. Berger and Blom looked at each other above the bright screens of their computers.

'It could still be Anders Hedblom,' Blom said after a while. 'Blocks of wood, hatred of mothers, pushchairs. He killed Helena and Rasmus Gradén, and Lisa Widstrand. And then "Sam Berger" came along and took over. Maybe they were already partners in crime, and that was how Anders knew this man called himself Berger, but now "Berger" wanted to work alone. He'd had enough of sharing the pleasure with someone else.'

Berger tilted his head.

'Bodybuilding loner Anders Hedblom in a creative partnership with not just the madman, but the madman's girlfriend? I've got my doubts about that one.'

'Let's just keep an open mind about the possibility that Anders might not have been a particularly good boy. Speaking of good boys, the test results on his brother are back.'

'Karl in Säter?' Berger said. 'The blood test?'

'Yes. We were right about the methamphetamine. But it's a cocktail that also includes a significant quantity of phenazepam.'

'That rings a bell,' Berger said. 'The old Soviet drug?'

'But fairly new to Sweden,' Blom said. 'It's an anxiety suppressant, only seems to be manufactured in Russia and a few neighbouring countries. One of the strongest side effects is memory loss.'

Berger nodded.

'In other words, whoever is sending Karl Hedblom drugs wants him to lose his memory. On a different matter, I think I might have found more victims.'

Blom merely stared at him.

'You went off with the Internet,' Berger continued, gesturing towards the satellite phone. 'I was just about to get the results from an expanded search. I'm getting hits on the four-leaf clover. Let's see ... Wrong, wrong, wrong sort of drawing, wrong again. This one, maybe. A drawing of a flower on a murder victim's backside.'

'A drawing of a flower?' Blom exclaimed.

'A police officer could easily confuse a four-leaf clover and a flower. And it also happened a long way from Orsa, in March last year. No one made the connection. An Elisabeth Ström in Växjö, criminal record, had links to a biker gang. She was found tied to a chair in a run-down house that the gang had abandoned after a confrontation with a rival gang. There was still blood in the house, and the floor and ceilings were riddled with bullet holes. And there she sat, beaten to death and with severe knife wounds. The police linked her death to the feud between the bikers. They had a number of suspects in the other gang, but didn't manage to piece together enough evidence. The case is still open. Looks like she was killed on a particularly rainy spring night, so it wasn't possible to find any evidence outside the house, and inside there was masses of DNA from both gangs, but nothing else.'

'No semen there either?' Blom asked.

'Not that I can see from this summary. I'll try to get hold of the original files. Either way, Elisabeth Ström was found with a drawing of a "flower" on her left buttock; I'm hoping there'll be pictures in the preliminary investigation. She was thirty-five when she died, and had a fourteen-year-old son.'

'Another mother,' Blom said. 'And a son. I seem to recall Superintendent Sjölund in Gothenburg talking about Lisa Widstrand's "unborn son".'

'Christ,' Berger said. 'If we provisionally count Elisabeth Ström among the victims, we've got four murdered women who either were or were going to be mothers, three with boys, and Jessica Johnsson, who we just know was pregnant, child's gender unknown.'

'But on the other hand the killer could hardly have known what sex Lisa Widstrand and Jessica Johnsson's kids were going to be ...'

'True,' Berger said. 'It just feels so weird that Jessica was pregnant. Who by? The murderer? That adds another possible angle. Was the murderer the father of all the children?'

'We should probably try to calm down with our deductions here ...'

'They're not deductions,' Berger said. 'This is brainstorming. Without brainstorming police work would all be mechanical.'

'With the significant difference that we aren't police officers. Anything else?'

'I'm still looking,' Berger said, going back to his computer. 'OK, this one could be something: "ink marks on rear". Older, just six months after Orsa, April 2009. A Danish woman in Malmö.'

'Really? Malmö?' Blom said.

'At the time when Anders Hedblom was still living down there,' Berger said. 'Maybe we're getting a bit closer to the idea of partners in crime after all. Were Hedblom and this so-called Berger working together? Hedblom rational, "Berger" crazy. Eventually crazy enough to kill his own partner for kicks?'

'After shitting on his own doorstep in Malmö, Hedblom flees the field, pretty much as far away as you can get in Sweden, to Sorsele. The madman goes with him. Anders comes into contact with Jessica Johnsson, and could be the father of her unborn child. Anders and the madman plan a murder in Porjus, but the madman runs amok and kills his partner. But the plan remains in place, the madman is still capable of following the now-dead Anders' plan.'

'That was a record-breaking brainwave,' Berger said. 'But not at all unthinkable.'

'What about the Dane?' Blom said.

'Mette Hækkerup, forty-four, paediatrician, lived in Malmö with her husband and son, who worked and went to school respectively in Copenhagen, whereas she worked at Skåne University Hospital. The odd thing is that her death isn't classified as murder but as a road accident. No other vehicles involved, on the E6 out near Tygelsjö. Hækkerup was alone one weekend and had no real reason to be driving north on the E6. She went off the road in the middle of the night, slid along the safety barrier and smashed into a road sign. When the pathologist found evidence of "ink marks on rear" a different theory was checked out. A male colleague at the hospital lived in Tygelsjö, and it turned out that he'd been having an affair with Mette Hækkerup. The colleague admitted it but said he'd never drawn anything on her buttocks. The case was written off as an accident.'

'Hmm,' Blom said. 'If that one turned out to be our perpetrator, first we have a smart case of pin-the-blame-on-an-innocent-man in Orsa in October 2007, then an equally smart case of hide-a-murder-with-an-accident in Malmö in April 2009. That's hardly the work of a raving lunatic who doesn't know his own name.'

'At least not during his lucid moments,' Berger said. 'In those moments he's sharp, dangerous and mentally ill. A bad combination. But a year later, in September 2010, Lisa Widstrand's obviously murdered body is found lying in a hotel room in Gothenburg. So what's happened here? Is he openly challenging the police?'

'On the other hand, though, she was a prostitute,' Blom said. 'And it was just before the start of the book fair. He knows the case won't be a major priority. In a way, that too was partly concealed.'

'But someone like Jessica Johnsson was able to spot it. The fact that she mentioned Lisa Widstrand is what drew us into this crazy case.'

'And the fact that she talked about the "local press" writing about it, even though that doesn't seem to have been the case, indicates that she already knew about it. She had inside information. I think our theories are starting to fit quite nicely.'

'We really do need to know what her name was when she was living under a protected identity,' Berger said. 'From 2005 to 2011. Six years of her life that are a complete blank for us.'

'In spite of everything, though, she is just one of a depressingly rising number of victims ...'

'But also something of a key figure,' Berger said. 'She knew the murderer, she knew who he was. As soon as he came round in the clinic he drove to her house, cleaned the entire place, went and hid in the boiler room and waited for her to come home.'

'Hang on a moment now,' Blom said. 'He was discharged. And the van wasn't sitting waiting for him in the car park of the Lindstorp Clinic. The blonde woman must have come to pick him up again. And we know that the van was in the garage at Porjus when the murder took place. So if she did drive him there, she must have been present during the murder.'

'But there definitely wasn't a blonde woman in the house in Porjus when we were attacked there. We searched the house.'

'We searched everywhere but the boiler room,' Blom said. 'She could have been in there with him.'

'Doesn't it seem more likely that she went and picked him up from the clinic, and then he dropped her off somewhere? He was better by then, if that's the right word, and was in a fit state to drive himself. Like he did from Sorsele. She's probably just a friend, or a girlfriend.'

'Probably,' Blom said and shrugged her shoulders.

'We'll have to keep an open mind about that,' Berger said in a spirit of compromise. 'Hang on, what's this?'

'What?'

'"Tattooed leaves".'

'Now you're not making any sense.'

'It's just shown up here in my expanded search,' Berger said. 'One more possible victim. The police in Täby interpreted leaves on a victim's buttocks as a tattoo. She had a lot of tattoos elsewhere, apparently. But there's a picture of her buttock here – it's definitely a four-leaf clover.'

'What are we talking about here?'

'I've only just seen it myself. I'm reading as I speak, sorry if it sounds disjointed. Her name was Farida Hesari, she went missing somewhere around Täby shopping centre in July three years ago. Looks like she'd already run away from her family and had gone underground, but was temporarily living in her girlfriend's flat.'

'How did she die?'

'Let's see,' Berger said, and tapped at the keyboard. 'She went out to buy cigarettes one warm summer's morning and never came back. One and a half days later ...'

'Yes? You can't just stop.'

'Fucking hell,' Berger said.

'What?!' Blom snapped.

'Farida Hesari was found covered in blood in Stolpa Forest in Täby by a group of Scouts who were out camping.'

'Block of wood and knife?'

'Don't know,' Berger said. 'But she survived.'

23

They were walking in the forest. It was grey and bitterly cold, and about half the time she regretted the decision to set out for a Sunday walk in the Trångsund Forest. The other half supported the impulse: it could be the last chance before the snow and frost slapped their six-month-long lid on experiences of nature.

And she wanted to give Lykke as many experiences of nature as possible in a world that was becoming ever more virtual, ever more unnatural. It was actually possible to drag her away from Facebook and Instagram, even if Snapchat was harder: every now and then she saw her daughter glance surreptitiously down at her jacket pocket.

Johnny was still working weekends, so it was just Deer and Lykke and the seeming endlessness of the forest, which made the ringtone of her mobile sound even more jarring than usual.

They were standing in a glade that opened on to the dramatic drop down towards the water of Drevviken. Lykke was in one of her impetuous moods, and Deer was doing her best to calm her down. She'd be damned if her daughter was going to fall off a cliff just because she had answered her phone. Especially given the identity of the caller, she thought as she looked at the screen. With some effort she managed to stop Lykke, sighed and answered, 'What did we say about this, Sam?'

'We've found three more victims,' Berger said in a tinny voice.

'What?' Deer exclaimed.

'I've emailed the documentation to you. You've been searching every police register for alternative formulations of 'four-leaf clover on buttock', just so you know. You identified three potential victims of the same killer. You've now studied the files and can say with certainty that they all have an ink drawing of a four-leaf clover on one buttock. In Malmö, Växjö and Täby. You've been sitting in your garage in your own time working on this. That ought to satisfy the NOD.'

'You've certainly got the bit between your teeth up there, wherever you are.'

'Has Robin sent a report from Sorsele?'

'Only to say how delighted he was at the prospect of going up there on a Sunday morning. I don't think he and his team have got there yet; I got one of my contacts to call the police in Arjeplog, and then everything took its time.'

'Three victims, but not three bodies,' Berger went on. 'One of the women survived, badly wounded and severely traumatised after being held captive for a day and a half. She could hardly speak when the police spoke to her so wasn't able to provide any information. The Täby police decided to wait for her to recover, but when they got round to making another attempt she'd already discharged herself from Danderyd Hospital. A couple of days later she and her girlfriend checked into a flight to Manila. And that's where the trail goes cold.'

'Manila in the Philippines?'

'Yes. This was in July 2012, and since then there's been no trace of Farida Hesari, now twenty-six years old. Can you instigate an international search for her?'

'As soon as I've taken a look at the documentation, yes. Now I need to get on with my walk through this savage, brutal, harsh and wild forest.'

'You've got considerably more than half your life left, Deer. By the way, aren't you forgetting something?'

Deer stared with distaste at her phone, then eventually said, 'Thanks a bunch.'

Then she ended the call.

Berger spoke.

'She said thanks very much and asked me to send you her warmest regards.'

Blom just gave him a sideways glance and said, 'Come here and let's do this.'

He went round to her side of the table and sat down on her bed, just out of sight of the laptop's built-in camera. Blom clicked and a ringing signal rang out from the computer. The Skype window remained empty, but then an elderly woman appeared, and said with unexpected clarity, 'I skype with my grandchildren in the States, so you don't have to ask if I understand the technology.'

'Mrs Enoksson,' Blom said. 'I'm a police officer, Detective Inspector Eva Lundström. We've already emailed about what I'd like to talk to you about. Is that OK?'

'Call me Laura, and I'll call you Eva,' Laura Enoksson said.

'Laura, you were the social worker who handled the case of Jessica Johnsson and Eddy Karlsson back in the spring of 2005, weren't you? What can you tell me about that?'

'I was so sorry to hear about poor Jessica,' Enoksson said. 'I'm afraid it wasn't entirely unexpected; she had an unfortunate tendency to pick the wrong men. But Eddy Karlsson's dead, it can't have been him. He came back from Thailand four years ago, a complete wreck from too many drugs, just a shadow of his former, repugnant self. But even the shadow was pretty repugnant.'

'Did you see him then? When he came home?'

'No, he kept under the radar. But I saw his body. I *wanted* to see his body. Men like him are the reason I ended up getting burned out.'

'Tell me about it, right from the start, please, Laura.'

The old woman let out a deep sigh, and her slightly haggard face – which had evidently seen more than anyone should have to see – tightened slightly.

'Jessica was twenty-five years old, a nurse, a bit naïve, perhaps. Like I said, one of those young women with something of a father complex who tend to pick the wrong men. And Eddy Karlsson was definitely the wrong man.'

'Hang on,' Blom said. 'A father complex?'

'I don't really know that much about Jessica's background, but I recognise the type. It's often girls who don't have a real father – they're looking for a father figure who will both see and acknowledge them, and simultaneously set boundaries for them. It often goes wrong.'

'And Eddy Karlsson was definitely the wrong man?'

'Without a doubt,' Laura Enoksson said. 'He wasn't just violent and off his head the whole time, he was also manipulative and paranoid. He monitored every step she took. He was arrested after hitting her a couple of times, but was released because of a lack of evidence. And in the absence of a witness statement, like so many women in her situation Jessica Johnsson initially refused to give a statement. Eddy went underground but carried on bullying her. It happened after that.'

'It?'

'Yes, the assault. The most serious assault, I mean. It was terrible. Not only did she have a miscarriage, but she was very seriously injured. Seriously enough to make the police react. She was given a protected identity while she was in hospital, and was secretly moved to another one, a long way from Stockholm. And that was the end of my involvement.'

'So you don't know what her new identity was?'

'The whole point was for as few people as possible to know about it,' Laura Enoksson said. 'And I certainly wasn't one of them.'

'To backtrack a little,' Blom said. 'She had a *miscarriage* as a result of the assault? So Jessica Johnsson was pregnant?'

'With Eddy's child, apparently. He killed his own child.'

Blom fell silent and glanced quickly at Berger, just like they'd agreed not to do. But he understood, and the way he looked back gave her her answer.

'Do you happen to know what sex the baby was?' Blom asked.

'Yes,' Enoksson said. 'It was a boy.'

Another glance; it was unavoidable.

Berger felt his lips form the name Eddy Karlsson.

The bastard wasn't dead. He had faked his own death. He hadn't been in Thailand for more than a year or so before coming back to Sweden and starting to kill. He vanished in 2005 and was back in time for Orsa in 2007.

He had killed his own son and wounded the child's mother. Now he was going to do better.

And kill the mother at all costs.

The sickest thing was that it made sense. Berger couldn't see anything that didn't slot into place.

'It was so terrible,' Laura Enoksson said, shaking her head.

'Killing his own unborn son ...' Blom said, lowering her gaze.

Enoksson looked surprised.

'I was thinking more of Jessica,' she said. 'Of the injuries.'

'The injuries?'

'Jessica Johnsson's injuries. To her reproductive organs.'

'Right ...?' Blom said.

'Her womb was damaged beyond repair,' Enoksson said. 'They had to remove it. An emergency hysterectomy.'

Berger looked at the back of Blom's lowered head, faintly visible through her blonde curtain of hair. The cards were being shuffled again, and he felt he could actually see the brain cells working behind that hair. He heard her murmur her goodbyes to Laura Enoksson, asked her to get back if she thought of anything else, came up with a friendly but non-committal farewell, closed Skype and turned round.

They may never have stared at each other for so long before.

'OK,' Berger said in the end. 'For a moment there I was certain that Eddy Karlsson had risen from the dead. Now – God knows.'

'She *was* pregnant when we met her in Porjus, we've got a blood sample to prove it. An awful lot of blood samples. But ten years ago her wrecked womb was removed from her body in an emergency hysterectomy. In other words, she *can't* have been pregnant.'

They looked at each other again.

'Everything's gone pretty weird now, hasn't it?' Berger eventually said.

Blom shook her head and said, 'Was the woman we spoke to really Jessica Johnsson? Or was it someone completely different? Someone who was then murdered? But how could that work? A pregnant woman *pretending* to be Jessica and then getting killed pretty much in front of our eyes? How does that fit?'

'Are there really no photographs at all of Jessica Johnsson?' Berger asked. 'No driving licence or passport photographs? No old school photos?'

'I haven't found any,' Blom said. 'Get your Desiré on to it.'

'Is there something we're not seeing?' Berger said. 'Something that's right in front of our eyes, something that ought to be crystal-clear?'

Molly Blom shook her head so hard that the satellite phone started to ring. She recognised the number, lifted the receiver and said, 'Dr Stenbom, I presume?'

At that precise moment Deer and Lykke reached Sjöängsbadet. There was no one swimming, but a few dogs were sniffing at the water's edge. Lykke ran over to them, which Deer wasn't very happy about – the dogs' owners were over by the edge of the forest, anything could happen. But the dogs seemed friendly enough. Lykke could cling on to her naïve, trusting nature for a bit longer. She patted the dogs; everything was fine.

Deer gazed out across Drevviken. If the ice settled this year, this would be where the traditional skating race would start in February. It was said that Drevviken had the finest ice in the world, and Deer was thinking of forcing her whole family to take part. Even Johnny could manage to skate twenty kilometres on a pair of long-distance skates.

The dogs' owners came down from the edge of the trees, but the branches kept moving, as if someone was hiding there in the shadows. The thought was thrust aside by a persistent ringtone. Deer was about to answer angrily, then saw that the number wasn't the one she thought it was.

'Yes, Robin?' she said. 'News from Sorsele?'

'I'm in Linköping,' Robin said.

'What the—?'

'Don't worry, I've sent my team, they know what they're doing. I had to get to the bottom of that little white thread from the basement in Porjus, and for that I needed the best lab I could find.'

'And now you've found it?'

'Yes. Like I suspected, it's from a gauze bandage, and sure enough there was blood on it. Microscopic quantities, but enough to get DNA.'

'I'm listening,' Deer said keenly.

'The DNA belongs to a man called Reine Danielsson.'

'Reine Danielsson?' Deer exclaimed, watching her daughter down by the water. One of the dogs looked like it was getting a bit boisterous, it had started to growl in a slightly unnerving way. She called to Lykke and she started to amble back, presumably after noticing that the dog wasn't quite so friendly after all. Then Deer glanced up towards the trees. The branches were still moving, but in a different place now, as if someone was moving along the treeline.

And, simultaneously, this absolutely fundamental piece of information.

'Yes,' Robin said. 'Reine Danielsson, thirty-three years old. I haven't got anything else on him yet, I called as soon as the result came through. I'll text you his ID number and date of birth.'

And with that the conversation was over. Deer saw the text arrive, and quickly began to type another number, one that wasn't in her list of contacts. But then her phone started to ring again. The call was from the number she had been halfway through entering.

'Deer,' a voice said excitedly. 'We've found out the identity of the man calling himself Sam Berger at the Lindstorp Clinic in Arjeplog.'

'Reine Danielsson?' Deer asked.

The silence that followed felt almost definitive. Even so, it never occurred to her that the signal had broken.

A sudden clarity arose.

Reine Danielsson. Unknown. But nothing less than a genuine serial killer.

The silence lasted so long that something made its way into the clarity, like a grain of sand under a contact lens. Vision blurred as it itched and stung. There was something about the name Reine Danielsson ...

'How the hell do you know that?' Berger finally said from the other side of the Arctic Circle.

'The correct question is: how the hell do *you* know that?' Deer said.

'We've had the DNA in some skin fragments from Arjeplog analysed.'

'You've "had the DNA in some skin fragments analysed"? How the hell did you manage that? Are you leaving a trail of evidence behind you now? A trail that's going to lead back to me and take my head off?'

'Unofficial channels,' Berger said. 'Nothing to worry about.'

'That makes me feel so much happier.'

'How did you get hold of the name?'

'There was a thread found in the boiler room in Porjus. A white thread, not black like the balaclava. From a gauze bandage, and Robin found traces of blood on it. The thread had caught on the wall, at head height for a man 1.85 metres tall if he was sitting on the floor. Could it possibly be the case that "Sam Berger" injured his head at the clinic?'

'His face,' Berger said. 'We were told he ran straight into a bus.'

'Sounds like we're dealing with a highly intelligent serial killer, then.'

'He's only highly intelligent intermittently. The rest of the time he seems to be locked into the delusion that he's someone else.'

'You need to send me everything you know,' Deer said. 'This is only going to work if we're completely in sync.'

'We've got an audio file of our conversation with Senior Consultant Jacob Stenbom. I'll send it to you. And we've got a bit more information about Jessica Johnsson's background. For instance the fact that she can't have been pregnant when she was murdered. Can you help us get hold of a photograph of her?'

'I'll try,' Deer said, as the dog walkers slowly began to move away from the shore. Lykke was sitting on a rock openly looking at Snapchat, clearly in protest at her mother's constant telephone calls.

'Have you found out anything about this Reine Danielsson?' Berger asked.

'I've only just been given his name. But ...'

'Same here. But ...'

'I haven't had time to process it yet,' Deer said. 'But something doesn't feel right.'

'I know,' Berger said and hung up.

He turned to Blom.

'Something doesn't feel right.'

She frowned unhappily and tapped at her computer. Berger saw rolling text reflected off her irises. She shook her head.

'I can't find a Reine Danielsson,' she said. 'Not in any search at all. Which probably means, for instance, that he's never paid tax in Sweden.'

'And anyone who doesn't pay tax in Sweden either has a pair of luxury yachts in Monaco or no income at all.'

'If we set the luxury yachts to one side for a moment, why would someone not have an income?'

'Down and out? Or ...'

'Yes?'

'For fuck's sake!' Berger blurted and threw himself at the large stack of paper beside the computer. He pulled out the thick file on the Helena Gradén case and leafed through it frenetically.

Blom watched his outburst of energy and said tentatively:

'I thought you said it when I was having a shower. You babbled a load of names instead of handing me more water. We were talking about farm names from Dalarna.'

Berger shook his head in disbelief and pointed at the file.

'There,' he said. 'Reine Danielsson, one of the other residents of Karl Hedblom's care home in Orsa. Bloody hell.'

Blom rubbed the corners of her eyes and said, 'Reine built the shelter. Reine abducted and killed Helena and Rasmus Gradén. Reine held them captive for almost two whole days and still held himself together in the hostel. Reine planted his fellow resident Karl Hedblom's DNA at the scene. Reine can't just have been an ordinary resident in that group.'

'We questioned him,' Berger said and felt the colour drain from his face.

'We? You personally?'

'Me personally,' Berger confirmed. 'And Deer personally. The pair of us personally.'

He picked up the satellite phone and called a familiar number. The call was answered as good as immediately.

'Orsa,' Deer's tinny voice said. 'It was Orsa, wasn't it?'

'Yes,' Berger said. 'We interviewed him, you and I interviewed him in the police's provisional base in Orsa, in the hotel, if you remember. I can see in the file that that's what happened, but I can't say that I remember it. Do you?'

'There were so many, a steady succession. But maybe ...'

'No, I can't dredge up anything,' Berger said.

'You've always been bad at the past,' Deer said. 'I think I remember a fairly big, awkward lad, he could well have been 1.85 metres tall and have had size 45 shoes. He may have been around twenty-six years old, which would fit the date of birth. But can I remember anything about the interview itself? God knows. I need to think about it and get back to you.'

'I've got the transcript in front of me,' Berger said. 'I'll be in touch once I've read it and you've done your thinking.'

'We should be home in half an hour or so,' Deer said. 'It's starting to get dark here at Sjöängsbadet. We've been playing hopscotch.'

'Well hop quickly,' Berger said. 'You need to be at police headquarters at five o'clock.'

'What are you telling me now?'

'And I'm afraid you'll also need five thousand in cash.'

'What exactly are you dragging me into this time?'

'Robertsson,' Berger said. 'In the police store. He's going to give you some videotapes.'

Deer let out a very deep sigh.

'One more thing,' Berger said. 'Something that's only just struck me.'

'Yes?'

'If I made such a deep impression on Reine Danielsson that he called himself Sam Berger during a deranged episode eight years later, there's a risk that he remembers you too, Deer. Let's not forget that the letter was addressed to you personally.'

Deer fell silent for a short while, then said, 'What are you trying to say, Sam?'

'Just be careful.'

'I can take care of myself,' Deer said and clicked to end the call.

She looked over towards Lykke. After reluctantly learning to play hopscotch on the sand she had gone back to her rock. In the rapidly growing dusk her face was lit up by a bluish glow from her mobile, where Snapchat was in full flow. The still, dark water of Drevviken was coloured faintly by the setting sun, a pink cloak foreboding the darkness. The dogs and dog owners were gone, mother and daughter were alone in the gathering dusk. Peculiarly alone. There wasn't a sound, the silence was absolute. The pink cover thinned out across the water, replaced little by little by darkness.

Something rippled down Deer's spine and burst into a shiver.

Reluctantly she looked round at the edge of the forest. The trees had been still for a long while now, she had long since dismissed the movement of the branches as the result of the autumn breeze, falling pine cones, nut-gathering squirrels. The car was over in the car park just a couple of hundred metres away. She studied the pine trees in the dusk light. There was nothing moving, everything was still.

'Lykke?' she said, and it felt like her voice was echoing through the deserted suburban forest.

Lykke looked up from her phone but didn't say anything. Her still childish face was shining bluely.

'Time to go,' Deer said as gently but firmly as she could manage.

From one corner of her eye she saw Lykke get reluctantly to her feet, still staring into the depths of her mobile. From the other she saw the trees move.

Deer turned her head quickly in that direction. The branches of one pine tree were trembling lightly, like an aftershock. Nothing else happened. A quick glance at Lykke: she was ten metres away, still not looking up. Back at the forest again. Nothing. The swaying of the branches came to a stop. Stillness spread across Sjöängsbadet again, across Drevviken, across the whole of Trångsund Forest.

Lykke reached her, and Deer held out her hand. Her daughter took it, their hands were ice-cold, neither able to warm the other.

They had stayed too long.

They started to walk slowly up the path towards the car park. Dusk was falling with unexpected speed. Now Deer could only just make out the edge of the forest.

But the movement stood out all the more clearly.

At first it was just one branch trembling, then everything became still again. Deer stopped, squeezed Lykke's hand, stared at the forest.

Then the movement again. Darting from branch to branch, as if someone were running through the trees.

Heading their way.

Deer crouched down, picked up a large stone, for the first time in a very long while missing her service pistol. She remembered telling Sam where they were; that was an unexpected consolation, as if it meant something beyond the fact that their bodies would be found.

The edge of the forest came closer, no more than a couple of metres from the path. The very closest tree trembled. The forest opened up. Someone sprang out with terrible speed.

Reine Danielsson, Deer thought, raising the stone. You're *not* getting my daughter. I'll fight until there's nothing left of me but an arm clutching a stone.

The branches were pushed back, everything happened so incredibly fast yet in slow motion.

The figure running out of the forest came closer. And then it stopped, staring at her with death in its eyes.

Around the figure young were clustered, four baby wild boar around the huge sow. The two mothers stood still for a while, staring at each other, their eyes locked together.

Then it was as if they recognised the mother in each other, the mother that all life in the world depended on, the mother who would do whatever it took for her offspring.

The sow let out a grunt that was almost a roar. Then she turned abruptly and crashed into the forest. The piglets scampered after her.

Deer stood motionless for a long time. Eventually she realised she was clutching Lykke's hand too tightly. She let go.

But not the stone, she wasn't going to let that go. Not until they were safely back inside the car.

'They were so cute!' Lykke said, skipping with joy.

24

She didn't like the dark at all. There were animals in it, beasts. They crawled around her, invisible, tree branches trembled. At any moment some unknown monster might leap out at her in the gloomy corridor.

Crime doesn't rest, not even on Sunday afternoons. So large parts of police headquarters on Kungsholmen in Stockholm were both lit up and full of activity. That had been the case the whole way from reception, bright and full of people. But when she got out of the lift everything was black and silent, and she couldn't see far along the corridor at all. Even so, there was a peculiar logic in not looking for the light switch. She was in the world of duplicity now, and darkness reigned there, that was where the beasts thrived.

There was a coded lock on the door. She knew she'd be leaving a trail the moment she ran her card through the reader. There was a risk that all the spotlights would end up pointing at her.

Even so, she swiped her card and opened the door.

It was just as gloomy inside the store as it was out in the corridor. The long rows of shelving stretched off out of sight.

She took a few tentative steps towards the counter. Only when she got within a couple of metres of it did she realise there was someone sitting there watching her.

When he stood up she was struck by how flabby with alcohol his half-century-old face was.

'Robertsson?' Deer said, not recognising her own voice.

The man stared at her blankly for a long time. In the end he said, 'ID?'

Great, Deer thought, and put her police ID down on the counter. He read it and hissed:

'NOD, for God's sake. What was wrong with calling it National Crime?'

'Reorganisation,' Deer said without really knowing why.

'I recognise you,' Robertsson said, looking at her through the bloodshot slits of his eyes. 'You were up in Orsa, weren't you? You were pretty back then, really sexy. What happened to you?'

Deer had made her mind up from the outset that nothing this man could say was going to bother her in the slightest. Consequently she maintained a stoical silence.

Robertsson went on, 'At least you've got bigger tits now. That's one bright spot in the midst of the decay.'

She told herself that her silence was stoical. Not filled with hate.

'You've got something for me, I believe?' Robertsson said after a brief pause.

'Only if you've got something for me.'

He nodded. Then he shook his head, leaned down behind the counter and pulled out a black bin liner. It was half full, looked heavy, and rattled oddly when he shook it.

She slipped her hand inside her jacket and pulled out an envelope. She passed it to him.

He took it, opened it and started to count the five-hundred-kronor notes, and said, 'This is starting to feel like a production line.'

Deer looked at him.

'What do you mean?' she said.

'Never you mind,' Robertsson said, putting the notes back in the envelope and tucking it away in his inside pocket. He bent down and picked up the bag, and heaved it across the counter.

Deer took it, opened it and looked inside.

It was full of old VHS tapes.

On the top was a porn film that was closer to thirty years old than twenty. She picked it up, looked at the explicit photographs on the cover, then turned towards the grubby man behind the counter.

'An instructional film,' Robertsson said with a grin. 'Looks like you might need it.'

That was when Deer decided that Richard Robertsson's days in the police force were most definitely – and easily – numbered.

25

They were taking a breather in the makeshift staffroom in the hotel which, to everyone's surprise, functioned very well as a base of operations for the police. They would soon be going back in again; the next man in line. The coffee tasted of death, to put it bluntly: the leakings from a week-old corpse.

The young detective superintendent looked at his new partner. It was their second day working together, in a situation far removed from all glory and honour, and he still hadn't got used to the nimble movements of her slight body. He felt ridiculously clumsy alongside her.

It was when she emptied her cup with a grimace of disgust and looked up at him, simultaneously questioning and challenging, that it struck him.

A deer's eyes.

'Deer,' he said. 'From now on your name is Deer.'

'My name is Desiré,' she said sullenly. 'And your name is Sam. OK, let's get going again.'

'My name isn't actually Sam,' he said. 'My name is Samuel. But we can't be Samuel and Desiré, that sounds like the

232

nineteenth century's worst pair of cops. Sam and Deer, on the other hand. Snappy as fuck.'

'So you're basically going to call me darling? In that case you really are mad, Sam. I'm married, you're married, we've both got kids in preschool. You make that bastard Robertsson look like a monk. However much he sits there waving his escort catalogue.'

'I'm not married,' Berger said. 'I've got a partner. Freja doesn't see the point in getting married.'

'But on the other hand you've got two kids, I've only got one.'

'Fair enough. But I didn't actually mean deer as in darling, but deer as in deer. Roe or possibly fallow. Two 'e's, not 'ea'. You move like a deer.'

'Fuck off,' Deer said and opened the door.

With deer-like agility.

The room was nothing like a normal interview room. It was long and thin, more like some sort of reception room that the hotel used as an office. It felt like they were walking for a long time towards the two people sitting at the desk. They were a woman in a carer's uniform and a young man, and it was the young man who was the focus of the two young detectives' interest.

He was sitting still, watching them closely as they walked towards him. They must have looked a very odd couple as they approached the makeshift interview table, little and large, encouraging and dour. The roles allocated very early on.

And those surprisingly sharp blue eyes that seemed to take everything in.

He was another member of the group of care-home residents from Falun who had taken the fateful decision to spend a couple of weeks in the forest outside Orsa. One of the minority who, according to what they'd been told, it was possible to talk to.

'Our names are Sam and Deer,' Berger said. 'And you're Reine Danielsson.'

'Detective Superintendent Sam Berger and Detective Inspector Desiré Rosenkvist,' Deer clarified. 'I hope you feel ready to talk to us, Reine?'

There was no doubt that there was something not quite right about the young man's open, clear gaze. It was as if he could see something beyond the obvious, as if he were looking at a couple of invisible people right beside them.

Their doppelgängers, perhaps.

They had been through this before. They had spent pretty much the whole of this long thankless autumn Tuesday sitting opposite people with varying degrees of mental illness, usually with one of their carers present. And there was no doubt that there were an awful lot of different forms of mental illness in the world.

Reine Danielsson was really just one of many, and there was nothing that made him stand out from the crowd. He was relatively large, looked to be in unexpectedly good shape, with dark blond mid-length hair, a slightly round face that made him look rather surprised the whole time, and a half-open mouth, as though there was some difference in pressure between inside and out. But there was also that look, as if it was soaking up everything about the situation, saving it for the future.

'So, Reine,' Deer said gently. 'Did you build a shelter in the forest?'

Reine Danielsson shook his head and looked surprised.

'We're recording this,' Deer said, 'so you need to reply in words.'

'I'll reply in words,' Danielsson said in a weak voice. 'I haven't built a shelter, I don't know how to do that, but I'd like to learn. But no one can teach me anything, they tell me I can't learn anything.'

'So you've never been in the shelter in the forest?'

The young man shook his head, realised what he was doing, and said, 'No.'

'But you do know that there's a shelter in the forest?'

'They said there was, but I haven't been there. I haven't been out much.'

'You've spent most of your time indoors, in the hostel? What have you been doing there?'

Reine Danielsson's gaze drifted off between them again, as if he were talking to some third person. Someone only he could see.

'I draw a lot,' he eventually said.

'What do you draw, Reine?'

'I don't know. Things I see.'

'Real things? Things you've seen in real life?'

'I don't know. Maybe. I usually pretend I'm someone else. I see a lot more then.'

'What sort of things have you been drawing in the past few days, Reine?' Deer asked.

'Not much, really. It's been too noisy. I haven't been able to concentrate.'

'Concentrate?' Berger blurted. 'Too noisy?'

Reine Danielsson's gaze started to wander.

'No,' Berger said, leaning forward. 'Don't look at anything else, Reine. Look at me, look into my eyes.'

In the end Danielsson did as Berger said. There was fear in his eyes. Fear of Berger's authority? He hoped so.

'Now listen to me very carefully, Reine,' he said. 'Keep looking at me. We've looked at your drawings. We know what you've been drawing. Almost all of them look like dreams, things that don't really exist. But we also know it's a long time since you drew anything. In fact your last drawing is from the morning of 18 October. Early that afternoon Helena Gradén went missing with her son Rasmus in his pushchair. You haven't done any drawing for twelve days. That's almost two weeks, Reine. Before that you did a lot of drawing. And the police didn't show up and disturb your concentration until several days later. Why did you stop drawing on that day in particular?'

Reine Danielsson's gaze wandered off again.

'I have been doing drawing since then,' he said, casting a quick glance at the female carer. She nodded in encouragement. Even so, Reine started as if he'd been given a shock.

'So where have those drawings gone then?' Berger asked.

'I know what you're doing now. I've seen it on TV.'

'Just answer the question.'

'Good cop, bad cop, coffee cup. I've seen it on TV.'

'What did you do with the drawings, Reine?'

'I threw them away. They weren't any good.'

'And where are they now?'

'Gone. I burned them.'

'First you threw them away, then you burned them. Which is it?'

Reine Danielsson started again, then fell silent and stared into the gap between Berger and Deer as if someone really was sitting there. Deer shifted sideways to where he was staring. When she had caught his peculiar gaze she asked, 'Have you ever drawn a four-leaf clover, Reine?'

He just stared at her.

'Do you know what a four-leaf clover is?' she went on.

'They're unusual,' Danielsson said, wide-eyed.

'How are they unusual?'

'Almost all clover has three leaves. When you find one with four leaves you get to make a wish.'

'Does the same thing apply when you draw a four-leaf clover? Does your wish come true then?'

'I don't know ... I don't think so ...'

'What happened when you drew a four-leaf clover, Reine? Did your wish start to come true?'

Reine Danielsson started again, as if he'd been given an electric shock, and his eyes darted about.

'I haven't ...'

Deer leaned forward, and her voice was a miracle of gentleness as she went on, 'Did your wish come true in the shelter, Reine? Is that when you did the drawing that stopped you drawing anything else? The four-leaf clover? Where did you draw the four-leaf clover, Reine? How does it feel to draw on human skin? In the middle of all the blood?'

Reine Danielsson stood up and shook his clenched fist. The rest of his body was shaking too. The carer got to her feet and put her arm around him. She shook her head as if in disappointment, and without a word started to lead the disturbed young man towards the door. It swung shut behind them. They watched it close.

'How do you think that went?' Berger asked after a short pause.

Deer shook her head and said, 'I don't know. What do you think?'

'He might have to have a bit of a rethink about the whole good cop, bad cop thing ...'

'Did I go in too hard?' Deer asked.

Berger looked at her as if he was seeing her for the first time. Then he shrugged his shoulders.

'Your voice was very gentle, at least. Oh, I don't know. It does look like he's got a reasonable alibi, unlike Karl Hedblom. On the few occasions he's been outside while they've been here, he's always had a member of staff with him. Which makes me wonder how he managed to burn his drawings.'

'This feels like a dead end,' Deer said, looking down at a sheet of notes. 'He was neither cold enough nor angry enough to have done it. And as far as I can make out from his file he hasn't got anything against women or mothers. His condition is described as mentally unstable with a subsolid personality and a pronounced need to please other people combined with severe anxiety, confusion and depression. Seems to be happiest when he's left in peace to draw.'

'What if he wasn't *allowed* to draw?' Berger said. 'What if someone told him he couldn't?'

'Karl, you mean? Well, they're in neighbouring rooms at the hostel. They'll have had contact with each other. But as far as I understand it the doors are mostly kept locked.'

Berger nodded. Then he stretched and said, 'It's getting towards four o'clock. How many have we got left?'

'According to the timetable we need to do two more,' Deer said, consulting her brand-new iPhone, her pride and joy, a birthday present from Johnny.

'Shall we press on then?' Berger said and yawned.

Deer was still looking at the minor miracle in her hand as she said, 'Have we really got all we can from Reine Danielsson? Shall we put him on the reject pile?'

Their eyes met.

'We both know he hasn't got anything to do with this,' Berger said. 'Let's get this done.'

Deer nodded slowly. She glanced back at her phone.

'Just one thing,' she said.

'What?' Berger said.

'Don't forget that you can never see inside another person.'

26

That night winter arrived in Skogås. She didn't really understand how it woke her, but it did – too early. Maybe the glass of the window made a tiny crackling sound as the frost spread across it, maybe the frosted pattern on the glass refracted the moon's rays in a different direction to usual, maybe winter actually had a brittle, fragile sound of its own that put a damper on the flow of nightmares. It was a mystery that would never get a decent answer, she realised that at once, but there were plenty of other things demanding answers.

Johnny was sleeping like a log, of course, but she was now wide awake. She groaned when she saw that it was only 05.18. She could sense the lingering images of the wild boar's gaze from her dream, so she admitted defeat, got up, pulled on her dressing gown and slippers and crept through the ice-cold garage to her office. At least it was warmer there.

Then she sat down and read. She read everything. The whole case, one more time. Including the potential new victims, every preliminary investigative report. The as yet fruitless search for the survivor Farida Hesari; the unfaithful

Danish doctor Mette Hækkerup; biker chick Elisabeth Ström in Växjö; the mystery of Jessica Johnsson's hysterectomy and pregnancy.

At some point during those early hours of the morning she finally managed to get hold of a photograph of Jessica, despite the lack of a driver's licence and passport. It was a picture in the local press of the Christmas market in Porjus three years ago, and she was buying dried reindeer meat; she looked rather taken by surprise. Other than that, she seemed to have managed to avoid cameras altogether. Deer emailed the photograph to Berger and got an answer at once, as if he'd been waiting, as sleepless as her:

'Yes, that's her, the woman we met in Porjus. So the woman we interviewed was the real Jessica Johnsson. There goes that theory. Have you found out anything else about Reine Danielsson?'

Deer wrote back:

'Discharged from the care home in Falun just a few months after the trip to Orsa. No permanent address since then. Cutbacks in the social care budget probably the reason. Call me instead.'

Her phone duly rang.

'OK,' Sam Berger said. 'I spotted that he was discharged then as well, eight years ago. Out on his own since then. No income, no registered address. Where has he been? How has he survived?'

'No family,' Deer said. 'As far as I can see, Reine Danielsson is completely alone in the world. But he has surfaced on a couple of occasions. When he's been admitted to institutions like Lindstorp.'

'Lindstorp, from which he was discharged incognito, as "Sam Berger", unable to pay. We can probably assume that similar things have happened before. So he's actually been admitted under his own name as well then?'

'Yes,' Deer said. 'I'm trying to get hold of the details.'

'Three questions,' Berger said. 'Where? When? Who paid?'

'I'm working on it,' Deer said.

'Hold back on that for a bit. Let's just stop and think this through. The way things look right now.'

'Have you been thinking things through with Molly Blom?'

'She's out skiing.'

'What? It's not even eight o'clock. It must be freezing up there, not to mention pitch black. Winter's even arrived in Skogås now.'

'Don't worry,' Berger said. 'She's got a head torch.'

'What a relief,' Deer deadpanned.

Berger went on, 'Let's just think this through, you and me, like ordinary detectives. Let's pretend we're back in that open-plan office in police headquarters. This is a perfectly ordinary case, everything's fine, we're still working for Allan, we're partners trying to solve a murder, that's all. We'll ignore the fact that you're running a parallel investigation separate from your new employers, the NOD, and we'll ignore the fact that you've secretly employed a couple of freelancers who are on the run from the judicial system, and we'll ignore—'

'Thanks,' Deer said.

The silence that followed lasted a fraction too long.

Eventually Berger said darkly:

'There is no justice.'

'Just tell me you didn't kill Syl,' Deer said.

'For fuck's sake,' Berger said.

'A stroke,' Deer said. 'Sure. Syl dies, you disappear. How does that fit together, Sam?'

'It's better if you don't know, Deer.'

'No,' Deer said firmly. 'It's always better to know. Enough covering things up now. We do this together or not at all.'

'Is it enough if I say that it's the Security Service?'

'No.'

Berger sighed deeply and said, 'Syl was working for me, unofficially. She'd uncovered a load of strange connections between the top brass in the Security Service and Ellen's kidnapper. She went on digging, and just as she was about to tell me what she'd found, she was murdered. We found her in the boathouse. I had some sort of breakdown, and Molly got me as far away from there as she could. Since then we've been keeping off grid.'

'Bloody hell,' Deer said.

'Quite,' Berger said. 'But it doesn't change anything. We're really close now. This isn't the time to give up. Not now. You need to trust me.'

'But can I trust Blom?' Deer said. 'You're on the run from the Security Service, and *she is the Security Service*. She's an undercover agent, for fuck's sake, Sam, we've seen her in action before, she's bloody good at playing different roles. What have you done, Sam?'

'I've stepped on a real wasps' nest,' Berger said. 'And I can't get any sense of the bigger picture.'

'I had a feeling it was something like that,' Deer sighed. 'Just be careful.'

'There's only one person I trust implicitly, one single person, and that's you, Deer. I trust you. Can we press on as planned? We need to stop Reine Danielsson, not only to save your job, but also to make sure you're the hero of the hour. We can manage that. We just need to be able to keep two separate thoughts in our heads at the same time.'

'Two?' Deer exclaimed. 'Is there really any point in carrying on at all if your Molly bloody Blom is playing a double game? She could bring down the pair of us at any moment.'

'I don't think so,' Berger said. 'That's what my two thoughts are about, and they're splitting my brain. When it comes to me and the Security Service, maybe she is playing some sort of double game, but I'm convinced she's treating this case and serial killer Reine Danielsson with absolute seriousness.'

'The way you were once completely sure about Nathalie Fredén?'

Silence spread through Deer's depressing little garage again. She had a sudden vision of herself from far above, saw her unassuming life, her little family, her garage, her little terraced house as an absurdly exposed enclave in a world of betrayal and double-crossing and multiple loyalties, a tiny raft that was somehow still afloat on the surface of a seething witches' cauldron. And she saw Sam Berger appear out of the stinking brew, and she couldn't see his face because there were so many different faces on his head that it was impossible to make out any single one.

'Who the hell is Reine Danielsson?' Deer said.

'Yes,' Berger said. 'Thanks, Deer. Let's forget about the past for the moment: who is he now? He's suffered from periods of madness, is in and out of clinics presumably under a variety of identities. But it's when he's out that he's at his most dangerous. He spends a year or so in some unknown location, in some abandoned old house, with no money, and plans his murders. In all probability he targets the mothers of boys, but without drawing too fine a distinction between them: a pregnant prostitute will do just as well as a successful paediatrician with a teenage son. An awful lot of planning to then go on the attack with a lump of wood and a knife. He leaves no DNA behind, no semen, even though he's obviously killing for pleasure. Can you make any sense of that, Deer?'

Deer looked around her windowless study, at what was basically a dreary little converted garage. It was dimly lit, full of dark, dirty corners. But the cracks had closed up again, another dawn had come in spite of everything.

'No,' she replied. 'But don't we have to take as our starting point the fact that it's impossible to make any real sense of it? We're dealing with a psyche without any obvious parallels. A darkness that's sometimes so unbearable that he has to become someone else. And, most recently, between two brutal murders, he became *you*, Sam. There's no longer any possibility that that's a coincidence. He became you. And there we were, unable to remember if we'd even interviewed him. So he didn't make much of an impression on us, whereas you clearly made a huge impression on him.'

'That's all very well,' Berger said, 'but *I'm* safe here. *You*, on the other hand, Deer, you need to be really careful. Reine Danielsson is bound to remember you as well.'

'Like I said before, I can look after myself,' Deer said, thinking of the wild boar's eyes staring at her through the gloom.

'Have you read the transcript of our interview with him?' Berger asked.

'I've read everything else,' Deer said. 'I've spent hours sitting out here in the garage reading everything except that. I've been kind of skirting round it.'

'Putting off the inevitable,' Berger said. 'Me too. We can't put it off any longer. Read it – but try to remember the whole situation, every little impression, anything that could help us.'

'I'll try. And I've got Robertsson's fucking videotapes to go through. As luck would have it, I've still got a video player that works.'

'Molly's just got back. She'll read it too, to give her perspective, and then we'll pool our impressions and memories later.'

'OK,' Deer said.

Then she disappeared.

'What am I reading?' Blom asked in the darkness. She was radiating a mixture of heat and cold.

'The interview Deer and I conducted with Reine Danielsson eight years ago,' Berger said, passing her a sheaf of papers across the increasingly cluttered table; he hoped she didn't notice it shaking.

Blom took it and looked at it for a while, as if frozen to the spot. Then she handed the papers back to him and quickly turned round. She rushed to the door and stopped just outside, retching over the edge of the little terrace. Afterwards she scraped snow over the vomit and came back inside.

'You can't go on exhausting yourself skiing like that,' Berger said. 'I need you at your best.'

'Give it here,' Blom said, flashing Berger an angry look. She took the papers and sat down. She switched on the desk light and without further ado immersed herself in the old transcript. Berger picked up his own copy and tried to focus on it, failed, tried again, did a bit better. A whole world opened up, a world he'd forgotten a surprising amount about. The hotel in Orsa, the rush of activity in that hastily improvised police base, the extra staff, the constant flow of new people to interview. And then the staffroom, the sudden calm. And how he had seen Desiré Rosenkvist with new eyes – new: sure; better: hardly – and that was when she became Deer. He remembered them walking into the oddly stretched room and looking into Reine Danielsson's wide-open bright blue eyes which seemed to take in the whole universe.

He read on, diving deep into the tepid waters of memory, swimming around, exploring, looking in all the nooks and crannies before rising to the surface again. Only to meet a different pair of bright blue eyes. He didn't know what was hiding behind these ones either.

'Well?' Blom said, studying him. 'Do you think the pair of you did a good job?'

'That's exactly what I asked Deer afterwards,' Berger said.

'Not that it says that in the transcript. Which is why I'm asking.'

'Hardly,' Berger said. 'Dull, uninspired, failing to follow up things that look obvious in hindsight.'

'Such as?'

'Why did the question about the four-leaf clover upset him so much? Why did he stop drawing the same afternoon that Helena Gradén was abducted?'

'I was struck more by a couple of other things he said,' Blom said, leafing through the transcript. 'Here: "But no one can teach me anything, they tell me I can't learn anything."'

'He'd had it drummed into him that he could never learn anything,' Berger said. 'But that wasn't the impression I got.'

'The second quote is even more interesting,' Blom said. 'You asked if he drew things he'd seen in real life. And he replied: "I usually pretend I'm someone else. I see a lot more then."'

'Hmm,' Berger said, looking through the transcript until he found the quote. 'He did actually say that. He *sees much more* if he pretends to be someone else. *Pretend*, though? That suggests that he knows it isn't real.'

'You're thinking of something else?' Blom said, looking at him intently.

'There was something else, actually,' Berger said. 'There was a background file. Deer referred to it. We haven't found a background file for Reine Danielsson, though, have we?'

'No,' Blom said. 'The care home has closed down, the paperwork has been dispersed, and presumably none of it was digitised. Whatever's left of it is probably buried in the bowels of some council building in Falun.'

'I remember Deer saying something about a diagnosis. Reine Danielsson seemed happiest when he was left in peace to draw. He didn't seem to have anything against either women or mothers. Deer mentioned mental instability combined with a subsolid personality, along with severe anxiety, confusion and depression.'

'I'm afraid that sounds like a fairly standard diagnosis.'

'There was definitely something else too,' Berger said firmly. 'Yes, "a pronounced need to please other people".'

'That's a bit ambiguous,' Blom said. 'Easily led, then?'

'It's not entirely clear, is it?' Berger agreed. 'But some sort of outline of his character type is starting to emerge. Big and strong but also weak-willed and easily led. Someone who can be used.'

'You mean there could be someone sitting in the shadows directing him? That Reine Danielsson is some sort of remote-controlled murderer?'

'Domination,' Berger said.

'Haven't I heard that before?' Blom said. 'Once when you were questioning a suspect by the name of Nathalie Fredén. She was supposed to be the subservient slave of some master. Is this something personal? A fetish of yours?'

'This time it's real, though. Can't you see the outline, Molly? I can definitely see an outline, but I don't know what's inside it. It makes sense, and it doesn't make sense.'

Blom shrugged and dropped the transcript of the interview on the keyboard of her computer.

'I'm sorry,' she said. 'But I can't see anything here but an extremely unlikely murderer. Maybe we're on the wrong track altogether. He was in the Lindstorp Clinic for the simple reason that he's mad. The real killer must have come across him somewhere and taken a microscopic piece of gauze bandage down into the boiler room with him.'

'What about the van then?' Berger said. 'The once yellow-white Volkswagen Caddy that's now covered with Fjord Blue foil? It was stolen from Anders Hedblom in Sorsele. It drove Reine Danielsson to Lindstorp. It scraped the wall of Jessica Johnsson's garage in Porjus.'

'I know,' Blom sighed. 'But I don't see how—'

'There's no way in hell that a nutter like Reine Danielsson would have a driving licence,' Berger declared and stood up. '*She's* the one driving.'

'She?'

'The blonde outside Lindstorp, the woman who dropped him off. She's the brains behind this, she's there the whole time. She was there when Reine murdered Anders in Sorsele, she dropped him off at the clinic and picked him up again when he discharged himself, she drove to Porjus, she helped him get rid of any DNA inside the house. I bet there were two people in that boiler room. She sent him out at just the right moment. Your phone fell over when he slammed the cellar door shut after rushing upstairs with his balaclava on and Jessica Johnsson tucked under his arm. Then she followed him up. They killed Jessica together in the most brutal way possible. We shouldn't be looking for lovers from Jessica Johnsson's past. This was a friend, a female friend somewhere in her missing circle of acquaintances, someone close enough to her that Jessica didn't want to give her up.'

'Why not a female lover?' Blom said, staring out at the growing light of dawn. 'That could be a possibility.'

'Killing for kicks, and no semen,' Berger said. 'Bloody hell.'

The satellite phone rang. They stared at it as if it had come from outer space. Then Berger snatched up the receiver and answered, 'Deer, have you read the interview transcript yet? And did you manage to sort out Robertsson's videotapes?'

'Later,' Deer said quickly. 'Robin just called. With some really weird information. From Serbia, of all places. If it had been somewhere in the EU it would have happened much faster.'

'I have absolutely no idea what you're talking about right now.'

'The blood,' Deer said. 'It was circulated once it had been analysed – that happens almost automatically.'

'Sorry, but I still don't understand.'

'For fuck's sake, Sam. Wake up! The blood in Porjus. The bloodbath.'

'Jessica Johnsson's blood?'

'No!' Deer yelled. 'That's the whole point! *It wasn't Jessica Johnsson's blood*. And the hairs on the hairbrush in the bathroom weren't hers either. None of the DNA in that whole damn house was Jessica Johnsson's. Do you understand what I'm saying?'

Berger was left speechless. He looked over towards Blom. She'd heard, and he thought he saw her flushed face grow paler. She didn't say anything either.

'Are you still there, Sam?' Deer asked eventually.

'Yes,' Berger said. 'But we sat opposite her, we had tea, she scratched her head several times. It must have been her DNA.'

'And yet it wasn't. It belongs to a Serbian woman whose name is – or rather was – Jovana Malešević. She was travelling alone through the north of Sweden and hasn't been heard from since the morning of Sunday 15th, when she was in Arjeplog.'

'The day Reine Danielsson was discharged from the Lindstorp Clinic just outside Arjeplog,' Berger said. 'Are we absolutely sure of this, though? The Serbs couldn't have made a mistake?'

'We've got fingerprints too,' Deer said, 'even on Jessica Johnsson's old typewriter. They were Jovana Malešević's too.'

'And the blood upstairs? The blood in the shape of a human body on the sheet? The buttock with the four-leaf clover?'

'And the blood on the snow from the trunk,' Deer said. 'It's all Jovana Malešević's.'

'But,' Berger said simply. He felt lost for words.

'One other thing,' Deer said. 'The reason she was travelling so far from home is that she had a big decision to take. Jovana Malešević needed peace and quiet to decide whether or not she was going to keep her baby.'

Berger said, 'Jessica Johnsson wasn't pregnant, because she'd had a hysterectomy, but Jovana was. And hers was the only DNA found in the house.'

'Apart from a few molecules of Reine Danielsson's blood, yes.'

'Do they know what sex the baby was?'

'Jovana Malešević was fifteen weeks pregnant, and the previous week she'd had an ultrasound back home in Novi Sad. It was going to be a boy.'

'Dear God,' Berger said.

'Not that he seems to have much involvement in this,' Deer said. 'I'll look through Robertsson's tapes and get in touch if I find anything.'

And with that she was gone.

Blom stood up, still in her skiing gear, and walked over to the display on the wall. She stopped and looked at it.

'Some of this needs rearranging,' she said matter-of-factly, but her voice was trembling.

Berger stood up and went over to stand beside her.

'Is it even possible to reconfigure this?' he asked.

'Blonde wig,' Blom said. 'As good a disguise as any ...'

'The perpetrator isn't hidden in Jessica Johnsson's past,' Berger said. 'The perpetrator *is* Jessica Johnsson. She's directing the weak-willed Reine Danielsson, she's got him firmly in her grasp. Jessica is his master.'

'We were right about one thing, though,' Blom said. 'There were two people in the boiler room. But it wasn't Jessica sitting in there with Reine, it was a kidnapped Serbian woman called Jovana Malešević.'

'Robin was sure someone had been living in there,' Berger said. 'And the person who spent three nightmarish days in there before she was ritually slaughtered was poor Jovana.'

'There's more than that,' Blom said, swivelling quickly towards him. 'Much more. They *summoned* you.'

'What?'

'Jessica kept on about the four-leaf clover and Karl Hedblom being innocent until the police ended up ignoring her. She kept going on about it, but no one took the bait. She had to try even harder. When she and Reine for some as yet unknown reason murdered Anders Hedblom in Sorsele, she left a note with the name Berger on it. Then she drove the increasingly psychotic Reine to the Lindstorp Clinic and made sure he registered under the name Sam Berger. Then she wrote that fake letter and sent it directly to your former partner, Desiré Rosenkvist. Jessica Johnsson summoned you, Sam. She's issued a challenge.'

'But I've never met her.'

'You don't know that. She seems good at dressing up, and she lived under an assumed identity for several years. But maybe it was enough that your interview with Reine made such an impression on him, maybe she's summoned you for Reine's sake.'

'You don't think you're taking it a bit far now?'

'She wants you to look for her, Sam. And she's got her way. Now she knows that you're trying to find her.'

'We sat at that table with her, Molly. We sat and questioned her. There was nothing at all to suggest that she recognised me.'

'Because she was expecting you, she was well prepared,' Blom said. 'She'd scattered the clues, all she had to do was wait for you. It probably happened sooner than she'd been expecting, but when Desiré called to say that you were on your way they set to work cleaning the house. Then, once the deed was done, they cleaned up some more. Washed the teacups, hoovered the dining table.'

'But Deer didn't call to say that I was on my way,' Berger said. 'She just said that she was sending a couple of police officers. And when we got there we were Lindbergh and Lundström, that's all.'

'When Desiré Rosenkvist – your partner eight years ago – called, Jessica probably guessed that it was Sam Berger who was on his way rather than anyone else. The culmination of all her dreams. Now she could really draw you into the series of murders. She'd get Reine to commit murder while you lay helpless in the basement. That would infuriate you; you wouldn't give up until you caught her.'

'I still don't get why she'd be so obsessed with me. Among my limited number of skills is a very good memory for faces, and I'm sure I've never met her before.'

'You probably have, one way or another. Maybe she's a good actress.'

'Like you?'

Blom held his gaze for a while, then said, 'There's no need to go that far. OK, let's get to work.'

Berger let out a deep sigh, turned away and said, 'Now we really need to know what Jessica Johnsson's name was when she was living under an assumed identity.'

27

Monday 23 November, 09.46

Winter flooded in through the crack in the door. In the time it took for him to open it as quietly as possible, his fingers had begun to stiffen. He only just managed to get his mobile phone going.

Even so, the sun was shining just as intensely as yesterday. Its knife-sharp rays sought their way into Molly Blom's eyes as she stood facing the other way out into the snow; it was clear that she was having trouble making out the buttons of the satellite phone in the bright light reflecting from every direction. Once again she sought shelter from the harsh sunlight under the projecting roof of the little cabin, and held the satellite phone up in the shadow in order to see it. Then she dialled the number.

Berger zoomed in with his phone's camera. When Blom's voice rose towards the infinite blueness of the pole of inaccessibility he gently closed the door, put his frozen mobile on the table and held his hands out towards the radiator. Even though he knew what was under the red cloth nearest the window he raised it briefly and looked at the two pistols from the jeep; they radiated both security and danger.

Then he waited.

Time passed. The circulation got going again in his hands, pumping pain through his body. It was life-giving.

In these times of betrayal and double-dealing he could at least rely on the pain. That was his and his alone.

It took an unexpectedly long time. As if Blom was actually getting somewhere for the first time. Had her contact in the Security Service finally put a bit of effort in?

Frustration and hope grew in tandem as she remained outside.

Eventually she came in, and her blanched face probably wasn't only the result of the cold.

'Got it,' she said. 'At last.'

Berger waited, and a new warmth joined the pain that was still coursing around his body. Blom went on, 'When Jessica Johnsson was under protection, her name was Lena Nilsson.'

Berger felt his eyebrows frown; it was as if the muscles of his face were outside his control. Something that could hardly be larger than a single brain cell decided to go walkabout in his otherwise frozen brain.

'Typical name for an assumed identity,' Blom went on, flapping her arms to warm herself up. 'As bland and commonplace as possible. But I've also got her ID number.'

'I'll be damned,' Berger said. 'Lena Nilsson.'

'What? Do you recognise—'

Berger didn't wait for the end of the sentence. Instead he dived into the ten-centimetre-thick bundle of documentation covering the investigation of the eight-year-old double murder in Orsa. The papers flew around him. Finally he stood there clutching one sheet of paper in his hand.

'We're back in bloody Orsa again,' he said, pointing at the document. 'The staff from the care home. One of them was called Lena Nilsson. It could have been her. She looked after both Karl Hedblom and Reine Danielsson. It's not impossible that she manipulated Reine to murder one of the town's inhabitants, Helena Gradén, along with her fourteen-month-old son Rasmus. And then pinned the blame for the murder on another of her charges, Karl.'

Blom snatched the sheet of paper, read it, then nodded.

'The ID number matches,' she said.

Berger went over to the wall covered with the ever-expanding investigation and looked at the only known photograph of Jessica Johnsson, the one Deer had found from a Christmas market in Porjus.

'What if she was there all along?' Berger said. 'Maybe she was lurking in Orsa, completely anonymous. If she was, I must have seen her. But I don't remember her at all. Lena Nilsson ...'

Blom was sitting at her computer now, tapping away at it.

'Jessica Johnsson may not have a driving licence,' she said, 'but Lena Nilsson's got one. It may have become invalid once Eddy Karlsson died and Jessica was able to go back to her real identity, but it was never formally withdrawn.'

'New idea,' Berger said. 'Did they kill Eddy Karlsson as well?'

'We need to look into the circumstances surrounding his death,' Blom said.

'Driving licence,' Berger said slowly. 'She would have been driving from Sorsele after they'd killed Anders Hedblom.'

'Who questioned her eight years ago in Orsa?' Blom asked.

'Robertsson,' Berger replied with a nod. 'One of his crap interviews. The recording might still exist ...'

'We need to go through it in detail.'

'We will,' Berger said, tearing his eyes away from the wall. 'We need detail, as much detail as possible. But what we need more than anything is some sort of overview. Shouldn't we start by taking it all from the beginning again? What we've got so far? Who is Jessica Johnsson? Who is Reine Danielsson? Who are these people we're up against here?'

'A couple,' Blom said. '*Are* they a couple? A loving couple?'

'That can't be right,' Berger exclaimed. 'Think back to the basement in Porjus. You rigged up your mobile, neither of them knew about it, they weren't putting on a show for the camera. Reine rushed out from the boiler room and attacked us. Then he dragged Jessica to the stairs and tied her hands. She sat there captive while he moved us over to the radiators. Then he cut her free and dragged her up the stairs so violently that it dislodged your phone. That didn't exactly look like a creative partnership.'

'It could have been a ritual,' Blom said. 'Some sort of kinky foreplay.'

'And then murder and sex? But without semen ...'

'Obviously they clean up after themselves, get rid of any DNA. But it's still a bit strange that there's never any semen in the blood ...'

'This is too sick,' Berger exclaimed, shaking his head. 'Sure, there's not much we haven't seen, and as seasoned cops we know that nothing we can imagine, however hard we strain our imaginations, will ever come close to what reality has to offer. Even so ...'

'We need to think beyond the boundaries of a normal psyche,' Blom said, walking over to the wall. 'And we need to think beyond our usual prejudices. Women don't commit sexually motivated murders, everyone knows that. But what if they do under certain circumstances? Certain extreme circumstances far beyond anything that could be considered normal? We need to delve deep inside a soul that's unlike anything we've ever encountered before.'

'Deep inside, in the deepest part of the interior of the country,' Berger said.

'We sat opposite her, Sam. Neither of us had the faintest idea what was going on inside her head. She didn't make much of an impression, not then, and evidently not eight years ago either. And if you actually think about all the things that came together for her around that dining table in Porjus – all the long, complex planning that was in the process of coming to fruition – you have to admit that she was as cold as ice. To an almost super-human degree.'

'As cold as the interior of the country,' Berger said. 'Shall we try taking the whole damn thing from the start? So, where does it start? When does Jessica Johnsson become as sick as this? There are no indications of it anywhere in her past.'

'But there are, though, aren't there?' Blom said, gesturing vaguely towards the wall. 'Eddy Karlsson is one indication. Jessica was a girl who chose violent men; there's nothing unique about that, it's all too common. But perhaps it's a sign that she liked danger even when she was younger, that she rejected the safe, the normal. And this unusually repulsive man got her pregnant, assaulted her repeatedly, finally so badly that she lost her child, her unborn son, and with him her womb and her identity. It seems plausible that something like that could trigger a pretty strong hatred.'

'But it would be directed at Eddy Karlsson in that case, or maybe at men in general. But the murder victims are women.'

'Women with sons,' Blom said. '*Precisely* what she could never be. Isn't she using Reine to help her reconstruct and restage Eddy Karlsson's abuse of her?'

'But she didn't die. The women she sets Reine loose on die, even if their sons don't always. Which would make it a kind of suicide by proxy. Something along the lines of her needing to die too.'

'But that would make it depressive,' Blom said, 'life-denying. And both you and I see something different, a sexual, almost manic element. A grotesque act of affirmation. An ecstatic ritual. And as part of that, Reine has to attack her, drag her off with him. The way he dragged her up the stairs in Porjus.'

'And then the murder of a woman? I don't really know if I—'

'You're blinkered, Sam, the way you always have been. You idolise women. But we're just as capable of grotesque deeds. The more liberated we become, the more dangerous we are.'

Berger nodded slowly. That was certainly true.

The phone rang. Berger clicked the speaker button and answered:

'Yes?'

'It's me,' Deer said. 'It really was there.'

'What was?'

'A video recording of our interview with Reine Danielsson,' Deer said. 'The afternoon of 30 October 2007. I've filmed the television screen with my mobile, it's still reasonable quality. I'm sending you the whole recording now, but I've already sent the most important bit, the end of the interview. Have you got it?'

Berger checked his email. Sure enough, the file was there.

'Yes,' he said.

'Take a look at it,' Deer said. 'I'll stay on the line.'

Blom stood up and went round to Berger's side of the table. He clicked the file. A film started to play, and he paused to get an idea of the context and perspective.

His memory hadn't been too far out. There were four people sitting around a table in the oblong office in the hotel in Orsa.

The camera seemed to be above his and Deer's shoulders, you could mostly see just their backs. On the other side, facing the camera, sat twenty-five-year-old Reine Danielsson. He was caught in a moment of agitation. Beside him sat an anonymous carer staring down at the table.

Berger clicked Play. Deer's voice sounded unexpectedly girlish when it said, 'Does the same thing apply when you draw a four-leaf clover? Does your wish come true then?'

Reine stared at her uncomprehendingly.

'I don't know ... I don't think so ...'

'What happened when you drew a four-leaf clover, Reine? Did your wish start to come true?'

Reine Danielsson jerked, and his eyes darted about.

'I haven't ...'

Deer leaned forward, and her gentle voice went on:

'Did your wish come true in the shelter, Reine? Is that when you did the drawing that stopped you drawing anything else? The four-leaf clover? Where did you draw the four-leaf clover, Reine? How does it feel to draw on human skin? In the middle of all the blood?'

Then Reine Danielsson stood up, so agitated that he was shaking. The carer got to her feet and put her arm around him. It was clear that Reine couldn't speak. He looked pale, and it all seemed to be getting too much for him.

Then Berger stood up. He raised his right hand, extended his index and long fingers to form a double-barrelled revolver. He aimed the imaginary weapon at Reine and made a shooting sound. His hand jerked up, as if recoiling.

The carer shook her head and looked up at Berger.

'That was uncalled for,' she said.

Berger replied:

'Stick to what you're good at.'

Deer chuckled. For a brief moment the carer's eyes darkened as she flashed him an unexpectedly sharp look.

Then she took hold of Reine's hand and led him out of the room without another word. Berger sank onto his chair again and asked, 'How do you think that went?'

The recording came to an end. Berger replayed it and watched the short sequence again. He paused it just as the carer stared darkly at him; it was the first time he really saw her face.

'Bloody hell,' he said, feeling the colour drain from his face.

'Is that ...?' Blom said.

'It most definitely is,' Berger said. 'That's Lena Nilsson.'

'Are you sure?'

'Of course I'm sure. That's the young Jessica Johnsson. I never actually looked at her back then. Not properly.'

The satellite phone crackled, and Deer's voice said, 'It's her, isn't it?'

Blom zoomed in on the carer's paused face.

'There's something about that look,' she said.

'Yes,' Deer said. 'She wasn't at all happy with what you said there, Sam. Or me laughing. Looking at it again like this, we didn't exactly show a lot of respect.'

'Ugh,' Berger said. 'The memory puts a gloss on a lot of things.'

'I didn't remember that pistol gesture at all,' Deer said.

'Nor me,' Berger said.

'We interviewed the murderers,' Deer said. 'And we let them go.'

'But they remembered the two of you,' Blom said. 'Look at the way she glares at you, she's making a note of that moment, Sam. Eight years later Reine is admitted to a mental hospital under the name Sam Berger, and Jessica addresses her letter directly to you, Desiré. They've had the two of you in their sights for a long time.'

'But what the hell do they want?' Berger exclaimed. 'What does Jessica want with me?'

'Don't know. Maybe she wants an audience, a strong father, someone to set limits and stop her. Maybe she just wants to show off. I don't know. But you're the person she's after, Sam.'

'I need to think this through,' Deer said and disappeared.

'One more time,' Blom said.

They watched the clip again. Blom paused it in the middle of Deer's line: 'What happened when you drew a four-leaf clover, Reine? Did your wish start to come true?'

'Look carefully at Reine now,' Blom said and pressed Play.

Reine Danielsson jerked as if he'd been given an electric shock. Blom paused again.

'What's going on there?' she asked.

The interview table covered the lower part of Jessica and Reine's bodies. Even so, Berger thought he could see. He said, 'You have a tendency to put your hand on my thigh when I'm about to lose my cool or say too much.'

'Happens a bit too often,' Blom said. 'But I see what you're getting at.'

'Reine jerked several times during the interview. Lena Nilsson didn't just put her hand on his thigh, out of sight – she pinched him as well. And that stopped Reine at exactly the right moment. She'd drilled him but didn't dare leave him unsupervised. So she sat there, inconspicuous, like some animal tamer.'

'She was directing the conversation without it showing? By that point she'd worked with people with mental illnesses for a while and had evidently figured out a way of guiding some of them. But we need to go even further back. What do we know about her childhood in Rågsved?'

'Nothing,' Berger said. 'Nothing at all.'

'She was an only child,' Blom said. 'Went to high school in Huddinge. Then there was that unexplained year she spent in the USA immediately afterwards. She came back, did her nurse's training with the Red Cross, worked the night shift in psychiatric units and geriatric wards. Got her qualifications, started working as a bank nurse at St Göran's, mostly on psychiatric wards. It was while she was working there that she met Eddy Karlsson.'

'Was that at St Göran's?' Berger asked. 'Was Eddy a patient?'

Blom shook her head.

'Maybe Laura Enoksson, her old social worker, knows more about this; we'll have to contact her again. Either way, Jessica Johnsson became Lena Nilsson in the spring of 2005. Two years before Orsa. Can I just take a quick look online?'

Berger reluctantly turned the laptop towards her.

'These two blank years need to be examined in much more detail,' Blom said as she tapped energetically at the computer. 'Yes, as soon as she gets her new identity she moves to Falun and starts work at the care home where both Karl Hedblom and Reine Danielsson were already living, where she was able to wrap weak-willed Reine around her little finger. She knew about Karl's background, with his mother and the block of wood, and stole the MO. She handed in her notice not long after Orsa, in October 2007. And Reine left the care home a month or so later. It's not beyond the bounds of possibility that Reine moved in with Lena Nilsson.'

'Was she still living in Falun then? Unemployed? New job?'

'Hmm,' Blom said, staring at the computer. 'This is where it gets interesting. She soon got a new job, in the psychiatric unit at Skåne University Hospital in Malmö. She was working there when one of her colleagues, Mette Hækkerup, had her car accident on the E6. Six months later she got a new job at the Sahlgrenska University Hospital ...'

'In Gothenburg,' Berger said. 'So she was living in Gothenburg when Lisa Widstrand was murdered in a hotel room in the Gothia Towers?'

'Yes. A few months later that same year, 2010, Lena Nilsson bought the house in Porjus, looks like she moved there then. The house was transferred automatically to Jessica Johnsson's ownership when she switched back to her real identity. At that moment all traces of Lena Nilsson's involvement in the purchase were erased.'

'So Reine lived with her in the house in Porjus?' Berger said.

'He probably lived with her in Falun, Malmö and Gothenburg as well, without ever being seen. I've got a bit more on Eddy Karlsson here. The police didn't know he'd come back to Sweden from Thailand because he'd have gone straight to prison if they had. What he did to Jessica was classified as aggravated assault, and that doesn't lapse for fifteen years. It wasn't until he took a fatal overdose in a basement in Bagarmossen in the autumn of 2011 that he was identified as Eddy Karlsson – by a DNA test as well. Can you guess what drug he overdosed on?'

'I'm starting to wonder if it might have been a cocktail ...'

'Correct,' Blom said. 'A cocktail of methamphetamine and phenazepam. Eddy had injected himself with five times the fatal dose. Fellow addicts said under questioning that Eddy had smuggled a load of that particular combination back from Thailand with him. According to one witness statement, he's supposed to have said, "This time no fucker's going to steal this shit from me." The remainder of the stash was never found.'

'Because it's being sent little by little to Karl Hedblom in Säter,' Berger said. 'So Jessica got some use out of Eddy in the end ...'

'But should we interpret that to mean that she'd stolen drugs from him before? "This time no fucker's going to steal this shit from me." She'd done it before. Maybe we've just found the answer to how she and Reine have been supporting themselves.'

'Not impossible ...'

'It's not clear how she found Eddy, though,' Blom said. 'And she refrained from leaving her signature on the body. No block of wood, no knife, no ballpoint pen, no four-leaf clover.'

'Not the right time to leave any evidence, I guess,' Berger said.

'There is one detail here,' Blom said, leaning closer to the screen. 'From the post-mortem report. Eddy had been castrated.'

'Castrated?'

'No half measures, either. His entire genitals had been removed, the whole lot.'

'That's mad. Surely that should have triggered interest from the police? It was pretty obviously murder. In which case surely Jessica ought to have been a suspect?'

'The wounds were well healed, the scar tissue intact. The cause of death was an overdose, nothing else. It was assumed that he'd had an accident during his time in Thailand. It's worth noting that the other addicts hadn't seen Eddy for a couple of months, and the basement where he was found was in an abandoned house they'd never been to.'

'Hang on,' Berger said. 'A couple of months?'

Blom groaned and said, 'I'm imagining a scenario that fits with what we're starting to assume about Jessica Johnsson's nature.'

Berger could feel the colour draining from his face as he went on, 'She and Reine caught Eddy, took him down into the abandoned basement, tied him up and very slowly cut his cock off during a controlled but excruciating medical procedure. Probably involved plenty of antibiotics and transfusions of blood and plasma – everything but painkillers. Eddy survived, but the pain he experienced would have been like nothing on earth, and he would also have been suffering acute withdrawal. Jessica kept him alive long enough for the wound to heal and for scar tissue to form. Only then did she give him the fatal overdose.'

'Eurgh,' Blom said. 'A final act of revenge.'

'Christ,' Berger said, looking at the two photographs of Jessica Johnsson: the calm exterior beneath which hell reigned.

'It's probably worth pointing out that this was one of the few occasions when Reine Danielsson surfaced. The secure psychiatric unit of the Löwenströmska Hospital. Severe psychosis. He was admitted under his own name.'

'He must have suffered a serious breakdown in that basement in Bagarmossen,' Berger said.

'What happened next, after Eddy?' Blom went on. 'They went back to Porjus, then when it was almost summer the following year they attacked Farida Hesari in Täby. But somehow Farida managed to escape. Then it was almost two years until Växjö, and Elisabeth Ström and the biker gang. They managed that one with great precision. That was only last year. Things began to escalate. Jessica had spent several years trying to get your attention, Sam, so now she was forced to try a bit harder. About a month ago Jessica and Reine went to Sorsele to attack Anders and leave the note with the name Berger on it. Reine had another breakdown during the torture and needed to go back to hospital. A couple of weeks of meticulous planning followed. During that time Jessica typed another letter on her typewriter, but this time she addressed it directly to Desiré. At the same time she identified the pregnant Serbian traveller, Jovana Malešević, in Arjeplog. When Jessica collected Reine from the clinic they took the opportunity to kidnap Jovana. Desiré called on the morning of 18 November to say that she was sending two NOD officers. Jessica assumed that one of them would be you. She also needed to be seen in Porjus, to make it look like she'd been gone from the house for several hours. Because it was supposed to look like she'd died, attacked by an unknown assailant, her own DNA had to be replaced everywhere by Jovana's. Hairbrush, toothbrush, Jovana's fingerprints had to be on the typewriter. And then we showed up at three o'clock, and she set the final act in motion. And she definitely wanted you there for the final act, Sam.'

'Holy fuck,' Berger said.

'Afterwards they put Jovana Malešević's body in a trunk, dragged it out to Anders Hedblom's van and disappeared. Hey presto – gone.'

'Hey presto indeed,' Berger said. 'So where are they? And what are they planning next?'

Blom looked at him.

'I'm guessing that the odds were raised in a rather exciting way when you introduced yourself using a fake name, C. Lindbergh. Jessica realised that you were no longer a police officer but were still in contact with Desiré. That made the game even more fun. And now she really does want you to chase her.'

'I still don't see why this is anything to do with me,' Berger said. 'Why me?'

'Because of what we saw on that video clip,' Blom said. 'Because you pushed Reine so hard. Because she thought you'd be a worthy adversary.'

'I still don't get it.'

'Jessica Johnsson wants you to stop her.'

28

The observer is on tenterhooks. He's spent the whole of his adult life on hopeless, drawn-out surveillance jobs, and he shouldn't be on tenterhooks. This is part of ordinary life for him. He knows that, this has always paid his wages.

He spins his Sig Sauer P226 again and again, never letting it stop. No truth, no dare.

And the time passes.

It feels like his sight is getting worse with each passing second. As if every moment kills a cone, slices off a rod. If feels like he's suddenly in a rush, just when keeping a cool head is the only thing that matters. He really does need to be able to see the Rock of Gibraltar one more time, from his own terrace, in his own house, and he really does need to stop being alone. He's been alone for long enough.

The cabins are sitting there on the two screens, like fossils, encased in time that has turned to ice that has turned to stone. Nothing is moving. Nothing except the pistol on the table. The pistol that never stops.

A life of absolute loyalty and fidelity. A life based on never questioning orders.

It's extremely cold in the room. It's as if it's been blasted right into ice-draped stone. As if he's sitting inside the rock at the pole of inaccessibility, ready to burst out.

Time must pass. He is losing control of it. It can no longer be measured, counted. And he's on tenterhooks. The whole time.

Something needs to happen now.

If nothing happens, he'll have to make sure that something happens.

This can't go on. The observer has waited long enough.

While the pistol spins he pulls on the thin leather gloves properly. Then he puts his hand on it. The Sig Sauer stops, pointing towards the screens where the man and woman are noticeable by their absence.

Today the observer doesn't write anything.

Instead he picks up the pistol and walks towards the door.

29

Berger looked at the time. They were sitting almost motionless, waiting for a specific moment. The usual tense activity had petered out. Now most of the activity still going on was taking place internally.

There was a sudden scraping sound outside the cabin. Their eyes met for an instant. They waited, ready for anything. It was a strange noise, sweeping, almost as if something was moving inside the wall.

Then nothing but silence.

Blom took a small step sideways, closer to the table. Right now all their attention was focused on their ears.

Then the sound came again. A quick, sweeping, dragging sound along the wall, clearly moving towards the door.

Blom leaped into action. She threw herself at the table, pulled the red cloth aside, tossed one pistol towards him, and as it spun through the air with peculiar slowness Jessica Johnsson's typewritten words echoed through Berger: 'Because I can hear the noise again, the rapid shuffle, a swift dragging sound. It's never been this close.'

He caught the pistol as the shuffling turned into a couple of definite steps out on the veranda. By then Blom had already rushed past him with her pistol raised, and they both emerged onto the porch, ready to fire.

There was no one there.

It was completely empty.

They stood there with the temperature down to almost minus thirty degrees, scanning the entire area in front of them. There was only whiteness. A completely white surface. Nothing was happening there, there were no signs to interpret.

Berger ran out into the snow, past the place where they showered. He heard Blom behind him, covering his advance. He was behind the cabin now, she was still with him. Nothing. Then round the last wall; nothing there either.

They were back where they had started, both breathing hard. Blom examined the snow around Berger's clumsy footprints. She moved closer, crouched down.

Then she gestured with her pistol. He couldn't see anything. He moved closer and crouched down beside her.

Then he saw the tracks. Small circles made up of smaller circles, like flowers in the snow.

'Arctic fox,' Blom said. 'They're almost invisible, camouflaged white.'

Berger couldn't speak. He looked out across the expanse of snow. He still had a distant look in his eyes.

They went back inside the cabin, tried to calm down. Life-giving heat enveloped them.

Blom's computer made a sudden, persistent ringing sound. Her expression changed as she realised what it meant. And then an elderly woman's face appeared on the screen.

'I told you I knew how to skype,' Laura Enoksson said.

Berger sat down beside Blom, out of range of the camera. He could feel how badly he was shaking.

'I didn't doubt it for a minute,' Blom said, keeping her chattering teeth under control. 'Thanks for getting back to me, Laura. I've got a couple more questions.'

'So I understood,' Enoksson said. 'Shoot.'

Berger saw Blom close her eyes for a moment, which seemed to indicate that she was clearing her mind of irrelevant thoughts and concentrating hard. And quickly.

'How much do you know about Jessica Johnsson's past?' she asked the computer.

'Not much,' Laura Enoksson said. 'A single child from Rågsved. We never talked about her parents, but I could tell it was a sensitive subject.'

'She spent a year in the USA in her late teens,' Blom said.

'She didn't talk about that either.'

'Nothing at all? You saw her after she was assaulted by Eddy Karlsson, you must have spent a lot of time with her, just the two of you. At a very sensitive time.'

'I certainly did,' Enoksson said. 'Little Jessica. Poor girl. Sometimes I felt she had to absorb all the evil that our patriarchal society had to offer. And there was a lot of it.'

'Was she angry?'

'Determined. As if she was waiting for the right moment.'

'The right moment?' Blom said.

'I can't really explain it,' Enoksson said slowly. 'She turned in on herself, as if she was storing everything up. But Ebba probably knows more about all this.'

'Ebba?'

'You must have spoken to Ebba? Her aunt in Gällivare?'

'No, we weren't even aware that she had an aunt in Gällivare.'

'Her name is Ebba Hult,' Laura Enoksson said.

The hearth spread a magical light across the living room of the small one-room apartment. Through the window they could make out the illuminated white shape of Gällivare church. In front of them on the coffee table steam rose from three cups of brewed coffee, alongside a plate laden with seven different types of biscuit, in line with the age-old custom.

Berger stirred his coffee and looked up at the woman. Even though she was in her sixties and her hair completely white, some of her features resembled Jessica Johnsson's. Not least her clear if somewhat restless gaze, and her stern manner.

'So, Mrs Hult,' he said. 'Tell us about your relationship with Jessica.'

'She was my sister's daughter, my niece,' Ebba Hult said. 'As for the state of our relationship, I didn't even know that she was living in Porjus. Not until I heard about what had happened.'

'But she grew up with you in Rågsved?'

'From the age of eight until she was eighteen, yes.'

'Why didn't she live with her parents?'

Ebba grimaced and sipped a little of her coffee.

'Help yourselves to biscuits,' she said, gesturing to the groaning plate. 'I don't get many visitors.'

'Thanks,' Berger said, taking one. There was little doubt that it had sat in the freezer for a number of years.

Ebba nodded. 'My sister Eva and I moved to Stockholm to study, that must have been 1973. She became a preschool teacher,

I became a speech therapist. She met Ove Johnsson and got married in 1978. They had Jessica two years later.'

'But you never married, Ebba?'

'Let's just say that I prefer female company,' she said with a brief smile. 'Especially if the alternative was Ove Johnsson.'

'So you weren't particularly fond of your sister Eva's husband?'

Ebba held her hands up. 'I don't suppose there was really anything wrong with Ove. He was very intelligent, some sort of academic. But he always seemed a bit distant. I don't think he was ever particularly close to his daughter, for instance. After the disaster he just vanished, got away as far as he could – he got some sort of job at the University of Dunedin.'

'And where's that?'

'The South Island of New Zealand,' Ebba said with a wry smile. 'Literally as far away as it's possible to get.'

'You're going to have to tell us about *the disaster*, Ebba.'

Ebba Hult went on nodding for a while, then shook her head instead.

'Everything seemed fine,' she eventually said. 'There was nothing to suggest otherwise. After eight years of being an only child, Jessica was going to get a little brother. Eva was so happy, they'd been trying for so long. What Ove thought remained a mystery, obviously. And I never talked to Jessica about it, but there was no sign that she was unhappy about it.'

'So what happened?'

'A sudden haemorrhage. Some sort of complete placental abruption. Eva was on her own in the house, didn't stand a chance of getting to the phone. It was Jessica who found her. She was eight years old, she had her own key, she got home from school and found her mother and unborn baby brother lying dead in a bloodbath. I looked after her; Ove went off to Dunedin, I don't think he even said goodbye to his daughter. I got custody pretty quickly.'

Berger and Blom looked at each other. Blom closed her eyes and nodded, and Berger went on:

'How did Jessica react? She must have been referred to a child psychiatrist?'

'Yes,' Ebba said. 'Of course. She saw a therapist for a year or so. With me she was always remarkably stable.'

'What about later on? You had custody of her for ten years ...'

'She was calm,' Ebba said. 'Even puberty was uneventful. But there was a distance there. She kept me more and more at arm's length, until she suddenly announced on her eighteenth birthday that she was going to the USA. She was an adult, I couldn't object. Besides, I'd also started to think about moving back to Gällivare.'

'It sounds like you weren't particularly close to each other?'

'We were probably as close as people like her and me could be. I had my secrets, and I dare say she had hers. We each kept to ourselves, fairly shut off, I suppose. I never told her I was a lesbian, for instance.'

'She must have had some sort of interests,' Berger said. 'What did she spend her teenage years doing?'

'She was interested in the Internet,' Ebba said. 'She spent a lot of time in the 90s in various "online communities". I think that's how she came into contact with someone who encouraged her to go to the USA.'

'How about friends?' Berger said. 'She must have had a few friends, at least?'

'She said she did, but they never came to the house.'

'What about boys? Boyfriends?'

'None, as far as I know. I did try to raise the subject a few times, but she just brushed it off.'

'So, the USA,' Berger said. 'What makes you think that had anything to do with online communities?'

'That was one of the few things she used to talk about. How the Internet had given her the opportunity to talk to people who were like her. Not least people in the States.'

Molly Blom leaned forward and spoke for the first time:

'What did "people who were like her" mean? She must have felt different, or she wouldn't have said that. In what way was she different? What were "people who were like her" like?'

Berger added, 'Because to be honest we're not really getting any real sense of who she was. Did you really spend ten years living with Jessica, the ten most formative years in a person's life?'

'She's dead,' Ebba Hult said quietly. 'What does it matter now? Let her rest in peace.'

'She experienced something horrific,' Berger said. 'As an eight-year-old she found her mother dead in a pool of blood, completely out of the blue. That must have left scars, deep-seated scars. You have to give us something more, Ebba. She won't rest in peace if she's resting on a lie.'

'Your parting doesn't sound like it was particularly harmonious,' Blom said. 'Jessica waited until the day she turned eighteen to announce that she was planning to go to the USA, alone, at that age.'

'She must have said why she wanted to go to the States,' Berger said. 'Was it to meet other "people who were like her"?'

'I suppose so,' Ebba said, looking down at the table. 'She said she wanted to see reality, naked reality. Not the protected bubble I'd kept her shut up in.'

'And had you kept her shut up in a protected bubble?'

'Naturally I tried to protect her. She'd been through something no eight-year-old should have to experience.'

'But did you give her security, Ebba?' Blom asked. 'Or did you just give her silence and emptiness.'

Ebba Hult's armour suddenly cracked. Both Berger and Blom saw the past pouring through the gaps in the metal. Or were they witnessing the metal itself melting?

'I tried,' she cried, and her voice broke. 'I really did try. I became a mother very suddenly. I didn't want to be a mother, I'd never planned to be a mother. I didn't know what to do. I thought peace and quiet were what she needed.'

'You couldn't talk to her?' Blom said.

'It was impossible, it was like we were speaking different languages.'

'Even so, you still had to try to find out what she wanted, didn't you? You felt it was your duty as her guardian. What was this "naked reality" she wanted to see? Who were these "people who were like her" that she needed to meet? You must have looked at her computer when she wasn't home? You must have looked at the browsing history to see what sort of "communities" she belonged to? What did you find? Was it something that – if you were to say it out loud – would prevent her resting in peace?'

'I'd like you to leave now,' Ebba said in a fragile voice.

'I'm afraid we're not going to,' Berger said. 'Not until we've found out what we need to know. Which, fortunately, is a pretty good match for the things you need to get off your chest, Ebba.'

She shook her head. Tears dripped onto the table next to the seven different types of biscuit. Blom leaned towards her, stroked her arm, and asked, very clearly:

'Why did Jessica go to the USA, Ebba?'

'She needed to meet other people who were like her, who had experienced serious trauma in their family. She belonged to one online community for people who had seen too much blood, blood from blood relatives, "blood from blood", as they put it. And another one called "absent father". She'd put together a list of names and addresses all over the USA.'

'That sounds almost healthy,' Blom said. 'She wanted to meet others in the same situation, see what survival techniques they'd developed. That seems sensible from a therapeutic point of view. So it can't be that stopping you from talking. What else did you see on Jessica's computer?'

The old woman went on shaking her head. She didn't say anything more. Blom went on, very gently:

'Jessica spent ten years living with her nightmares. I'm glad that there was a positive plan of action, that she – in the absence of being able to talk at home – found other people in the same situation to talk to. But there was something destructive as well, wasn't there, Ebba? Perhaps something self-destructive?'

Ebba picked up a sugar lump, put it between her teeth and reached for her coffee. Slowly she tipped a little coffee into her saucer, then slurped the now tepid liquid into her mouth through the sugar lump.

'Coffee from the saucer,' Blom said with a smile. 'My grandma used to do that too. Said she found it comforting.'

Ebba swallowed the sweet coffee and gave a brief smile.

'Jessica was so quiet. She hardly ever spoke. But when I looked at her browsing history I realised how much was going on behind that tranquil façade. Still waters ...'

'What did you find out, Ebba?' Blom asked calmly. 'What did you see running deep in those still waters?'

'Sex,' Ebba said.

'But not just ordinary sex?'

'I'd never seen anything like it. I used to sneak about online, looking at lesbian porn. But this was something altogether different.'

'What was it, Ebba?'

'She was seventeen,' Hult exclaimed. 'She shouldn't have been looking at things like that. She shouldn't have been talking to people like that.'

'What was it?'

'I don't even know how to describe it. Domination, perhaps. Rough sex, violence, submission.'

Blom cast a quick glance at Berger. His face was completely neutral, giving nothing at all away.

'Porn then?' Blom said eventually. 'But not just porn? She was *talking* to people of that sort as well?'

'It was a community …'

'Based around sadomasochism?'

'I suppose that's what it's called … She chatted a lot with a girl called Joy. And then, when she filled in all those complicated forms to get residence and work visas and all that, she gave Joy's name as her contact in the USA. When I think about the things they talked about …'

'So Jessica applied for a work permit too?'

'She hadn't worked while she was in high school,' Hult said. 'And I didn't have much money I could give her. She was planning to work over there, that much was very plain.'

'Did you confront her about that?'

'I did … I yelled at her, asked if she was planning to work as a whore in the USA. I'm ashamed of it now, so horribly ashamed.'

'And was she thinking of working as a whore in the USA?'

'I don't think so, I just blurted that out. But Joy knew someone she could work for, she'd been working there herself for a while. I don't know what happened in the end.'

'Jessica gave Joy as her contact in the USA,' Blom said. 'So you sneaked a look at the forms? You saw what Joy's surname was?'

'Her name was Joy Wiankowska, and she lived in Hollywood.'

'Hollywood, Los Angeles? The real Hollywood?'

'Yes, it said California.'

Blom turned demonstratively towards Berger, but when she saw that he was already busy googling she went on:

'Did Jessica call from the USA to ask for money? Did she mention Joy then?'

'Yes, they were room-mates in Hollywood. A couple of months had passed, and then I didn't hear from her again until towards the end of her stay. By then I'd already moved back here. With Elena.'

'Elena?'

'We lived together for four years,' Ebba said with a little smile. 'Then she got cancer and died. She's buried out there.'

She gestured towards the church outside the window.

'In the cold,' Hult added. 'In the frozen ground. I suppose Jessica's buried somewhere similar.'

'It's probably even colder where she is,' Blom said, glancing at Berger again. He held up three fingers.

Three Joy Wiankowskas? In the USA? In Los Angeles? Now wasn't the time to ask. She just nodded encouragingly at him.

He stayed silent, recognising that it was better to let her do the talking. Maybe he had learned something after all.

'Thank you, Ebba,' Blom said, leaning closer to the sobbing woman and giving her a quick hug.

'You were right,' Ebba said, with tears running down her cheeks. 'I needed to say that. I needed to let it out.'

'If you feel even the slightest bit guilty about Jessica, Ebba, you can stop that right now. I promise you, she isn't worth it.'

'Perhaps you'd like to see some pictures?' Hult suddenly said, wiping her tears. 'I've never been all that interested in photographs, I've hardly even got any of Elena, but Ove had a sort of – I don't know – *clinical* interest in photography.'

She stood, considerably more nimbly than when she had opened the door to them, and darted out to a door in the hall. She opened it to reveal a magnificently well ordered closet. She vanished inside it, and they could hear her bustling about in there.

Berger whispered, 'Three Joy Wiankowskas in the whole of the USA. With a bit of luck we'll be able to get in touch today, tonight.'

Ebba Hult emerged from the closet clutching a shoebox. She put it down heavily on the coffee table, knocking some of the biscuits off their plate. Then she lifted the lid.

The photographs in the box were the classical sort. None of them had been anywhere near any sort of digital processing, they were yellowing and had evidently been developed in a darkroom, and they weren't arranged in any discernible order.

Berger and Blom's reaction was a combination of deep sigh and silent jubilation. Berger pulled out almost all of them in a messy bundle and divided it roughly in two. In the meantime Ebba Hult put another old-fashioned sugar lump between her teeth, filled her saucer with coffee, and let the sugar dissolve as she drank from the saucer.

Berger leafed through the photographs and saw Blom doing the same. They were mostly pictures of a toddler, as if Ove Johnsson's interest had waned after that. Sometimes, completely out of order, a photograph of a slightly older child would appear. It was definitely Jessica Johnsson, at various ages and in traditional contexts. Midsummer, Christmas, snow, skiing, swimming, at the beach. There was hardly anyone but Ove, Eva and Jessica in the pictures, and occasionally, always in the background, a young Ebba Hult. Berger found himself speeding up, as if he was gradually realising that there was nothing useful to be gleaned from the heap of photographs. He saw Blom going faster as well, and he very nearly missed the photograph altogether.

He stopped, went back, stared.

He saw Blom stop to look at him. She put her own pile of pictures down.

He looked more closely at the photograph. It was high summer, the sun was glinting off what looked like a small lake in the background. In the foreground sat a child of about eight. The child was holding something up towards the camera with a broad if somewhat forced smile. It was large and green, and the photographer had managed to gauge the shutter speed and focus so well that nothing in the picture was blurred in spite of the obvious differences in distance.

It was all crystal-clear. The lake in the background, the strangely smiling eight-year-old Jessica Johnsson in the centre, and in the foreground the plant she was holding up towards the camera.

The four-leaf clover she was holding up towards the camera.

Because it was so close to the camera it was impossibly large, almost as big as young Jessica's smiling face.

Berger held the photograph up towards Blom, then passed it to Ebba. She took it, looked at it, shook her head blankly and turned it over.

'I don't know when or where this was taken,' she said. 'But there's something written on the back.'

She picked up her glasses case from the table, and fumbled for a moment before managing to put her reading glasses on. Then she said, 'It's very childish writing. It must have been written by Jessica herself.'

She moved the photograph closer to her face.

'The writing's tiny,' Ebba said. 'It's very hard to read.'

'Try,' Berger said as he looked at the picture of Jessica and the four-leaf clover.

She tried. And read out, '"When you find a four-leaf clover you get to make a wish."'

Berger nodded. Blom nodded. Ebba Hult went on reading, '"I don't want a little brother."'

30

The possibly lethal meat soup had long since been replaced by coffee. Black, vicious coffee, the sort that gives you little choice but to stay awake all night. They were sitting in Blom's cabin, staring hollow-eyed at the empty computer screen.

The soup had been preceded by a stop at a petrol station outside Gällivare and a couple of potentially even more lethal hot dogs, but they had tasted divine. After that Blom had gone to the toilet while Berger quickly hurried back out into the cold. He had loitered by the refuelled jeep, facing away from the security camera, watching a video clip on his mobile, a very short film that consisted of an index finger moving across the keypad of a satellite phone. Then he made a call.

'Yes, Sam?' Deer said at the other end.

'Urgent and top secret,' Berger said. 'Have you got access to one of your decoys?'

'Not again.' Deer sighed. 'Another body?'

'I'm shocked that you'd think that of me,' Berger said, trying to sound upset.

'Nothing would surprise me any more,' Deer said. 'What's this about?'

'I need someone to call a mobile number, someone who can't be traced back to either you or me. I want them to listen very carefully to whoever answers. Hopefully this person will say their name. After that it would be good if the caller could do some drunken shouting, make it look like a genuine wrong number. Could that be arranged?'

'Obviously without me knowing what this is about?' Deer said.

'For your own safety's sake, yes,' Berger said. 'Can it be done?'

'Not right away,' Deer said.

'As soon as possible,' Berger said. 'Answer via email, not any other way. Using our old code?'

'Ah,' Deer said. 'It's like that, is it?'

Then Berger gave her a mobile phone number and hung up.

And now Berger and Blom were staring wide-eyed at a computer screen that looked dead.

'Already eleven minutes overdue,' Berger said.

He looked at her through the darkness but said nothing more.

Time passed. Twelve minutes, thirteen. Fourteen.

Berger took another slurp of cold pitch-black coffee. It trickled down his throat as slowly and sluggishly as the seconds ticked past inside the dark cabin.

'Her father,' Berger said. 'Ove Johnsson. A professor of neuro-endocrinology in New Zealand. Worth contacting?'

Blom just shook her head.

'Aren't you even curious to find out what neuroendocrinology is?'

Another headshake, more emphatic this time.

Eighteen minutes overdue. Nineteen. Berger said,

'She was eight years old, and had got used to being an only child. Her mum got pregnant, was expecting a boy. She found a four-leaf clover. She got to make a wish, and she wished not to have a little brother. Not long after that her wish came true, in the worst, most nightmarish way. The four-leaf clover is a sign of her destroying the relationship between mother and son.'

'Can't you just be quiet?' Blom said.

Berger fell silent. He agreed with her.

He ought to keep quiet.

At twenty-two minutes past two a call came through on the computer, and the apparently dead screen lit up with a Skype window that initially showed nothing but static. A voice emerged from the stripes.

'Hello?' it said in English. 'Did I call the right number? Ms Bloom?'

'Yes,' Blom said. 'This is Molly Blom. We have a slight problem with the picture. Is this Ms Wiankowska? Joy Wiankowska from Los Angeles?'

'That's about right,' the stripes said and slowly started to settle into the outline of a person.

And then the picture was suddenly there. The orange glow of dusk lit up the darkened cabin, showing them what the sun could look like. The silhouette gradually came into view, until eventually the image was clear: a slim woman in her early forties, gently Slavic features, with a multicoloured, multi-layered cocktail in front of her. It matched the sky behind her, where the sun was busy drowning. In a slightly exaggerated Californian accent she said, 'If I understood you correctly, this isn't an official statement regarding a police operation?'

'I'm a private detective,' Blom said in unexpectedly precise Oxford English. 'Nothing you say will go outside my office.'

'Not that I've got anything to hide,' the woman said.

'This isn't actually about you, Ms Wiankowska. I'm interested in an old friend of yours, and none of what we discuss will have any negative repercussions for you.'

'An old friend? A Swedish friend? A girlfriend? Jessica?'

'Exquisite deduction,' Blom said. 'As I understand it, you and Jessica Johnsson were room-mates in Hollywood for a while in 1998. Is that correct? You were both young, had come into contact with each other over the Internet, and eventually you helped Jessica to get a job?'

'It's all a very long time ago,' Joy Wiankowska said and frowned. 'I was living a different life back then. Mixing with the wrong people.'

'Like Jessica, perhaps you had a fairly turbulent past,' Blom said. 'I'm in no position to make any moral judgements, and I don't have any intention of doing so. But when Jessica left Sweden, she gave your name as her contact in the USA.'

'God, yes,' Wiankowska said. 'We'd talked a lot about it on an online forum. Back then I hadn't really found the right way of dealing with my past. We're talking about a time before a hell of a lot of hours of therapy.'

'Tell me what you remember. Is it OK if I call you Joy?'

'Seeing as you probably can't pronounce Wiankowska.' Wiankowska laughed. 'That's fine, Molly, I can hardly pronounce it myself any more. Anyway, my surname will soon be Cabot. Joy Cabot. And then the transformation will be complete. Right now I'm sitting on one of four balconies belonging to the Cabot Estate in Santa Barbara.'

'You and Jessica Johnsson came into contact online?'

'That's right,' Wiankowska said. 'We shared a certain type of curiosity.'

'Curiosity?'

'It was like ordinary sexual expression wasn't really enough for people with our background.'

'A traumatic background?'

'Yes, a background soaked in blood. I did get a sense that Jessica was something of a poser rather than someone who was genuinely looking for a solution to her problems. But we still got close to each other in cyberspace. I'd just left a position as private secretary to Madame Newhouse, and suggested that Jessica should take over from me.'

'Who was Madame Newhouse?'

'She's been dead a couple of years now, but she was on the periphery of one of the wealthiest families in the USA. She was famous for arranging some of the most extravagant parties in Hollywood. And she took a liking to Jessica. She was calm, sensible, controlled and something of an exhibitionist. She got the job.'

'And what did the job consist of?'

'Like I said, private secretary. Jessica managed, very competently, the more private parts of Madame Newhouse's organisation. A large PR company had responsibility for the official parts.'

'And what did the private parts of the organisation consist of?'

'Private parties,' Wiankowska said. 'Unofficial. Not always entirely above board.'

'I'm afraid I'm going to have to ask you to be a little more explicit, Joy,' Blom said.

Wiankowska turned and looked out across the deepening pink of the Pacific Ocean. When she turned back her expression had changed. She said seriously, 'She invited people to parties. Featured in video films that in turn functioned as invitations.'

'And what did "featured in" mean?'

'I'll leave that to your imagination, Molly.'

'But these were sadomasochistic parties?'

Wiankowska turned away again towards the vast ocean and watched the last sliver of sun disappear over the horizon. The pinkness melted into a darker shade of red for a moment until all light disappeared from the surface of the water.

'You could call them that,' Wiankowska said. 'If you want to keep things simple.'

'You're going to have to speak plainly now, Joy. Just a few days ago Jessica Johnsson murdered a young pregnant woman in a particularly cruel way, for kicks. And I need to get hold of her. You can help me understand.'

Wiankowska's expression didn't change much. She stared straight up at the darkening sky and kept her eyes there. Then she slowly nodded, 'I don't suppose it's possible that Jessica could have used a ... slave?'

'A slave?'

'A strong but not particularly intelligent man whom she guides and dominates? Purely hypothetically?'

Berger watched as Blom's face moved closer to the screen.

'Hypothetically, that's a very strong possibility,' she said.

Wiankowska grimaced and said, 'At those unofficial parties Madame Newhouse was able to be herself. She was the foremost dominatrix in Hollywood. She had a domestic slave, Rob, an extremely strong but seriously troubled man who obeyed her every whim.'

'Whim?'

'Guests knew that attending Madame Newhouse's unofficial parties wasn't entirely free of risk, that was part of the excitement. There was always a risk of running into Rob, whether you were male or female.'

'Violence? Sex? Assault?'

'Yes to all of the above,' Wiankowska said. 'Anything that managed to reach Madame Newhouse's high appetite threshold.'

'Appetite threshold?'

'Come on, Molly, you're not a child. Anything that could turn her on. She was fairly detached most of the time, it took an awful lot to get her going. But when that happened, the whole party went along with it.'

'Including her private secretary?'

'Absolutely. You were only there because you shared a particular type of desire, something more demanding than plain old vanilla. But occasionally you could end up seeing a bit too much.'

'Did that apply to Jessica too?'

Wiankowska leaned back and frowned.

'I don't honestly know,' she said. 'I keep coming back to the word poser when I think of Jessica. She had a certain detachment that meant things didn't really affect her. I can't help wondering if she was more interested in the impression she made rather than what she was actually experiencing. It was all about being seen the whole time.'

'Seen by whom?'

'Anyone who could validate her. For most of us those sado-masochistic games were deadly serious. I'm not sure the same thing applied to Jessica. And I'm not sure that Jessica stopped because it got too much for her. It was more like she'd exhausted that world and was ready to move on to the next one, where some father figure could validate her by offering moral judgement and maybe even trying to stop her.'

'A father figure, you said?'

'There was a big father complex there, yes. As if she'd always felt the lack of having someone to rebel against. And now I can hear the unmistakable patter on the stairs that can only mean that Grumpy, Happy, Sleepy and Bashful are on their way up to the balcony. Once I've been showered in Great Dane saliva, it's time for the prince himself, Barron Cabot, to enter the stage. I must bid you farewell, Molly. I hope you catch your murderer.'

'One last question,' Blom said. 'Are you happy, Joy?'

Joy Wiankowska laughed loudly and said, 'It's probably fair to say that my appetite threshold is pretty high.'

The Skype window went dark. Just a very, very faint light filtered out into Molly Blom's cabin.

They sat in silence. After a while they looked at each other. Both of their faces were hard to read.

'Bloody hell,' Berger eventually said.

'Pieces of the puzzle,' Blom said. 'In a funny way I kind of hate it when they all fall into place.'

'Rob,' Berger said. 'And Madame Newhouse.'

'And the father figure,' Blom said. 'Daddy Sam Berger who shoots with his fingers.'

Suddenly it felt like the light in the cabin grew brighter. They both looked at the computer screen, but nothing had changed there. Berger stood up and went over to his laptop, but that too was dark. Blom leaned over towards the window and gazed up at the night sky.

Then she stood up and grabbed Berger's hand. She pulled him towards the door. She opened it and they stepped out onto the small veranda.

And the sky was burning. A yellow-green ribbon was sweeping quickly across the heavens, like a vast curtain in a wild, gusty wind. It divided and danced into shades of blue that gradually turned red and formed an immense arc. There was a faint crackling sound and a weaker whining, and then the ribbon turned into rays that shot out across the whole of the visible sky.

'The Northern Lights,' Blom whispered breathlessly. 'The aurora borealis. I never thought I'd get to see it.'

Berger put his arm around her and pulled her closer to him. She put her arm around him in turn.

They stood like that for a length of time that could never be measured.

In the end Berger said, 'What sort of world have we ended up in, Molly?'

31

The worst of it was that she could feel it in the air.

Deer was sitting in her room off the NOD corridor in police headquarters, and had a very clear sense that the prevailing peace was merely the calm before the storm.

Even so, she didn't really have any idea of exactly how much was about to happen. All at once.

In the short time he had been her boss, Superintendent Conny Landin had never made anything but a completely ridiculous impression. But the stern look on his wide face as he threw her door open suggested a seriousness that she hadn't thought was in his repertoire.

Landin got straight to the point, 'You used to work with Sam Berger, didn't you?'

When you live a double life, you're constantly tense. The initial reaction when you are finally found out is a paradoxical feeling of relief. Only in the second wave do you think about the consequences of the revelation. Deer was in the middle of the second wave, in the middle of thinking that they probably wouldn't be able to afford to stay in their little terraced house, when she realised that the look on Conny Landin's face signalled something very different. There was no accusation there, but something else. This was about Sam, not her. Another brief burst of relief ran through her.

'Yes?' she said.

'OK,' Landin said and scratched his head. 'These earlier victims with four-leaf clovers on their buttocks that you've dug out, Mette Hækkerup, Farida Hesari, Elisabeth Ström ... I had a tip-off ...'

'What's happened, Conny?'

'I've had an anonymous tip-off that some of the evidence was ignored. The Hækkerup case is down in Malmö, and Ström is in Växjö, but we've got Hesari here in the store. I went down to see what we've got, and sure enough, there was a small evidence bag that hadn't been dealt with. Biological material. I sent it off for analysis.'

'Analysis?'

'DNA,' Landin said. 'It was Sam Berger's DNA.'

'Hang on,' Deer said. 'What are you saying? What sort of material?'

'Hair,' Landin said. 'There was hair from your old colleague in the blood on Farida Hesari's abused body. The Täby police never looked at it in their investigation. My theory is that Sam Berger somehow got to them, persuaded them to overlook the strands of hair.'

Deer just stared at him. He went on, 'I've asked Malmö and Växjö to look through their old material – I'm hoping to get a response soon – but there can hardly be any doubt that we're dealing with a rotten ex-cop here, and in the worst-case scenario, a serial killer. And we can't get hold of him. I'm on the verge of issuing a national alert. Desiré, if you know where Berger is, now is the right time to say.'

'I've got no idea,' Deer said. She could feel that her face wasn't looking quite the way she would have liked.

Conny Landin walked out. Deer sat still, unable to bring herself to move. What was all this about? She needed to process the information. Just how smart was Jessica Johnsson? Then she thought about the police store and the deeply unpleasant Robertsson. 'This is starting to feel like a production line.' The old investigations were about to be opened up again: had Jessica managed to slip Sam's DNA into them all?

Or was it simpler than that? Was Sam Berger a serial killer?

Like hell he was. She had to warn him. But she daren't call him, not now. She started to write an email ready for encryption: 'Sam, we need to talk asap. Important.'

She didn't get any further that that before her unofficial mobile phone rang. She saw who it was. Tompa, one of her anonymous decoys. She had to take the call, but before she answered she pressed Record.

A few minutes later she emerged from a conversation that under any other circumstances would have left her deeply shocked. But right now it did no more than make a few ripples on the surface of the water. She saved the audio file, added it to the email to be encrypted, and went on writing: 'Sam, we need to talk asap. Important. More important than ever that you stay below the radar. National alert being issued, explain later. Also had a call from one of our shared assets, you'll recognise the voice, I'm attaching the file. We can discuss that under quieter circumstances.'

While she was typing an email arrived and immediately caught her attention. It contained a telephone number. She called it at once. As she waited for the call to be picked up, she permanently deleted the email containing the number.

'Yes?' a voice answered after a couple of rings.

'This is Detective Superintendent Desiré Rosenkvist from the National Operations Department of the police. I've just received an email. Have I called the right number?'

'Yes, you have,' a quiet female voice said. 'The carbon dioxide plant in a quarter of an hour. Don't look for me, I'll find you.'

And with that she was gone.

Once again Deer looked at her mobile before staring into space for a while. What was it Sam had said? 'There are too many questions again. I'm shutting down.' Deer felt that she was coming very close to shutting down. She stood up and walked towards the door. Halfway into the corridor she stopped, went back inside, finished the email, encrypted it and sent it off to Berger. Then she removed all trace of it.

She walked back to her car and got in.

The carbon dioxide plant, she thought. She knew it was in the old Lövholmen industrial area, on the edge of Liljeholmen, somewhere close to the Paint Factory, which had been an art gallery for the past couple of decades. She crossed a number of bridges, the big Western Bridge, then the Liljeholmen Bridge. As she approached the waterside the ramshackle carbon dioxide plant appeared in marked contrast to the renovated industrial units.

It lay opposite the Paint Factory, down by the water of Liljeholmsviken. Against the metallic grey November sky the dilapidated buildings looked like a scene from an apocalyptic disaster movie.

There was a boom across the main entrance, and she wandered along a fence that felt endless until she finally found a hole and crept through it. Instinctively she put her hand to the left side of her chest and felt her service pistol throb like an extra heart.

It was probably her own heart beating so hard that it was making the gun bounce.

Graffiti by the entrance announced in English ENTER BUT BEWARE, and the area was littered with so much rubbish that it felt almost artistically arranged, as if the Paint Factory had been involved. Old electronic equipment, syringes, paint tins, mattresses, mouldy porn magazines. And then suddenly a concrete wall topped with barbed wire.

Feeling increasingly disheartened, she made her way along the wall until she found a ladder leaning against it. She climbed it, jumped down the other side and made her way into what seemed to be the main building, clambering through a broken window.

In the first room there was a stub of candle on a half-rotten table next to a mattress with a duvet that had stiffened in a very odd position, as if some sort of liquid had stuck it to the wall when it dried. Deer switched on the Record function on her phone; it was starting to feel like it was time. Just as she was skirting a large hole in the floor a figure appeared in a doorway.

Deer unzipped her jacket as she stared at it but made no further move. Then she recognised the figure.

'Farida?' she said. 'Farida Hesari?'

The cropped-haired woman walked away, and Deer followed her through rubbish-strewn corridors until they reached a larger room. Streaks of metal-grey November light filtered through gaps in the ceiling, illuminating a space that looked like it had only just been cleared. There were two chairs. Farida Hesari sat down on one of them, Deer on the other, facing her. She said, 'You look well, Farida.'

Farida snorted; it could have been a laugh.

'Seriously,' Deer went on. 'You look like you're in good shape.'

'I'm never going to feel that defenceless again, I can promise you that. I'm here to tell you what happened in July four years ago, nothing else. Do you want to listen?'

'I want to listen,' Deer said.

'I heard you were looking for me. Have you lot finally decided to give a damn about the fact that those sick bastards are still on the loose?'

'We definitely give a damn,' Deer said. 'But you've been hard to get hold of. You disappeared to the Philippines four years ago and haven't been back since.'

'Do you want me to tell you or not?' Farida said.

'One question first,' Deer said. 'Were you pregnant when it happened?'

Farida's eyes narrowed.

'Are you messing with me, bitch? That showed up in the tests they did at Danderyd, and you know that. I'm here to tell you the truth, so why are you trying to trick me?'

'Sorry,' Deer said, honestly. 'I was wondering if you or your girlfriend had managed to hide it somehow. Because that plays a significant role in this case. These two only seem to attack the mothers of boys, women who are either already mothers, or about to be.'

'I already had a son,' Farida said. 'For José Maria's sake, if nothing else, I had to survive that shit.'

'His name's José Maria?' Deer said and smiled.

'After José Maria Sison,' Farida said, and what could have been the shadow of a smile crossed her face.

'The Philippine revolutionary, right?'

'Clever cop,' Farida said. 'The NDF is the only seriously functional movement in the world. And right now the situation

300

in the Philippines is completely fucked, thanks to that bastard Duterte's reign of terror.'

'But your son José Maria isn't registered here in Sweden? He doesn't have a Swedish ID number? So he was born outside the Swedish system? I can't help wondering how Jessica found out that you had a son ...'

'Jessica? Is that her name? The monster?'

'I thought it was Reine who was the monster?'

'Like hell it was! That big bozo just acts as an extra pair of arms for her. Or whatever body part you care to pick.'

'Can we come back to that? So you were living in the centre of Täby, in those big curved blocks?'

'Grindtorp, yes. On Meteorvägen.'

'You were hiding from your family, is that right? Were you being threatened at all?'

'Religion is the opium of the masses,' Farida said. 'My family follow an evil faith. A volatile mixture of patriarchy and religiosity.'

'Did you go out in Grindtorp with José Maria? Out in public?'

'I stayed hidden for a hell of a long time. I was eighteen when Ritva and I decided to have a child. A revolutionary comrade, adopted from the Philippines, actually, gave us some sperm. Apart from our friends, no one knew about Ritva. I stayed hidden in her flat in Grindtorp. I spent something like a whole year indoors. We handled the birth ourselves, obviously. Then eventually I started to go out with the pushchair. No one knew who I was, hell, there was no better place to be anonymous in the whole of Sweden.'

'That must have been when Jessica saw you,' Deer said. 'You were very lucky you didn't take José Maria with you that July morning when you went out to buy cigarettes.'

'I realise that now,' Farida said, shaking her head. 'I may think my family are sick, but they're nothing compared to those perverted capitalist pigs. Typical fucking hierarchy.'

'So, Farida, it was a Sunday morning?'

'Yes, there was no one about in Grindtorp. I knew I'd have a long walk to find a shop that was open. But I didn't get very far. She was sitting on a bench just a few stairwells away. She had long blonde hair and she smiled at me, asked what time it was. I heard a noise behind me, a sort of whistling sound, but it was too late. I felt a flash of terrible pain at the back of my head, then everything went black.'

'You were hit on the back of the head,' Deer said. 'Do you know what with?'

'A block of wood,' Farida said. 'I'd soon get to know that even better.'

'Please, go on if you can.'

'That's why I'm here. So, Jessica and Reine, eh? Nice, traditional Swedish names ...'

'Straight from the masses,' Deer said with a wry smile.

'I woke up in a cellar,' Farida went on. 'I was tied with those plastic strips you have to pull to tighten, to a chair that must have been fixed to the ground. And I was naked. The walls and ceiling were covered in some sort of fibreglass insulation, but there was a window with very thick glass at ground level, facing what looked like forest. They'd covered it with some sort of thick curtain, but a bit of light was getting in. And you could see the trees.'

'What happened when you came round?'

'There was a table. On the table were a large knife and a block of wood. There was also a sofa. They were sitting on the sofa. You could hardly see them in the darkness.'

Farida fell silent. She looked up at the gaps in the ceiling. The light filtering through the factory was coldly neutral, passing no judgement on either the living or the dead.

'They were sitting still,' Farida went on. 'It only started when I woke up. It was like the curtain had been raised. The first thing I saw was her pulling her hair off.'

'Pulling her hair off?'

'It was a wig, a blonde wig. Beneath she had brown hair, cut in a sort of bob. Then she leaned back in the sofa, into the darkness again.'

'Into the darkness? Did it feel like the lighting had been carefully arranged?'

'When she leaned forward I could see her, when she leaned back she disappeared. I think it was to do with the curtain over the window. Carefully arranged? Yes, I think so. Blood was running into one of my eyes, so I could only see them through a red mist.'

'What were they doing?'

'I don't really know. They were naked. The sofa was covered in plastic, and then I noticed that the floor was as well. I remember the sound of their buttocks squeaking against the plastic ...'

Deer let out a deep sigh. She wanted to stop now. She wanted to say that was enough, pull back, think about her family, her wonderful daughter Lykke, spend some time trying to come to terms with the endless insanity of the world. Like she had done so many times before. Instead she said, 'Then what happened?'

'Vague movements,' Farida said. 'It looked like sex, but I don't really know.'

'Did Reine have an erection?'

'The crazy thing is that I'm not sure. It was like it was happening behind some sort of screen.'

'She must have said something?'

'She never spoke to me directly. But she kept telling him what to do to me ...'

'Sexual acts?'

'No. I think he might have been impotent ... No, she told him to hit me. I kept drifting in and out of consciousness. It hurt, it really fucking hurt.'

'She told him to hit you?'

'And how. She told him how. I remember that. One time I passed out properly. I thought I was dying. I remember screaming Ritva's name, José Maria's name. I was happy those were the last words to pass my lips in this rotten, shitty life. It kind of made up for some of the crap.'

'But you regained consciousness?'

'I came round and found that I had been untied, at least briefly. My legs were free, and were being held up. The weird thing is that she was doing the lifting. Because he was busy doing something else.'

'Is it hard to talk about?'

'It's all hard to talk about. He was drawing on my backside with a pen.'

'He was the one doing the drawing? Not her?'

'It was him. It was the only time he seemed happy. But I've got no idea what he was drawing.'

'A four-leaf clover,' Deer said, still somewhat taken aback. 'What happened next?'

'She said something about the knife. He picked it up, held it up towards me. I saw it sink into my arm. It took several seconds for the pain to register. I could see things happening in the darkness, I could see movement again. I watched my blood pouring out. I saw the way he raised the knife again. The important thing was that I saw the way he raised the knife. If there was going to be another chance ...'

'Go on if you can, Farida,' Deer said. She could feel her hand shaking in her lap.

'I came round again,' Farida said, and then it all came tumbling out. 'I don't know how much time had passed this time, but I could see it was dark outside. Again. And then I saw my body, how covered in blood it was, maybe there was some moonlight or something. I was fading away. And she was actually asleep on the sofa now, I could hear her snoring, but he was awake, staring at me. I begged him, I remember begging him with all the strength I could muster, quietly, so I didn't wake her. I begged him to let me go, I pleaded and begged, and he did actually get to his feet without her waking up, and he walked over to me, and I looked into his eyes, and they weren't as dead as I had thought, there was something there, life, maybe even some sort of kindness in the midst of all the insanity, and he took hold of the knife, but not the way he did before, not to stab or kill me – and I didn't know if I was dreaming – but more to cut me loose than to cut me, but then she woke up with a start, sat up abruptly and roared something that I've only just realised was his name: "Reine!" and he jerked back, cowering, then changed his grip on the knife, more aggressive again, ready to attack, and I recognised the posture because I'd kept on practising my martial arts even though I was pregnant, and I knew I would only get one chance, and that was when he was holding the knife just above my wrist, and it happened, the knife came closer, and I threw myself forward as hard as I could, making that fucking knife cut into my wrist, I remember, it cut a chunk of skin off, but it also cut through that fucking plastic strap, and I managed to grab the knife, I took it off him with my right hand, jerked it up and hit him hard in the neck with the handle, and he collapsed on top of me, and I cut through the other strap in a flash and then hit him in the neck again, and there was a crunching sound and he slumped down, and sort of dribbled down my legs and just lay there, and she jumped up, shrieking, and I leaned forward and felt all kinds of stuff pouring out of me, but I managed to reach my ankles and cut those plastic straps too, stood up, kicked his curled-up body in the neck with my heel, then trod on him hard, pressing him into that bloody plastic, and she came at me, but I had the knife and managed to get up the stairs. She was roaring at me like some crazed animal, it was like she was putting on a performance. There was a key in the cellar door. I turned it, then took the key. Then I threw the knife right at her, ran out and locked the door behind me. Then I felt my way through the dark house until I found the door. The forest was right outside, and I ran until I collapsed and the first rays of the July sun were peeping through the trees. I stared down at my body, it was red with blood. And I still didn't think I was going to survive, not even when that little boy in that ridiculous uniform, his face whiter than any I've ever seen, was staring at me with both hands pressed to his mouth.'

Farida Hesari fell silent. She was standing up now, at some point during her story she must have stood up without Deer noticing. Everything felt rigid and stiff, the interior of the old factory had frozen to ice.

Deer got to her feet. She held her hands out awkwardly towards Farida. They stood like that for a while. Deer could feel tears running down her cheeks, and it didn't even occur to her to wipe them away.

Then Farida fell into her arms. They stood there hugging each other for a long time. The light surrounded them and they conquered its icy indifference, unable to let go of each other.

Just as they were about to part Farida whispered:

'I lied.'

Deer was still holding her upper arms tenderly, looking at her. They hugged again, more perfunctorily this time.

'What did you lie about, Farida?' Deer asked.

'He cut me loose,' Farida whispered. 'He freed me and let me go. She was asleep the whole time.'

Deer closed her eyes.

Of course.

Any sort of ninja activity would have been impossible in the state she was in. She had been lying to herself. Deer whispered:

'Did he say anything? Did anything worth remembering happen?'

'No,' Farida whispered. 'He was completely silent. The whole time, I think. But there really *was* a sort of kindness in his eyes.'

Deer stepped back slightly and said, 'Farida, I really hope that you've got past this now – I kind of feel that you have. That there's a life beyond it.'

'Not here, though,' Farida said. 'Not in Sweden. José Maria is still in Manila. That's where our lives are now. But we're probably going to move out to one of the islands soon. I just came back for this.'

Deer looked up at the ceiling and said, 'I'll find my own way out.'

She left Farida deep inside the old carbon dioxide plant. She looked so tiny. Even so, she seemed to be lit up from inside.

Deer walked to the door, made her way back through the dilapidated corridors. When she saw the table and half-burned candle and the mattress with the stiffened duvet she realised that the window she had climbed in through was only a few metres away. The greyish light shining through it felt nothing but comforting.

Deer took a couple more steps. Then she heard a creak and a whistling sound behind her.

Then everything went black.

32

Where were Jessica Johnsson and Reine Danielsson?

That was all they needed to know.

That was it.

Berger was reading through all the available preliminary investigations as hard as he could. Sooner or later something would pop up, soon he was bound to hear the familiar sound of a penny dropping.

Blom was engaged in something more concrete. The printer was churning out pictures. She was cutting and pasting and wandering over to the wall and pinning things in place.

'What are you doing?' Berger asked.

'Gathering together pictures of the victims,' Blom said, pinning up the most recently printed photograph. 'Photographs taken from the time they were attacked. I'm think I'm getting close to some sort of conclusion.'

'Feel free to let me know when you get there,' Berger said.

He had been reading without a break for at least two hours; he even found himself longing for some of that meat soup. His laptop pinged, an email that had somehow been delayed in the ether, sent at 10.24. That annoyed him.

He opened it. The sender was encrypted, as was the email. He decrypted it, saw it was from Deer and read it.

'Sam, we need to talk asap. Important. More important than ever that you stay below the radar. National alert being issued, explain later. Also had a call from one of our shared assets, you'll recognise the voice, I'm attaching the file. We can discuss that under quieter circumstances. I have to go out for a while now, I'll let you know how I get on. // Deer.'

Berger stared at the message. A national alert, he thought. Who for? For him, Sam Berger? What the hell for? What was going on?

He had to put that question to one side, it was impossible to get his head around it. Instead he looked at the attached audio file. He took out a pair of earphones, stuffed them in his ears and pressed Play.

Deer's voice appeared in his head, 'Tompa, have you made the call?'

'Yes, course I have,' a wasted-sounding voice said. 'Sten.'

'What do you mean?'

'Sten gun. Stentorian. Yeah, stentorian. You know who Stentor was? An ancient Greek – my neighbour told me, she's some sort of professor, I think. Something like that. "The Greeks' herald during the Trojan War had a voice so powerful he could drown out fifty other men." So there, Des'reeeeee. A big, deep, stentorian voice.'

'None of this is making any sense, Tompa.'

'I called the fucking number. The guy who answered said, "Sten." I was like: "Sten what? Sten gun?" I didn't come up with that thing about Stentor quickly enough? You always think of the really smart things to say when it's too late, don't you?'

'OK ...?'

'And then he cleared his throat and said, "This is August Sten, to whom am I speaking?" And I sang so loudly, I swear I nearly bust the fucking phone: "Hammarby! Hammarby! Always leave Djurgården and the Rats on their knees! Hammarby! Hammarby! Best team in the whole fucking city!"'

And with that the audio file came to an end.

Berger closed his eyes and listened one more time.

Not Sten, he thought. Steen.

August Steen.

The head of the Security Service's Intelligence Unit.

He sat perfectly still. Scorching anger and sorrow were coursing through him.

Molly's contact in the Security Service was August Steen.

One of the spooks behind Syl's death.

She had called him as recently as yesterday. To get hold of Jessica Johnsson's secret identity.

She was obviously very close to him.

The whole of their existence up to here was based on a lie.

No matter how much he didn't want to do it, it was time to confront her. He took out the earphones, then pulled out his mobile phone and played the short sequence of film showing Blom's fingers moving across the satellite phone's keypad, without making any attempt to hide it. He even held it up towards her.

But at that moment the satellite phone between them rang. He pulled his mobile back, she put it on speaker and answered, 'Yes?'

'Yes, hello,' a male voice said. 'I don't know if I've got the right number? Am I talking to Detective Inspector Eva Lundström?'

'That's right,' Blom said.

'This is Dr Andreas Hamlin from the secure psychiatric clinic at Säter – I don't know if you remember me?'

'Oh, yes,' Blom said. 'The man with the iPad at Säter. What can I do for you?'

'You asked me to get in touch if Karl Hedblom received any more letters. There was one in today's post.'

'Have you opened it?' Blom asked, moving closer to the phone.

'Yes, very carefully,' Andreas Hamlin said. 'Inside a blank folded sheet of A4 was a white powder that's been sent for analysis. I think we both know what the results will show.'

'A cocktail of methamphetamine and phenazepam,' Blom said. 'It's vital that it's handled with forensic care and sent to the National Forensics Centre at once.'

'I was about to get it couriered down there,' Hamlin said.

'Hang on,' Berger said. 'This is Lindbergh, the other detective who came to Säter. Was there a postmark on the envelope?'

They heard the rustle of paper.

'Yes,' Hamlin said. 'Normal stamps and a postmark. No sender's name or address, though.'

'Is there a date on the postmark?'

'It's a bit blurred, but yes. It's postmarked 23 November. Yesterday, in other words.'

Berger and Blom exchanged a glance. Berger went on:

'Is there a place name on the stamp as well? A town or city?'

'It does say something here, yes. Let's see. Skogås. I don't even know where that is.'

'I do,' Berger said and clicked to end the call.

He stood up and pointed to Blom. He said, 'Deer lives in Skogås. Fucking shit. It was Jessica Johnsson, letting us know she's planning to take Deer.'

Blom looked shaken. She went over to the wall and looked at the sequence of photographs. She removed the three male pictures, Rasmus Gradén, Eddy Karlsson and Anders Hedblom. That left a row of women: Helena Gradén, Mette Hækkerup, Lena Widstrand, Farida Hesari, Elisabeth Ström and Jovana Malešević. They all had dark hair, and they all had their hair styled in various lengths of bob.

Blom went back to the table and rifled through a shoebox. She took out a yellowing photograph, returned to the wall and pointed at the photograph of the eight-year-old Jessica Johnsson with the four-leaf clover. Immediately beneath it she pinned up a photograph of the same girl, slightly younger, sitting on her mother Eva's lap.

Her mother, Eva Johnsson, née Hult, had dark hair at the time of her death, cut in a mid-length bob.

Berger pulled out his mobile and flicked through with his hand shaking to a picture in which he was messing about with a former colleague. That former colleague's name was Desiré Rosenkvist, and she had mid-length dark hair.

Cut in a bob.

'What if they aren't just out to get you, Sam?' Blom said in a hoarse voice. 'What if Desiré made just as strong an impression in Orsa?'

The silence lasted a few more seconds.

The terrible silence of realisation.

Then they leaped into action. Berger yelled, 'Email and text all the colleagues we can reach. Find neighbours, family, friends, grandmothers. Make sure that Lykke and Johnny are safe.'

Berger himself called Deer on both her official and unofficial mobiles. The satellite phone rang disconsolately, unanswered. He left messages everywhere he managed to get through.

Then he called the National Operations Department, got through to a switchboard, hung up, and started to type frantically on his computer. Blom took over the phone and after a while he heard her talking to someone who could have been the head of the NOD, the acting head of the national police force. He tried to remember the name of Deer's immediate boss, trying out Ronny Lundén and Benny Lundin before he got to Conny Landin, grabbed the phone, called. No answer. He tried again, no answer. What the fuck was that hopeless excuse of a human being doing? He called Robin, who merely said in surprise that he hadn't heard from Deer in a long time. Blom looked up from her computer, took the phone, dialled a number.

'One of the neighbours is on the case,' she said with her hand over the receiver.

A couple of text messages appeared on his computer: none of their colleagues seemed to have any idea where Deer was.

'What about her boss?' Berger roared. 'You spoke to the head of the NOD, didn't you?'

'He didn't know anything,' Blom said, then managed to say into the receiver: 'OK, thanks for your help.'

'Email from Conny Landin,' Berger said, tapping his keyboard.

'The neighbour saw her leave the house just before seven this morning,' Blom said. 'Looked the same as usual when she set off for work, but appeared to have a bag of gym gear with her. Sam, you must know at least one of her friends? A gym buddy? A tennis partner, anything?'

'No,' Berger said. 'And Johnny's not answering. Conny Landin just says there's a national alert out for me. He doesn't give a shit about Deer.'

'A national alert?' Blom exclaimed.

'Just keep going,' Berger said, trying to formulate a convincing reply to Conny Landin.

'What about your sources, your informants?' Blom said. 'Could she have gone to meet one of them?'

'I'll try them,' Berger said. 'Pass me the phone.'

'We've only got one phone,' Blom said. 'We need to do everything on it.'

'Like fuck we have,' Berger blurted and pushed her aside. He pulled the bed away from the wall, dug the hatch open and pulled out the second satellite phone. He slammed it down on the table in front of a very pale Molly Blom.

'So get fucking calling!' he shouted. 'Call your fucking Security Service contact and get an alert issued for her, for her car. Get August fucking Steen on the case, and Roy and Roger.'

Blom picked up the phone, speechless, silent. Made a call.

Berger got hold of Johnny at work. The coverage in the ambulance he was presumably driving was poor, he sounded like a robot. Berger tried again, no answer. He got hold of Deer's mother's name, called, pretended everything was fine, got Lykke's mobile number and called it. He reached her voicemail three, four times. Obviously she was at school and her phone was switched off. Unless she'd been abducted, assaulted, murdered. He called Conny Landin again. Got through. Persuaded him to go to Deer's office and look at her computer. Nothing, nothing, nothing.

'I've called her daughter's school,' Blom said with her hand over the receiver. 'The secretary's on her way to the classroom.'

Berger stopped and looked at her warily. The colour hadn't completely returned to her face, she looked chastened. The way people do when they have a guilty conscience.

'She's outside the classroom now,' she said. 'She's going in. Hello, is that Lykke? Lykke Rosenkvist? Great. Do you think you could go with the lady who just came into your classroom? You'll have to go to the staffroom for a while. Is that Mrs Lindh again? Good, take Lykke to a safe place, call the police and request immediate protection. Yes, by all means get the PE and science teachers to help. Great, thanks.'

'So Lykke's safe, then?' Berger said, then went on shouting into his satellite phone: 'For fuck's sake, Landin, forget the bloody national alert for a minute. This is about her, you're her boss, you must know where she is. Did she really not say anything?'

'Looks like she's safe, yes,' Blom said. 'For the time being. A patrol car's on its way.'

Berger tossed aside the receiver with a completely impossible Conny Landin still on the line and started to type frantically on his computer.

'We've got an alert out for her car now, anyway,' Blom said. 'What are you doing?'

'I'm sitting here at the arse end of the fucking universe while two deranged psychopaths are assaulting my partner. Fucking fuck! There, two tickets booked.'

'What have you done?'

'Flight from Gällivare to Stockholm, 16.00,' Berger said, pulling on his clothes. 'Come on, we can make it, we can get there in two hours. Then I'm going to clear the fucking shit out of the stables.'

'But we're—'

'Hiding from the Security Service?' Berger yelled. 'While you provide regular updates on your sedated partner's condition to the head of the Security Service's Intelligence Unit? While we carry on pretending to hide? While you convince me that I suffered a psychotic episode? For fuck's sake, Molly, did you help them murder Syl too?'

'What are you actually saying?'

'That all this fucking undercover bullshit is just that – bullshit. You've already blown it sky-high. We're not hiding from anyone, it's all a fucking sham. The Security Service have been watching us the whole time, watching me. The plane tickets are booked, so get your bloody clothes on.'

'But I don't get it.'

'We haven't got time for this crap now,' Berger roared, already on his way out of the cabin. He threw the big white padded jacket at her and more or less pushed her ahead of him on the long trek to the jeep.

Berger drove. Blom sat beside him. He drove like an absolute lunatic through the snow-covered icy wasteland. When they reached Kvikkjokk it started to snow. He passed her his mobile and she watched the video clip of her fingers dialling August Steen's unofficial mobile number. She gave the phone back without a word. Then she just stared stiffly ahead of her.

'We can talk about that later,' was all Berger said.

The snow poured down, swirling around the car as if they were driving through a horizotal tornado, a wind tunnel full of blood-doped skiers. He drove like a man possessed. Blom kept calling all of Deer's phones non-stop.

No answer.

No answer at all.

After an hour or so Blom said, 'Desiré hasn't got a son.'

'That's just another fucking red herring,' Berger said tersely. 'Jessica's another bloody actress, just like you. The whole thing is just some sort of perverse performance by an infantile, narcissistic, megalomaniac overgrown baby with a pathetic father fixation. Fuck her.'

They drove in silence for a while longer. Then Berger said, 'You haven't got a younger brother, have you?'

Blom lowered her gaze and looked down at her lap. Then she looked up at him with an expression that contained many different types of sorrow.

'No,' she said. 'I haven't got a younger brother.'

They slid into Lapland Airport in Gällivare, parked illegally in a disabled parking space, ran at full pelt through the small departure hall, found the right gate, saw that the clock was very nearly four o'clock, and heard their names being called out over the tannoy system.

The final call.

Berger ran to the departure desk, waving the electronic ticket lit up on his mobile. That made him notice his phone again, and he stopped and called Deer's phone for the hundredth time.

And someone answered.

He froze. Airport staff were fussing around him, but it all washed off him like water from a duck's back.

'Who is this?' he asked, concentrating hard.

A woman's voice that didn't sound anything like Deer's said something inaudible, something tinny.

'For God's sake, who is this? Is that you, Jessica?'

It really did sound like he was in direct contact with the realm of the dead. Hellish flames seemed to lap at the phone from within.

Then the voice at the other end settled and became normal.

'Hello?' a more natural female voice said.

'Who is this?' Berger repeated, but something inside him had already reacted.

'It's me,' Deer said. 'I'm in hospital.'

Berger couldn't move. It was a physical impossibility.

'In hospital?' he said. 'What's happened?'

'I fell through a floor,' Deer said. 'The old carbon dioxide plant in Liljeholmen. I lay there unconscious for several hours. But I'm OK.'

The sigh that emptied Sam Berger's lungs at that moment was the deepest of his life. It also emptied his body, then breathed fresh life into it. He felt his face relax beneath the mane of beard.

Then he felt a smile spread across his whole face. He turned to tell Blom.

'Deer's OK,' he said.

But she wasn't there.

Molly Blom wasn't there.

He looked around, scanning the departure lounge hard, but she was nowhere to be seen.

There weren't many people so it was easy to get a good view. He shouted and called out, he ran towards the women's bathroom, yanked the door open and shouted for her, louder and louder, opening the doors to all the cubicles. Nothing. Then the men's toilets. Same result.

He ran from counter to counter, and was finally informed that neither Sam Berger nor Molly Blom had boarded the flight to Stockholm. He spent another hour running around Gällivare Airport. He spoke to everyone he met, every single person, but no one had seen a blonde woman in a white padded jacket.

Not a single person had seen her.

Eventually he was pretty much alone.

When he walked out into the car park he felt peculiarly empty. It was a completely white surface. Nothing was happening, there were no signs of life.

And the snow fell indifferently through space.

His soul slowly turned numb as he watched the flakes falling through the air, gently and lightly and lightly and gently.

He got in the jeep. It too was empty.

He switched the windscreen wipers on. The thick covering of snow disappeared from the glass. Yet there was still something there.

He wasn't surprised.

He got out of the jeep, grabbed the envelope that was caught beneath one of the wipers and sat back inside.

He opened the envelope and pulled out the drawing.

He knew what it was going to be. And it was.

It was a drawing of a four-leaf clover.

IV

33

What he can see is Marcus and Oscar in the coltsfoot ditch. Oscar is smiling, Marcus laughing. The fixed point. The still point of the turning world.

One day he'll figure out where he went wrong. One day he'll understand what he put Freja through. The mother of their sons.

He's been disqualified as a father.

He's been disqualified as a lover.

Even so, that's what comes back to him right now. He knows he's asleep. He can see so many images of himself. Psychosis, drugs, sedatives. Lying knocked out for weeks. Yet he's up and moving about, like a zombie. He sees sudden moments of lucidity swathed in unconsciousness, hidden behind that unconsciousness, veiled in forgetfulness. He sees one moment in his bed, two people next to each other, a pause in the chaos. Looks deep into those eyes. Great sorrow, overwhelming emotions. And then he sees an act of lovemaking, a woman's breasts rising and falling in front of him, he feels hair brush his face and realises that he's inside the woman, that she's riding him, and all the terrible things have suddenly turned to pleasure, and he doesn't know if he's asleep or awake, if this is really happening or if it's just the materialisation of a multitude of mechanisms to help him cope. Because now the pleasure is real, he takes hold of the woman, caresses her, hears the groaning and whimpering, impossible to tell apart, feels the subtle, rolling convulsions of the female climax, and he's close now, he comes hard and long, and all the crap is wiped out, and when the woman finally leans over him he sees a star-shaped birthmark just below her right breast.

'Molly!'

And his own cry wakes him. He sits up on the edge of the bed and waits until time catches up with him. As if that could ever happen. And it was as if he touched down, came to rest, properly, inside the cabin.

He had a job to do.

He opened the watch case, selected his pride and joy, the watch that had solved a case, his Patek Philippe 2508 Calatrava. He noted that it was still telling the correct hour. And that there might, possibly, still be time.

Then he carefully got dressed and pulled on his unused ski suit. After grabbing the key to the jeep, he stepped out onto the terrace and opened the narrow door to the ski store.

In one corner of a large windowless room frantic activity was taking place on the computers in front of two well built men. They were sitting on either side of a desk, each staring at his own screen. One of them had a cheap diver's watch on his thick wrist, and couldn't hide his irritation when he noticed a dramatic change in his colleague's level of activity.

'What the hell are you doing?' Roy Grahn asked.

'We've got something here,' Kent Döös replied.

'Where?'

'No idea. Position: 67°19.034'N, 17°09.867'E.'

'Where the fuck's that?'

'Should be Lapland.'

'Why the hell would we be getting an alert from up there?'

'No idea,' Kent said, 'but sometimes it can be worth checking the surveillance programme.'

'Hook me up,' Roy said without any enthusiasm.

It took just a couple of seconds before a satellite image emerged from the darkness of the screen. It was completely white, and it took a while for Roy to realise that he was actually looking at snow.

He zoomed in. Eventually something became visible in the midst of all the white. It looked like letters, like writing in the snow. Roy zoomed in even closer, until finally he could read some sort of text. He spelled his way laboriously through it:

'AS! Urgent. M̶. Point 0. 1630.'

'What the fuck is this?' he exclaimed.

But his colleague had already grabbed a sheet of paper from the printer and was rushing off.

Roy caught up with him by the lifts. Inside the lift he said, 'Where the hell are you going?'

'Didn't you read it?' Kent asked.

'But it was just nonsense. As urgent as what?'

'Maybe,' Kent said. 'But it was in an area triggered for alerts, so there's a chance it could be important.'

Unlike Roy, Kent couldn't be bothered to let himself be irritated by the usual minute it took before the door to their boss's office made its low buzzing sound. If everything fell into place, he had just pulled away from Roy on the final sprint towards a job as an internal resource. And he held the key in his hand.

August Steen, head of the Security Service's Intelligence Unit, was sitting behind his desk with his usual stone-like stare. His cropped metallic grey hair looked like iron filings around a magnet.

Kent got straight to the point, held out the printout and said, 'Satellite image from coordinates 67°19.034'N, 17°09.867'E.'

He gave Steen a few seconds to absorb and interpret the information. Then he went on:

'Someone has written in the snow in an area triggered for alerts. Very large letters. The start could be your initials, boss. There are lower-case letters after that.'

Without bending his ramrod-straight back, August Steen's face twitched slightly in a way that might indicate approval. Kent felt like punching the air. He resisted and went on in a neutral tone:

'But I'm having some difficulty interpreting this letter.'

He pointed at the И.

August Steen nodded slowly.

'Good,' he said. 'I want you to concentrate on this symbol. I wonder if I haven't seen something similar in one of the Asian alphabets, maybe even among non-linguistic symbols. Full focus on that, I'll expect a report by the end of the day.'

August Steen didn't bother to look up at them as they left his office. All his attention was focused on the printout in front of him:

'AS! Urgent. И. Point 0. 1630.'

Someone wearing a pair of skis had written this message at the Swedish pole of inaccessibility. And, without any doubt, it was addressed directly to August Steen.

He sat for a while looking at the symbol И. He hoped he had managed to steer Kent and Roy away from the meaning of the message when taken as a whole. Which he thought he was beginning to see.

~~M~~. For a brief moment he was overcome by a wave of emotion.

Then he stood up, clutching the printout in his hand, and walked towards the door.

The observer is back. He watches the screens. Nothing is happening there. His pistol, the Sig Sauer P226, is spinning in front of him like it had never stopped.

It's close now. He knows it's close.

It's so terribly cold in his snow cave.

When he takes off his computer-terminal glasses he can't even make out the screens, let alone see what's on them. They really are terminal glasses.

The terminal stage for his sight.

He wouldn't be able to work for much longer anyway, his time is up. All that remains is a reasonable pension. Reasonable considering the amount of effort he's put into his work. All unreasonable jobs need reasonable compensation.

He has to see it one more time. The house on the slopes outside Estepona, the terrace with its view of the Rock of Gibraltar, the scents of thyme, rosemary, lavender. He has to be able to link the wonderful evening warmth to a view that he can share with ♀. That she can convey to him.

She can save his sight. She can save his life.

The observer thinks about ♀ and ♂. He thinks about their relationship. He thinks about the fact that he hates ♂. The observer thinks about how he set off after her, pulled her from ♂'s hard grasp, tenderly embraced her and found that he was loved. The observer thinks about how wonderful that was, how divine closeness can feel. The upper screen goes on showing events in real time while he rewinds the bottom screen, going backwards through the neglected recording.

The observer thinks to himself that he really ought to have done that, but then he loses himself in fantasies again. The hand in the thin leather glove absentmindedly spins the pistol on the table, but it still loses speed. The barrel isn't pointing at him when it stops; this time the observer doesn't have to choose between truth or dare. Because the truth, as always, is far too complicated.

Then he realises that he's wound the film back too far. It starts to play automatically. The image floats and flutters, the screen shows sky, then snow, then a face darts past. Then the picture stabilises and shows footprints. Footprints that seem to come from far away and get larger and larger, until eventually they lead all the way up the hill to here, towards the camera.

Then the face looks into the camera, adjusts it, concludes that everything is OK, then moves away up the slope to set up the next camera. ♀ is already gone before the observer sees her properly. She was just as beautiful then, when she was setting up the cameras.

Now it's time for him to rescue ♀ from ♂.

August Steen yanked the door open as hard as he could. The man behind the desk jumped but simultaneously clicked a joystick so that the image on the lower of the two screens in front of him changed.

'God, it's cold in here,' Steen said, rubbing his arms.

'It's like a snow cave,' the man in the computer-terminal glasses said. 'We've complained, but there seems to be something seriously wrong with the thermostat.'

'Those glasses look ridiculously thick,' Steen said. 'Your RP isn't getting worse, is it? You know you have to tell me immediately if that happens, Carsten.'

'I know,' Carsten said sadly. 'But all the evidence suggests that my retinitis pigmentosa is developing slowly.'

'We'll have to see,' Steen said. 'There haven't been many reports from you lately. The other shifts report regularly, but you've been falling behind.'

'I was just sitting here trying to catch up,' Carsten said.

'Is Molly in position?'

'She must be. But she hasn't shown herself yet.'

'I haven't received a report about that, Carsten.'

'I know. Like I said, I'm trying to catch up.'

Steen grimaced and said, 'There was an ambiguous report from Frans last night. He wasn't sure if Molly came back yesterday evening; the night-vision camera wasn't functioning satisfactorily. OK, have we had any activity from Berger? Anything recent?'

'He was moving about outside a quarter of an hour or so ago.'

'Show me.'

Carsten clicked the joystick, brought up a couple of menus on the lower screen, clicked and rewound.

After a while Berger appeared on his porch, opened the door to the ski store, pulled out a pair of skis and attached them to his boots with some difficulty. Then he set off towards the open expanse of snow a short distance away. Only his head was visible above the ridge of the snow, moving in strange patterns.

'Carsten, for God's sake. We want real-time reporting here. If you can't handle this I'll have to bring in a replacement.'

Carsten said nothing. He knew it was true. Darker sides of him had taken over. And yet he was known as the most professional of all the Security Service's internal resources.

'What's happening there?' Steen asked, pointing towards the top screen.

'Berger's coming out,' Carsten said and zoomed in. 'This is real time. He seems to have changed his boots, he's wearing thick snow boots now. And he's got a rucksack on his back. He's not heading towards Molly's cabin, he seems to be taking the short cut towards the car.'

Steen nodded and put the printout down in front of Carsten.

'What's your interpretation of this?' he asked.

'Is that …?'

'I'm having to rely on external resources, who are dealing with this a hell of a lot better than my internal resources. Interpretation, please.'

Carsten looked at the printout, and the message written on the snow:

'AS! Urgent. M̶. Point 0. 1630,' Carsten said, 'It's definitely intended for you, boss: "AS!" Then the need for an urgent meeting at "Point Zero" at 16.30. I don't know what that other character means though.'

Steen took a deep breath and said, 'It's a crossed-through letter M.'

Carsten looked at him, and fear slowly filled his considerable frame. Steen looked back at his clearly blanching face and went on:

'If we're lucky, it means that Molly is missing. If we're unlucky …'

'It means she's dead,' Carsten said hoarsely.

Steen glowered at him, and said, 'All we know for certain is that you and I are going to secure "Point Zero" by this afternoon.'

Carsten nodded.

His eyes hurt.

34

The meadow grass that had once reached his chest lay flat on the ground. The snow had fallen brutally and snapped the tall stems like driving rain. Then it had got bored and melted away again. In the flickering beam of the torch his childhood play area resembled a field of giant rotten asparagus stems.

The moon had just emerged in the dark sky, and was mirrored in the distance off the still surface of the water; the reflection reached him in fragments through the patch of forest by the shore. Eventually he saw the building glint as if lit from an innate glow.

As if covered with luminous paint.

When he got closer he saw that the rowing boat was still there, bobbing beside the jetty; it would probably be there until the ice settled properly. Then it would freeze solid and be shattered by the ice.

Without pausing for a moment he hurried up the steps towards the entrance.

The door opened before he had time to knock. He couldn't see anything but the Sig Sauer P226 that a gloved hand was pointing at his chest.

The pistol waved him into the darkness. He felt himself being patted down professionally. Then a weak light was switched on.

A tall, older man in a suit with angular chiselled features and cropped steel-wool hair was standing at the edge of the light cast by the lamp. He was leaning nonchalantly against a pair of wooden posts that rose from the floor. There were chains of various sizes hanging from the pillars.

'So, *Point Zero*,' the man said. 'The centre of the mechanism. Where it all started, and where it could all end.'

'Steen,' Berger said with a nod. 'If you were planning to kill me, you'd have done it by now.'

'It's possible that the ground rules have changed,' Steen said. 'Why the struck-through Molly? Have you kidnapped her?'

'Of course not. But she has been kidnapped. By seriously bad people.'

'And why are you turning to me?'

'Because she works for you. Because she was acting on your orders when she was taken. And because you're not heartless.'

'But it can't really be said that *you* work for me,' Steen said. 'Why should I listen to you – or even let you live?'

'Because I'm the only person who can find her,' Berger said.

'Go on,' Steen said.

'I don't give a damn that Molly betrayed me, I don't give a damn that she was in contact with you the whole time up there. And right now I don't even care that you murdered Syl with a black fucking sock. I just want to get Molly back. Alive.'

'I assume you've already tried searching for her mobile?'

'Yesterday. It was in a ditch outside Lapland Airport.'

'You still haven't told me why I should listen to you.'

'Because her kidnappers are after me. It's me they're trying to communicate with, me and only me. The murderer needs me for some reason, she wants me to see her, hunt her, catch her. She's picked me as some sort of father figure. The statistics suggest that Molly's still alive, but there isn't a lot of fucking time. All I need from you is a little assistance. Just once, right here and right now, then you can do what you like with me.'

'Assistance?'

'What do you know about this case?' Berger asked. 'The one we've been unofficially working on?'

Steen turned to his colleague, who was sitting somewhere in the darkness just beyond the reach of the light. Some sort of exchange took place. Berger felt a sharp, unexpectedly malicious stare being aimed at him from the gloom. Steen nodded and said, 'Not much. I got a report that you were offered a sort of unofficial freelance contract by a superintendent in the NOD.'

'A report from Molly Blom?'

'Correct,' Steen said. 'My verdict was that the case was a dead end, but that it could hardly do any damage. Anything to keep you occupied, below the radar.'

'Why was it so important to keep me below the radar?' Berger exclaimed.

There was a pause, and August Steen grimaced. He said, 'I thought you didn't care about anything apart from saving Blom? But perhaps I was wrong. We may have to reconsider the ground rules for this conversation.'

'You helped Molly get hold of Jessica Johnsson's protected identity,' Berger said.

Steen nodded.

'Finding out a protected identity isn't easy,' he said, 'even for me. You always leave evidence.'

'Yet you still did it. You still took a disproportionately large risk. Why?'

Steen didn't answer. He just stared straight ahead of him in the old boathouse, into nothing.

'Because Molly Blom was your protégée, your charge,' Berger said. 'Because you've been her mentor ever since you brought her into the Security Service. You don't have the sort of face that betrays your emotions, August, but I could see how sorry you were when you were forced to fire her. You're not heartless. And now you want to rescue her just as much as I do. If I thought the Security Service could crack this case and free her I'd happily hand everything over to you right now, but I *know* that the person whose details you pulled from the files will only talk to me. And Lena Nilsson, alias Jessica Johnsson, is a seriously unpleasant person who at this very moment will have Molly tied to a chair somewhere while she gets a slave called Reine Daniels-son to beat and cut her without any trace of pity. Molly Blom isn't just your *responsibility*, August. She's also your favourite. Help me to help her. I don't give a damn about anything else.'

Steen looked at him intently without any change of expression.

'What happened?' he asked.

'We suddenly realised that all of Jessica's victims looked like her mother. Deer has similar features, and we managed to locate Jessica in Skogås, where Deer lives. And Deer was missing, we couldn't get hold of her anywhere. We were just about to catch the plane to Stockholm when Deer answered her phone. And Molly vanished.'

'At the airport,' Steen said.

'Yes,' Berger said. 'In Gällivare.'

'So what are you doing in Stockholm? And how did you get here so quickly?'

'I drove very fast to Lapland Airport and got a lift on a transport plane. I doubt the perpetrators are still in Lapland. They keep picking new locations. And I needed to talk to you face to face. And be closer to Deer.'

'So who's this Deer?' Steen asked tersely.

'The acting superintendent at the NOD who arranged our so-called freelance contract,' Berger said. 'Desiré Rosenkvist.'

'And why would she be a potential target for this unusual murderer?'

'Because eight years ago she and I conducted an interview with the murderers. They sat together in the same room while we questioned them. They've been trying to get our attention for a while. And now we need to work together again.'

'You and Superintendent Rosenkvist? Is that what you want from me?'

'That's secondary,' Berger said. 'Deer and her family have been moved to a secure location, under guard. It would be good if we could get qualified Security Service surveillance of her home in Skogås. She's got the entire investigation there, in her garage.'

'Her garage?' Steen said, clearly sceptical.

'We need to keep working under the radar,' Berger said. 'Otherwise we'll waste unnecessary time on a whole load of bureaucratic nonsense, time we haven't got. But like I said, that's a secondary request. My main request is for something else.'

'Namely?'

'That you beat the big drum, August, and activate the whole of the Security Service's considerable surveillance machinery to find a bright blue or possibly yellow-white Volkswagen Caddy with the registration number LAM 387 somewhere in Sweden.'

Steen stared at him.

'Is that the best you've got?' he asked in astonishment. 'A van?'

'Stolen,' Berger said. 'Can you do that?'

Steen looked at him. He may not have had the sort of face that betrayed his emotions, but the variety of expressions in his eyes still seemed endless.

Then he nodded.

Deer was sitting in the black car looking at her family. She looked into Johnny's eyes and realised that something had changed, that everything would be different now. Nothing had come between them, nothing had broken their faith in each other, but he would never really dare to trust her job any more. Only now had he realised just how dangerous it was. For her and for him too, and – most importantly of all – for Lykke. Deer could see in his eyes that he couldn't forgive her for that. Lykke herself, on the other hand, seemed to think it was mostly all very exciting; she'd never seen so many guns before, or such elegant vehicles and well dressed men and women. She was chattering away happily, and above her head her parents' eyes were locked on to each other's.

They arrived. Were led into the terraced house. Split up.

Deer heard Johnny call out in a slightly forced voice, 'Liverpool.'

And Lykke burst out laughing, 'But it's only Wednesday, Dad!'

Then they moved out of hearing.

Deer shivered as she walked through the cold garage, nodded to the Security Service officer outside the door and pressed the door handle.

Berger was pinning things up on her whiteboard. He turned and looked her in the eye. Between them they said more than a thousand words.

'National alert?' Berger said.

'Conny Landin received an anonymous tip-off,' Deer said. 'Your DNA was found on Farida Hesari's bleeding body.'

'Oh shit.'

'Obviously we know that it wasn't. But there was a "neglected" evidence bag in the store. And probably something similar in Malmö and Växjö too.'

'What was in the bag? Skin? Blood?'

'Hair,' Deer said.

Berger took hold of the hair above his ears and held it away from his head. His hair was definitely shorter on the left.

'I know I usually go to a cheap barber,' he said, 'but it doesn't usually end up quite this bad.'

'Ah,' Deer said. 'Porjus.'

'Jessica hit two birds with one stone in that basement. She set me up and running on the case, and she cut off some hair so she had my DNA. What I don't understand is how the hair got into the store.'

'The police store,' Deer said. 'Our friend Richard Robertsson intimated that I wasn't the first person to show up there offering money. Presumably Jessica paid to get access to the Farida Hesari evidence.'

Deer shook her head and held out her arms. They hugged, quickly, awkwardly.

They sat down. Deer sighed and took out her mobile phone.

'Speaking of Farida Hesari ...' she said.

She pressed Play, and the interview from the carbon dioxide plant echoed around the garage. It ended with a whooshing sound, a scream that could have been an oath and a crash. Then silence.

'I saw the hole in the floor on the way in but not on the way out,' Deer said.

'I figured that out,' Berger said and felt his armpits. Sweaty.

'A pigeon flew past me through the derelict building,' Deer said. 'That could be what made me fall.'

'I think it's more likely that Hesari was the cause,' Berger said, gesturing towards the phone. 'That's not the sort of thing you just shrug off afterwards.'

'I don't know if I've ever conducted a tougher interview,' Deer agreed. 'I hope Farida Hesari is as strong as she seems.'

'What's your view of Jessica Johnsson's motive?'

'I'm just an ordinary suburban mum, Sam,' Deer said. 'I can't understand it.'

'And yet you did. You asked the right questions. It sounded like you understood.'

'In social terms, yes. I see Jessica's journey, a spiral into hell that I can't get a grip of. Not wanting a little brother. Her mother and unborn brother's grotesque deaths. The guilty conscience leading to self-destructive sexuality. Those bizarre events in the USA, sexualised violence. Her relationship with Eddy Karlsson, the rapes, miscarriage, hysterectomy. Her protected identity, her growing envy of mothers with sons eventually turning to hate. The ability to direct someone with a particular type of mental disorder, the way Madame Newhouse directed Rob. But psychologically? No. Never.'

'I also think that Jessica developed a Teflon coating very early on,' Berger said. 'Things don't affect her. She's playing a game. She hoped she was a sadomasochist, but she's really just empty. Nothing touches her. She solely wants to impress us.'

Deer nodded, then changed the subject, 'OK, so I disappeared, I fell down a hole. This was a bit over the top, though, wasn't it? Calling everyone you could?'

'They could have taken Lykke,' Berger said.

Deer understood. She would have done exactly the same thing in that situation.

'And they took Molly Blom instead,' she said.

'She betrayed me,' Berger said. 'Doesn't stop me wanting to save her though.'

'We don't sleep until we've drained every last bit of information from what we've got,' Deer said. 'It's all here.'

She pointed at a number of piles of paper on the desk.

Berger's shoulders slumped.

'This one's got to me.'

'I know,' she said. 'We can see the animal inside us peering out. The beast.'

Berger straightened up and pushed his shoulders back.

'Two central questions,' he said. 'The first is obvious. Is there anything in all the material we've got that gives even the slightest indication of where Jessica and Reine are right now, with Molly?'

'And the second question is just as obvious,' Deer said. 'How the hell did they know that you were going to fly from that damn airport in Gällivare at that exact time?'

Berger nodded.

'It was a spur-of-the-moment decision, to put it mildly,' he said. 'When I couldn't get hold of you I booked two plane tickets. And Jessica must have seen the booking somehow.'

'And must have been in the immediate vicinity. How?'

'When we got to Porjus she must have realised that we hadn't come straight from Stockholm. But she couldn't have known that we were hiding out in a couple of cabins at the pole of inaccessibility.'

'The Security Service knew,' Deer said. 'Could Jessica have a contact in the Security Service?'

'I'm having trouble thinking that,' Berger said. 'She's running her own race. But she's much better with computers than she pretended to be – all that business with the typewriter. I'm guessing she had some sort of surveillance on all flights out of Lapland to see if my name cropped up.'

'I agree with you that I make a far more plausible candidate though,' Deer said, stroking her dark bob and thinking about her daughter's similar appearance.

'To be honest, I think you're safe now, Deer. The fact that they took Molly means that they're after me, not you. They want to get at the cop who shot them with his fingers, the cop who mocked them in Orsa. Jessica took Molly to hurt me. She evidently assumed we were a couple.'

'So did I,' Deer said with a brief smile. 'In spite of that damn beard.'

'I never get time to shave it off,' Berger said with a grimace.

They sat silent for a while, thinking back.

'I've never trusted Molly Blom,' Deer said.

'I know,' Berger said. 'But the two of you were the ones who agreed this whole thing, without me.'

'She betrayed you,' Deer said. 'She drugged you, lied to you, manipulated you.'

'I know,' Berger said. 'OK, let's get going.'

35

They read so much that their eyes started to bleed. Deer looked up from the pile of papers, pointed first at her own eye, then at Berger's. He touched the corner of his eye with his finger and saw blood on it.

The imagery wasn't lost on them.

She handed him a handkerchief and her powder compact. He looked at the compact with evident bemusement, and she gestured silently to show him what to do. He clicked and opened it, and looked in the small mirror.

Blood was seeping from his eye.

He wiped it with the handkerchief and said, 'Nothing?'

'The geographical spread looks random,' Deer said, flicking the pile of papers. 'I can't see how we can figure out where they are. It's impossible.'

'It must be possible,' Berger snapped and got to his feet. 'For fuck's sake, it must be possible. She's dying!'

'They were in Gällivare, but that was a day and a half ago. With decent transport they could be anywhere on the planet by now.'

'They're in Sweden,' Berger said, sinking back down onto his chair.

'I know,' Deer said. 'But Sweden's big. Orsa, Malmö, Gothenburg, Bagarmossen, Täby, Växjö, Sorsele, Porjus. There really isn't a pattern.'

'It's here,' Berger said. 'I know it's here.'

But his voice was very weak.

There was a knock on the door, and it opened at exactly the same moment. A man with a boxer's nose and very thick glasses walked in. He was carrying two empty suitcases.

'I don't even know your name,' Berger said quietly.

'Carsten,' the man said as he opened the suitcases. 'You can call me Carsten. I've got a Bell ready for you.'

'OK, I'm hearing words but not getting any sense from them.'

'The fastest possible way to get to Dalarna,' Carsten clarified and gestured towards the suitcases. 'Take all the material, all the computers.'

'But my family,' Deer said, taken aback.

'Obviously we'll maintain our presence here,' Carsten said. 'Your family's safe. But the two of you need to go.'

'Where?' Berger said as he started to fill one of the suitcases.

'We can't give you any official support,' Carsten said. 'This is completely unofficial. You're going to have to do this yourselves. But we can get you there. To Särna.'

'Särna?' Deer said, starting to pack the material just as frantically as Berger.

'It's the repetition that's important,' Carsten said.

The black car drove faster than Berger had ever travelled on land before. On the long straight section of the E4 leading to Arlanda Airport, past the massive pig farm, he thought he saw the digital speedometer hit the magical figure of three hundred.

He glanced at Deer, who was frowning hard. Then he leaned forward towards Carsten, who was sitting in the passenger seat.

'The repetition is important?' he said.

'We've spotted a bright blue Volkswagen Caddy with what appears to be the registration number LAM 387 at four locations in the country,' Carsten said, adjusting his thin leather glove. 'Speed cameras near Arvidsjaur and Östersund, and at petrol stations in Vilhelmina and Särna.'

'Sounds like the Inland Highway,' Berger said.

Carsten nodded and said, 'Almost exclusively the E45, yes. But not Särna. The Inland Highway turns south at Sveg. They've carried on into the north of Dalarna. Sighting a vehicle somewhere doesn't really signify much. It just means it's on its way somewhere and is already gone. But if the sighting is repeated then there's a strong likelihood that the vehicle is hanging around, for one reason or another.'

'And this has happened at Särna? In northern Dalarna?'

'Yes, at the OKQ8 petrol station on Särnavägen. I'll text you instructions.'

He fell silent. Berger looked at his heavy face and those thick glasses.

'Anything else?' he asked.

Carsten removed his glasses. There was something odd about the look in his eyes when he said, 'Just make damn sure you rescue her.'

They were above Sala when Berger suddenly realised what Bell meant. A Bell 429, the light twin-engined helicopter that the Swedish police had recently purchased seven of. And Berger and Deer were sitting in one of them behind a pilot who had evidently been told not just to take them to Särna but also to remain silent. He wasn't showing any sign of saying a single word throughout the entire flight.

They landed in a deserted field outside Särna. The only thing in sight when the cloud of snow had settled and the Bell 429 had disappeared into the night sky was a solitary cottage at the edge of the field. When they got closer they saw a garage beside the house. Berger peered through the garage window; there was a black car parked inside. They strode over to the house, and Deer pulled out her mobile and read Carsten's instructions. She dug about for a while in the lightly frozen gutter and pulled out a set of keys. They walked up the steps and let themselves into the house.

It was warm but bare. The windowless living room didn't look the way a cottage in Dalarna ought to. The textured wallpaper was bland, and there was a birch-veneer table as well as a side table with an indefinable assortment of technical equipment. There was a set of car keys on the living-room table, the electricity worked, there was a whiteboard beside the table with both magnets and marker pens, and a wireless router was flashing in one corner. It was exactly how Berger had imagined Security Service safe houses, but this was the first time he had ever been inside one.

There were still a few hours of night left. They began to unpack. To keep the living room clear for use as a possible interview room they moved the whiteboard and other equipment into an inner room which soon resembled a perfect blend of Molly's cabin at the pole of inaccessibility and Deer's garage in Skogås.

Not that that made them feel any brighter at all.

It was still extremely dark outside.

Deer glanced down at her phone.

'That wasn't the end of it,' she said.

They were in the inner room. They'd just set up the camera on the wall of the living room, dragged the side table into the inner room, checked the camera facilities on their laptops and wheeled the whiteboard in. Berger paused in the middle of pinning up a map of northern Dalarna.

'Wasn't the end of what?' he asked.

'Carsten's text,' Deer said. 'First some instructions about the keys in the gutter, WiFi password and so on. Then there are some blank lines before the message goes on. I've only just noticed.'

'Goes on?' Berger said.

Deer walked into the bedroom for the first time, over to the wardrobe in the corner. She opened it and pulled out a thick plastic briefcase. She carried it out, put it on the side table next to the computers, turned the lock to the right combination and opened it.

The briefcase was full of liquid-filled tubes.

And a keyboard. And a screen.

Deer looked down at her mobile again and said, 'The rest's in the car.'

They stopped in complete darkness; not even the car's unusually powerful headlights could uncover anything but snow. Snow, snow and more snow. Berger switched the engine off and turned towards the passenger seat. Deer hadn't taken her eyes off her mobile for a single second.

'Two hundred metres on the right,' she said. 'There's supposed to be a path.'

They got out of the car and quickly concluded that there was no path. There probably had been before the snow arrived. Deer switched on her torch, followed by Berger. The GPS on

Deer's mobile told them that they were walking along the path, but there was nothing in their surroundings to suggest that might be true. There was only thick snow.

Thick snow and two people carrying an unfeasibly large weight through the wilderness in the middle of the night.

What loomed up before too long just beyond the reach of the torches looked like a medieval castle, all turrets and towers. As they got closer the towers turned into transformers and breakers, the turrets into serial condensers and disconnectors.

The darkness was intrusive. Nowhere in the sky was there even the slightest hint of light. It remained medieval.

If there had been a medieval castle, they would have been standing in front of the moat now. As it was, there was just a sturdy gate made of unwelcoming galvanised chain-link fencing and crowned by rusting barbed wire.

Berger picked up the bulky bolt cutters and cut through the coils of barbed wire. Eventually he was able to reach the thick chain, positioned the jaws of the cutter around one of the links and pressed the handles together.

The chain unwound under its own weight, loop after loop, and Berger pulled the heavy gate open.

They were in an area that felt like it was crackling; there seemed to be electricity in the air itself, everywhere around them.

Deer looked down at her phone and headed towards what seemed to be one of the central buildings. They found themselves facing a huge steel door. It was locked.

'Careful,' Deer said.

Berger pulled out the doughy lump he had found in the boot of the Security Service vehicle. He pushed it as far into the keyhole as he could, then attached two wires and unwound them. The two of them took several steps back. Then Berger connected the battery.

Nothing happened. They waited. He rubbed the wires clean and tried again.

The explosion was more powerful than they'd expected. They were both thrown backwards and lay on the snow looking at each other. Deer nodded, and Berger nodded back. They got up, pushed the door open and made their way into the inner sanctum.

Then shone their torches around. They were surrounded by power-generating technology. Deer stared at her mobile and searched the flashing displays.

'Here,' she said.

Berger wasn't going to argue. He carried the plastic briefcase over to what looked like a gigantic transformer. He placed it exactly where Deer was pointing. He opened it and stepped back.

Deer took over. She followed the instructions to the letter. She tapped a code into the little keypad in the briefcase. A screen lit up. When Deer tapped in the last digit the numbers 08.00 appeared on the screen.

'Does this mean we're going to be without electricity all night?' Berger asked.

'Not us,' Deer said.

The screen was still showing 08.00. She moved her finger to the Enter button and said, 'Not us, we're in a safe house, we've got a generator. But the rest of Särna and the surrounding area.'

Then she pressed her finger down.

Now it read 07.59.

They left, running through the thick snow. At one point Deer fell forward. Berger helped her up, but all she was bothered about was brushing the snow from her mobile. The screen said 04.12.

When they reached the car she showed Berger the screen; it read 02.46. He had to turn round on a largely non-existent road. By the time the car finally drove off the screen showed 00.21.

Berger scratched the corner of his eye. Something ran down his cheek. He turned the rear-view mirror and saw that it was a drop of blood.

Then the world exploded behind them.

36

This isn't the first time Molly Blom gets out of the jeep in the disabled parking space at Gällivare Airport; on the contrary, the sequence of events keeps repeating in an endless loop.

That was the last time she breathed fresh air.

She saw Berger from behind up ahead, on his way through the main entrance, and was about to run after him. Instead she heard a whistling sound and felt her head explode.

She drifted in and out of consciousness, bumping and bouncing, heard the sound of a car engine, saw nothing. She was lying in a space that was more tightly sealed than a car boot usually was, a claustrophobically enclosed space. Eventually she figured out she had been squashed inside a case, a trunk.

Then she realised that what she could smell was blood. Dried blood.

Jovana Malešević's blood.

The realisation sent her back once more to the moment when she steps out of the jeep at Gällivare Airport and sees Berger ahead of her and gets ready to run after him.

Then she was sitting on a heavy metal chair, and everything was spinning around her in murky semi-darkness. Her head was pressed forward, down. She looked into a white enamel washbasin. Water ran through her hair into the basin. At first she thought it was blood mixed in the water, swirling down the plughole, but then she realised that it wasn't the right colour. A towel was thrown over her head and her hair very roughly dried. Then her head was released, and she sat there with her hands and feet tied to the chair, and saw a brown-haired figure within a picture frame, saw the figure shadowed by someone in a black balaclava who was approaching fast. A pair of scissors cut the air. Then a hand was pressed over her eyes and the scissors dived into her hair, cutting furiously for a long, long time. Then the hand disappeared from her eyes. It took a while before she could see into the mirror in front of her again.

She looked at the gilded mirror, looked into her own eyes and eventually recognised her face. That was when she realised that the brown hair she had seen reflected in the mirror was actually hers.

And now it had been cut into a bob.

The figure in the balaclava was standing behind her and put the scissors down. A hand stroked her hair gently. Then something else erupted behind the balaclava. An inhuman roar echoed through the unknown room. A considerably larger figure in a matching black balaclava threw itself at the smaller one.

Then everything went black again.

She gets out of the jeep in the disabled parking space at Gällivare Airport. She sees Berger from behind, on his way through the main entrance, and is about to run after him. Then she hears a whistling sound.

She gets out of the jeep in the disabled parking space at Gällivare Airport. She sees Berger from behind, on his way through the main entrance, and is about to run after him.

Then she woke up.

She opened her eyes. The cold had already eaten its way into her. It took a little too long for her to understand why. She was naked, completely naked. The heavy metal chair seemed to be screwed to a concrete floor, a cellar floor from the look of it. The chill, mouldy smell assaulting her nose seemed very cellar-like. She tugged a little at her arms and legs; they were firmly fixed with cable ties.

There was total silence.

It was very nearly totally dark as well. A few metres away she could make out a sofa, and on the sofa she could make out a couple of figures.

Perhaps it was the sound that made her realise that everything was covered; it sounded like bare skin on plastic.

But she couldn't see anything, could only vaguely detect movement. Then darkness again.

Then she wakes up again, senses two bodies on the sofa. Bodies without heads.

Until she realises that they're wearing black balaclavas. She senses movement on the sofa. Snake-like, squirming. Nothing else.

Just darkness and silence. Then the smaller of the figures leans forward. Until it reaches something that resembles light. It's a woman. Her upper body is bare, but she's still wearing the balaclava. Then she disappears again.

It's like a slow but insistent stroboscope.

Once again she senses movement on the sofa, but the movements seem to belong in a parallel universe. They don't reach her, not really.

Then the woman leans forward again, into the weak light, into the spotlight. She slowly pulls off the balaclava, but it isn't until Jessica Johnsson removes her blonde wig that Molly Blom recognises her.

The man leans forward too, pulls off his balaclava. Reine Danielsson has aged significantly since he was questioned in Orsa; Molly has only ever seen pictures of him as a young man. Anything childlike about his appearance back then is long gone, replaced by dark, furrowed experience. By unrelenting loneliness.

Then the pair lean back on the sofa again and are replaced by darkness. She's in darkness now, immense darkness.

She hears the sound of the pair's grotesque pantomime, senses naked skin on plastic, is struck by how ridiculous the whole charade is. The whole performance, which no one seems to be getting any pleasure from.

When her sight returns Reine is standing up. She sees herself, sees her naked bound body as if from a completely different part of the room.

Reine comes closer. Then she sees, right at the edge of the faint strip of light, a table. On the table is a large knife.

Darkness again. Receptive, deceptive darkness. Pain in her head. Spreading through her body. And this is only the start.

She doesn't want to know how the rest of the pain feels, she really doesn't want to know.

She wakes up. Even though her every instinct is to open her eyes, she keeps them closed. Time passes, she tries to orientate herself in the room, in her own consciousness. Her nose is filled with the stench of mould, her body. She tries to understand what's going on.

A woman's voice says, 'Eyelids aren't just thin, they're also revealing.'

She opens her eyes. Reine is standing in front of her. He's holding a block of wood in his hand. Almost completely hidden behind him she sees Jessica leaning forward on the sofa, sees her head, her faintly smiling face, not much more. She goes on:

'Three minutes and eight seconds have passed since you woke up. Was that long enough for you to work out where you are?'

'I know where I am,' Molly says, as calmly as she can.

'And where is that?'

'In the darkness,' Molly says.

Jessica laughs loudly. It's a warm, happy, bubbling laugh that doesn't belong in this cellar.

None of this belongs together.

Jessica stands up and stretches.

'If only you knew how right you are,' she says.

She walks forward to stand beside Reine. They're just a metre away from Molly, side by side. Two naked people.

Jessica leans forward and inspects Molly. She puts her hand under her chin and tilts her face from side to side, as if she were looking at it through a magnifying glass.

'I thought your name was Eva Lundström for far too long,' Jessica says. 'It took quite some time to figure out that you're really called Molly Blom.'

Then she straightens up and, without taking her eyes off Molly's, says:

'Reine. Hit her.'

Molly feels herself jerk as her head is knocked sideways, back and forth. Her whole body prepares for the pain.

'We'll make do with the upper arms for now,' Jessica says. 'Then you cut her.'

Molly isn't going to close her eyes. She isn't going to close her eyes.

She looks straight into Reine Danielsson's eyes as he raises the block of wood, and she doesn't take her eyes off him even when it slams into her upper arm. There's definitely no pleasure in those eyes. More a peculiar lethargy. If she gets the chance, maybe she can use that to her advantage.

He hits her left arm, then her right arm, and she keeps her eyes on him the whole time, every moment. When the third blow strikes her left arm she feels numb, and the only sensation when it's time for her right arm again is a strange dullness. Numbness. As if her body were shutting down.

Then Reine swaps the block of wood for the knife.

Molly sees it sink into her lower left arm. She sees the blood pour out. It feels like someone else's blood.

Like someone else's body.

Then Jessica is there, staring with those clinical eyes at the blood pumping out of the wound. And she holds up a test tube and removes the cork from it. She moves the test tube towards the arm, the flow of blood, and fills it. She holds it up against the weak red light and shakes it; the act looks professional.

Jessica is about to say something when the light goes out. The cellar is completely dark.

'Not again,' Jessica exclaims.

Reine mumbles something, Molly can't make out the words. Jessica says:

'I think there are more fuses. We talked about buying candles. Did we?'

'No,' Reine says.

It's the first time Molly has heard his voice. It's balanced, sounds almost veiled.

She knows she can work with that.

If she gets a chance.

'Go up and replace the fuse,' Jessica says.

Reine disappears.

Molly stares into the darkness and thinks about the absurdity of it. The absurdity of everything. But particularly the absurdity of listening to a serial killer having an everyday conversation. Perverse normality. Fuses blowing. Forgetting to buy candles.

It's as if there were suddenly something like everyday life again.

And her arm hurts really badly.

'Let's call this a ceasefire,' Jessica says.

Molly is aware of how heavy her breathing is. There's nothing to say. And Jessica doesn't say anything else.

As if she didn't have anything to say.

Time passes. Then she hears footsteps on the stairs. Reine's voice, saying, 'It's something else. The fuse hasn't blown. I changed it anyway. It didn't work.'

'Damn,' Jessica says somewhere in the darkness.

Molly wishes she could stem the flow of blood from her arm. But that's impossible. She can't move.

She hears things in the darkness. She hears the springs of the sofa, as if someone is sitting down. Then a small light goes on, the light from a mobile phone. She sees Jessica on the sofa, sees her push aside everything lying there and look at the test tube. Reine goes over to her with a trolley that was parked somewhere. There's medical equipment on the trolley, laboratory equipment.

Molly tries to understand what she's seeing.

But the only thing she understands is that she doesn't understand anything.

And that she's been granted a respite.

She closes her eyes and knows, *knows* that every minute works to her advantage. Because every minute she can stay alive, Sam Berger is getting closer.

She *knows* that.

37

The announcement was made during the night. Berger and Deer heard it on local radio, saw it online. The local electricity substation was out of action. Älvdalen Council, to which Särna belonged, had been smart enough to withhold any suggestion that it was an explosion, a deliberate attack. And by seven o'clock in the morning the news hadn't been deemed interesting enough to warrant national coverage.

During the small hours the council website issued the following information to the residents of Särna and the surrounding area: 'We are working to reroute the electricity supply. Every household must log on to the website with an individualised code that can be collected from the address below in Särna from 08.00 on Thursday morning.'

The location given was Särna church, and by ten to eight people had already started to gather. Särna wasn't big and, as luck would have it, the white church was blessed with a large car park next to the petrol station on the other side of the road. And to start with it seemed to be going well.

They were waiting in a strategic position close to the entrance. It was already starting to get seriously cold inside the car.

The grey sky was just beginning to break, and pale white streaks of dawn were starting to filter through the reluctant clouds.

'So Carsten was right,' Deer said from the passenger seat.

'He seems very keen for us to rescue Molly,' Berger said quietly.

Deer looked down at her mobile and read:

'The electricity grid is digitally controlled. An individual code is required to reroute the supply and must be collected in person. Knocking out the power supply is the only way to get people out of their houses.'

'Now there's a man who knows how to carry out attacks,' Berger muttered.

Time crept past. As it grew brighter the temperature inside the car sank. The gradual build-up of traffic in the car park in front of Särna church meant that they could switch the engine on and run it in neutral from time to time without attracting attention. There was now a queue of people snaking towards the church; the gathering was slightly chaotic but still good-natured. It was getting more and more difficult to distinguish individual people, even individual vehicles.

Berger and Deer had sat in surveillance vehicles together so many times before that this felt almost routine. Yet at the same time it was also completely alien. As if they were taking part in a play about the distant past. Everything was familiar, nothing was familiar.

The circumstances were radically different.

The chaos in the car park was getting worse. Drivers were blowing their horns, one man was gesticulating wildly at their parking space, apparently demanding that they vacate it. The vehicles were crammed together, people were shouting at each other, waving their fists, making obscene gestures. The blaring horns formed a cacophony of their very own. A truck pulled up in front of them and stopped, blocking the whole row. Completely unconcerned, the driver began to unpack a delivery for the filling station.

After ten minutes or so Berger had had enough and got out. He walked around the truck and tried to get an overview of the chaos. He glanced over towards the queue winding towards the church; there too the initial amused hubbub was threatening to spill over into something more threatening. Where had all these people come from?

That was when he saw it. In an out-of-the-way parking space, there it was, a Fjord Blue Volkswagen Caddy with the registration number LAM 387. And it was empty.

He hunched down and hurried back towards Deer, beckoned her out, pointed to the van. They pulled their hoods up and made their way as normally as they could towards the queue leading to the church. They then began to stroll along on either side of the jostling line of people, not without a good deal of protest from those in the queue. It was at least ten degrees below zero, people were well wrapped up and it was hard to see their faces. On two occasions Berger was obliged to show his fake police ID; he would have preferred not to have to do that.

The atmosphere grew increasingly heated the further up the queue they progressed, and Berger couldn't help thinking it had the makings of a lynch mob. Just as he was reaching through the queue to grab Deer out of the hands of a huge red-faced man, a figure in a camouflage-green hooded jacket detached itself from the queue some twenty metres ahead. He managed to free Deer from the giant as he kept his eyes on the figure. It slipped away to the right, onto a path that had been cleared between the snow-covered graves.

Berger set off with Deer close behind. Someone stuck their foot out and tripped him, causing him to fall flat on his face. Harsh laughter filled the white air. Deer carried on past him, and from his prone position he saw her reach the path leading into the graveyard. He stood up, pulled free and ran after her.

The figure in camouflage green had stopped. There was no face visible beneath the hood. The figure seemed to be watching them. It was standing twenty metres away on the icy path between the graves when Berger passed Deer and once again fell to the ground, this time entirely through his own fault. The path was like an ice rink. He got to his feet, sliding about on the spot. The figure was standing perfectly still, invisible eyes staring at them from inside the hood. It was as if it was waiting, waiting for something. As if it knew something they didn't.

Berger didn't like it. The figure was standing between two headstones, just waiting for them. While he tried to get a grip on the path with his boots, he glanced over his shoulder. Deer was gone. The moment he started off, as well as he could, the figure set off towards the right; there was evidently a track there between the graves. And the figure was managing to find its footing in a way that he couldn't hope to, probably thanks to snow studs. It ran off towards the car park. He hadn't even reached the junction of the paths when he saw the figure vault the snow-covered hedge facing the car park like a world-class hurdler. He made a little progress, slipped again and struggled to find his footing as he watched the green hood pass among the cars, heading for the VW Caddy.

Fucking hell, the situation was slipping from his grasp.

By now the queue stretched back almost to the entrance to the churchyard. The figure was running smoothly towards the entrance when something happened.

38

Berger walked in. The door closed behind him. It was all very clinical. The textured wallpaper was as bland and nondescript as the empty birch-veneer table. There was some unidentifiable technical equipment on the side table. There were no windows in the room, but two chairs. One of them was empty.

And on the other sat Jessica Johnsson.

Her wrists were fastened to the armrests with cable ties. She had a number of cuts on her face, some covered with plasters, others still seeping a little blood. Berger recognised the strange little smile playing at the corners of her mouth. But she said nothing.

Berger sat down, switched on the recording equipment on the side table and said, 'Where's Molly?'

Jessica didn't answer. Instead she looked around the bare room, analysing it. Berger went on, 'It's over, Jessica. Surely you can see that?'

No reaction.

'If nothing else, spare a thought for Reine,' Berger said. 'Your Reine. Don't make him commit one last murder. Don't force him into another psychotic breakdown.'

Forcing himself to hold back was genuinely painful. All he wanted to do was launch himself at her and tear her to pieces. But Deer, who was directing him via his earpiece, had persuaded him that that wouldn't be particularly effective.

'Get under her skin,' she reminded him now, in his ear.

And he had to try, he really did have to try to crawl under the skin of Jessica Johnsson. But how the hell was he supposed to find his way in?

They'd had heated discussions about the arrangements. Should Deer be present during the interview? Or should Deer conduct it on her own? In the end they came to the conclusion that her absence would probably have most impact. At least to start with.

After all, it was Sam Berger whom Jessica had been after.

He leaned across the table and said, 'If you tell me where she is, you'll probably get a fixed-term sentence. Otherwise it'll be life, a full life sentence: you'll already have taken your last breaths as a free woman.'

Jessica sat in silence, watching him, mysterious, determined, absurdly strong. Infinitely sick. This really wasn't going to be easy. He needed to summon up all his patience. It seemed unlikely that Reine would attack Molly on his own. Assuming she was still alive ...

Jessica seemed to read his mind. Her first words were, 'Reine knows what to do if I don't come back.'

Berger felt like he was going to be sick, throw up across that stupid birch-veneer table. In his ear he heard, very calmly, 'And what is Reine going to do?'

He managed to sit still and said, 'And what is Reine going to do if you don't come back?'

Jessica smiled, momentarily, fleetingly, joylessly, 'Finish the job,' she said.

'Farida Hesari,' Deer said in his ear.

'Reine becomes a different person when you're not there,' Berger said. 'While you were asleep he let Farida Hesari escape from that house in Täby.'

Jessica nodded slowly, as if something had just dawned on her.

'You've done your homework,' she said. 'You've been very clever.'

'Just as you wanted,' Berger said as calmly as he could.

'Reine's done his homework too,' Jessica said, shrugging her shoulders. 'He won't make that mistake again.'

Berger looked deep into Jessica Johnsson's averted eyes. For a brief moment he thought he could see all the artifice in her. As if she realised how much pain she ought to be feeling but wasn't capable of. The question was whether she actually felt anything at all, or if it was all just a sick game.

'We know about everything you've been through,' Berger said.

'Everything?' Jessica laughed. 'Stick to what you're good at.'

Berger fell silent. He vaguely recognised the phrase.

Jessica went on, 'Is she chattering in your ear again, Sam? Like she did eight years ago?'

The scene in Orsa came back to Berger. Him raising his hand towards Reine and the nurse. Forming his fingers into a pistol. Shooting Reine. And saying to the nurse: 'Stick to what you're good at.' Then Deer laughing.

A gesture, a few words, a laugh. And that combination had taken root and grown like some insane cancerous tumour.

Against all the odds he managed to return to the present, and his outward calm surprised him, 'We know what you've been through,' Berger said. 'But we can't get it to make sense. When you were eight years old you found a four-leaf clover. You got to make a wish, something you really wanted, but you weren't allowed to say it out loud. And what you really wanted was not to have a little brother.'

She was staring at him now, and their eyes got caught in each other.

'Because you wanted to be alone,' Berger continued. 'Like a true narcissist you couldn't bear the thought of having to share your parents' attention. I wonder if you were even shocked when you found your mother in a pool of blood at the age of eight. I can't help wondering if you actually killed her? Did you poison her? If you were going to have to share her with someone else, then she had to die.'

Jessica tore her eyes from his and stared into the wall. He thought he could see her jaw muscles tense.

He needed those tensed muscles.

'And there's the whole business with your father,' Berger went on. 'You never did get his attention. Perhaps you could get it now, now that the threat had been removed?'

Her jaw remained tense.

'But that didn't happen, did it? Quite the reverse, in fact. Your dad moved as far away as it's possible to get on the planet. I think he moved to get away from you, Jessica. He was frightened of you. He could see how dangerous you were. How sick you were. Did you tell your dad about your wish? Have you murdered him too?'

She smiled, but her jaw was still tense. The combination was a very odd expression.

'You saw a child therapist,' Berger went on. 'You realised how you *ought* to feel. But you couldn't. You couldn't feel it then, and you can't feel it now. Your hinterland is completely white, Jessica. A perfect blank.'

Their eyes met. There was something in her gaze now, something almost content. As if she wanted this out in the open. As if this was what she was after. It wasn't pain that was driving her, it was the search for pain. The search to feel anything at all.

'While you were stuck with your poor clueless Aunt Ebba, surfing the Internet for the very worst things you could imagine, you realised that you ought to feel something self-destructive. Perhaps you ought to be drawn to sadomasochism? You adopted the self-punishing role, moved to the USA, saw how Madame Newhouse handled her high boredom threshold. A slave you could order about, perhaps that would be worth trying? Someone who could enact your sickest fantasies, someone who would *see* you. Because that's what you want, to be seen. You're nothing but an attention-seeking drama queen.'

'Stop there,' Deer said in his ear.

Berger stopped. Looked at Jessica Johnsson. She met his gaze again. He tried to read the look in her eyes, but it was very, very difficult. Was that something broken he could see in there? Could he see a desire to correct, adjust, change anything he had said?

He didn't know, so he waited, hoping that Deer might have been able to see more than him. But his ear remained silent.

'Why should you be the first person in the world to understand?' Jessica said with a little smile. 'What would qualify you for that?'

'You've been trying to get my attention, Jessica. You've been calling to me.'

Her eyes narrowed. Berger went on:

'Reine wasn't enough, was he? You realised that he wasn't the audience you needed, way back in Orsa. You wanted someone who could both see you and condemn you. Who could stop you. Because what you're doing is utterly meaningless, and you're all too aware of that. You think that sooner or later you're going to feel something, but I think the fact is that you genuinely *can't* feel anything.'

Jessica Johnsson looked away. He could see something in her eyes, her smile had been wiped away.

'I'll soon be able to feel something,' she said quietly.

Berger waited, hoping to hear something from Deer, anything at all, but nothing came. His ear was silent.

What the hell did 'I'll soon be able to feel something' mean?

'Eight years ago you chose Deer and me as some sort of replacement parents,' Berger went on. 'Deer was tough on Reine when we were questioning him, I pretended to shoot you with my fingers. Something back then triggered you. Over the years, while you got on with your hideous series of murders, you've been trying to contact us, get us to notice you. Get us to understand and stop you. But then something happened, a few weeks ago you *really* needed to get us moving. What was it that happened then?'

Jessica suddenly smiled again, as if to herself.

'I already told you in Porjus. I saw you on television.'

'You said you saw Deer.'

'You were both on television, you were still working together. She said something about the Ellen case, you were standing in the background.'

'But why did you need us now?'

'I want to see your pain,' Jessica said with a beaming smile.

Lightning flashed through Berger. He wanted to use force. Brutal force.

'Keep calm, Sam,' Deer said in his ear.

Berger closed his eyes, managed to control himself.

'You want me to validate your pain, Jessica,' he said. 'I'm not going to do that; there is no pain. But I can validate your emptiness.'

Was that disappointment he saw in her face? Had she been hoping for him to validate her suffering? Had she been hoping that he'd dignify her feelings, make them nobler than they were?

So, what would be most effective now? To go along with her? Or to push even harder? He was going to have to decide. Deer had stopped him. That would have to guide his decision.

'Unless perhaps you did feel something when you took such extreme revenge on Eddy Karlsson in that basement in Bagarmossen?'

She seemed to brighten up a little.

'You can't say he didn't get what he deserved,' she said.

'Hang in there,' Deer said in his ear.

'I don't actually know what Eddy Karlsson did to you,' Berger said.

'You're not going to find out either,' Jessica said.

'It seemed a pretty straight eye-for-an-eye transaction. A cock for a womb.'

Jessica laughed.

'Smart, eh?' she said.

Berger looked at her and said, 'Are you really such a banal serial killer, Jessica? Have you really called me here simply so I can admire you? So I can be impressed by how *smart* you are?'

She blinked again, but this time she didn't look away. He thought he could see a bit of anger in her eyes.

'I've stopped you now,' he said. 'And you're not really that smart. And you probably haven't ever felt anything.'

'Soon I'll be able to feel something,' Jessica repeated.

'And how's that going to work after thirty-five years of feeling nothing?'

'I want to look into your eyes when Molly Blom dies.'

Everything turned white. A world without markers.

'Keep calm, Sam,' Deer said immediately into his ear. 'Take it very gently now. Does that mean she knows exactly when it's going to happen? Has Reine been given a time when he has to deliver the fatal blow? How do we find that out?'

'Don't be ridiculous,' Berger said with hard-won calmness. 'You didn't even know Molly existed until we showed up at your house in Porjus.'

'And at the time I thought her name was Eva Lundström,' Jessica said with a slightly more confident smile. 'But the important thing was that I saw that you were a couple.'

'A couple?'

'It was very obvious.'

There was a crackle in his ear. Deer said, very clearly:

'Don't let her get to you, Sam. Just keep going.'

He couldn't. He genuinely couldn't keep going. So Jessica did instead, looking past Berger, straight at the camera, 'Right outside your daughter's school, Deer, is a postbox. School was over for the day, Lykke was walking straight towards us. I was standing there with the letter to Säter, to Karl, poised in the mouth of the postbox. Reine was standing next to me, awaiting orders. I had to take a quick decision. What would hurt more? Taking Deer's daughter or Sam's lover? Lykke is the same age I was when I picked the four-leaf clover; she actually reminded me of myself, with that hairstyle and everything. We were all set to snatch her. But right there and then I changed my mind. It would be more of a challenge to find and capture Molly Blom. I dropped the envelope in the box and let Lykke walk past. If I hadn't, your daughter would be dead now, Superintendent Rosenkvist.'

'Stay where you are, Deer,' Berger said out loud.

He heard Deer sob in his ear, but nothing else.

He had to get control of the conversation. He said, 'How did you manage to get to the airport in Gällivare ahead of us? We thought you were in Skogås.'

'That was the point,' Jessica smiled sweetly. 'Once I'd decided that we weren't going to snatch Lykke we flew back to Lapland.'

'That doesn't answer my question,' Berger said.

Jessica shrugged and said, 'I realised that you were up north somewhere, within reasonable distance of Porjus. The airlines up here run systems that are very easy to hack into, and we'd positioned ourselves between Gällivare and Arvidsjaur, the two potential airports. All we had to do was set off once your booking popped up. Any more exciting technical questions you'd like to ask?'

'Anders Hedblom, Karl's brother,' Berger said. 'Why did you kill him?'

'Berger did that,' Jessica said with another smile. 'It said so on the note.'

'Did you move to Malmö because of Anders?' Berger asked as calmly as he could.

'That's not very interesting,' Jessica said scornfully. 'He came to visit his brother up in Orsa, we started seeing each other. I moved down to Malmö to be with him, but he wasn't that interested in me. To keep hold of him I suggested that Karl was innocent and let slip a bit too much. Then he moved north after I did, and started to blackmail me. So he's only got himself to blame.'

'He wasn't a good enough dad,' Berger said. 'So he ended up being one of your ten victims.'

'Ten?'

'I make it ten. Helena, Rasmus, Mette, Lisa, Eddy, Farida, Elisabeth, Anders, Jovana and Molly.'

'I count them completely differently,' Jessica said. 'There are six.'

'Explain,' Berger said.

'Farida escaped, she doesn't count. Eddy and Anders don't count, they were just unavoidable. And Anders was a way of getting my message to you, Sam.'

'I still make it seven, Jessica,' Berger said.

'Rasmus Gradén doesn't count. He belongs with Helena.'

'I don't understand what you mean.'

'It's not six victims,' Jessica said. 'It's six times two.'

Berger waited, thought, listened. But Deer didn't say anything, his ear was quiet. And his thoughts weren't adding up.

Jessica went on with repellent calmness.

'There are always two, a mother and a son, none of the rest matters. Helena and her son. Mette and her son. Lisa Widstrand and her son. Elisabeth Ström and her son. Jovana Malešević and her son.'

'That's only five,' Berger blurted, feeling his head start to boil. 'Five times two.'

'Right jacket pocket,' Jessica said.

Then she said nothing more.

Berger got to his feet, stumbled out through the door to the hall, returned with Jessica's padded jacket, put his hand in the right-hand pocket, pulled out some sort of plastic tube, looked at it, saw a window and a small line in the window.

'I started with a blood test,' Jessica said. 'The result was surprising but strangely logical, as if even fate had helped me to make the right decision. Then I did the more usual pregnancy test as well. Urine.'

Berger stared at the line, at Jessica Johnsson, at the wall.

'Molly Blom is pregnant,' Jessica said. 'Less than a month, though.'

Berger stared at her. He wondered what was dribbling out of the corner of his mouth.

'Six times two,' Jessica said with a broad smile. 'The number of victims is six times two.'

39

It was the cold that woke her. That or her wounds. Not that it really mattered: they both hurt.

Everything hurt.

But most of all it was awareness that hurt. Awareness of the situation she was in.

She tugged at the cable ties. All four limbs were held as tightly as ever. Only then did she open her eyes.

It didn't make much difference. Some sort of vague background light was filtering into the cellar, that was all. She could just make out the sofa, and could sense a figure on it, sensed that he was no longer naked, sensed that he was wearing some sort of tracksuit, sensed that he was asleep.

Sensed that he was alone.

She looked around her at the gloomy cellar. There was nothing there. There was the sofa, there was the man, there was the table with the block of wood and the knife, and there was her. There was nothing else.

Molly Blom looked down at her body. She tried to estimate the extent of her injuries. Just seeing her arms so blue, so swollen, so bloody was a shock, but it was the itch in her buttock that really bothered her. She tried to lean forward, in tiny increments over a period of time she couldn't be bothered to try to estimate, reaching a little further each time. Eventually she was able to look between her legs. She could make out a faint shape on her buttock. She realised that it was ink.

And that she was probably looking at a four-leaf clover.

Jessica was gone. Molly had no idea when she might have left, but something had happened during the night, Jessica and Reine had sat huddled in front of the computer discussing something in subdued but agitated voices.

Molly had no idea what time it was. The faint background light suggested that it might be daytime, that a few rays of daylight were slipping past a poorly fitting cellar door, something like that. Because of the problems with the fuses or whatever it was, it could hardly be electric light.

Then she heard something beyond Reine's snoring. A more persistent, more regular sound. Ticking?

Very, very faintly, but it was there, it was definitely real.

There was a ticking sound behind her back.

She was relatively fit, not least thanks to all the skiing she had been doing recently, and she had already stretched her neck and back trying to see the four-leaf clover. Even so, it took her several attempts to be able to look behind her. There was a clock on the wall. Its hands showed a quarter to eleven, and it looked new, didn't seem to be part of the normal furnishings and fittings, just like the red velour sofa. Which meant it had been put there for a reason.

For Reine's benefit, presumably.

Molly might not have been especially awake during the journey here, inside the trunk soaked with Jovana Malešević's blood, but it had taken a long time, at least six hours, she guessed. They could have driven north, of course – towards the point where Sweden, Norway and Finland met, or even further north than that, towards Finnmark, Honningsvåg, Hammerfest, the North Cape. But it felt more likely that they had driven south. Towards more densely populated areas, in other words. Which suggested that Jessica Johnsson had been gone a fairly long time. Rather longer than necessary.

This sort of logical analysis was vital.

Her life was on the line, and she wasn't about to spend what could be her last minutes worrying about metaphysical speculation. What happens after death? Had she lived a good life? Not a chance. This was all about survival now.

On or off, yes or no.

She was Molly Blom. And she wasn't going to depart this world without fighting to the very last drop of blood.

And right now her opponent was a bona fide idiot. If she couldn't handle this, then she didn't deserve to survive. Despite the cable ties and a razor-sharp hunting knife.

Jessica would never have left without some form of insurance; she was too smart for that. If it was true that too much time had passed – best-case scenario if Sam Berger had got her – then she would have given Reine something to go by. And there was only one possible thing for him to go by: the newly installed clock. So, a specific time. And Reine hardly seemed capable of dealing with thirteen minutes past eleven, say, or 11.47. But he'd be able to deal with whole hours, and possibly half-hours.

The clock was ticking towards ten to eleven. Perhaps eleven o'clock was too soon. Perhaps Jessica had given Reine until half past eleven, twelve o'clock.

But there was a time when he was going to kill her.

She listened to the snoring. If that time was eleven o'clock, then an alarm clock, possibly a mobile, ought to start ringing any moment now. Jessica must have been aware of the risk that

Reine might fall asleep. She must have set an alarm clock. And poor Reine would need at least ten minutes to wake up before he set about committing yet another murder. On Jessica's orders.

Which meant that the alarm ought to be ringing now.

Which meant that Molly Blom – in spite of the fact that she had only one functioning limb – had to be ready to mount a counter-attack the moment the alarm clock rang.

So she got ready. Steeled herself. In case eleven o'clock was the designated time.

Time passed. It felt almost like a session in the gym, repeatedly having to look back over her shoulder at the clock. The hands passed eleven. So she probably had another thirty minutes, possibly an hour. Did she have any alternative courses of action? Hardly. Her body was firmly tied and was also in pretty poor shape. All she had, the only thing that was still intact, was her head.

Somehow what she said to Reine had to be stronger than what Jessica had said, and Jessica and Reine had lived together for eight years, and Jessica had spent a decade training him. Taming him. Brainwashing him.

Even so, she hadn't seen evil in Reine's eyes. He had a slave's eyes.

Molly could use that as her opening. She could. She could talk him past the allotted hour.

She had to believe that.

At quarter past eleven something rang in the pocket of Reine's tracksuit. She had guessed right.

Quarter of an hour to prepare.

Quarter of an hour of life left.

Reine opened his eyes and stared around the cellar. It took him a while to pull his mobile from his pocket and switch it off. She looked at it and thought about triangulation, tried to think logically: if Sam had caught Jessica, he might have found Reine's phone number among the contacts in her mobile, and would be working on triangulating their position.

The likelihood was fairly slim, of course, but the fact that it was even a possibility gave her the strength to go back to her original plan. She said in her very gentlest voice, 'Good morning, Reine. Did you have a nice sleep?'

He rubbed his eyes and looked at her through the semi-darkness. What those eyes saw was very unclear.

'It's very cold in here,' she said and tried to smile.

She saw his eyes look past her shoulder at the clock. She thought she saw the penny drop.

She saw from his expression that he knew what he was supposed to do. He glanced over at the table, at the knife.

'Did you use to call Jessica Lena when you first met?' Molly asked. 'Her name was Lena back then, wasn't it? Do you remember that, Reine? When you lived in the home in Falun?'

Reine blinked several times, still sitting on the sofa. He said nothing.

'That's where you grew up, Reine, do you remember?'

'I'm not allowed to listen to you,' Reine said.

'Was it Lena or Jessica who told you not to listen to me, Reine?'

Reine looked at her, met her gaze for the first time.

'Who do you like best, Reine? Lena or Jessica?'

'I'm not allowed to listen to you.'

'But perhaps you're not Reine? Are you Sam? Sam Berger? Do you remember Sam? And Deer, you remember Deer, don't you? Sam and Deer?'

'I'm not allowed to listen to you.'

'Do you remember the needle in your arm, Sam? You were really clever that time, bending the needle so the liquid in the drip didn't go into your bloodstream. Because you wanted to run off through the snow, Sam Berger. You looked like a snow angel as you ran through the snow. You remember that, don't you?'

'I'm not—'

'You wanted to stop that bus with your bare hands, Sam. You remember the bus, don't you? It was going to save you. You wanted to escape then, Sam, you wanted to get out, get away. You never wanted that when you lived in the care home. Back then you just wanted to sit and draw, do you remember? Are you allowed to draw these days, Reine? Lena was nicer than Jessica, wasn't she?'

Reine stood up and said, 'I want to do more drawing.'

Molly glanced over her shoulder, seven more minutes to live, seven more minutes to unlock the latent consciousness tucked away inside Reine's limited brain.

'Jessica's the only one who draws now, isn't she? The four-leaf clover. Did you watch when she drew it on my bottom last night?'

'That's the only thing I'm allowed to draw,' Reine said and moved towards the table. She saw him glance at the clock again.

'Is it you who draws the four-leaf clovers, Reine? Or is it Sam? Sam Berger? Why do you like Sam and Deer?'

'I don't like them. They're nasty. They said nasty things.'

'But you *are* Sam, you know that, don't you? You do nasty things too. Lena was nice when she first came to the care home, wasn't she? You didn't need to run away then, Reine. But then Lena became Jessica. And Jessica is nasty. You want to run away from Jessica, Sam, and that's what you did, through the snow. Do you remember Farida?'

'Farida,' Reine said and stopped halfway to the table.

'Yes, Farida,' Molly said. 'Farida with the tattoos. You remember her, don't you? You let her run away to the bus, Reine. You were nice to her, you let her run away. Do you remember?'

'She didn't want to die,' Reine said, standing still.

'I don't want to die either,' Molly said, feeling tears trickle down her cheeks. 'Please, Reine, let me go, let me go and we can run away to the bus together, Sam. There's a bus that goes past right outside, we can run away from Jessica together. Jessica was so horrible to you when you let Farida go. You remember how horrible she was, don't you? That was when she dipped your fingertips in acid to make your fingerprints disappear, wasn't it?'

'I'm not allowed to listen to you,' Reine said in a louder voice and took another step towards the table.

'My name is Molly, Sam. I want to run away with you. Molly. Are you going to kill Molly, Reine? Are you really going to do that?'

Another look over her shoulder. Three minutes left.

Reine moved closer to the table and shouted, 'I'm not allowed to listen to you!'

'But you want to listen to me, to Molly, don't you? You want to run away from Jessica. We can run away together. The bus goes right outside here, Sam. We can get on it together, we can fly away like snow angels, as beautiful snow angels. Sam and Molly, just the way it should be. My name is Molly, I'm a person. You don't want to kill me, Sam.'

Reine reached the table, picked up the knife. She saw it tremble in his hand. She felt tears fall.

Reine walked slowly towards her. The knife was shaking violently in his hand.

'You can draw as much as you want to with me, Reine,' Molly sobbed. 'You can have a room of your own and all the paper you want. Come on, let's run away, Reine.'

Reine stopped and stared at her with an odd look in his eyes.

'I keep trying to kill you, Jessica, but it never works. You always come back.'

'I'm Molly, Reine! You're Sam and I'm Molly and we're going to run away from Jessica together. We can kill her together. Then you can do as much drawing as you like.'

He crouched down in front of her, looked into her eyes, moved the knife towards her.

'We'll catch the bus, Reine,' she said. 'We'll catch the bus to freedom, Sam.'

The knife stopped, still shaking, just above her right wrist.

'I have to kill you now, Jessica,' Reine said.

40

Berger couldn't remove his hands from his face. It was impossible. It was like they'd frozen in place.

Deer was watching him. They were sitting in the inner room. The interview was frozen on the screen. Jessica Johnsson was smiling, and as a still image her smile was terrifying. It was as if she hadn't been real until then.

There, on the screen.

'I don't get it, I really don't,' Berger said.

'I have a feeling you get it all too well,' Deer said.

'She threw up,' Berger said. 'After she'd been out skiing.'

'If I understand your story correctly, the two of you were isolated up in those cabins for almost a month. But we can't rely on Jessica Johnsson to tell the truth. Molly could very easily be two months gone, in which case she got pregnant long before the two of you even met. Or she went off while you were drugged and met some local hotshot in Kvikkjokk or something.'

'But I remember her body.'

'What do you mean?'

'A birthmark under her right breast that looked like a star.'

'You could have seen that at any time.'

Deer went over to the map of northern Dalarna pinned to the wall. She said, 'She's in this area somewhere. OK, let's go back in together and finish this.'

She walked towards the door and pulled it open.

'How lovely,' Jessica said and smiled. 'Now Superintendent Rosenkvist comes crawling out of the woodwork. Like a newly hatched house borer.'

'Where is she?' Deer roared, one centimetre from her face.

'It's all very clear when I look around this room,' Jessica said calmly. 'You're on your own, none of this is official. Which means that we could actually do a straight swap. Sit down.'

Deer clenched her fist several times before she moved back slightly. She went around the table and sat down. Berger sat down beside her.

In a tone of voice that sounded almost formal, Jessica said, 'At a designated time Reine is going to kill Molly. However he has a mobile phone, I can phone and stop him. We can do an exchange. You get Molly, Reine gets me. Everyone walks away happy.'

'We've checked your mobile,' Berger said. 'There are no contacts, no calls made, no calls received.'

'For reasons of security neither his nor my phone has ever been used,' Jessica said, tapping her head. 'But I've got the number in here.'

'So call him, for fuck's sake!' Berger shouted.

'First we need to agree on the procedure,' Jessica said, glancing over his shoulder at the clock on the wall. 'We've got fifty-two minutes.'

Deer and Berger both turned to look at the clock.

'Half past eleven, then?' Deer said.

Jessica shrugged.

Berger and Deer's eyes met, and they looked at each other for a few moments, reading each other.

Then they left the room. Behind them they heard Jessica's voice:

'Remember, the clock's ticking.'

Berger slammed the door shut and said, 'She's never going to make that call. This is another attempt at sadistic pleasure. She wanted to get caught, she's happy now. All she really wants is to look into my eyes when Molly dies, but she won't feel anything then either. She wants to see if I try to kill her. Then maybe she'll finally feel something.'

'I agree,' Deer said, then seemed to get an idea. 'Something's just struck me. It looked like Jessica stepped out of the queue at Särna church. But what if she didn't?'

'What do you mean?'

'What if she'd already been to the church to get her Internet password?'

Berger stared at her.

'Her van wasn't there long enough. It's just not possible.'

'But she's smart, isn't she?' Deer said. 'She could have jumped the queue somehow, her daughter's respirator was running on backup and they desperately needed to get the electricity back on. Something like that.'

'In which case she'd have it written on a piece of paper,' Berger said. 'I've already checked her pockets. There was nothing there.'

Their eyes met.

'The churchyard,' Deer said. 'It's a long shot, but she could have ditched the password when she was running through the headstones.'

They went back into the other room. Berger dragged Jessica over to the radiator and fastened her to it with a cable tie. Then they walked out without bothering to look at her.

They heard her yell after them, 'Three quarters of an hour now. Don't you want me to call?'

The car skidded into the car park outside Särna church. There were still plenty of vehicles, but the queue leading up to the church seemed to have diminished slightly. Berger didn't even attempt to park the car properly, just abandoned it and rushed through the entrance to the churchyard. People watched as he slid and danced about on the path leading to the graves. Deer was right behind him, and held him up when he was about to fall.

'You take this one,' Berger yelled. 'I'll go round the other way.'

He slid towards the junction and started to search the glass-like surface of the path down towards the hedge. Everything was white, covered in snow. He saw nothing that stood out against the whiteness, not even a piece of white paper. He reached the hedge with a growing sense of desperation. He hadn't found a damn thing.

'Look at this,' Deer called out.

Berger turned. He saw her step into the deep snow between two of the larger headstones. He set off, slipped, kept going and turned left. Deer was just bending down beside one grave not far from the entrance to the churchyard. Then she stood up. In her outstretched hand was a ball of crumpled paper.

She unfolded it and looked down. Then she clenched her fist.

Berger saw the gesture, understood. Against all the odds they had guessed right. They ran to the car, threw themselves in and drove off fast. Staring down at the unfolded sheet of paper Deer said, 'There's even a bloody address. In a village called Mörkret.'

'Mörkret? You're kidding? A village called *Darkness*?' Berger exclaimed as he reached the turning onto Särnavägen. Right or left, that was the question.

'Which way?' he said.

'Hang on,' Deer said, opening her laptop. Her fingers danced balletically across the keyboard. Then she peered at the screen.

'Mörkret,' she said. 'A village in the parish of Särna, in Älvdalen Council District. Twenty-five kilometres west of here. In other words, right.'

The car slid badly as Berger turned sharp right. Blom tapped at the car's GPS, adding the address on the sheet of paper. Then she held her breath.

And got a result. The GPS zeroed in on the address and gave a distance of twenty-seven kilometres. It all seemed to fit.

Deer leaned back as Berger slid the car again, held tight and then looked down at the laptop once more.

'It's as far inland as you can get. Quote: "Just to the east of the village of Mörkret, in the shadow of Fulufjället, is the point on the Scandinavian peninsula that's furthest from the sea, just over two hundred and twenty kilometres to the coast of Hälsingland, the Trondheim Fjord and the Oslo Fjord."'

'Mörkret,' Berger said, avoiding another slide. 'The innermost point of inland Sweden.'

The road grew increasingly contorted, and it got harder and harder to keep the car on the road. Berger wasn't sure he was actually breathing.

Deer sat in silence. Her gaze was glassy.

'Twenty-three minutes,' she said after a while.

Berger was driving against the clock. The world had assumed truly sick dimensions. The passage of time stuttered, twitched, sped up. The gleaming white road snaked off between equally gleaming white mountains and fir trees.

Everything was white. Absolutely white.

His brain as well. His own innermost recesses.

Molly, he thought. The accelerator pedal wouldn't go any lower. He saw Reine's knife coming closer and closer to her body. He saw the block of wood.

The car moved in fits and starts along the icy tarmac.

'She wrote it,' Deer said. 'This endgame has been planned for a very long time.'

'What do you mean, wrote it?' Berger snapped as he put his foot down again.

'In her letter,' Deer said. 'In that letter she sent me. We even commented on it. She said, apropos of nothing, "I am in Darkness." On a separate line, with a capital letter.'

'Of course, because she's so fucking smart,' Berger said.

They drove on in silence for far too long.

The clock moved on, and now read 11.27.

Three minutes left until Reine Danielsson started sticking the knife into Molly Blom. Berger stared at the GPS. Another seven kilometres before they reached the address in Mörkret.

They were never going to get there in time.

Berger would never be able to explain what happened to time at that point. It kept jerking and twisting, never quite making sense. As if everything was slightly out of joint. And he drove like he had never driven before.

Should they have tried to persuade Jessica Johnsson to make the phone call after all? Could they have forced her? Tortured her? Torn her fingernails out?

But the bitch would only have enjoyed that.

The only option was to put his foot down. And drive like a fucking lunatic. Through time's absurd stuttering.

When the clock showed half past eleven everything was still nothing but white. A more nauseating white now, though.

They didn't get the directions wrong once. Even so, they arrived eight minutes too late.

Time stopped acting weirdly, no more jerkiness.

Berger threw himself out of the car and ran towards the house. He heard Deer behind him, heard her release the safety catch on her pistol. He didn't give a damn about weapons right now, he just ran. The front door was slightly ajar, he threw it open, ran through a sitting room, searching frantically from room to room until he eventually reached an open cellar door.

And plunged down the stairs into the heart of Darkness.

He saw a clock on the wall, a red velour sofa covered in plastic, a table with a block of wood on it. Saw an empty chair with the remains of cable ties hanging from it, saw a knife on the floor, saw a figure in a pool of blood, ran over to it. Turned it over.

It was Reine Danielsson, blood was running down his head, his breathing was laboured and rattling.

Berger turned on his heel, and now he saw the trail of blood he'd blundered straight through as he ran down the stairs. Saw the amount of blood, hurried back upstairs, heard Deer call out in a weirdly muted voice, 'I've got a trail of blood in the snow!'

He emerged, saw Deer pushing through the snow ten metres away, saw the trail of blood that she had partially obliterated, and set off after her. Ran past her.

The trail of blood led into the immense whiteness, up a hill, disappeared beyond it. He tried to take a first step up the slope but fell flat on his face, and somersaulted into the metre-deep snow. His mouth filled with it and he couldn't breathe.

It lasted slightly too long and he started to panic. An avalanche of panic. But he got to his feet, and this time his legs didn't give way. He spat out snow, blew snow from his nose, vomited snow, but crashed on up the slope. His progress was painfully slow. Like moving through quicksand. Eventually he reached the brow of the hill, and stared with an unsteady, faltering gaze down the other side.

And there she lay.

She was lying on her front, her arms stretched out in front of her on the snow, and around her right hand a circle of blood was covering an ever-growing area of white.

Like a fallen angel.

With her hair cut in a brown bob.

He crouched down beside Molly Blom, turned her over, saw no movement behind her closed eyelids. Her body was a pale blue colour, but she couldn't possibly have frozen to death already. He checked her breathing, her pulse; both were weak, almost non-existent.

He stood up, tried to look back over the hill, couldn't see Deer, she seemed to have disappeared inside the house.

He pulled his padded jacket off and laid it over Molly's body. Then he very gently lifted her right arm. A large slice of flesh had been cut from the base of her thumb up to her wrist. The blood was literally gushing out, but it wasn't clear if the artery had been completely severed. He tore his fleece pullover off as well and tried to rip it into strips, but failed. He heard steps pulsing through the snow on the other side of the hill, saw Deer's face appear, bleached of all colour. She passed him a couple of blankets and said, 'The air ambulance is on its way.'

Then she saw the wound to Molly's wrist, and the blood pumping out, and said,

'Fucking hell.'

'What?' Sam said, finally managing to tear the fleece.

'Molly acted out Farida Hesari's fantasy.'

'What the hell are you saying?' Sam exclaimed, tying a tourniquet around Molly's arm.

'How is she?' Deer said instead.

Sam shook his head. Together they wrapped Molly's blue-white body in blankets and the padded jacket. Berger picked her up.

Snow began to fall slowly. Through a fog of tears he saw snowflakes floating down towards him. They fell so infinitely breathlessly. As if they wanted to swathe the innermost part of the hinterland in a cloak of forgetfulness.

He carried her carefully through the drifts of snow. He gazed down at her face.

Molly Blom looked dead.

The snowfall grew heavier as they walked, and just as they reached the house a bus drove past on the road.

41

Jessica Johnsson was sitting still, pressed up against the radiator, watching the clock on the wall as it hit 11.30. That was the moment when everything came to fruition. And it was happening at that very moment.

It was as if all the energy, all the tension, all the drive just drained away from her.

It was complete.

She was complete.

Molly Blom was dead, Sam Berger destroyed. And Jessica Johnsson had power, she had real power over life and death.

She was God. She was the goddess of death incarnate. She had killed Daddy's girlfriend.

But now it was over.

Had she felt anything? Not really. It was too late for that.

She knew Berger would come back before too long. Perhaps he would kill her. There was a morbid logic to that. He would get the life sentence, not her. Her life was over anyway. And perhaps she would even feel something during her final seconds.

Naturally it had never even occurred to her to call Reine and get him to stop the process.

She couldn't help wondering what would have happened if she hadn't found that four-leaf clover.

She remembered the day so vividly. The walk along the shore from Fagersjö to Farsta. The little family had walked there from Rågsved, it wasn't very far. The shimmering water of Lake Magelungen. Her dad, Ove, with his camera, her mum, Eva, whose belly had just started to grow. The little cluster of trees, the dense patch of clover. The path leading to it. Her Sunday dress had swayed coolly around her calves. The wind had got up slightly, making her dress stroke her skin.

She sank slowly into the patch of clover.

That was the last time she felt anything. She felt how good everything was then. Admittedly, just before the family had set off her mother had told Jessica that she was going to have a little brother at last. But it hadn't really sunk in. Not until she settled down in that little patch and found the four-leaf clover, and at the very moment she held it up towards her dad's camera the wish had come to her. At the precise moment she heard the click she wished not to have a little brother. A week or so later she was given the picture after it had been developed. She remembered writing her wish down then, on the back of the photograph. That meant it was fixed. And her dad, Ove, had read what she had written; he wasn't supposed to, but he read it. He had turned pale. But as usual he didn't say a thing.

It was true, actually. Berger had been right. Her dad, the man of science, had without question been frightened of his own daughter. He had moved to get away from her. All the way to the other side of the world.

She hoped he was still alive. And felt ashamed.

The cowardly bastard.

And then she was there. It was unavoidable. Not even now, just before she died, could she avoid seeing the key being pushed into the lock. She couldn't help seeing her feet walk towards the kitchen, and there, on the threshold between the living room and the kitchen, seeing her mum's pale, dead face, seeing the horrific chaos of blood spreading across the floor.

And she looked her dead brother in the eye.

She thought those barely formed eyes were saying, 'You're never going to feel anything ever again, Jessica.'

Then she heard a car, heard footsteps on the porch, and she prepared herself.

It was time.

She closed her eyes. The heat from the radiator she was tied to was strangely pleasant. She hoped Berger would make it quick.

She felt she'd suffered enough. She really didn't want to have to deal with having her fingernails pulled out.

She heard the front door open, heard footsteps coming inside, heard the internal door open, heard steps in the room, heard him sit down on the birch-veneer table.

Surely he ought to be screaming and wailing? He shouldn't just sit down there without a sound, not when she'd just murdered his lover.

She opened her eyes.

The man sitting on the table wasn't Sam Berger. It was a large man with thick reading glasses. He pulled on a pair of extremely thin leather gloves not without care. Then he looked up at her, smiled and said, 'Well, then, Jessica, that's the end of your games. I hope it was worth it.'

'Who are you?' Jessica Johnsson exclaimed.

'My name is Carsten,' the man said. 'It's been rather difficult to find you.'

'But ...' Jessica said. 'I thought ...'

'I know what you thought,' Carsten said. 'But I've looked through your entire CV, and what strikes me most is how *little* you deserve to know. You've been a very bad girl.'

'You have to understand ...'

'I don't have to do anything at all,' Carsten said, pulling a well polished Sig Sauer P226 from his inside pocket.

'Who on earth are you?'

Carsten smiled and said in English:

Life's but a walking shadow, a poor player
That struts and frets his hour upon the stage
And then is heard no more: it is a tale
Told by an idiot, full of sound and fury,
Signifying nothing.

'What the hell ...?'

'Sometimes,' Carsten said, 'I think the real punishment is complete ignorance at the moment of death. Some people simply deserve to die without having the faintest idea why. They don't get to take even a glimpse of atonement with them down to hell. Because that's where you're going, Jessica, be in no doubt about that. Let them know that I'll be along soon.'

'What the hell do you mean?' Jessica said and started to pull at the cable tie.

'The whole point of this is that you die in absolute ignorance,' Carsten said and shot her three times, right in the heart.

And during her last second of life Jessica Johnsson did actually feel something. She felt immense surprise.

Carsten took his thick glasses off and blinked several times. He wiped a tear from the corner of his eye.

Then he walked over and stuffed a thick black sock deep into Jessica's throat.

He stepped back to admire his handiwork.

His sight really was getting worse and worse.

And he would end up alone on his terrace in Andalusia.

Signifying nothing.

42

The corridor Deer was walking down seemed endless. Through the endless row of windows she could see that ice had begun to settle on Årstaviken. She could see that even through the heavy snowfall.

It was going to be a long winter.

Södermalm Hospital was full, as usual. When she opened the door the only thing separating the body from the other three beds in the room was a faded curtain. The room also felt disrespectfully full of strangers. Three men dressed in white were talking in low voices around one of the beds, a nursing assistant was changing a catheter bag by one of the other beds, and a cleaner was scrubbing the floor through an open toilet door. And beside Molly Blom's bed in the far right-hand corner stood a wide man with a wide face and an even wider moustache.

Deer let out a deep sigh. This was the last thing she needed.

'Conny,' she said.

Conny Landin, detective superintendent with the National Operations Department, more usually known as the NOD, said, 'Desiré.'

'How is she?' Deer asked.

'Don't know,' Landin said. 'One of those doctors is coming over as soon as they're done there.'

Deer nodded. She looked at Molly Blom and wondered what she was feeling. Instruments were moving in time with Molly's breathing. Deer wondered if she could actually breathe without assistance.

Landin cleared his throat and said, 'I presume you've seen the tabloids?'

'How could I miss them?' Deer said, still looking at the array of equipment surrounding Molly Blom's body. It made her unconscious body look very small.

Almost like a child's.

Landin shook his head and said, 'Obviously I know you lied to me and were working on some secret mission for the Security Service together with Berger. And sure, the normal rules don't apply when it comes to the Security Service.'

Deer sniffed and shook her head. Landin went on, 'Even so, headlines like EX-COP HUNTED FOR MURDER OF SUSPECT aren't really what we want at a time like this ...'

'No,' Deer said.

'Your Jessica Johnsson was shot with Berger's old service weapon, a Sig Sauer P226 that he should have handed in. Add the fact that his DNA has been found in at least three old cases relating to the same investigation and it's hardly surprising he's gone underground. I presume you appreciate that Internal Investigations are going to want to question you?'

'So I understand,' Deer said quietly.

'You went with her in the air ambulance to Falun, then? But not Berger?'

'There wasn't room, there were two people in need of urgent treatment. But we had a car, Berger drove to Falun.'

'Yes, the car was found in the hospital car park. And there the trail goes cold. Obviously he went back to the house in Särna on the way and shot Jessica Johnsson. That was the conclusion of the Dalarna police.'

'I suppose we'll have to see what Internal Investigations say,' Deer said as one of the doctors came over to them and asked,

'Police, I assume?'

They introduced themselves. The doctor said, 'So, Molly Blom. Are there really no next-of-kin?'

'I'm probably as close as you're going to get,' Deer said. 'How is she?'

'Her condition isn't yet stable,' the doctor said. 'We're monitoring her closely to see if the heavy loss of blood has led to permanent brain damage.'

'And ... the baby?' Deer said almost under her breath.

'The foetus is fine,' the doctor said. 'That, if nothing else, means that she's going to be here for at least another eight months.'

Deer stared at him uncomprehendingly. He realised and corrected himself, 'If we were to end up in a situation of *atria mortis*, I mean.'

Then he realised that the clarification didn't exactly make things any plainer.

'Brain death,' he explained.

Which was an admirably clear explanation.

'But we're not there yet?' Deer said as calmly as she could.

'No, no,' the doctor said quickly. 'For the time being the prognosis is merely uncertain. Her other stats look good. We'll do a magnetic resonance tomography as soon as it's medically safe to do so.'

'A what?'

'Commonly known as an MRI scan,' the doctor said. 'To give us a clearer picture of brain activity.'

He walked off. Landin turned to Deer and said, 'I want a full verbal report later today, Desiré. Shall we say in an hour's time? Twelve thirty, my office?'

Deer nodded and watched the thickset man slip out of the room along with the medical staff. Then she turned back towards Molly Blom. She walked up to the bed and took her hand. It was pale and felt cold.

Deer was feeling extremely low.

The cleaner emerged from the toilet. Deer only saw him from behind, mournfully squeezing out his mop. She turned back. Suddenly he was standing beside her.

'I hope your heart's in good shape,' the cleaner said.

Deer whirled round and stared up at him, and found herself eye to eye with Sam Berger's still far too bearded face. She closed her eyes and shook her head.

'What the hell happened?' she said once the initial shock had died down.

'What was that I heard about brain death?' Berger said, walking over to Blom.

Deer let him take Blom's hand.

'Just that it's not clear,' Deer said. 'She isn't brain dead, Sam. And the baby's OK.'

'Whoever the father might be,' Berger said, slowly stroking Blom's hand.

'What's going on, Sam?'

It was a while before Berger answered. When he did, he spoke very slowly, 'While I was driving to Falun I heard a report on police radio about a murder in Särna. When I listened more closely I realised someone had gone into the house and shot Jessica. And bearing in mind the fact that someone was already trying to frame me, I decided to lie low until I could find out what had happened.

Then came the news that she was shot with my old service pistol.'

'Yes, what's going on there?'

'Don't know,' Berger said. 'Obviously I left it in the gun cabinet in police headquarters when I was fired. Someone's stolen it in an attempt to frame me. You have to believe me, Deer.'

She looked up at him, and for the first time in a very long time he was reminded of a deer's eyes.

'Yes,' she said. 'I believe you. But everything went wrong.'

'I don't know,' Berger said. 'At least Molly's still alive. Thanks to you, Deer.'

He passed Blom's cold hand back to her and stepped back slightly. Deer stroked the hand and felt pain welling up inside her.

What she needed right now was a big hug.

She turned round. But Berger was gone.

Out in the corridor he pulled the cleaner's uniform off and looked at his vibrating phone. The screen read:

'Point 0.'

The solitary aspen leaf clung to the outermost twig of a lone branch. He stopped in the swirling snow and watched the leaf until it fell. It drifted slowly down and landed beside his feet without a sound. Then he carried on across what had once been the playground of his childhood towards the faintly luminous boathouse.

Out in Edsviken the rowing boat was getting more and more covered by snow. And ice had begun to form.

He climbed the steps to the boathouse. This time he wasn't met by a Sig Sauer P226. Instead the door was opened by the apparently unarmed head of the Security Service's Intelligence Unit. His cropped metal-grey hair still looked like iron filings around a magnet, but the look on his face was very different, more conciliatory. It was as if the man whose face gave nothing away had expanded his repertoire.

There was also the fact that he said, 'Good that you could come.'

Berger looked at August Steen. They sat down on either side of the boathouse's old workbench. Steen nodded for a while. Then he pushed an iPad across the bench.

A video started to play. Berger instantly recognised the interior of the Security Service safe house in Särna, up in Dalarna. Jessica Johnsson sat tied to a radiator at the far end of the room. Her eyes were closed. Then a man came in; so far only his back was visible. He sat down on the table. Jessica opened her eyes, and a silent conversation went on for a while. In the end Jessica started to pull at the cable tie. Then the man shot her in the chest three times. He remained seated for a while, then went over and forced a thick black sock deep into the dead woman's throat.

When he turned round Steen paused the film.

And it was very clear that the man was Carsten.

'No sound?' Berger said.

'Unfortunately not,' Steen said. 'A microcamera but no microphone. He found everything else.'

'This is *your* man, Steen,' Berger said. 'And a close one, at that. He was here with you last time, when everything was so top-fucking-secret. What is this?'

'Do you feel like watching another little film?' Steen said instead of answering. 'I dug it out just before I came here. It's a couple of weeks old.'

Berger nodded. Another clip started.

It showed an open-plan office. Even though it was dark, it looked familiar. It took Berger a moment to recognise his old workplace, where Allan Gudmundsson's team had grappled with the Ellen Savinger case. A man came into the picture, and the footage switched to night vision, all green and white shapes. The man walked straight over to the gun cabinet, opened it without any difficulty and removed a pistol.

Steen paused.

'You can clearly see which part of the cabinet he takes it from,' he said.

'Mine,' Berger said.

Steen pressed Play again. When the man turned it was clear once again, despite the night vision, that it was Carsten.

'This gets me off,' Berger said.

'But this will never be made public,' Steen said.

'What's to stop me grabbing the iPad and running off with it?'

'Nothing,' Steen said and smiled cheerlessly. 'But the files are time limited. They'd be gone before you even made it through the door. It would save time if we could manage not to under-estimate each other.'

Berger looked at him.

'What's going on?' he asked.

'It's a long story,' Steen said. 'With your permission, I'll give you the short version.'

'You murdered Syl, you bastard,' Berger snarled.

'No,' Steen said calmly. 'The short version?'

Berger said nothing. Steen nodded and said, 'Sylvia Andersson was murdered because she tried, on your instruction, to reinstate a number of files in the deepest part of the Security Service archive, isn't that right? Files that were erased at the start of the new year? That's your theory, isn't it, Sam?'

Berger looked at him in the gloom of the boathouse without the slightest change of expression.

'It's true that I was the person who erased those files,' Steen went on. 'Because about a month earlier it started to become apparent that we had a mole in the Security Service.'

'A mole?'

'Excuse the Cold War terminology.' Steen smiled. 'A traitor, a spy, a leak, call it what you will. I had to make sure that the mole didn't get hold of those files.'

'Are the Pachachi family the key?' Berger asked.

August Steen pulled a more animated face that Berger had ever seen before.

'That was why we had to get rid of you,' he said. 'Because you realised that. Out of reach. And protected from the mole.'

'So you used Molly?'

'You have the wrong idea about Molly Blom,' Steen said. 'She'd broken away from us, she was ready to go into business as a private detective with you. She saved you when you had a breakdown here in this boathouse, a serious psychotic breakdown. We only contacted her later. She agreed to keep you out of sight; she understood that it was the mole who had murdered your Syl.'

Berger stared at Steen.

'That was the short version,' Steen said after a pause. 'Pachachi is extremely important to us, and the only person who knows his true identity is me. But then a mole popped up, trying to find out. I quickly had to erase all the files related to him. He made other attempts, he murdered a senile old woman with a thick sock, a woman who could have identified Gundersen, and it was Gundersen who helped us get Pachachi here. He murdered Sylvia, even though it doesn't look like she had any information about Pachachi to give him – certainly nothing

401

we were aware of, anyway. But above all, he got hold of Pachachi's daughter. She was kidnapped by—'

'William,' Berger said, even though he couldn't really speak.

'The mole has her now,' Steen said. 'He went in and snatched Aisha before the labyrinth at Stupvägen was finished. He ignored all the other kidnapped girls and just took Aisha. Now he's keeping Pachachi quiet because he's got his daughter. But the mole only gets his thirty pieces of silver once he's murdered Pachachi. Considerably more than that, by all accounts.'

'Where's the money coming from?'

'IS, probably. I've been hunting him for a year. And now he gives himself away just like that. Mad.'

'Carsten?' Berger exclaimed.

Steen shook his head slowly and said, 'His primary motivation was probably that he needed a scapegoat. Obviously it would have been better to pick someone from inside the Security Service, but seeing as you were already responsible for Sylvia Andersson digging about in the most sensitive parts of our archives, you were actually a plausible mole.'

'He murdered Jessica to make me your mole?' Berger blurted.

'Primarily, yes,' Steen said. 'It's always passion that gives moles away. The perfect spy is a castrated spy.'

'Hang on. Carsten is trying to frame me because …?'

'Secondarily, yes. Because he's jealous. There's a lot to suggest he thinks you've taken Molly away from him. There are indications in his reports from the surveillance of the two of you. If you know what you're looking for. Which I didn't until it was a little too late.'

'So where is he now, then?'

'Probably still in Sweden somewhere. Together with the kidnapped Aisha Pachachi. I think he's waiting for Daddy Pachachi to make him an offer. Waiting for him to sacrifice himself for his daughter.'

'And why am I here? What do you want with me?'

Steen looked at him for a drawn-out moment.

'We're on the brink of something big,' he said. 'Dangerous people are on their way into the country. If Carsten manages to silence Ali Pachachi, they'll be able to go ahead without any problem. And we will be facing the worst act of terrorism in Swedish history.'

Berger stared at him.

'What do you want with me, August?' he said.

'You're better than you think you are, Sam.'

'Molly's lying there, possibly brain dead. With a baby inside her that might actually be mine.'

Steen shook his head.

'Like I said, the perfect spy is a castrated spy,' he said. 'But Molly isn't brain dead. The situation is merely unclear. And I believe that the issue of paternity is also somewhat uncertain.'

Berger stared at the ruins of the clock he had been chained to not all that long ago.

'What do you want, August?' Berger asked.

August Steen pushed a mobile phone and a sizeable bundle of cash towards him and said, 'I just want you to be ready; I'm going to need you before long. And don't forget that there's a national alert out for you. Stay under the radar.'

'I'm starting to get used to it,' Sam Berger said with a wry smile.

43

In the falling snow it was very nearly impossible to see just how well guarded the newly built Helix secure psychiatric unit in Huddinge was. Even so, the driver of the car got through, equipped with fake authorisation from the highest possible source. He parked and switched the engine off.

Sam Berger adjusted the rear-view mirror and looked at his freshly shaven face. He didn't recognise himself.

And he felt horribly alone.

There was a definite new-building smell in the remarkably pleasant corridors. The female doctor was walking in front of him with a trim, bouncing gait. Without turning she said, 'It's a shame you've had a wasted journey.'

'What do you mean?' Berger asked.

'There's a complete ban on all communication before the trial,' the doctor said. 'But you can take a look through the window.'

The doctor stopped abruptly a couple of metres from a door containing a small window. Then she turned on her heel and set off back the way they had come.

'You've got five minutes,' she said over her shoulder. 'Then the staff will come and get you.'

Berger waited until she had gone. Then he slowly approached the window and peered in.

The first thing he saw was a large window. Through the heavy snow he caught a glimpse of a bus driving past down on the road.

Then he saw Reine Danielsson. He was sitting at a table, drawing. The table was covered with paper and a variety of coloured pencils. He had a look of extreme concentration on his face. There may even have been a trace of happiness hidden behind his focused expression.

At first it was hard to make out what he was drawing. Then Berger saw that there were also drawings on the walls. The motif slowly became apparent.

Four-leaf clovers. The whole of Reine Danielsson's cell was decorated with extremely detailed drawings of four-leaf clovers.

Then he looked up at Berger. He smiled and raised his right hand as if to wave. Instead he stretched out his index and long fingers so that his hand resembled a double-barrelled revolver.

And then he shot him.

penguin.co.uk/vintage

ECONOMY
CLASS

SEAT NO.
14D

SPECIAL SERVICE

SERVICE INFORMATION

PAX NAME
MENAKER/DMRS